WHEN THE STORM DIES

THE DEADLY WOLDS MURDER MYSTERIES
BOOK 1

JACK CARTWRIGHT

CHESTNUT PRESS

ALSO BY JACK CARTWRIGHT

The DCI Cook Murder Mysteries

A Winter of Blood

A Secret to Die For

The Wild Fens Murder Mysteries

Secrets In Blood

One For Sorrow

In Cold Blood

Suffer In Silence

Dying To Tell

Never To Return

Lie Beside Me

Dance With Death

In Dead Water

One Deadly Night

Her Dying Mind

Into Death's Arms

No More Blood

Burden of Truth

Run From Evil

The Deadly Wolds Murder Mysteries

When The Storm Dies

The Harder They Fall

Until Death Do Us Part

WHEN THE STORM DIES

A Deadly Wolds Mystery

PROLOGUE

Water licked at the doorstep. It wasn't the type of water one might bask or bathe in, where tropical fish darted to and fro while the sun's dying rays refracted off of the gentle ripples of an evening tide. It was the devil's water, frothing with fury, and laden with forest debris carried down into the gully across land dried by one of the long, hot summers that British residents were told to expect more of.

But while the heatwave had raised smiles during those hot and sticky months, the surface of the land had solidified, scorched to an impenetrable crust that had gone unnoticed by most, save for the farmers.

But now people were noticing. Now people were sitting up and paying attention. And now the brown froth that licked at Sophie's door was rising faster than she could think what to do.

There was no use in shouting out, for nobody would hear her in the storm. Only two dwellings occupied that part of the shallow gully, and hers was one of them.

The phone. That was it. She ran to the telephone stand by the door, only to sink a sodden slipper into the encroaching water.

This was why Edward had always wanted her to keep her mobile phone with her, she realised. Exactly for moments like these.

The doorstep was below the surface now. Three inches it had risen in as many minutes, or less. How long it had taken no longer mattered. What mattered was action of some description.

She picked up the phone. She was torn. Part of her desperately tried to be Edward. What would he have done? Sandbags, maybe? They had none. But no doubt he would have fashioned something from nothing. He was good like that.

The other part of her wanted to leave. To run into the night, leaving it all behind with nothing but the clothes on her back.

She watched as the water level rose higher than the carpet pile, darkening the feet of her mother's old telephone table and likely ruining it forever. The old oak would suck the water up like a straw until it was bloated, forever tarnished.

In the end, the decision was made for her. Darkness fell in an instant as some rogue trickle found a bare wire and plunged the house into an inky-black gloom. There hadn't been a giant bang like the movies might have portrayed it, or a shower of sparks lighting her fear for the briefest of moments. The light was there and then it was gone. There may have been a click as the breaker kicked in, but she hadn't heard it over the rushing of water along the road, the pouring rain on the porch roof, and the howling wind outside.

The only coat within reach was the light denim jacket she had been wearing earlier in the day, when the skies had been blue and the clouds white. It slid easily over the long t-shirt she had been sleeping in, and she pulled the jacket tight around her before heading out into the deluge.

And so she left. Forced from the life she had been building for decades, groping her way through the darkness, sodden, and drunk on adrenaline.

In an instant, she realised the denim jacket had been a mistake, but she soldiered on with the water lapping at her knees.

Submerged branches grazed her shins like the bony fingers of the dead, and with the smell of waste stuck in her throat, she pushed forward, trying hard not to imagine what else was in that foul water.

It was only when she reached the end of the front garden that she recalled the conversation she'd had with Edward when they had bought the place. How he'd dreamed of having a house with land, remote and wild. And how she was happy to have the land, but wanted a neighbour or two within eyesight, at least.

How happy she was to have made that demand. From the gate, she could see the light coming from the Tuckers' kitchen across the road.

Blinded by the angry sky blocking all natural light, she stumbled forward, pushing against a raging torrent with that single light as a guide. Twice, she stumbled, and once she fell to her knees, forcing her to grip onto the Tuckers' gate, which had been forced open in the torrent.

"Florence," she called out, when she was close enough to make out the TV in their living room. "David?"

She hadn't expected them to have heard her, but the pang of disappointment she felt was cut short by a loud thud nearby, followed by the sound of breaking branches. She pulled herself past the Tuckers' garden wall just as the remains of a small, dead tree soared past. Its lethal branches whipped across her frozen knuckles as she held onto the gatepost and her scream was lost to the storm.

She could have just let the water take her. Part of her wanted to, the part that gave in easily. The part she hated. The part that, many moons ago, she used to hide from Edward. The road ran down from the hill to the east and up the hill to the west, and the houses sat in the gully between, alongside a stream that, in all the time she had lived there, had been little more than a pleasing trickle, a stark contrast to the raging torrent it was now. An angry force of nature that could swallow her whole.

But no. She'd been through too much to give in now. All she had to do was reach high ground. Somewhere out of reach of the river's burst banks.

But not without helping the people who likely didn't want her help.

"David? Florence? Are you there?" she called out, wading through water which was over her knees now and nearing her waist in the surges that rolled through like a strong tide.

The Tuckers' house sat lower than the road, and although she'd walked down their path many times, her memory eluded her, leaving her stumbling over unseen objects – rocks that had been dislodged from David's rockery, maybe?

The current eddied around her, pushing her towards the house with force. She lost her footing on one of those rocks and felt her slipper slide from her foot, and for a terrifying moment, she plunged face first into the wrath.

Only through instinct alone, she reached up, blindly groping for something to hold on to, and her trembling fingers found the window ledge. She pulled herself up, and banged on the glass with hands that were so white they seemed to glow in the near darkness, peering through only to find the living room empty and the rising water breaching the coffee table inside.

A shadow passed across the wall near the door, or maybe it had been a trick of the light. She pressed her face to the window, clearing a spot on the glass only for the incessant rainfall to dot it once more.

But as fast as hope had roused its weary head, it bent down again without warning. This time, there was a bang as the water level breached an electricity circuit, and a shower of furious sparks captured her fear in the flash.

And then there was darkness and only the sound of the wind, the rain, and the gushing water to drown her cries.

She banged on the glass with the flat of her hand again.

"David? Florence? Are you there?" she called. "We've got to get out."

There was no answer.

Even when she hauled herself along the window ledge to bang on the front door, nobody responded. She was alone, with nowhere to go except to make her way up the hill to higher ground. But even then, the nearest neighbour was a five-minute walk along the winding lane.

And if she was honest with herself, she didn't really want to go there.

She leaned on the door, letting her head sag between her arms, and she let the tears run free. A single sob rose through her chest and burst like a bubble of air.

Then she felt it. An icy hand on her shoulder in the darkness, and she started with a scream that was silenced as icy fingers reached from behind and clamped firmly over her mouth.

CHAPTER ONE

Ten years. That's how long it had been. Ten years since a much younger version of himself had walked through that front door with his wife on his arm, George Larson thought, finding himself staring at the oak threshold over which he must have stepped...

How many times?

He welcomed the distraction of running the calculation.

If he had passed over it twice a day for ten years, that would be three hundred and sixty-five multiplied by ten, multiplied by two.

"Good God," he muttered, shaking his head. *That's over seven thousand times that I've passed through here.*

He held up a dress shirt in his hands, picked off a piece of lint from the shoulder, and carried it upstairs to the bedroom. Then he laid it in the small suitcase on the bed, adding to the pile to make five in total. Once more, George shook his head when it dawned on him that he'd slept in that bed for close to four thousand nights.

But then, spurred by the photo on his bedside table, he wondered how many of those nights had been spent alone, and found the distraction of the calculation far too arduous.

Three pairs of trousers, underwear, socks, belts, and braces followed by a pair of sturdy shoes, leaving just enough room for his toiletries, pyjamas, and waistcoat, which he laid on top of the various piles. Then he closed the lid before the temptation grew to add more items.

He tugged the zip closed, then sat down, finding the whole process utterly exhausting. It was an odd feeling. Nearly four thousand nights beneath that ceiling, and now he was starting again. If he had a choice, he would have taken everything – the furniture even, the mirror in the hallway George checked his hair in before leaving the house, the old, tattered dining table from their first house together, and the dresser that had been Grace's mother's, with its small, crystal animal figurines. No, all that was all too large, bulky, and heavy with memories.

But there was one last thing he would never leave behind.

He removed the photo from the bedside table and ran his thumb across the image to wipe away the dust. The frame was small, gold-leafed, and classic. He reopened the case and slipped it inside one of the shoes for safekeeping, then hauled the case to the front door and set it beside the other few bags he had arranged.

Of all the furniture in the house, he would miss his old armchair the most. Perhaps, if things went well, he would have it sent down to him. He lowered himself into the seat, and instinctively his hand reached for the side table where, on a silver-plated tray, he kept a decanter and a single crystal glass.

He poured a good measure, then set the bottle down, making a mental note to give Clive down the road a call. He could use his emergency key to let himself in and take the whisky, plus a few other perishables.

The whisky burned his throat and the memories of Grace sitting opposite him burned his eyes with the heat of suppressed tears. They wouldn't fall, though. The same tears had been there for years and hadn't once fallen. They just burned, as if to taunt him.

From his armchair, he was afforded one of the greatest views he'd ever known. It wasn't of a mountain range, or a field of wild-flowers, but of his home, his world, his everything, including the little window beside the parlour door which wasn't just dotted with specks of rain; it was being hammered by the downfall.

He shoved himself out of his seat, strolled over to the front door, and opened it with caution.

"Good God."

The light from the house spilled onto his neat flowerbeds, revealing roses that sagged under their weight and a landscape that hid in the shadow of an impenetrable sky. He shook his head in dismay, closed the door, and leaned against the wood, taking stock of the old house one more time.

He sipped his whisky, savoured the burn, then turned to stare out the window at the dismal night as a flash of distant lightning cast a silhouette of the horizon onto his mind for eternity. It was a view he knew so well, one he could never forget.

The smell from the windowsill too was familiar, of a slight damp from the storm. But in a comforting way, like the smell of sturdy old boots, or a dog after a long walk.

Still, he didn't have much time to spare. It was best to get going.

He downed the rest of his drink and winced, stirring those same burning tears once more. He'd have to leave eventually, George knew. He couldn't just keep touring the house in melancholy. And if the storm outside was getting worse, the time was now.

So, with his future looming over his shoulder like one of those great, dark clouds, he rinsed out his glass and returned it to the tray. The room had that same cleanliness as a newly rented house. Everything in its rightful place. A fresh start, albeit a fresh start he wasn't sure he was ready for.

And as George returned to the front door, he repressed a long, loud sigh.

Just this once, he let his eyes travel to the spot above the fireplace he had tried so hard to avoid. There was a lighter patch of wall where a painting had once hung. No. Not just a painting. His favourite painting. The most beautiful painting he'd ever seen.

Its absence was an art in itself. The lighter patch stained the wall like a charming birthmark. It belonged.

But art as it may have been, that empty space was such a reminder of what his life was lacking. In all that he had, all that George admired about his home, one key element was missing. And that space above the fireplace only reminded him of it. Even in the corner of his eye, that painting's absence was blinding.

How long George stared at that patch of wall, he wasn't sure. But eventually, he blinked his gaze away. As he'd done at least four thousand times before, George turned to check his hair in the hallway mirror before leaving his house.

His hair was grey and thinning, but still more present on his head than many men his age. The wrinkles around his mouth and eyes were deepening each year, but George didn't mind. He'd always been a calm, inquisitive man, who thought before he spoke, mature at heart, more at home in an old garden than a young crowd, and it was reassuring to see his face catching up with his soul. He wiped his thin-framed glasses on the sleeve of his woollen sweater, the comfy, wrist-holed one he reserved for car journeys, which he wore beneath his rain jacket, placed them back on his nose, and straightened his shoulders.

Then he turned to face the front door, pulled it open, and grabbed a bag in each hand before stepping outside.

The storm howled, and the sky wept great bucket loads of rain. It was far from inviting. The night was deep and dark. It had settled hours ago, and the storm was embracing its shadows. He'd left it as late as he could to leave the house.

But now it was time.

"Once more unto the breach, old boy," he muttered to himself, feeling the splash of raindrops on his shoes. "Once more."

CHAPTER TWO

"What the bloody hell are you doing?" Sophie yelled, as she pulled away from the hand on her mouth. She turned and saw Lucy standing in the rain with her finger pressed to her lips and her eyes wide with fear.

"*Shush*," she hissed.

Although Sophie didn't really know Lucy to speak to, she'd watched the girl next door grow up from afar, and easily recognised her blonde, straight hair, now wet and tangled from the rain, her amber, autumn-like eyes, and youthful features – chubby cheeks that would slowly hollow with time, smooth skin that would dry out, and wide, bright eyes that would tire of life.

"Where's your mum and dad?"

"In bed," Lucy replied, her voice youthful and scared. "Please don't tell them I wasn't home. I was at Jay's. I was supposed to be back at seven. Dad's going to hit the roof."

"Somehow, I don't think that you staying out late is going to be at the top of their priorities," Sophie replied. "Come on. Help me wake them up. Do you have your key?"

Lucy fumbled in the pockets of her waterproof coat and pulled out a small bunch, then trudged over to the front door.

The water was up to their ankles near the door, and the current gripped their legs like spectral fingers.

"Tell them to get dressed as quickly as they can, and to leave everything. There's no time. This rain is getting heavier. If they stay up there, they'll end up being trapped."

Lucy slotted the key into the lock, then looked Sophie in the eye, her hand poised to turn the key.

"Lucy, don't worry about your dad. Come on, we've got to get to high ground. We'll go to Connor's. Now, hurry up."

She lingered a second or so more.

"Lucy, come on."

Eventually, Lucy snapped out of her fearful state, took a deep breath, and then pushed the door open through the foot-deep water in the hallway.

The women waded into the house and Lucy forced the door closed behind her, more to prevent debris from entering than water.

"Don't—" said Sophie, but the door was already shut, and at least the respite from the raucousness of the storm was welcomed. It was now a distant din, like a waning headache, along with migraine-like whistles through gaps in the outer walls.

"Oh God," said Lucy, distracted by her waterlogged childhood home. "Look at this place."

Sophie sighed. "Don't worry about that now. Just hurry. Get upstairs and wake them up."

Sodden, Lucy trudged up the stairs, her wet boots staining the cream carpet that David Tucker had always been so protective about. Sophie recalled the times she'd had a cup of tea with Florence in the kitchen after a Sunday walk, interrupted by David emerging from his study, enraged at the dirt on the carpet.

But that had been a long time ago. Another lifetime.

She was surprised he hadn't replaced the carpet by now. Well, the insurance would replace it for them, and if David had any sense, it would be a darker colour or, better still, bare wood.

Sophie continued to stare down the long hallway until it began to extend and shake as if she had tunnel vision. She stood still, trying to stabilise the nostalgia, dread, and stress from the rising waters – now to her calves – that made her feel dizzy. Best not to move from the doorway, she thought. Best not to fully enter a house in which she knew she wasn't welcome.

Her misty gaze was broken only by the sound of Lucy's tumbling footsteps down the stairs. Sophie braced herself for the disgust on Florence and David's face when they saw she was in their home.

But Lucy was alone.

"They're not here," she said, and looked up and down the hallway as though her parents might be hiding.

Sophie frowned. "What do you mean they're not here?"

"I mean they're not in their room. The bed's empty."

Sophie looked at her thin-strapped watch, which miraculously still ticked even though its face was soaked with water. "It's eleven p.m."

"I know what time it is," Lucy huffed.

"Well, where could they be?"

The dread in Sophie was rising at a similar rate to the flood water.

"How do *I* know?"

Sophie swept forwards. "David?" she called up the stairs. "Florence?"

Lucy rolled her eyes, as though frustrated at Sophie questioning her capability to find her own parents. The only reply was a sinister groan that seemed to come from the entire house. It was old and creaking, and who knew where its weakest points were, or when they would succumb to these new forces?

Lucy looked at Sophie in the fearful way a child does when an adult is present and they expect them to take control. Wherever David and Florence were, they weren't here. For now, Lucy was her responsibility. And if they weren't careful, they'd soon become trapped in the hallway, unable to open the door.

"They must've gone to higher ground already," said Sophie with as much authority as she could muster. "I didn't see the car outside, come to think of it. Maybe they got out."

"Without me?" said Lucy quietly.

Sophie trudged towards the front door. "Come on. Let's go."

She reached for the bronze pull handle, but hesitated, preparing herself for the rush of water about to enter the house. In that moment of hesitation, came a soft, vulnerable voice.

"Sophie?"

She turned to find Lucy standing behind her, hands wringing with fear.

Sophie looked between the girl and the door impatiently. "What?"

"Are we really going to Connor's?"

"Yes," said Sophie quickly. "Come on."

"But he's..."

Sophie span again. "What, Lucy?"

Lucy grimaced. "He's...*weird*."

"He lives at the *top* of the hill, Lucy. That's all I'm worried about right now." She gripped the door handle again, then said over her shoulder. "Hold onto something."

With one yank came an onslaught of water, gushing through the doorway like the bottom of a bucket falling through. Sophie held the handle with such force, she was surprised the bronze didn't warp in her grip. Lucy flung her arms around Sophie's waist. It would have felt comical almost, if their lives hadn't been on the line.

In the short five minutes they had been in the house, the water levels had at least doubled by Sophie's reckoning. Before long, they would lose their footing, and, more likely, be dragged under.

With that thought came another ominous groan. This time, it

was more localised and louder, coming from the living room. The two women's eyes met just briefly, before Sophie led the wade out of the house and into the howling night.

But just as they crossed the threshold, the strength of the water must have taken Lucy by surprise. She lurched forward, her hands scrambling for purchase. Just in time, Sophie grabbed the doorframe with one hand and Lucy's arm with the other. The surge of water forced Lucy's legs from the ground, as if a dozen submerged hands grappled at her clothes, hungry to carry her away, to pull her beneath the frothing surface.

Between screams, the teenager's face vanished once or twice, only for it to return gasping for breath. She was panicking, frenzied. Her fingers gripped Sophie's arm so tightly, Sophie worried it might cut off her blood circulation.

But the girl was strong enough to regain her footing, if only she calmed down.

"*Help!*"

"I've got you," Sophie screamed over the wind. "Now stand up."

The water was now past her knees. They had no time for setbacks, no time for seconds lost to terror.

"I can't."

"You can. Just pull yourself up," said Sophie, trying to pull the girl in encouragement. But she was a fifty-five-year-old woman, no match for the strength of a sixteen-year-old. Lucy had to help herself. "Come on."

"You're going to let go."

"I'm not going to let go."

Sophie looked over Lucy's head. Large panes of glass and splintered pieces of wooden window frame carried through the living room doorway into the kitchen.

"Look at me, Lucy."

The young girl's darting eyes focused on Sophie's with something between fear and trust.

"Trust me. You're not going anywhere."

With that, Lucy's face twisted into resolve. She pulled herself towards Sophie with such a tight grip that Sophie knew it would leave bruises on her skin. Without as much effort as expected, Lucy was standing once more, and with her two feet grounded, she stepped towards the doorway so that both women could rest their weight on the frame.

They took a moment to breathe amidst the whipping rain.

"To Connor's?" said Sophie, waiting for a willing confirmation.

Lucy wiped away the wetness on her cheeks that could've been anything between tears, sweat, and rain. Or all three. Then she nodded in defeat. "To Connor's."

CHAPTER THREE

Sophie trudged through the Tuckers' front door holding Lucy's hand, one dragging the other forward through the torrent, then the other wading ahead and doing the same. They used the house where they could, grabbing its window sills and garden fence where possible. But the little, picture-perfect gully that changed with the seasons was filling faster than the water could drain into the fields downstream.

With a quick glance towards her own house, Sophie said a silent goodbye. The house would never be the same. And then she saw it. A faint glint of light reflecting off a shiny surface. The roof and windows of the car were all that remained visible as the Tuckers' black four-by-four had been carried off to the side of the road and was being devoured by the flood water.

"They must have walked," Lucy said, when she saw the subject of Sophie's gaze.

"Either that, or somebody picked them up." She looked at the girl sadly. "Some friends in the village, maybe?"

Lucy didn't reply. She didn't have to. The guilt in her eyes spoke volumes. But Sophie didn't have time to consider the possibilities any further. The waters were unrelenting, and soon she and Lucy were forced to break free of each other to focus on themselves, pushing their bodies forward step by step with raised arms. The hold of the current pulled them backwards like a lover pulling them back to bed. But they pushed onward with the promise of safety not far away.

Spiky branches and perilous splinters of farm gates sailed past. Every time Sophie stepped on something soft, she tried not to think of what it might be. Just mushed leaves, she told herself. And when her thoughts grew darker, she blinked away the images of dead animals in the water, foxes and badgers whose dens had been flooded in the nearby fields.

Many times, she gagged at the smell of waste that had dried on her face and hands. She shuddered at every strange touch in the water and continued on. It was all she could do until the ground started its incline. The storm was waning. Now she was on her hands and knees, crawling up the tarmac slope with her numbed fingers digging into the hard surface, searching for the tiniest of gaps to hold on to. A river of rainwater flowed down into the hollow like a water slide, but still she held fast, grateful to be out of the worst of it.

But her moment of relish was brief. She sat up in a start and frantically searched the darkness behind her for a blonde head dipping beneath the surface. And then she heard it, above the chaos and the wind, she heard it, and somehow she managed a smile. At the sound of heavy breathing beside her, she turned to find the girl on her back and panting, clearly past caring about the deluge of mud that had ruined her jeans and her oversized, pink rain jacket.

Shivering now, Sophie stood. With one slipper lost to the deluge, she limped over to the girl and held out a pale arm to help her to her feet. Lucy shook her head, in the same way Sophie imagined she might shake her head at Florence when she didn't want to get out of bed.

"Come on," said Sophie.

Without children of her own, the chore of coercing a teenager to her will was alien and immediately exhausting. It was only when a rogue branch on the downhill stream grazed the top of her head that Lucy stirred.

She cursed, and then reached for Sophie's hand to drag herself to her feet. They took a moment, the elation of survival somewhat doused by the bitter cold and the prospect of the task ahead of them. And then they laughed. They laughed at Sophie's white legs, her drenched nightshirt, and the way her entire body seemed to shake with cold. They laughed at the way Lucy's waterproof coat had actually contained water in the folds, and how her sodden jeans were almost impossible to walk in. But the laughter was a front, and it was brief.

They focused on one step after another until the hill topped out. One hundred yards, no more, and they could see their way out of the trees. With the cruel lash of the rain against their faces, the silhouette of Connor's house beckoned, and they continued with renewed yet reluctant vigour.

Shivering and soaking wet, they trudged up to Connor's house and banged on the large front door.

"Connor?" Sophie yelled. "Ruth?"

They were probably locked up inside and unable to hear them, such was the roar of the rain. Connor's doorstep was in a perfect crosswind for the rain to beat their faces, and when they realised nobody was going to answer, both women instinctively ran for cover around the side of the house.

Sophie shaded her eyes to peer through a window, but the dark living room was empty. She banged on the glass, with no luck.

"What now?" asked Lucy, as though Sophie had all the answers.

Sophie looked around the soaking yard. Water streamed from a rusty piece of metal that was probably once used for harvesting, falling like a decorative waterfall, and the tapping of rain on the tin roofs of the outbuildings was a light percussion compared to the frequent growls of thunder. Even in the storm, she could see the yard was grassy and overgrown, with quick fixes to damage like pieces of cardboard over broken windows, which were now soaked and peeling away. It reminded Sophie of an old, disused children's playground – toys left out in the rain, orange tractors and Lego-like fences.

In the far corner of the yard, she spotted an open door swinging in the wind. It banged back and forth against the door-frame, adding to the symphony of din. It was the entrance to one of the smaller yard buildings and looked the flimsiest of them all, with gaps below the walls and holes in the roof. But the rest of the buildings were padlocked shut. It was their only choice.

"This way," Sophie said with an illusion of authority.

They ran across the yard, their feet splashing in the puddles, so wet now that their saturated clothes could take in no more water.

Sophie held back the swinging door while Lucy ran inside. She followed and pulled the door to her with resistance, then bolted it from the inside. She'd never been so grateful for a roof over her head. Shelter from the storm, at last. Although the wooden panels bled rain like blood from an artery, it was dry enough for now.

Peeling off her heavy denim jacket, Sophie took in her surroundings.

The workshop was small and void of life except for her and Lucy, but packed full of objects. There was a pile of tyres in the corner, of various sizes, from tractor-size to motorbike. A large bookcase dominated one wall, not filled with novels but gears and cogs and screwdrivers, and multiple small, metal pieces Sophie couldn't identify. The floor was barely walkable, as cardboard boxes took up much of the space, overflowing with muddy sheets and plastic coverings. There were two old wooden chairs, one of which Lucy had already occupied, a woodworking bench, and from the ceiling beams hung orange lawnmower cords and cables of all kinds.

Dangling in the middle of the room was a single, unshaded lightbulb with precarious wiring that distributed light in the worst way possible. Some corners were too shadowy for Sophie to see.

"Well," said Lucy, picking up a bolt from the worktable then throwing it back onto the surface with a *thunk*, "at least it's dry."

"Yeah," Sophie replied.

She walked back over to the entrance and looked through the generous gap between the door and its frame. As she stood there, the rain appeared to slow. The thunder became more of a far-away purr. The sky seemed to grow thin and turn to a lighter shade of grey.

It wasn't the first flood she'd experienced living in The Wolds and surely it wouldn't be the last. They'd never been this bad before. Not so dangerous. She shuddered at the thought of what could have happened to her and Lucy trapped in the Tucker house. But still, they'd escaped. The storm always moved on. The next morning always came, bringing a welcome sun for the locals to view the damage.

Sophie sighed and looked over at Lucy, who sat heavily in the chair with her arms crossed.

"Looks like the worst of it is over," she said. "We should be safe here, at least."

CHAPTER FOUR

The rain was so relentless that George could barely see through the windscreen of his car. Some part of him had longed for a warm, moonlit welcome to The Wolds, but what he'd received was far more reminiscent ‒ wild, remote, and unrelenting forces of nature. The storm had picked up considerably since he'd left forty minutes ago. Now, only one mile from the house in Bag Enderby that he'd soon call home, he'd be relieved to get there.

But, from the smudged sight of distant blue lights through his windscreen, he deemed the storm to have other plans.

Larson had worked in the force for long enough to recognise an imminent diversion when he saw one, and considering the rain that was now running down his windows in bucket-loads, he guessed it had something to do with flooding.

He followed the road until the lights became bluer and brighter, and stopped just before the road began turning downwards into a hill. Between frantic and tireless windscreen wipers, he could just make out more blue lights on the other side of the gully in the road. Clearly, this intense dip in the road had been flooded, and police were stopping cars from driving into the basin of floodwater that had gathered.

Larson slowed and rolled down his window for the officer approaching his car.

The poor lad was sodden. His clothes looked like uncomfortable weighted blankets on his shoulders. Water poured from his cap, rather than drip from the shiny rim.

"Evening, sir," he said. "Can't get through this way, I'm afraid. You're going to have to turn back and take the long way around through Hagworthingham."

"Flooding, is it?" George said, nodding across the small valley. On the other side, in the distance and around the corner, he saw more police lights.

"That's right, sir. The whole road is totally waterlogged at the bottom of the dip. Water coming down from both sides. No-one can get through."

Larson looked at his watch and rested his head back on the car's headrest. He'd hoped to be in bed asleep by now, ready for tomorrow.

"Going through Hagworthingham will take me twenty minutes," he said, more to himself. Still, the officer replied with a guilty shrug.

"Sorry."

George looked at the officer closely. The boy was young and shiny-eyed, almost tearful; although that might have been on account of the rain, they were big and brown, and, in these conditions, puddle-like. He couldn't have been long out of school. George wondered if he was one of his, if they'd work together, and was already considering how he might mentor the lad to buck up and not apologise for the weather to members of the public.

"What's your name?" asked George.

"My name?"

"Your collar number then?"

"I–"

But the officer's radio interrupted, crackling with resistance against the water that had soaked into the creases of its speaker.

Due to the rush of the wind and the officer turning his body to listen in privacy, George couldn't hear what had been said. But from the look on the officer's face, it was serious. He had flinched when receiving the information. Shakily, he pulled out his notepad and jotted something down before the rain smudged the ink. In all this water, he was clearly out of his depth.

George stared down his car's headlights at the rush of groundwater beneath his car. There was a stream gathering beneath him, adding to the torrent of rapids speeding down the steep hill. The trees lining the road looked skeletal and spindly, deformed by the heavy power of the rain. On either side of Larson, he remembered, were fields which probably now resembled swamps more than farmland.

With another watery crackle of the radio, George tweaked his well-tuned ear into the muffling that came next.

"...calling paramedics now."

The officer seemed to be dazed, and was shocked to find George still sitting there with the engine running when he asked, "What's happened?"

The officer took a breath then replied, "Nothing to worry about, sir." Then he gestured to the turning at the side of the road, as though inviting a guest to leave a house. "Please."

Larson didn't feel like torturing the poor lad, so he pulled his warrant card from his inside pocket and gently passed it to him through the window.

"Serious, is it?"

The officer looked at the ID, then at Larson, and even seemed a little relieved that a higher official was there to take control. He nodded. "We found the car first, stuck in the waterlogged gully. A few officers looked for the owner, and it looks like they found her."

"Alive?" George asked.

"Drowned," he replied. "She probably thought she could get through. They don't realise the power of the water, you see."

Larson grimaced. Some poor soul trying and failing to escape their car.

The rain cleared a little, as though to offer George some clarity. He looked at the scene, the sudden dip of the road, its tight curvature, the two houses up ahead. He could only make out their roofs from where he stood, so low were they in the gully, and although the gloom had cast a shadow over the scene, it was clear they were traditional white thatched cottages. He remembered the two houses well. Too well, in fact.

Lost in the valley's water, they were storybook-like, cute, a spacious home for a middle-aged couple, or a cosy home for a young family.

It was like breaking a dream, the way the memory came back to him.

It flooded his mind, the same way the water flooded the gully below – the black, wooden door he'd knocked on to deliver the news, the forest behind their neighbour's house that he'd trudged through countless times, kicking up leaves, desperate for a sign.

He suddenly realised where he was. It was Somersby Road. Of course it was. He couldn't believe it had taken so long, considering how much he'd analysed this whole area, on maps, in person, on body-finding missions.

Then the calm passed, and the rain continued to slather them. He was back in The Wolds all right, and, George thought, looking up at the pouring sky, it was quite the baptismal return.

A thought hit him.

"Who is it?" George asked the officer.

"Sir?"

"The body," he said, putting a hand on the car window frame. "Has it been identified?"

"Well...yes, actually," said the officer, looking at his notepad. "We have an initial ID. My colleague was taught by her in school."

"Her name, lad," Larson said urgently. "Who is it?"

"Florence," he said. "Florence Tucker."

Larson leaned forward with a rush of recognition, held his steering wheel, and rested his head on his knuckles. He was calming a brewing storm in his chest, whether one of regret or anger, he wasn't sure.

The officer eyed him. "Do you know her?"

Larson sat straight in his seat and then zipped up his rain jacket before answering, "I used to." Then he opened his car door and stepped out into the full force of Lincolnshire's wild, unrelenting forces. "Right then, lad. Let's get to it, shall we?"

CHAPTER FIVE

"Sir," said the officer, jogging to keep up with George's long strides as he marched down the hill. "Sir, I'm not sure you're allowed to–"

"Oh, I'm allowed to, son," Larson told him.

It was unlikely that the lad could hear him over the raging wind. Either way, he didn't try to stop George anymore. Instead, he muttered an apology once they reached the bottom of the hill, where his colleagues watched them arrive with a curious stare.

"DI Larson," George introduced himself, taking out his warrant card again. "What have we got here?"

The older of the two officers reached out to take his ID and read it. She was a brown-haired woman with a bun wrapped so tightly on top of her head that George wondered how she formed facial expressions. She glanced between George and the warrant card like a passport controller.

"A body," she said, handing it back. "Female. Drowned. Paramedics are on the way."

"And you've identified her," Larson confirmed. "Florence Tucker."

He looked around as he spoke and quickly found what he was

looking for. On the other side of the road, in the ditch beside the tarmac, was a lump – a dark shadow that didn't seem to fit the nature that surrounded it.

"Yes, guv," the younger of the two officers said. He was in his thirties, George guessed, with cropped, ginger hair, and like his colleague, held his cap against his chest. "She taught me English at school." He looked a little pale and swallowed before he added, "I recognised her face as soon as a I saw her, guv."

Larson held the man's stare until more flashing lights stole his eyes away. An ambulance slowed to come down the hill and stopped close to where they were standing. It took a few moments for the doors to burst open and two paramedics rushed out.

"Where are we going?" asked one of them, his eyes darting, taking in the scene, ready to act at a moment's notice.

The older policewoman shook her head. "She's already dead," she said, and nodded at the dark lump in the ditch.

Shifting into a state of reverence rather than urgency, one paramedic walked over to Florence Tucker's body and crouched beside it. Larson followed. He looked over the man's shoulder to see the woman he recognised. She was ten years older now, wet through and awkwardly positioned, with blueish skin and haunting, open eyes.

Larson stared at her, his face impassive. "Time of death?" he asked the paramedic.

The paramedic shook his head and took a breath. "Impossible to say," he replied, arbitrarily checking for a pulse. "But it can't have been long. Definitely looks like drowning though." Then the paramedic looked at his watch. "Confirmation of death, 11:31 p.m." George made a mental note of the stated time and surveyed the scene again. "Are we to leave her for CSI, sir?" the paramedic asked, tearing George from his thoughts.

"Leave her here much longer and she'll be halfway to the coast before they get here. No, get her out of here," he said, then pointed at the young uniformed officer. "Photos. I need photos before she's moved."

"You want me to take pictures, guv?" he replied, the thought appearing to horrify him.

"No, perhaps not," George said, and then found the camera app on his phone. He took a few wide shots of the scene, asking the uniformed officers to shine their torches where required, and then took some close-ups of the body, her face, and her clothing. "You never know when you might need it," he told the paramedic, who was professional enough to retain a grave expression during the process. George gave the nod for the paramedic and his colleague to lift the corpse onto the gurney.

In the chaos, George had barely noticed the easing of the rain and the quieting of the storm that finally allowed him to hear his own thoughts. He scanned the scene with a fresher mind and noticed something in the huge puddle that had formed in between the two houses on either side of the gully. The roof of a black four-by-four in the water. It was at the deepest point of the pool. Its wing mirrors stuck out just above the surface like ears.

George nodded at it. "Have you identified the car?" he asked the tight-bunned policewoman, who was clearly in charge.

"Black Toyota RAV4," she answered. "But no registration plate yet. We'll have to wait until the flood levels fall."

"And no other bodies?" George asked.

"No," said the officer, and she eyed Larson. "Why?"

"She has a husband." George nodded at the ditch in his peripheral. "David Tucker. And they have daughters." George shook his head and blinked hard. "A daughter," he said. "Lucy Tucker."

"No sign of anyone else," said the woman. "How do you know all this?"

George ignored the question but nodded at the partially submerged cottage a little further into the huge puddle. "That's their house," he said, and eyed the waterlogged banks on either side. "Stay here," he instructed, and took a step forward. "I'll go and take a look."

"No," said the woman, holding an arm up to block his way.

George stopped and looked at her. "No?"

In his peripheral, he saw the young officer look between his two superiors nervously. Expressionless, George merely stared at the older officer until her arm dropped to her side once more.

"I can't let you do that, guv," she said. "It's not safe."

George nodded and paused. Then he said, "What is your name?"

She hesitated but raised her head a little. "Campbell, guv," she replied. She glanced down at the bright yellow tunic that concealed her epaulettes.

"Sergeant?" asked George.

"Constable, guv."

"And you?" George turned to the young officer, who responded to his look like a deer in headlights.

"Byrne," he said quickly. "PC Byrne."

George didn't need to remind them of his own rank. The message was clear.

"Thank you for your concern, PC Campbell," he said calmly. "I'm sure I'll be fine," and he stepped past them into the shallows of the puddle.

George waded further into the water, up to his knees. He rolled up his sleeves, then stepped onto the corner railing of the Tucker's garden fence. Most of the fence on the other side of the gate had been entirely dragged away, but this side was surprisingly stable. He sidestepped along it, gripping the upper railing. Only once did his foot fall through the rotting wood and threaten to drop him into the deepening water.

But for a man of sixty-six, George Larson was quite strong. His weakness was his agility, or lack of, as was the case. So, once he'd sidestepped to the gate and it was time to swing his leg over and climb down the other side, he did so slowly and with great caution, and in the back of his mind, he knew his knees would suffer the next day.

Still, soon he was wading up to the front door, water up to his waist, ruining his favourite woollen driving jumper. The pea-green door looked the same as it had ten years ago when he'd knocked on it to deliver dreadful news on one of his worst days on the job. Except this time, it was wide open.

He fished his little Maglite from his pocket and turned the head until a wide beam lit the awful scene.

Water slowly drained through the kitchen and out through the broken back door, holding an eery stillness like swamp water, dark and menacing, so thick and dirty he was unable to tell what lay beneath. With that thought, a fallen coat stand floated by slowly like a long alligator.

The inside of the house was just as he remembered, and his memories of the place only added to its spectral quality. The same green-marble kitchen tiles, the same bulbous lampshades, and the same apricot-white wallpaper, bland in the glow of the torchlight.

Of all the things George had expected of his first hour back in The Wolds, he hadn't expected to be forced to exert his authority over potentially new colleagues, or to clamber along a garden fence, or be up to his knees in floodwater.

But least of all, he hadn't expected the step he was about to take next. The step into the Tucker house. The step over this threshold and into a past he'd long since chosen to forget.

CHAPTER SIX

Sophie wasn't sure how long they'd been sitting there, with Lucy slumped and moody on one of the wooden chairs, and herself straight-backed and anxious on the other. They sat beside each other, staring in the same direction – at the wooden slats of the front wall that bled water. They might have been two patients in a waiting room, but waiting for what, Sophie wasn't sure.

For the first time that evening, she felt awkward being close to Lucy. David and Florence wouldn't have liked it. They wouldn't have liked it at all.

The silence lingered, and Sophie shuffled uncomfortably.

Lucy, on the other hand, seemed immune to the disquiet, staring into space, and pushing her tongue into her bottom lip as though pushing around a hidden piercing. Sophie wondered if she was still at that age where the concept of awkwardness hadn't yet kicked in. When the world felt more like something to be taken than something that takes.

How could she know? Sophie had such little experience with teenagers, or kids at all. In the last ten years, especially, she couldn't even remember being in the same room as one.

The night had grown still and quiet, and in the silence, Sophie actually missed the distracting sounds of the rain. How long did they have to endure this? She'd rather take her chances in the storm.

"Do you–" Sophie said, right at the same time as Lucy spoke.

"Can we–"

"Oh," said Sophie, cringing. "You go first."

Lucy rolled her eyes at the absurdity of the situation. "Can we leave?" she said. "The storm's stopped."

"I think it's best to wait," Sophie replied. "Do you have your phone?"

Lucy took a phone out of her pocket. It was so large, Sophie wondered how it even fit. She held it up and a collection of rain dribbled over the dry concrete floor.

"It's dead," said Lucy, and threw it onto the worktable. "It must have flooded when I fell."

Whether the battery was dead or the phone had drowned in her pocket, it didn't matter. There was no way of calling Florence and David. Sophie had never owned a mobile phone. She was one of the few who still had a landline, including a William Morris address book and telephone stand by the front door.

Sophie looked at her watch. It, too, had given up, which was hardly surprising. The time read 11:03, though she knew it was later than that. If they'd left the house just after eleven, it must've been nearing half past by now.

Sophie stood up again, restless, and looked around the workshop. She approached the nearest cardboard box and opened up its flaps. There were the tarps that would soften the ground and some bubble wrap they could use for pillows.

"What are you doing?" asked Lucy, as though offended.

Sophie sighed and looked around for something to keep them warm, blankets or old coats. "We might have to sleep here."

At this, Lucy stood. "What?"

Sophie continued searching. "Well, we can't exactly go home, can we? It'll be midnight soon. Best to just wait for the morning then we can go and find your parents."

"Absolutely not," Lucy said, and Sophie was surprised by the level of authority coming from the voice of a young girl.

Sophie turned around. "Lucy–"

"No," she said, and even stamped her foot a little. "I am not staying here. Mum and Dad will be worried sick, for one. And I need to find out where the hell they are anyway." She walked over to the door.

"Where are you going?"

The floor of Connor's workshop seemed strangely inviting for a nap, and Sophie leaned on a workbench, wearily, while Lucy fiddled with the bolt, which was rusty and stuck.

"I'm getting the hell out of here," she mumbled.

Sophie rubbed her eyes. "The storm has stopped but the whole area is still flooded. It's not safe to go wandering about in the middle of the night. Be logical."

"Logical?" Lucy spun to face Sophie dramatically. "Logically, I don't want to spend the night in that weirdo's dirty workshop."

"Lucy, don't call–"

"What? He *is* a weirdo," she argued, and continued to fumble with the door bolt. "I'm *not* staying here."

"He's not a weirdo," said Sophie softly. "Connor's harmless. You know that."

"How do you know what I know?" Lucy gave up on the bolt and slapped the door in frustration, then turned once more to confront Sophie. "You don't know anything about me. My whole life, you've lived across the road and barely said a word to me. How do you even know my name?"

This time, Sophie didn't reply. She longed for the awkward quiet. Anything was better than this – the dreaded conversation she'd never planned on having. The very reason she'd stayed away from the girl in the first place.

Lucy walked over slowly, her frown deepening, and asked

quietly, as though it was a question she'd never expected to ask out loud, "Why do my parents hate you so much, anyway?"

Again, Sophie knew not to speak. She knew when no words were better than anything she could say in defence. That is, if there was any hope of defending herself.

"Stay away from that house, I was always told. Cross the street. Don't walk past the windows. Don't wave to Mrs Gibson. Why, *Sophie?*" Lucy pushed, using her first name with malice. "Why shouldn't I be talking to you?"

But Sophie just shook her head and stared at the floor like a scolded pet. The wave of tiredness was almost overwhelming. She gave in to Lucy. There was no point resisting. She had no leg to stand on. And anyway, this was a conversation she was happy to walk away from.

Sophie stood up, walked to the door, jiggled the bolt, and unlocked it. It was stiff, but she had strong fingers from gardening and the kind of patience that sixteen-year-old girls lacked. Then she pushed the door open so the still, black night filled the entranceway. So that Lucy could see it was also an exit.

"If you want to leave, then leave," she said. "But I don't think it's a good idea."

Lucy joined her by the door and stopped to add one last scathing remark. She was shorter than Sophie, but in this moment, she seemed much taller. "Lucky for me, I was raised not to trust a word you say."

But as she went to leave, the girl stopped. Sophie felt a wave of cold rush through her soaked skin to her bones. Lucy lingered in the doorway. On the horizon came a flash of lightning, followed by a roll of thunder. Further away than it had been, but still close enough to make Lucy jump.

And the same young vulnerability that Lucy had exposed during the survival moments of the flooding shone through once more. The flash enlightened her profile – her round cheeks, her wide, scared eyes.

Oh, thought Sophie. *I get it.*

This was another secret of teenage behaviour. She'd never known one well enough to understand – they lashed out when they were scared. And, like everyone, even teenagers were scared of the dark.

"Well, if you're going..." said Sophie, pulling on her still-not-dried denim jacket. It creased and stuck to her body. She'd never felt so uncomfortable in her own skin. "I'm going with you."

Lucy didn't look at her. But just as she had after her moment of fear in the flood, she relented and nodded her head in defeat. And the two women went to step outside, back into the cold, dark night.

But before they could leave, a voice from outside spoke. An unfamiliar voice.

"No."

Lucy gripped Sophie's forearm in surprise.

From around the corner of the workshop, dripping with rain and covered in mud, from specks on his chin to the dark patches on his knees, walked Connor. He looked even skinnier than usual, like a dog after a bath, when its fur is flattened against its ribcage, such was his old, flannel shirt flattened against his chest. His thin, blonde hair was sodden, revealing a receding hairline unprecedented for a twenty-something-year-old man. His face had always been flat, Sophie recalled, even as a baby, and without strong, defining features, the water from his hair flowed down his nose and cheeks like a stream over pebbles.

Connor shook his head sadly, his eyes roving Sophie's bare legs.

"You're not going anywhere."

CHAPTER SEVEN

George stepped over the Tucker threshold and waded into the hallway.

"David?" he called up the stairs. "Lucy?"

But nobody replied. The house was silent, except for the occasional splash of a drop falling from some piece of furniture into the larger pool that had engulfed the downstairs.

After a quick look around in the kitchen, George made a beeline for the stairs, ignoring the dirt and debris that pushed up against him in the water. With trouser legs weighted with rank water, he climbed the stairs, reminded of days long gone when his muscles would feel heavy after a session at the station's gym.

"David," he tried again. "Are you here?"

But when he reached the landing hallway, the emptiness of the house could be felt in its cold, lifeless walls. He could have sworn, last time he'd been there, that those walls were full of family photographs – rosy-cheeked faces and lips smeared with chocolate ice cream. But these walls were blank. Yet it was clear the house was lived in. A laundry basket in a corner by the bathroom overflowed and marks from doors swinging open too wide had scuffed the paint.

A flash of lightning lit up the hallway just briefly, like camera film exposed to a snapshot of light. Three rooms branched off the landing and a nook to his right held the bathroom door and enough floor space for the wash basket and an armchair that he doubted anyone used. A crack of thunder followed the lightning, and George did a quick calculation. The storm was about two miles away. It was leaving.

He headed towards the first bedroom on the right and opened the door. It was immediately obvious that this was a teenager's room. George did another quick calculation. Yes, he thought. That's right. Lucy would be about sixteen by now.

A poster of some internet cat meme George didn't understand dominated the wall above the bed, while the other three walls held collages of selfies and groups of friends spilling over each other on sofas or in classrooms. The bed was unmade, and half-empty cups of tea and Coke bottles had been laid on almost every surface.

George remained respectfully in the doorway.

"Lucy?" he called softly, as though he might be waking her from a nap. "Are you there?"

But he heard no reply. The room was empty. He shut the door again behind him.

The next door on his left was also firmly closed and its handle was dusty, as though nobody had touched it in years. He unsettled the dust and opened it.

Inside was neat and tidy, just a tightly made bed, an armchair with a single cream-coloured cushion, and bare shelves. There were no old teddy bears or child-sized school shoes or plastic toys. The whole room was beige and bland. It looked as though it had been redecorated, then forgotten, like it could be used as a guest room but never had been.

George wasn't surprised. He wouldn't want to stay in it. Its aura was distinctly inhospitable; haunting. Everything was too straight-lined, too in-place. It felt uncanny, like somebody had tried far too hard to make the room look like any other. Like it was normal.

But of course, it wasn't, George knew. This room still belonged to someone. Though they hadn't used it for ten years, and would likely never use it again.

He closed the door as peacefully as possible. Then he headed for the last door, the room at the end of the hallway. His heartbeat thundered in his chest, George noticed rationally. Something in his body was anxious about what he might find, and he pondered the wonders of a dark and empty house and the ideas it might tease into play.

Slowly, he pushed open the bedroom door. The first thing he saw was the double bed.

It was empty.

It had been made up with throws and cushions and not slept in all day. George quickly scanned the rest of the room, finding it, too, void of life.

"David?" George called quietly and, he knew, unnecessarily.

He doubted David Tucker was hiding behind the curtains. But then, where was he? Why had Florence been here alone late at night and during a storm? And why did she attempt to drive away in rising floodwaters, rather than run?

George walked over to the window. It was a sash window, the kind that lifted stiffly from the bottom. He checked behind the curtains, just in case, and felt like a child losing at a game of hide and seek. He pulled the window up and received a rush of cold air for his efforts, which went straight to his shin bones and hips, through the wettest parts of his body.

He leaned out and looked up and down the road.

To his left and across the way, Sophie Gibson's house loomed. The lights were off. He supposed somebody should check if she was home and safe. Or if she'd escaped the flood. Maybe she had slept through it, lucky soul.

But it wouldn't be him.

Behind Sophie's cottage was the woodland George had walked through what felt like a hundred times, though it couldn't have been that many. It was just that every hour, during those times, had felt like a week.

Down and to his left, George followed the line of the garden fence he had climbed, and spotted the circle of officers speaking with the paramedics. PC Byrne looked up, spotted him, and waved, like a schoolboy spotting his dad across the playground. George nodded and lifted a hand in return.

Perhaps sensing they were being watched, the paramedics opened the ambulance's large double doors, and one of them climbed inside and sat beside the gurney with its long, white sheet draped over the lifeless lump from the ditch.

Florence. George forced himself to name the lump. *Florence Tucker. Wife. Mother of two. Schoolteacher.*

He gripped the windowsill hard enough for his knuckles to complain, and he let go before cramp set in.

He looked to his right and up the hill. Beyond the curve of the road, he could just about see a sprawling farm with its cottage and spread of outbuildings. He knew the property, or at least he remembered it enough to picture it in the daylight. There was a decent amount of land to the rear, and the muddy yard surrounded the house on three sides, merging with the workable farmland.

But the thing that really caught George's eye was a single headlight in the darkness.

It was on the horizon and winding down the road, travelling fast towards the dip. It passed the ambulance, then slowed once it drew near to the farm house. But instead of turning into the driveway, the lonesome headlight came to a stop.

It stayed there for about half a minute, lighting the scene below like a beacon. Even at this distance, George could hear the low, loud rumble of either a heavy car or a motorbike engine. It felt more like the headlight was watching, absorbing the scene, rather than being up to no good.

Only once the headlight had grabbed the attention of the circle of officers below the window, and PC Campbell began climbing the hill to get a clearer look, did the vehicle perform a three-point turn and return the way it came.

The light became smaller and smaller until, like the last dying ember of a bonfire, it merged with the vast, damp blackness of the countryside that surrounded them all.

CHAPTER EIGHT

"Connor," Sophie breathed.

He just stood there with water dribbling from him like some starved and sickly Poseidon. Lucy's hand had not left Sophie's arm. If anything, her fingers gripped harder. Another flash of lightning illuminated the horizon, and in that brief moment, she could see that mud had crusted the ends of Connor's hair. He was staring at their feet, as though unable to meet their eyes.

"We were just taking shelter from the storm," Sophie said. She took Lucy's hand in hers. "We'll be going now."

But Connor said nothing.

He stepped forward, forcing the two women to take a step back.

"Connor?" said Sophie.

But the young man still didn't speak. He just stared at the ground with dark, lost eyes. And took another step forward.

"Sorry, we didn't mean to intrude," Sophie continued. Lucy's hand in hers was shaking, and she told herself it was from the cold. "We just needed somewhere to wait out the storm."

Slowly, Connor raised his head and stared between the two

women. His face was far from expressionless. It was filled with a
deep sadness.

"You see, our houses were flooded." Sophie began sidestepping, pushing Lucy along with a firm grip. "So, we came up the hill
to get away from the water."

With each backward step Sophie took, Connor took another,
so they were circling each other like fencing partners, matching
the other's movements. If she could just perform a half-circle, her
back would be to the door, and they could make a quick exit. All
she had to do was keep Lucy's hand in hers.

"So, thank you," Sophie said, trying to sound as sincere as
possible. "But Lucy's parents just called," she lied. "So, we'll go
and meet them now." She paused as Connor looked over at
Lucy's wet, dead phone on his workbench. "They're waiting
for us."

Finally, Connor spoke. His voice was so quiet and raspy, it was
hard to hear what he was saying.

"No, they're not."

"What's that?" Sophie asked, in the same jovial voice she used
with animals.

"They're not waiting for you," he said, monotone, then looked
Sophie in the eye quickly, and looked away again. "They don't like
you."

Even though it was true, the directness of the statement sent
a surprising stab to her chest. It hurt to have somebody dislike
you, let alone two people. And even more so when everyone in a
ten-mile radius knew of the ill-feeling.

"Mm-hmm," Lucy spoke up. Her voice sounded so high in
comparison to Connor's, and Sophie recognised the fear. "They
called me, not Sophie. They're waiting outside the house."

Their sidestepping had continued until Connor was the
closest to the workbench. He snatched up Lucy's phone, pressed
the home button to find a black screen, and then set it back
down.

"They didn't call you." Connor sighed, and his voice broke as he said, "You can't leave."

Sophie gulped. Her mind was in that state of disbelief when something unpredictable is happening. It felt surreal, like a dream. So, she played along. "Well, I'm not going to leave," she said. "Just Lucy." She lowered her head to catch his eyes. "I'll stay here for a bit, if you like?"

Connor shook his head but said nothing.

"Go on, Lucy," said Sophie, pushing her hand away and trying to let go. But Lucy didn't let her. "Go meet your parents. I'll stay here for a while." If Lucy could just make a break for it, she could probably run to the door faster than Connor from where they now stood. "Off you go now–"

"No!"

Connor slammed his fist down on the worktable, on top of Lucy's phone, so hard that the screen cracked. Even in the tension, Sophie heard a gasp from Lucy in her ear.

He looked up at them again with eyes sharp, green beneath that single bulb. They reminded Sophie of lily pads in a shallow pool, wet and surface-level, with not much going on beneath.

"You can't leave," he repeated.

The three of them stared at each other, each with tensed muscles, ready to fight or flee. It felt like an old western standoff, as if tumbleweed might roll through the workshop at any given moment.

Sophie had known Connor since he was a boy. At least she'd seen him around, riding his bike up and down the hill between their houses. When he was younger, he'd ride along with his sister Kelly, on her own tricycle beside him. But since she'd left, he'd ridden alone. Since then, he'd always been alone.

She'd watched him become a man and begin working on the farm with his mother Ruth, but he'd always been a strange, quiet and sad, little child, and had grown to become an even quieter and sadder young man. He was what people of her generation called *slow*. His outburst at Lucy's phone was the fastest she'd ever seen him do anything. But she couldn't imagine him being violent. He was probably just anxious from the storm.

Because he would never actually hurt them. Would he?

They continued their standoff in a triangle. Nobody moved an inch. Connor looked at Sophie and she at him, but his stare was off slightly, not making eye contact but looking somewhere closer to her chin. Just as Sophie was about to start talking again to ease the tension, the roar of an engine came from outside.

Sophie wondered if it was Ruth. But her car wouldn't make such a noise. This was so much louder. Like a sports car or a motorbike.

"Jay," Lucy whispered.

Sophie looked at her. The girl looked back, her eyes sparkling with hope.

"Jay," she said louder.

Sophie looked at Connor, whose gaze had moved to Lucy, a frown forming on his brow. Lucy bounced on the spot a little, as though overcome with hope.

"Jay!" she yelled. "JAY!"

Lucy finally let go of Sophie's hand and made a run for the door.

It all happened so fast.

In the same instant, Connor took two long strides over to the door and pulled Lucy back by the hood of her pink rain jacket. The collar tightened around her throat. So, her last "JAY!" was choked and stifled. As she squirmed, Connor placed a large, muddy hand over her mouth and held the rest of her body in his farm-strong grip.

Sophie moved forward instinctively but saw Connor's grip tighten in a way that threatened to cover Lucy's nose and her mouth, and she stopped. Instead, she stood still and held two hands up like a suspect approaching armed police.

The sound of the engine got closer, then further away, then

closer again in the time it took for Connor to restrain Lucy and for Sophie's future to flash before her eyes. If she didn't de-escalate this, who knew what Connor might do, whether on purpose or by accident? If anything happened to Lucy, the Tuckers wouldn't just hate Sophie anymore, she knew.

They'd kill her.

"Connor," she whispered. "What are you doing?"

His face held the same fear as Lucy's. Both young people looked at Sophie with wild, scared eyes and she wasn't sure which ones to meet or who to reassure. Lucy had stopped squirming. She seemed to be focused on breathing instead, and her breaths came out of her nose in noisy fits like a cornered bull.

Connor shook his head, but it was more of a shudder.

"You can't leave," he repeated.

"Why, Connor?" said Sophie, as calmly as she could. "Why can't we leave?"

His shoulders slumped and his grip on Lucy's mouth slackened, leaving bright pink marks on her cheeks where his fingers had dug into her flesh. Lucy blinked hard, with relief or fear, and a single tear fell from her left eye and landed on his knuckle.

Outside, the distant sound of the engine faded to nothing.

"You can't leave," he said one more time, then added, "I'm going to look after you."

CHAPTER NINE

George leaned on the kitchen counter and watched the kettle boil. It was old and layered with limescale and kept crackling like it might explode at any minute. He thanked God that he'd brought a small jar of instant coffee with him in his suitcase, and he thanked God that the gas supply was a large butane bottle stored to the rear of the house and not a mains connection, which would have surely been turned off by now. The cupboards were bare. Beyond bare – moulding in the corners, with doors hanging off their hinges.

The previous night had been much longer than he'd been expecting. And when he had arrived at the old house in the early hours of this Monday morning, the bed's lumpy mattress and creaky metal frame had offered little in the way of a good night's sleep. His brief dreams had been swimming with memories, bordering nightmares.

Like everywhere in The Wolds, the storm had penetrated the old place. Luckily, the house was positioned on a rise, which meant that groundwater hadn't invaded the space. But rainwater had entered the attic and through weak spots in the ceiling. So much so that George had almost sleep-walked into the garden in the early hours to gather whatever buckets, watering cans, and barrels he could find in the decrepit shed. So, all night, his haunting dreams had been punctuated by tip-taps, slowly becoming deeper in tone until he'd awoken and emptied them.

The kettle boiled with a sound more similar to the spin cycle of a washing machine than a kettle. Still, the smell of fresh coffee, however cheap and instant, was a welcome scent. George usually preferred his coffee with milk, but there definitely was none. His mistake of opening the fridge last night to a swelling scent of rot had told him that much.

He took a sip and turned to survey the room. It was an old-fashioned kitchen with sturdy enough features that had only become dated through neglect. But the black range oven would be a defining feature once cleaned, and if he had a chance to fill the grout between the terracotta, flowery tiles, they might regain their timeless aesthetic.

No, the bigger problems were more structural, he mused. The leaking roof, the single-glazed windows, the overgrown garden with weeds that had been left wild for so long, he imagined they'd tangled their way into the very foundations of the house.

It was a fixer-upper that George didn't have much time to fix-up.

He carried his black coffee into the living room. It was, objectively, a beautiful room. So long as one didn't look too closely at the details. A long, stained-glass window let in light from the top floor and stopped just above the solid-wood front door. Opposite it, a staircase hugged one wall and crossed into an open mezzanine balcony, so one could lean on its bannister at the top and look through the long window at the charming fifteenth-century St Margaret's Church.

But the devil was in the details. The fireplace was a veritable spider's nest, and although the house hadn't been abandoned overnight, it had an air of neglect. A huge, oak bookcase held a decorative layer of dust alongside its collections of old books, all of which appeared dogeared and weathered, from leather-bound classics to contemporary novels. The sofas were cream and dated from a time when floral and winged was the style. The rug that dominated the middle of the floor space had fringes at the end that were now limp and matted.

But mostly, the house was skeletal. It reminded George of those sadder gravestones in a cemetery. The overgrown graves that relatives either cannot or don't care enough about to maintain. The ones that never receive fresh flowers or carved stones or tearful and thoughtful visits.

George carried his coffee up the wide staircase.

He'd already learned, last night, that the third-from-the-top step had a dangerous softness to it that suggested rot and it was best to skip it. He was learning the house, George felt. He'd only been here for six hours. But one of its secrets, at least, he was familiar with now, and he wondered how many more there were left to discover.

The bedroom George had chosen was not the master, but the room to the left of the landing that had half-painted canvases and a box of dried-up brushes in the back of its closet. It had an ensuite, too, which must have been a later addition, plus a small but majestic view of the Lincolnshire Wolds, framed by a large, square window that made the view look like an artwork in itself.

There was a desk in one corner, an easel in the other, a lumpy double bed with scratchy blankets, and a door to the bathroom. Beside the bed, on the rickety table, he'd placed the only photo he'd brought with him from Mablethorpe – the one of Grace smiling as confetti rained down on them on their wedding day.

George put down his coffee on the desk. Usually, he'd use a coaster after years of conditioning by Grace. But the furniture in the old house seemed beyond saving, even if there had been one in sight.

Above the desk was an oval gold-leaf mirror, now tarnished and sad. It was as though somebody might have also used the desk as a dressing table. Above it was an empty pin board, which years ago may have held little memories, just like in Lucy Gibson's room. George studied his withered reflection. His eyes looked heavy and sleepless. It wasn't the restful night he'd been hoping for before his first day. But considering the face-slap of the past he'd received on his return, he was surprised he'd managed to get any hours at all.

Stepping into the bathroom, George expected little in the way of hot water. But he settled for a cold, dribbling shower, which did at least wake him up. There were no towels, and no bath mat either. All he could do was stand naked in the bathroom and dab himself with a t-shirt. Out of the open suitcase on his bed, George pulled his wash bag and brushed his teeth and, with no place to set down his toothbrush, set it back, wet, into the bag. He wet his fingers, and pushed back his strands of grey hair away from his face, into a rough style.

His experience of Bag Enderby so far had been wet. Wet ground, wet clothes, wet house, wet skin. He should make a list, he told himself, of things to buy in town after work. Towels were at the top of the list. He wanted to feel dry. He wanted to feel warm.

George blinked away the image of the soft, white towels back home, the thick duvet on his bed, and tartan blankets on his sofa by the fire. There was no point. He was here now. And he had to make the best of it.

He got dressed into his standard white shirt that was more comfortable than crisp. George hadn't ironed his clothes in years. He found it wasn't worth the effort when they creased so easily on the job anyway – up and down from a desk, in and out of a car, to and from houses and interview rooms and crime scenes. Over the top, he wore a sleeveless woollen pullover, striped in autumnal tones, along with his best argyle socks, grey tweed trousers, and smartest brown brogues.

He toured the upstairs to see what else could go on his list.

Though the house felt grand in some ways – its enormous fire-place, long, double-floored window, and dominating pieces of furniture – it wasn't huge. There were only three bedrooms, two with en suites, then the large open-plan living room slash entrance area and a spacious, square kitchen.

The other two bedrooms, George reasoned, could wait for bedding and towels. But if he was to stay there for a while, as was the plan, then he'd have to get around to them, eventually.

George leaned on the banister and looked through the misted, long window. The air inside the house made it too cold to see outside. But it was out there, waiting for him. The consequences of last night. The aftermath of the flood.

The handrail creaked, and George learned another of the house's deadly secrets – to not rest too much weight there. Nothing in this house was trustworthy. It had evolved to be alone. Or devolved, maybe? And his presence was threatening its delicate ecosystem.

But he felt it in his bones, the need for a project. The need to fix something. Recently, so much of his life felt out of his hands. The previous night had only proved how unpredictable and cruel the world could be. That, in his first hours back in The Wolds, he might come across the dead body of Florence Tucker. It was unbelievable; chaotic or synchronous.

But this house needed only sensible, straightforward fixes – the turn of screws, the wipe of a dust brush, the hammering of nails. It was something he could fix with his own hands. And these days, the ability to remedy was a novelty.

George descended the stairs, skipping the soft step. He took his keys out of the front door, then looked to his left instinctively at the empty wall. A mirror here, he added to his mental list, to check his hair before he left the house. He downed the rest of his watery coffee in one, like he'd seen young lads do with pints at the pub, then placed the empty mug on a side table.

There was a time when he wouldn't have been able to leave an empty cup anywhere but in the sink. But if he was honest, the house was a ship wreck. One empty cup left on the side wouldn't make a difference.

After all, there was nobody around to notice it but him.

George didn't check his hair in the mirror before he left the house. He just opened the door and stepped into the frigid February air. The winter had almost faded away. The frosty mornings were over, leaving the promise of greens and yellows. The time for snowdrops and misty mornings. The time for change.

CHAPTER TEN

Ivy Hart turned the engine off and sat for some moments in the warmth of her car. Still chilly from Jamie's frosty goodbye when she'd left the house, she was in no rush to face the lingering storm winds. Luckily, the floods hadn't affected her drive to work. But signs of its aftermath were everywhere. Even the station car park drains were struggling to deal with the residue.

Her watch told her it was 7:55 a.m., so she took a deep breath and prepared to brave the new day. When she opened her car door, she found the air warmer than she had expected, a reminder for Ivy to stay optimistic. She needed to begin the day with a positive attitude, to make good first impressions. They were everything she knew. And a positive attitude meant setting aside the image of her husband's disappointed eyes and the too-tight little hugs from Hatty and Theo that she'd received over an hour ago.

She'd made her choice. Now it was time to follow through with it. Still, her heart quickened to that rate many experience on their first day in a new job, with sweaty palms to match.

She walked around the side of the two-storey, red-brick building and over to the siren-blue main doors of the police station. She focused on switching her mask, from wife and mother and failure of her domestic duties to agreeable and capable detective sergeant who was ready for her new position.

As soon as she pushed through the main doors, she could see that the blue and white theme would continue throughout the building. Two straight, cyan lines stretched around the clean walls on every side of the room and plastic chairs – more of a sky-blue and bolted down so nobody could throw them – offered seating for waiting visitors. Straight ahead was a single door leading into a long corridor visible through the square-panelled glass, leading, Ivy knew, to the custody suite, interview rooms and a number of cells at the end. To the left of where she stood was the reception desk, the front of which was blue.

Ivy strode over and rested her hands on the counter, assuming a posture that she thought suggested confidence. The man on reception, an older, moderately overweight officer with red cheeks, clearly felt differently. He eyed her with suspicion.

"DS Hart," she introduced herself, then produced her warrant card, which he examined with a casual glance, or disinterest.

The man didn't introduce himself in return. He just nodded into the corridor and muttered, "Up the stairs. Chief Inspector Long is waiting for you."

Ivy tapped the counter once before walking away, feeling slightly annoyed with herself at having wasted some of her good-impression energy on the man. She waited for him to push the door release button, then pushed through into the corridor. The stairs were on the right, and she climbed with more than a little trepidation, stopping at the top to roll her neck and rearrange her mask once more. She rubbed her jaw so as not to appear tense, then took a final deep breath.

The first-floor corridor looked the same as any other corridor in any other police station in which Ivy had worked. But perhaps a bit smaller. After all, the Lincolnshire Wolds was not exactly a crime hotspot. She and George would be the only plain-clothed detectives in the building, accounting for the closure of Mablethorpe Station and covering the jurisdiction of The Wolds.

She supposed uniformity was a crux of the force, and the buildings were no exception. So given the choice of left or right, she went right, as she'd never been in a police station where the boss's office wasn't the last door on the left at the end of the corridor, closest to the fire exit and, therefore, the car park.

Still, she checked the signs on every door she passed. There were a few offices and a locker room. One was the kitchen. Another was the incident room door, outside of which was a floorboard that creaked. But she found the door she was looking for exactly where she expected it − the last door on the left, with a bronze nameplate that read, *DCI Long.*

As Ivy lifted her fist to knock a well-considered and confident three times, once more came the reliable flutter of her heart. She was familiar with nervous sensations. Life in the force wasn't a career for the faint-hearted. It wasn't that the job didn't scare her at times, more that she knew how to recognise when that feeling arose in her body and how to tune into it. Instincts were not something she feared − they were a superpower, telling her what might come before it came, feelings that had saved her life on more than one occasion.

So attuned were her senses that even the footsteps sounding along the corridor were recognisable; slow and steady. She knew to whom they belonged long before the familiar voice that accompanied them called her name.

"Ivy," George Larson said, speaking her name as though for confirmation and not a greeting. He was never one for formalities, even though their roles were part of a huge and comprehensive matrix of formal processes.

She turned to face her boss. The man she'd worked beside for five years. The man she'd followed here, regardless of the consequences to her personal life. He looked smart in his standard sleeveless pullover, beneath a long black coat, and his best brogues. His hair was slicked back, his coat was lint free, but to somebody who knew him as well as Ivy did, he also looked extremely tired.

She nodded once. "Guv."

Ivy *was* a stickler for formalities. However many times he'd told her to call him George, she only did so in the comfort of her own mind. Even though, ever since she'd known him, he had been more of a comforting presence than an authoritative figure. Unlike so many toxic members of the force, George had never succumbed to the power his rank could wield, however much responsibility he had been burdened with.

Each rung of the ladder he'd climbed with a compassionate nature, mostly due to his ability to make wise, calm decisions like a chess player thinking three steps ahead of everyone else. And so lesser colleagues, calculating only their next move, failed to understand how to read him. And George's stoic expression further served his enigma-like thought processes.

Indeed, he was infuriating to play chess with. She had never won a single game.

They said nothing more. They just stood side by side. Either could have asked the other, "Are you ready for this?" and possibly predicted the other's reply. But the words remained unspoken. Instead, George reached out and knocked twice.

Then, before anybody called out, he opened the door and held out a chivalrous arm for Ivy to enter the room first, just as a voice called, "Come in."

It was a smaller office than Ivy expected with standard, white furniture, a few framed certificates with writing too small to read from afar, and a large desk, in front of which were two empty chairs that were, of course, blue.

The man behind the desk stood as they entered. Ironically, DCI Timothy Long was rather short, the table top in line with his waist. He had salt-and-pepper hair that was especially grey around his temples, styled in a rather nondescript fashion.

"George," he said, beaming, and walked around the desk to shake George's hand.

Larson shook it back, and DCI Long placed one hand over the top, whether out of affection or to exert authority, Ivy wasn't sure yet.

"And you must be Sergeant Hart," he said, turning to Ivy, who also shook his hand, sure to hold tight and make a firm impression. "Chief Inspector Long," he confirmed.

"Nice to meet you, sir."

He looked younger up close, with wrinkles only in the most endearing places – around the eyes and mouth that suggested a lifetime of smiling. She wasn't sure she'd ever received such a warm welcome from a Chief Inspector. Still, from his younger features, he couldn't have been older than mid-forties. So it looked like he'd grown grey before his time, and Ivy doubted he'd climbed so high up the ladder through warmth alone.

"Sit, sit," he told them, and walked back to his chair behind the desk while George and Ivy took the two in front of it. "It's great to see you back, George."

Ivy had to bite her lip to stop from responding. *Back?*

"It's good to be back, Tim."

Ivy tried to read Long's reaction to his first name. She thought she might've seen a twitch of the eye, but again, she couldn't be sure.

"So," said Long, "straight to business." He clasped his hands and placed them before him on the desk. "I am sorry to ask you to start on a Saturday. But, as you likely already know, we experienced a hell of a flooding last night. Nearly a month's worth of rain in a single night." He looked between the two, who said nothing in reply. "I was going to ask you to help with the clean up. Ease you in. First day and all. But it looks like you're going to have to dive in the deep end."

He paused as though for dramatic effect. However, the next words didn't come from his lips, but George's.

"You found a body."

Long blinked at him. "Yes," he said. "A–"

"Woman," George said, cutting him off. "Drowned."

Ivy kept her eyes on Long. For Larson to be three steps ahead of everyone else came as no surprise to her, but she was curious to see her new Chief Inspector's reaction. He looked shocked, and a little amused, as though he too had played George at chess in his time.

"How do you know?"

"I was stopped by road traffic police last night."

Long paused and looked deeper into Larson's face. "So, you know who it is?"

Ivy thought she heard George grind his teeth before replying. "Florence Tucker."

Whatever game they were playing, Ivy thought, she was more than three moves behind. The name meant nothing to her, but from the serious expression on both men's faces as she looked between them, it meant a lot to *them*.

"I want to start looking for David," George said. "As soon as possible."

Long nodded, then straightened a piece of paper on his desk that was already straight, then looked up again. "Do you really want to do that, George?" he said. "Do you really want to get involved?"

This time, Ivy looked only at her boss, whose face, as usual, was infuriatingly stoic.

"I don't *want* to," George replied. Then he added with a rare vulnerability, "I think I *need* to."

CHAPTER ELEVEN

"Who's Florence Tucker?"

George strode down the corridor and waited until he'd pushed through the door to the stairwell before replying. "Local woman," he answered. "Wife. Mother. Schoolteacher."

Ivy hated it when he walked this fast, he knew, because she had to do an undignified half-run to keep up with him. But she was far too stubborn to ask him to slow down. So, he slowed of his own accord, and they cantered down the stairs side by side.

"How do you know her?"

George sighed. "Florence Tucker had a daughter, Kelly Tucker. Ten years ago, she disappeared. I worked the case."

He pushed through the fire escape doors, and they entered the car park and headed towards George's car. Ivy waited until they were pulling on their seatbelts before she asked something that wasn't really a question. George noted the tinge of hurt in her voice.

"I didn't know you used to work here," she said.

"It was a long time ago," he said, then, feeling overly ambiguous, added, "ten years now." He almost added, *five years before we met*. But she could work out that much for herself.

George took a moment of reflection with his hands on the wheel, contemplating how much to tell Ivy. She was his number two. She had followed him here. She had taken the risk. But she wasn't his confidante, though he trusted her with his life. Indeed, on more than one occasion, she had even saved it. Still, he chose not to say anything more, choosing instead to turn the key, start the engine, and pull out of the car park and into The Wolds.

The standing water rose off the fields as mist, the sun broke through the layer of clouds, the birds that had taken shelter in trees were once more in flight. And suddenly, George missed the sea. There was a landlocked dampness to this place. He wanted a wide, undisturbed view into nothing. But for now, all he had was rolling hills, farmland, and a smattering of church spires marking the various settlements.

It was a quiet drive. Ivy stared out the window at the view that was also new to her, and George felt that tinge of hurt growing between them. Anything growing between them, however much he didn't want to acknowledge it, was the last thing he wanted.

"I worked with Tim," he explained. "DCI Long," he added for clarity. "We were both DIs under Chief Inspector Rose, who is now Detective Superintendent Rose. It was a big enough station, with room for progression for a few. I moved to Mablethorpe with Grace. Tim stayed. He rose up to DCI. And that was that."

George hoped that was enough. Ivy, at least, didn't dig for further details, but simply nodded and offered him a brief smile to show that she'd been listening. He wasn't ready to tell her why he and Grace had moved to Mablethorpe all those years ago. Why the sea air had been so important in their lives. But she didn't probe. It was one of his favourite things about Ivy. She was personable without being pushy. He felt he had, in her, a capable, warm teammate who didn't prioritise getting ahead. They got on well. But she maintained a professional distance, too. And for a man like George, who liked to keep his personal life to himself, that was very much appreciated.

The Tucker house was only a fifteen-minute drive from the station, and when they pulled up at the diversion at the top of the hill, clean-up was clearly underway. The scene looked very different in the daylight. There were no shadows masking the extent of the damage. On either side of the lane were, as George remembered, fields, and they did indeed resemble something more akin to swampland.

The road below was littered with matted leaves, stray branches and empty drinks bottles that the floodwater had carried. At the bottom of the waterlogged gulley, the gardens of the two houses looked more like rugby pitches. And although the water level had now fallen, an ugly, muddy line showed where it had once been on the stained Lincolnshire stone.

George pulled the car to the side of the road and turned off the engine, and he and Ivy sat in a still silence for a moment, as though there was more to be said.

"You followed me here from Mablethorpe," George said, and turned to her. "I appreciate that, Ivy. We're in this together, and I should've told you the complete story."

She smiled a smile that, George saw with relief, reached her chestnut-brown eyes. He knew she was insecure about her eyes – that they were too close together. But George thought they were beautiful, and gave her the intense, majestic stare of a bird of prey. Along with her strong, masculine jaw, Ivy Hart looked as formidable a woman as any George knew.

"Thanks, guv," she said, and then paused. He watched her lips twitch before she asked, "Did you ever find her?"

George almost asked, *who?* Only to bide himself some time. But he knew exactly who she was talking about, and it was a truth from which there was no running. His arrival in The Wolds had made that very clear. He shook his head, raised his eyebrows, and answered in a voice that sounded sadder than he'd meant it to.

"No."

They endured a few more seconds of silence, watched a

kestrel dive for some rodent or other, evicted from its home, and then, in synchronisation, stepped out of the parked car.

George flashed his warrant card at the officer as they walked past the diversion. He was a different officer to the one last night and nodded them through without fuss.

Before descending the hill, they stood to observe the scene in its entirety. In the dip at the bottom, a red pump hummed as it sucked water from the gulley through a large, black hose, then regurgitated it somewhere amongst the trees away from the road. On the other side of the lane, a firefighter was setting up another, pulling at the starting cord just like George's lawnmower.

The submerged Black Toyota RAV4 he'd spotted last night was becoming more and more visible. Even from this angle, they could see it was completely wrecked, and although the windows had not been lowered, water had clearly seeped through gaps enough to destroy the upholstery and flood the footwells.

George and Ivy descended the hill. There were a handful of officers who were distracted talking to the fire brigade. Only one of them did he recognise as the police officer from the previous night. In his last few strides, George racked his mind for her name, and found it just in time.

"PC Campbell."

The woman turned to face George, the bun on top of her head as tight as ever. He noted her look of slight disappointment, as though he was an omen of trouble.

"Inspector Larson," she confirmed.

"DS Hart," Ivy said, stepping into the circle, and the two women nodded at each other.

"Any updates?" asked George.

Campbell shook her head. "We're still cleaning up, I'm afraid. We're focusing on opening this road up again to traffic. It's a major thoroughfare for the locals."

George nodded and eyed the woman. He found PC Campbell to be a confident, self-assured officer who didn't hesitate to respond. "We're looking for David Tucker," he said, bringing her into the loop. "Any sign of him?"

"The husband? He hasn't been home. I've been here all night."

George did one of his quick calculations. For someone who'd been on a night shift for at least ten hours, she seemed surprisingly alert. He was impressed.

"Well, let me know if you find anything."

Then, deliberately crossing her path to see if she stopped him, George headed towards the destroyed house closest to them. But PC Campbell kept her arms firmly at her side.

The walk along the Tuckers' garden path was far from welcoming. Its large paving stones had sunk into the ground like soggy biscuits. He hadn't noticed in the chaos of last night, but the front door had one of those doorbell cameras he'd seen a few times, which the flood line hadn't quite reached. George wondered if it still worked. He pressed it as he walked past, and noticed a little blue light on the device, but heard nothing from inside - most likely due to the power being out, which meant that the doorbell itself was battery-powered and may hold some clue as to David Tucker's whereabouts.

Then, for the second time in less than a day, George crossed the threshold into the Tucker home. Just like the outside, the inside appeared very different in the daylight. The rank water that had sat like a still, forgotten pool had been drained and left, in its wake, broken furniture, peeling wallpaper, and a dirt-ridden carpet that, if memory served George, had once been cream.

George and Ivy headed upstairs. This time, he didn't bother calling for David. David clearly wasn't home. Where on earth he – or Lucy, for that matter – was, that was anybody's guess. George just hoped the news of his wife's death didn't hit David out of the blue. Seeing as George had been the one to deliver the news of his daughter's assumed death ten years ago, he felt he should be the one to deliver the news of Florence's too.

As George entered Lucy's bedroom, the first door on the

right, he felt Ivy move past him straight to the end of the hallway – the master bedroom. They were good like that, at breaking up and dividing what needed to be done evenly. And rarely did either of them feel obliged to explain themself to the other.

This time, George didn't hover in the doorway. He entered the room fully and took a good look around. To his left was a desk with a closed laptop surrounded by crumbs and shavings from a pencil sharpener. He crouched to look beneath and found an overflowing waste paper bin. Atop the mound, only half-buried beneath a crisp packet, was a single used condom. The poor attempt to conceal it provided two possibilities. The first was sheer complacency, which wasn't entirely out of the question for a teenage girl. The second, however, was that it had been left there purposefully, the way a teenager might leave dirty dishes on the countertop just to rile their parents.

George stood up and wove between the furniture. He looked beneath the bed, inside the wardrobe, on the windowsill, but found nothing out of place. He turned to the walls.

The collages, it turned out, didn't just include photos of Lucy and her friends, but also images of her and someone who looked to be a boyfriend. With Lucy's lips pressed up against his cheek, the boy looked only into the camera with a straight, unmoved face. She was smiling in every photo. He, however, was not.

He had that fuzzy type of hairstyle that boys often wore. It wasn't a look for a full-grown man. It was cut short and dyed blonde, with an uneven fringe that encroached on his forehead. And he had hollow cheekbones that gave him a dark and dangerous look that George supposed a smile would betray. He didn't look much older than seventeen, but these days, George found youngsters looked older and older.

He selected the photo that best captured the boy's face head-on, the one most like a mugshot, and unpeeled it from the wall, before slipping the photo into the inside pocket of his coat.

"Guv?"

George turned to see Ivy standing in the doorway holding a piece of paper.

"In the bin," he said, then offered Ivy a sympathetic grimace. "Bag it, would you?"

From the corner of his eye, George saw Ivy look in the bin, groan, and grab a pencil from the desk, which she used to pick up the condom and drop it into one of the evidence bags she kept in her coat pocket.

"What is it?" he asked, and nodded at the paper she'd placed on the desk.

But before she could answer, a flustered PC Campbell appeared in the doorway, holding on to the frame as though for support. "DI Larson," she said quickly. "You're going to want to see this."

CHAPTER TWELVE

George and Ivy followed PC Campbell through the woodland behind Sophie Gibson's house. It was the same woodland George had trekked through many times before. He had led teams through the trees, searching for Kelly Tucker's body in a long, single line. The searches had included dog handlers and volunteers, some of whom had called Kelly's name incessantly.

The forest held a mishmash of trees, from spindly and peeling silver birches to yews with thick trunks that made the ideal climbing apparatus for fearless kids. The flooding had made the path indistinguishable from the wilder, root-filled soil surrounding it. Saturated leaves glinted in the absorbing sunlight; their dew drops sparkling like diamonds. But there were shadows too, in the deeper parts of the woodland where George didn't dare to look for too long out of some primal fear that he might just see what he was looking for.

Like the rest of the area, the ground was soggy. Some patches of mud gripped his ankles like quicksand. At one point, George tripped on a sticky patch and Ivy leaned forward to offer him her forearm. He held onto it, sturdy as a fence. Before letting go, she gave his arm a subtle squeeze, as though reminding him to not break an ankle.

Still, George couldn't focus on his footing, so distracted was he by the forest. Almost every tree held a memory of dogs digging at its roots, or local volunteers leaning against its trunk, exhausted. But no tree held such a strong memory as the oak in the middle of the clearing before them.

George stopped and gazed up at it, straight to the second branch from the bottom on the right. The thick and sturdy limb. The limb that any logical man might select, just as Edward Gibson had.

The tree was so bulbous and rugged that it resembled the Bowthorpe Oak in Bourne, England's oldest tree. It had a similar hollow trunk with triangular entrances to its shadowy centre. But George imagined that this tree had seen even more life than the famous oak had in its one thousand years. Or, more accurately, that it had seen more death.

Ivy stopped beside George. He felt her curious gaze on the side of his face, but he didn't turn to meet her eye to eye. Nor did he explain his hesitation to walk past this most haunted of trees, choosing instead to press on. After all, there was little time for nostalgia. He was restless to see what Campbell had to show them. Her findings could offer closure of some description.

"What is it?" Larson had asked Campbell back at the house.

"A body, we think," she'd answered, and then she had left it at that.

But as soon as they broke through the tree line, George saw what the fuss was about, and he knew that any closure around the Tucker family was nothing more than a pipe dream. There were only more mysteries to solve. More tragedies to face.

Just beyond the forest was a small stream fed by the water that flowed from two huge culverts. And like the fire-engine pump back at the road, they too had been draining the floodwater from the road, pushing it further along its natural course to find its way to the sea.

Except that something blocked one of the watercourses before him.

At the exit of one culvert, as though he'd travelled through the tube head-first, were the grisly remains of a man, held fast in the rush of water, as if seeking a way out.

Again, he felt Ivy's gaze.

"Is it...?" she asked.

"David," he said, finishing it for her, and nodding his confirmation. "Yes, it's him all right."

George had to look away for a second after identifying the man. The way the water ran across his lifeless, pale blue face was sickening. He'd been a father, a husband, a businessman, George reminded himself. But at this moment, David Tucker was no more than a blockage. A build-up of coffee grounds in a pipe. A collection of hair in a drain.

Poor Lucy. That was the first thing George thought when he saw David's body. The poor girl had lost everything. Everyone in her family. Dead.

Just like Florence, David too looked wide-eyed and scared. There was no peace in death, George reminded himself. Not even in drowning, for all its myths of shipwrecked sailors dying in harmony with the sea. Still, the look on David's face was far from peaceful. And from this angle, something about the shape of his head didn't seem right. It was distorted, somehow.

He stepped around to the other side of the culvert, beckoning for Ivy to follow. Campbell stayed back, as though her job of leading George to the scene was complete. And as George rounded the tube, stepping through the stream and wetting his brogues, the uncanny shape of David's skull made sense.

One side of it was concave. The skull had been struck with such force that it had dented. And the volume of blood that had consequently been released had been so high, it still stained

David's prematurely grey hair and the top of his ear, even though his body must have been bathing in floodwater for hours now. It had set as hard as glue.

Though the body's journey through the culvert had unlikely been smooth, George doubted that any debris in the water or loose lengths of pipe could have caused such a wound. No, this kind of head trauma was intentional. Somebody had done this to him, he thought, and imagined the weapon, along with the hatred of the person wielding it.

George remembered the steely grief in David's eyes, ten years ago, when George had told him they'd stopped looking for his daughter, the whitening of his knuckles around his wife's hand, his tightly clenched jaw. Even in that moment, David hadn't cried. And now, the drain's deluge over his face looked like it was making up for all those unspent tears.

George never had been able to offer the man closure. Nor Florence. Nor had he found justice for little Kelly.

There was only one person left whom he could help.

"I want Lucy Tucker found and brought to me as soon as possible," he said sharply to the group of officers, who'd all silenced at George's arrival and joined him in staring at David Tucker's body.

But only one of them replied.

"I'm on it, guv," Campbell said behind him, and he heard her march back into the woodland, presumably headed to her car, where she could start to plan a search under the authority of her superiors.

George crouched closer to the body, wetting his shins. Opposite him, Ivy did the same, and they both scanned David's body. Then they met each other's stare.

"That's some head wound," she confirmed.

With that observation, the phone in George's pocket began to vibrate. He pulled it out slowly and held it to his ear, still staring into David's dull eyes.

"DI Larson?" the voice at the other end jumped in immediately.

"This is he," George answered quietly.

"I was told to call you. Heard you're working the Florence Tucker investigation?"

With a longer sentence, George was able to identify the accent. From the stretched-out vowels and singsong tone, it was Welsh. He immediately imagined a small, humble Welsh girl in a green field chock full of sheep. He knew it was a stereotype, but George had spent little time there, and it always helped to put a face to a voice.

"That's right."

"Pippa Bell. I'm the forensic pathologist, here at Lincoln Hospital," the woman said, as casually as revealing herself as Florence's dentist. "I wanted to talk to you about my assessment of the body."

"Let me guess," George said, eyeing David's body and noticing the deep mud stains on his knees. "You don't believe her death was an accident?"

"Well, yes," the pathologist said, as though she wasn't used to people speaking her next words for her. "Exactly how do you know that?"

"I'm looking at her husband," he said, and met Ivy's eyes once more. "And I very much doubt that his death was an accident either."

CHAPTER THIRTEEN

For what felt like the hundredth time, Sophie watched Lucy stretch her leg across the workshop floor, trying to touch a spanner with her foot. The girl had been tiptoeing towards it for the last hour. What she expected to do with it once it was at her feet, Sophie wasn't sure. She'd already knocked over a box of bolts and a paint can.

Whatever plan Lucy had, it wasn't working. She was just making a mess.

Both their arms had been tied to the backs of their chairs. Their ankles, too, had been tied to the legs, so exactly how Lucy had freed one of her legs, Sophie wasn't sure. But it was not providing much benefit.

Since a rounders accident in her twenties, Sophie had always had dodgy knees, and now they were grumbling. She hadn't moved her legs all night, and what with the damp and cold air, her knees had locked at the same awkward angle. She hoped she'd be able to garden after this. Hell, she hoped she'd be able to stand.

Again, Sophie checked to see if there was any wriggle room in the rope that bound her hands. But every time she moved, the bindings only seemed to grow tighter. Cutting off the blood circulation to her fingers was becoming a real possibility and cause for quiet concern. But with Connor being born and raised on a farm, securing horses, building fences, she realised that his powerful hands would tie tight knots.

Even so, Lucy had managed to work an ankle free during the night, and since then, she'd been on a mission. Her foot had reached the spanner, and with the infinite flexibility of her sixteen-year-old body, her stretches had increased inch by inch. But in her excitement, she'd kicked the spanner a few centimetres further away, and it clattered on the concrete floor.

The teenager cursed under her breath, but loud enough that Sophie felt compelled to check that the noise hadn't stirred Connor. The two women sat facing each other, while Connor slept close to the door, curled up on an old blanket like a watch-dog. But he still seemed sound asleep.

Undeterred, Lucy began stretching again, endlessly hopeful about what Sophie deemed a pointless task. Still, she watched the girl with the same indifference with which she watched daytime TV. Against the backdrop, she let her mind wander.

She couldn't remember the last time she'd sat so long in a chair. Let alone with only her thoughts and a teenager's vague escape plans for entertainment. Sophie preferred to keep herself busy, pottering in the garden, helping at the food bank, or enjoying long and brisk walks through the fields. The latter forced her to focus on her breathing, something she had learned that helped with her anxiety. Since Edward had died, it felt as if she hadn't stopped moving.

But judging by the daylight that had started to seep through the panelling, Sophie wanted to say four hours ago – though it was a wild guess, really – she'd been sitting here for at least ten hours. She remembered her school friend, Irene, going on a silent meditation retreat after her husband left her for the au pair. It was meant to be a serene, soulful experience. Irene was going to find herself, find her purpose, in a commune in the French Alps. But instead, she'd told Sophie, her mind had travelled to dark places. Behind her eyelids was a whole world of malice – images of demons, existential anxieties. Doubts. Doubts about every choice she'd ever made, from shopping at Waitrose to marrying her husband.

It was a place that Sophie had no desire to go.

So, she turned her attention to Lucy. The marks where Connor had gripped her face still looked pink and swollen. Her arms, too, appeared much more strained than her own. While Sophie had sat still and let Connor tie her up, not wanting to spook him, Lucy had struggled the entire time. She had spat viscerally about what Jay would do to him when he found out. She'd threatened him with her dad's lawyers, her mum's maternal instincts.

But Sophie was convinced that Connor wouldn't hurt them. At least not on purpose. She looked over at him, curled up by the door. He looked like a puppy. He didn't have it in him to act out of cruelty. No, whatever his intentions, they were from a different source. One of mercy. Misaligned, sure, but not cruel.

He'd said he was protecting them. From the storm? From the flood?

It made little sense. The rain had long stopped. The waters would have lowered by now. Whatever he felt they needed protection from must have been a more constant threat. Something still out there.

Lucy's legs had found new limits. She could once more touch the spanner with her toes. She winced and pressed down on its circular head so that the other side lifted in the air. At this, she laughed with hope and tried again with renewed vigour. But she overcompensated, pressed too hard, and the other end of the spanner rose, performed a cartwheel-like movement, and landed with a loud rattle on the floor.

Sophie rolled her eyes. She checked Connor again. He stirred in his sleep and rolled over.

"What are you doing?" she whispered.

Lucy seemed surprised to hear her voice, as if she'd forgotten Sophie was there, so focused had she been on the spanner. Now it was closer, she could drag the tool across the floor under her shoe.

"Getting us out of here," said Lucy.

Slowly, she pulled the spanner to her feet, then stopped and looked at it. She watched, as though it might perform a trick. Then Lucy narrowed her eyes, contemplating her next move while biting her lip.

"Now what?" said Sophie. "Are you going to *unbolt* the rope?"

The girl didn't react but continued to stare at the useless spanner. The last thing Sophie wanted was to kill the girl's hope. But she was starving. Hangry, Edward used to call it, when she got like this. She was exhausted too, surviving only on a few brief and uncomfortable naps, each time waking from the agony of her predicament. And she too, was growing weary of Connor's delusions of protection.

Then, a noise stirred Lucy's hope once more, and she looked up at Sophie.

"Do you hear that?"

Sophie did. It wasn't so much a noise as a vibration. Something travelling along the main road outside, so big it seemed to create its own tremors, its own tides of sound. A digger, maybe? Or a fire truck, Sophie guessed. It wouldn't be the first time the fire brigade had been called in to drain the floodwater that had collected in the gulley between the Tucker house and her own.

As if to confirm her theory, then came the unmistakable sound of a siren, a short, loud blast. The sound of hope, the signal that help was coming.

And just like before, Lucy couldn't stop herself.

"Help!" she cried, her throat hoarse and dry from whispering through the night. She swallowed hard and caught her breath. "HELP US!" she screamed, louder this time.

Connor was up immediately, scrambling to his feet in a panic.

He stood still for a second, blinking his eyes awake and glancing between the two women for the source of the yelling. Sophie sat still, waiting for him to work out who it had been. She knew that nobody could hear them from the road, least of all through the firetruck's thick shell.

Opposite her, Lucy switched tack.

"FIRE!"

It was a trick they taught young girls these days, Sophie knew, to scream *fire* instead of *help*, because people were more likely to react when they thought a danger might affect them too.

Lucy managed one more cry for help before Connor's hand was over her mouth. But he quickly drew it away and shook it as if he had burned his finger on the stove, and he stared down at a bloodied knuckle.

"FIRE!" Lucy continued to yell, and she shook her chair so vigorously she was at real risk of toppling over and banging her head. She glared up at Connor, baring her bloodied teeth like a savage dog.

"Lucy, calm down," said Sophie.

Connor didn't cover her mouth again. Instead, he began rummaging through a box on one of the metal shelves further into the workshop. Out of one, he pulled an old and oily red bandana, the type a mechanic might use as a rag to wipe his hands.

He stepped up behind Lucy, held one end in each hand, and the next time she opened her mouth to curse him, he shoved it between her teeth, finishing by tying the ends at the back of her head. The sudden loss of air caused Lucy to gag on her next scream, and although her words were muffled, their vile meaning was more than apparent.

With obvious agitation, Connor crouched down in front of Lucy, who stared down at him with wide, suspicious eyes. She pulled her head back, drawing her face as far away from his as possible.

"Why are you doing this?" he asked quietly, appearing almost hurt.

Sophie replied for her.

"Why are *you* doing this, Connor?" she said. "Look at us. What are you doing?"

The boy spun on his haunches to face her instead. She knew his next words before he spoke them, and Sophie wondered how many more times she could hear them before she lost it.

"It's okay," he replied, his voice almost childlike, and he placed a hand lightly on her knee. "I'm going to look after you."

CHAPTER FOURTEEN

It took less than half an hour for the Forensic Medical Examiner to arrive. George recognised the man's lengthy gait immediately and felt a rush of warm affection. Campbell led Doctor Saint through the forest from the road, and they both stopped at the tree line to take in the scene.

He was a little out of breath from the short hike, and from a pocket in the side of his leather doctor's bag he pulled a handkerchief, which he then used to dab at his red face. Perhaps he was a little older, a little rounder around the middle, yet his stubbornly dark hair was still somehow free of grey hairs. Even though the man must have seen hundreds of bodies in his career, his face saddened at the sight of David Tucker.

Yes, thought George, it was definitely him.

Peter Saint stepped forward to get to work. George had worked with him many times in the past, and couldn't quite believe that the man was still working. Though sometimes, George couldn't believe *he* was still in the job himself. For some people, retirement was a last-case scenario kind of option.

Saint was so focused on the body he hadn't even noticed

George, let alone recognise him. He carried his medical bag over to the body and knelt down beside it. George approached from the other side and crouched, even though it meant the flood water staining his trousers. He was glad, as predicted, that he hadn't ironed his shirt. In this job, there wasn't much need for good brogues or ironed shirts. He was already wet and muddied, and he considered overalls to be more suitable attire for a detective.

He looked up at the man currently shining a small torch light into David Tucker's eyes, then saw him take the temperature from the deceased's mouth, looking between the thermometer and his watch.

"Any idea of time of death?" asked George.

Saint leaned back on his haunches. "Hard to tell since the body has been in freezing water. But I'd say no less than twelve hours. Estimate of between ten and eleven p.m. yesterday," he replied, nodding to himself. He looked up at Larson briefly, then back at the body.

Then he did a double take.

"George?"

George smiled back at him. "Hello, Peter." It wasn't the most appropriate time for a reunion, but in their line of work, it was hardly unusual.

"I'll be," said Saint, looking him up and down. "You're back from Mablethorpe then?"

"Looks like it," George said.

In the corner of his eye, George felt Ivy's stare. He knew it must feel strange to her, to see him reunite with old colleagues when she'd assumed it was a fresh start for them both.

"So, let's say 10:30 p.m.," George said, then cast his memory back to the previous night. "I'd have still been in Mablethorpe. That's about an hour before I arrived here." He had a sudden thought. "Campbell," he called from the ground at the officer with the tight bun, who watched every interaction as if she was taking mental notes. "How long had the traffic diversion been in place last night before I arrived?"

"Not long," she said, stepping forward. "You were one of the first cars PC Byrne stopped."

"Specifically," George pushed her. "Minutes?"

"Ten," she said solidly. "At the most."

Somersby Road may have been a major thoroughfare for locals, but wouldn't have been busy in the middle of the night.

George turned back to Saint. "Cause of death?"

"I can give you a theory, but that's not really my–"

"A theory will be fine, Peter," George clarified. "Between us."

Even though they were surrounded by officers who, including Campbell and Ivy, were definitely listening in, Saint put his trust in George, and allowed himself to venture off-piste. "Well," he said slowly, "judging by the injuries to his head and the congealed blood in his hair, it would be remiss of me not to suggest blunt force trauma. Of course, the pathologist will be able to–"

"So, this didn't happen after he died?" asked George, gesturing at David's skull. "It wasn't a piece of debris in the water?"

"No," said Saint confidently. "Even if something had struck his head whilst in the water, the blood would never have congealed. He was killed at least ten minutes before he entered the water, more most likely." He watched for George's reaction, then shook his head, further convincing himself of his own theory. "Anyway, even in the flood water, and especially through this tube, he wouldn't have been travelling fast enough to cause such a wound. His skull has been fractured in several places." He looked up at George with serious eyes. "You should be looking for a weapon, George."

George met his gaze and nodded, then both men peered back down at the body. They sat the way parents sit on either side of the bed, watching a child sleep. But David Tucker was not sleeping, and neither did he look at peace.

"Thanks, Peter," George said finally. "I'm afraid you've confirmed my thoughts."

He stood up and walked away from the culvert, leaving Saint to finish up – completing his legal requirements, like noting the official pronouncement of death and recording the temperature of various bodily cavities, as well as the smaller kindnesses, such as closing David's eyes.

"So," George said, walking over to Ivy and voicing his thoughts out loud. "David and Florence get in their car. They go to escape the floodwater. But they're stopped. They're attacked."

Ivy nodded. "And the killer leaves their bodies in the car, knowing it will look like they drowned in the flood trying to escape," she finished.

"No," George said, shaking his head. "Impossible."

"Why?"

"Because the windows and doors were closed."

Those last words were neither Ivy's nor George's, and they both turned to find the owner. In the peripheral of their conversation, listening in like an auditor, was Campbell. Ivy's expression morphed into a sneer, and George felt her energy shift, like the accumulation of static before a lightning strike. DS Ivy Hart was about to teach the young constable a message about rank and respect.

But George got there before she had a chance.

"And why does that matter?" he asked. "Why does it matter that the car windows were closed?"

Campbell's eyes darted between Ivy and George, as though choosing a side, and she continued, "If they'd died in the car, their bodies would still be in there."

"So?" George said.

"So, they must have been killed *outside* the car. For their bodies to have travelled through the flood."

"Hmmm," George said. Then he stayed silent and eyed the officer long enough for her to shuffle uncomfortably. "Very good."

Then he shifted into action. "PC Campbell, I'm putting you on the car. The black Toyota. I want it identified. I want to know when it was last picked up by ANPR and who was seen driving it."

Campbell processed her new role for a few seconds before speaking.

"Yes, guv," she said, then hesitated and George raised his eyebrows expectantly. "It's just that my superior needs me to–"

"Who's your superior?"

"Sergeant Kerrigan, sir."

"I'll handle Kerrigan," he said, then lowered his head to study Campbell over his glasses. "Off you pop."

In his peripheral, Ivy clenched her jaw but said nothing. At least not until Campbell had disappeared once more through the trees. "Do you really want to trust her with this, guv? She was on traffic duty a minute ago."

"So, who better to identify a car?" asked George. Then he grinned at Ivy, who softened. He looked around the scene – a few lingering officers and Doctor Saint, who was now packing up his case. "Anyway, we need a team, Ivy. This is now a murder investigation."

"Speaking of," she said, nodding to a group walking through the trees with such unfazed purpose, they could only be one thing. The old codgers, George remembered Tim used to call them, because they'd seen it all.

"CSI," said the woman at the front, making a beeline for George with a raised hand showing her ID, as though she was used to spotting the Senior Investigating Officer. "Katy Southwell."

"Inspector Larson," George introduced himself, and Ivy followed suit.

"Sergeant Hart."

The first thing George noticed about Katy Southwell was her

shockingly blue eyes. They reminded him of early summer mornings in Mablethorpe, when the rising sun glittered on the sea. From her athletic frame, George guessed she was a runner, slim and average height for a woman in her mid-thirties. But it was hard to tell if her perfect posture was from running or from the firm confidence with which some people moved through the world.

Behind Katy, Saint nodded his goodbye to George before heading back to the road.

"So, what have we got?" said Katy, looking around and glancing over at the dead body blocking the culvert as though it was only one element of a complete picture, as commonplace as the surrounding trees.

"A body," George said. "Estimated time of death ten-thirty p.m. yesterday. Local man." He forced himself to say his name. "David Tucker."

At this, Doctor Saint turned.

"Tucker," he repeated from the tree line. "As in..." He looked at the body he'd just examined, as though seeing it for the first time. "David Tucker?"

George met his eye. "Aye," he said. "His wife Florence was found last night, too."

As the two men shared a moment of acknowledgement, so did Katy and Ivy share a moment of confusion. The names, he guessed, meant nothing to Katy. Even to Ivy, they meant very little. But to him, and to the people who worked on the case of Kelly Tucker ten years ago, they meant so much more. Loss, tragedy, and not least of all, failure.

Saint shook his head. "That poor girl," he said quietly, before heading back to the road.

Only George knew who Saint was talking about. Not Kelly Tucker. Not the girl who had been lost for a decade. Whose body had never been found. Who had been exposed to God-knows-what in her all-too-short life? No, not her. But the girl who,

George hoped beyond hope, still lived. The girl who had now lost everything.

Lucy.

Katy looked between the two men and Ivy, then shook herself free of curiosity and snapped into action. "I'm going to need to clear the area," she said, waving her team over.

That was their invitation to leave. George and Ivy skulked back to the shadows of the woodland. Investigations were a finely tuned rehearsal. Everybody knew their role. And for George and Ivy, their act was over. The body had been found. Now it was time for CSI to take centre stage, and for George and Ivy to reassess their options.

"One more thing," he called out to Southwell, and she glanced back at him. "There's a black Toyota RAV4 that also needs a good going over," he told her. "It's back at the road."

"I'll get somebody on it," she replied.

Before they left, George added one last request. "Fast-track this one for me, won't you, Miss Southwell?"

As she removed a large, white canvas from a bag, Katy Southwell smiled the smile of a woman who'd heard that request more than once before.

"Of course," she said, without looking up, and with more than a hint of sarcasm in her tone. "I expected nothing less."

CHAPTER FIFTEEN

In Ivy's eyes, Sophie Gibson's cottage was quintessentially idyllic. The kind pictured in English children's stories and fables. But, preferring location over aesthetics, Ivy deemed the house as not one in which she would choose to live. Surrounded by trees, in a dip on a through road, prone to flooding every few years. No, she would choose her cramped, little terraced house by the sea any day.

She followed George through the garden, which had received the same level of flood damage as the Tucker's across the road, though Ivy guessed that the owner of this one might be slightly more devastated. The flattened and petal-less flowers had been organised in rows and squares. The hedges beneath the windows now bore loose leaves and accumulations of mud as if from neglect.

Inside the house, too, was neater than the Tucker house, more in tune with a lady living alone than a family with a teenage daughter. It was minimal, with far less furniture, fewer bits and bobs on the higher shelves that hadn't been washed away. The dining table, for example, was quite large, taking up the entire backside of the kitchen. But it only had four chairs, which the flood had dumped unceremoniously into one corner, and one of which looked far more worn than the others.

Even in the damage, Ivy could tell that everything matched. A colour scheme had been considered, from the coasters to the curtains. It was the kind of house decorated by a woman with plenty of time on her hands. Still, some objects were a necessity rather than a decoration. Objects that stood out like grisly gargoyles against fine masonry, items that anyone living in the middle of a country lane must keep by the door – an iron scraper for muddy boots, a high-powered torch, albeit broken, and a well-used doormat, one without any kitsch, homey message, that Ivy imagined had looked scruffy even before it had been subjected to floodwater and carried through the house.

On the longer wall of the hallway was a large canvas painting.

"She's got good taste," George mumbled, stopping to admire it. "I'll give her that much."

To Ivy, it looked like a standard landscape, the kind sold on any Lincolnshire high street – of trees and hidden rooftops, the white blobs of sheep in fields, and interlocking spurs continuing on to the horizon. She almost asked George what he meant, but he'd already wandered into the kitchen and could be heard opening and closing drawers. She looked to the corner of the painting, but the signature was illegible.

Leaving him to his own devices, she headed upstairs to find a spotless landing. And while the house had a similar layout to the Tuckers', it felt entirely different. There was something haunting about the Tucker home, with its lack of photos and untouched third bedroom. But Sophie Gibson's home, ironically, felt full of life. Its walls were adorned with framed photos of a couple who seemed very much in love — from youthful, grainy photos taken with a Polaroid to more mature, digital snapshots of their life together.

Walking past them slowly, as though looking through glass at a museum, Ivy saw the same two faces over and over again. At weddings, on beaches, with a dog, then a different dog, at Christmas, on a park bench, in the snow. The woman, Sophie, looked as similarly put-together as her house, in branded gilets with shoulder-length, styled blonde hair. She had a bright smile that reached her amber eyes. The man, too, was smiling, though his eyes were the kind of blue that were always bright. Piercing.

She reached the bedroom at the end and pushed the door, whispering, "Sophie?"

But the room was empty.

On the far side of the room, enjoying the best views of the fields beyond the property, a large double bed stood proudly. It was the type of bed that Ivy imagined a married couple enjoying a cosy morning in, perhaps with a tray of tea to drink while they discussed what they might do that day. Directly opposite the door was a dressing table, on which Ivy found the kind of jewellery she had expected – expensive charm bracelets and silver earrings.

But hanging from one corner of the mirror, given its own spot to dangle, was a cheap, gold necklace with daisies along the chain.

"What's that?" George said behind her, and Ivy closed her eyes in shock.

But she answered as though unfazed, not bothering to tell him it was a necklace. That wasn't what he'd asked. Not really. He'd asked why it caught her attention.

"Nothing," she said. "Just, well, she has a jewellery box, so why hang this one from the mirror?"

George shrugged. "Maybe she was planning on wearing it."

As a woman, Ivy knew that her favourite pieces of jewellery didn't go back in the box at the end of the day. They stayed out, either on the side or hanging from the mirror, ready to be worn the next day.

"True, she said, letting it fall from her fingers. "Probably."

But George didn't seem to hear her. He had moved on, and was still beside a large chest of drawers, staring down at one of the many framed photos on its surface. The only sign of distress on his blank face was the sudden paleness of his skin. Ivy approached cautiously.

"Guv?" she said, looking up at grey, windowless eyes. "What is it?"

But George's jaw seemed too locked to move. He'd been that way all morning, grinding unspoken words between his teeth rather than verbalising his thoughts. Something was weighing on him, a heaviness that he'd been unable, or unwilling to hide. She felt as if she was watching him carry three loads of shopping in each hand, while both of hers were free.

"What aren't you telling me?" she asked gently. "What is it about this investigation?"

All of a sudden, George released his tensed muscles and leaned on the chest of drawers, his long arms locked, and he hung his head between them. "I told you," he said. "Kelly Tucker disappeared ten years ago. I worked the case."

"You must have worked a hundred cases, guv."

He shook his hanging head and then looked up, arms bent under the weight of his chest. "It's not often I've worked the same case twice. The same family, Ivy."

"But it's more than that, isn't it?" she said, after a while.

George stayed silent, continuing to stare at the old photo.

"Guv, whatever it is, it's–"

"I failed them, Ivy," he interrupted quietly. "Florence and David. I should have stayed. I should have carried on looking for Kelly. They deserved that much." He rubbed his forehead. "But I didn't. I left. And the case remained open. Right up until they died, they never knew the truth. They were never able to bury their little girl."

If George had been a different man, his voice might have broken. But whatever emotional storm was brewing in his chest, it didn't shake his voice. Only someone who knew him as well as Ivy could recognise his suffering.

She stepped forward knowing there would be no comforting

him or trying to relieve his guilt. George Larson was a strong-minded man. If he thought he'd failed the Tuckers, then there was nothing Ivy could say to convince him otherwise. So instead, she voiced her own question.

"Where did you go?"

"To Mablethorpe," he said with an affectionate smile. "With Grace."

"But is that why you left?" she asked. "Because you couldn't find Kelly?"

George shook his head. "No," he said, taking a breath and straightening. "No, it was already planned. We'd bought the house on the seafront. I stayed as long as I could, but we had to move eventually."

Ivy almost took this moment to ask why he and Grace had moved to Mablethorpe. His private life was something he had always been vague about, a topic she hadn't broached for five years and if she was honest, had never really needed to.

But she'd asked enough questions for one day.

Then something clicked that made George's attachment to the investigation make even more sense. "Kelly was your last investigation," she said. "Before you moved, I mean?"

"Yes," George said simply. Then, his eyes turned dark again. "And do you want to know the worst part?"

Now the gates were open, he had more to say. Ivy let him continue, the way she'd been trained to let suspects talk themselves into a confession. "Everyone knew who killed Kelly." Ivy's frown deepened. George turned to face her before reiterating, "*Everyone*."

"How?"

"There was an inquiry. It all came out. It was obvious. Clear as day. He'd been abusing Kelly for months. You know how it is when you *know* when someone is guilty. The timeline, the order of events, it all adds up. But that doesn't hack it in this job. You need evidence." George sighed. "And we didn't have any. Not a shred of it."

Ivy *did* know how it was.

Some investigations that she had worked on had suffered the same fate. The feeling of failure was something that just came with the job. She could picture the faces of the victims if she thought hard enough. But the knowing grins of guilty men as they walked free were almost impossible to forget. Some frequented her dreams, of course. That was standard for a detective working a harrowing investigation. But those involving children, abuse, and violence, they were impossible to let go. Yes, Ivy knew, those were the ones that stuck with you.

George sighed, removed his glasses, and pinched the bridge of his nose. Ivy had never seen him look so tired, so resigned to the dark corners of his mind.

"The community helped," he went on. "Of course they did. People joined the searches. But after a few weeks, less and less turned up. They wanted to move on with their lives. Resources are reallocated, et cetera, et cetera." Ivy had seen it countless times during her career – justice not being served. "We never found her," George said. "So, we could never use her body in evidence to bring him down."

"So, the man walked free?"

"No." George shook his head. "Not quite. He killed himself. Hung himself from a tree." He spat the next words. "Like a coward."

"Before he was caught?"

"Maybe," said Larson. "But he killed himself the same night that Kelly Tucker went missing. So we'll never know."

"What a coincidence," Ivy said.

"Isn't it just," he replied, sneering at the photo. "Why would a man kill himself the same night the little girl next door disappears? A man with a long list of character witnesses calling him a creep, people who'd pointed out red flags to teachers, neighbours, employers."

"Who?" asked Ivy, whispering now. "Who was it?"

"Him," spat George, staring ahead.

Ivy finally followed his gaze to the photo. It was of the man from the pictures in the hallway, his blond hair messy and out of place. In his hand, he was holding a large fish by a gaff, which had pierced the poor thing's mouth so deeply, that the tip was almost in its eye. By contrast, the man looked delighted. His palms were stained with the fish's blood.

On her boss's face, she saw a hatred she'd never imagined he could feel.

"That's him," he said, quietly, then turned to look her in the eye. "Edward Gibson."

CHAPTER SIXTEEN

Sophie Gibson heard his name echo around the courtyard, and the three of them froze.

He stood suddenly, as straight as a dog's perked ears, then checked his watch with fearful eyes. He scratched at the stubble around his mouth that might one day become a beard and looked between Lucy and Sophie before doing a last check of the bindings around their wrists.

"Connor!" came another rough, aggressive call.

Connor rushed to the door, then stopped, turned back, and looked Sophie in the eyes.

"You hush, now," he said. "Don't make me come back here."

It sounded like less of a threat and more of a genuine statement, as if Sophie was the adult and therefore in charge of her own kidnapping.

"It's okay, Connor," Sophie said, softly. "I'm not going to make any noise."

At the next call of his name, Connor winced, then rushed through the door, slamming it closed and sliding some kind of mechanism into place.

Sophie looked up at Lucy, who stared down at her sad, little spanner on the floor as though she'd missed some kind of opportunity.

"Are you okay?" she whispered.

The girl looked up at her with eyes that conveyed numb emotions. She was strong, or at least she was getting stronger. Lucy nodded. Her gagged mouth was reminiscent of a radiator grill, teeth showing in a frozen kind of growl. Sophie didn't know what to say to ease her worry. She tried to remember the last time she'd even spent this long with someone so young.

They had decided before they were even married that children were not for them. They just didn't suit the way of life they had both envisaged, and having each other was enough.

They had dreams, of course. It had been Edward's dream to live in the country, in a storybook-like cottage, the opposite of the big-city flat he had known as a boy. It had been Sophie's dream to follow him wherever he went, to find his perfect house, and to live there by his side.

She had been enamoured with him since they had first met. In Lincoln, he would come into the pub where she worked, all curly locks and full of charm. A tall blond in a suit was a far cry from the farm boys that she had gone to school with. She would have followed him anywhere.

Lucy's hopeless eyes returned to the spanner.

Edward would have known what to do. He would have known what to say. How to comfort the girl. He had always been good with kids. He had a familiarity with them that Sophie had always lacked, able to soothe them, able to joke with them, able to crouch down to their level.

Whatever cruel rumours had spread about Edward after his death, Sophie had never believed them. She'd barely listened. They were so unimaginable. She knew what they really were – a way for the community to process their grief. To find meaning in the meaningless. Kelly's Tucker's disappearance had been a tragedy. But it was no one's fault. No one's except a stranger in town, or the current of a river, or a hit-and-run driver.

But it had certainly not been Edward's.

He had found peace, thank God, before the rumours had reached him. So, when the grief of losing their daughter turned the Tuckers' minds, she had been the only one around to absorb their misplaced sorrow. As anger. As hatred.

But the truth was that she and Florence had been friends. Edward and David, too. They'd spent Sunday lunches together, quiz nights down the pub, New Year's Eves, letting off fireworks in their shared lane. Sophie had held Lucy when she was only days old. Kelly, too.

They'd tried to run her out of town, of course. But Sophie had no reason to run. That house had been Edward's dream, and however much the Tuckers resented her, she would never leave it. Not while she lived. Not while Edward's spirit walked the woodland behind it. If she had her way, she would be buried in the garden to join him in endless walks through the trees.

And, of course, the Tuckers would never leave. Just in case Kelly ever came home.

So, they had lived in a dark homeostasis. Borne of hatred, Florence and David had since avoided Sophie. And out of love and pity, she had stayed away from them.

But now their daughter was tied up opposite her, and she had no idea how she could help.

Lucy's stare still hadn't moved from the spanner. It was obvious to Sophie that she was slipping into hopelessness, her eyes misting over like the sun behind a cloud, turning the room cold. She had to snap the girl out of it. *What do teenagers like?* Sophie thought desperately.

Jokes? No. She didn't know any, anyway. She hadn't been told a joke in years. That had been Edward's job; to make her laugh.

Films? She had no idea what was popular these days. The last film she'd watched in the cinema had featured Colin Firth at his peak. Edward had held her hand between the seats.

Music?

Music...

Sophie remembered something she had seen, but her mind was only just catching up. She looked around the room at the jumbled boxes and cluttered shelves. And there it was. On the second shelf from the top to her right. An old radio, the alarm clock kind that she had kept beside her own bed since the nineties.

She followed the route of its wire with her eyes, from its back, down the side of the metal shelves, and, she noticed with relief, into an electrical outlet in the wall.

"Lucy," she hissed. "Look."

The girl looked up with those sad, deadened eyes, and Sophie nodded at the wall.

Lucy looked over her shoulder at the plug, then back at Sophie, raising her eyebrows in a way that made Sophie almost hear her the testiness in her voice saying, *What?*

"The radio," she said. "It's plugged in."

Lucy's eyebrows raised again, this time sneering; *so?*

"Use your foot," said Sophie, nodding at her freed ankle. "Turn it on."

Sophie had never been so excited at the prospect of music before. These days, she only listened to Edward's old record collection, dancing around the kitchen, pretending he held her in his arms. But that was all eighties ballads and sixties folk. She hoped there was something on the radio that Lucy might enjoy.

Lucy looked over her shoulder again, and Sophie saw with relief that her eyes filled with the same determination as when she'd been stretching to reach the spanner. After a few useless bounces on the seat, she jumped a little higher, as much as the bindings allowed, and swung her body to the left. The chair shifted a little each time, and it took a while before those small efforts began to make a difference. From where Sophie sat, it looked exhausting. But Lucy's face was resolute.

Eventually, she'd turned to face the wall and shuffled forward a bit more.

For a minute, she just sat there, staring at the plug in the same way she'd stared at the spanner – *what now?* Sophie knew what Lucy had to do next, but she let the girl work it out herself. And eventually, Lucy began grinding her heel against the leg of the chair, trying to remove her shoe.

After a few tries, the wet shoe peeled off, and she kicked it to one side. With her big toe pressing through her damp sock, Lucy reached for the plug socket. Stretching forward awkwardly, she nudged the switch until it flicked on. The radio crackled into life, and the orange display on the clock flashed to tell them it was midnight, despite the light coming through the cracks in the old wooden walls.

Sophie laughed the way that people did when a joke suddenly made sense, or when they had turned a corner to discover a shockingly beautiful view. Lucy's reaction was hidden from her, but she hoped it was glad.

The radio wasn't very loud. Connor didn't seem the type to listen to loud music, even in the privacy of his own workshop. He seemed more likely to not want to disturb anyone. Even the silence of an empty yard outside. But still, it was on loud enough to hear the heavy bass and screaming lyrics that the kind of pop music Sophie despised seemed to be full of.

She'd never been happier to hear it.

In a series of shuffles, Lucy returned the way she'd come and was once more facing Sophie.

Her eyes looked a little brighter, her mouth a little more smile-like and less of a growl. She looked at Sophie, who wriggled her shoulders off-beat, pretending to sing along with the crescendo of the chorus.

A huff of air came through Lucy's gag that Sophie believed was a laugh. Her eyes were sparkling again.

Relatively, things were looking up, she thought, turning towards the door.

But for how long?

CHAPTER SEVENTEEN

"So, do you think this investigation could be connected to Kelly Tucker's disappearance?" Ivy asked, and George winced inwardly.

They had left Sophie Gibson's house, agreeing to check in with the only neighbours who weren't either dead or missing, which left only the individuals in the farmhouse at the top of the hill. George was walking fast again, and Ivy struggled to keep up. But instead of forcing her to run a little, he slowed down.

"No," George said. "Why should it be?"

"It just seems odd, that's all. The daughter disappears, then the parents die, and God knows where the other one is."

"There's ten years between the two incidents, Ivy."

"Oh right, yeah," she said, with more than a sprinkle of sarcasm. "I forgot that parents tend to forget about a missing child after a decade."

"Listen," he said, almost exasperated. "All we know is that David was killed. Nothing more. It could've been a robbery for all we know. A robbery gone wrong. Florence might have died looking for him. She could have just been swept away by the flood water. We don't know, Ivy. We can't jump to conclusions."

She shook her head at him, braving a reprimand.

"You don't believe that any more than I do," she said. "And I'm sorry if I'm being outspoken, but we have to at least consider the possibility."

"Well, until we know more, that's what we have to believe," he replied. "For all we know, Florence Tucker might be the culprit. The possibilities are endless. Our job, Ivy, is to reduce those possibilities until we are left with only one."

"And how do you suggest we do that?" she asked. "I'm guessing you're formulating a plan of some kind."

"We find Lucy," he replied, curtly. "We find her, we find out who wore that condom, we check the doorbell footage on the Tucker house, and we talk to the neighbours. Until then, and until we talk to the pathologist, all we've got is one murder."

The hill proved to be steeper than he had expected, and he surmised that he had been right in thinking that his adventures in climbing the Tuckers' fence during the previous night's escapades might catch up with his knees. They were already aching.

Halfway up the hill, his attention was drawn to two men wearing bright, high-visibility jackets studying an old oak tree that had fallen during the storm and was now sprawled across the field adjacent to the road, its branches encroaching onto the damp tarmac road. The obstruction wasn't enough to declare the road unsafe for drivers, but in the grand scheme of things, perhaps it would be for the best if the road was closed for a while.

The two men were fettling chainsaws, presumably preparing to dissect the tree into smaller, more manageable chunks. It was these little details that life on the coast had almost erased for George. Those little touches of country life. The things many people take for granted, especially those who rarely venture from the security of a city. Like much of the British countryside, in certain areas of Lincolnshire, floods were so much more than irritating pools of water that closed roads. They uprooted decades-old trees, drowned crops, destroyed livelihoods, homes, families and, in some instances, entire villages. The cost to the local farmers following the previous night's flood would be astronomical. But the cost to the Tucker family, George knew, was already beyond any financial burden.

Taking the excuse to catch his breath, he stopped to watch the men at work, and Ivy, who was as fit as anybody George had ever known, stopped beside him, saying nothing of the unplanned halt.

"Guv, what if they *are* connected?"

"What if what are connected, Ivy?"

"You know?" she said, and then let her expression rephrase the question.

"After ten years? No," George said, rubbing his kneecap. "Anyway, they can't be. Edward Gibson is dead. I saw his body with my own eyes."

"What if it wasn't him?" Ivy mused, and her doubt sent a ripple through George's eyebrows. "What if someone else killed Kelly Tucker?"

"No," George said sharply, and continued the walk up the hill. "It was him. I know it."

Ivy could have reminded him of the lack of evidence, but she didn't. George appreciated it was her job to consider all the options, to voice any idea, regardless of how absurd it might be. She was committed to her job, whatever the effect on her personal relationship. She always had been. Still, she seemed to word her next question sensitively. The noise of the first chainsaw firing up was enough for them to press on up the hill, and the higher they climbed, the greater the pressure of Ivy's silence. Until finally, it gave.

"Guv," she said. "I don't want to push it, but how can you be so sure?"

It was an odd sensation at the top of the hill, where the wide open space and cool breeze were as far removed from the suffocating gully, where the trees and hills loomed. Another few hundred yards of contemplative silence, and George turned left to enter the old farm. The frontage bore not so much a garden path and more of a desire line – a section of dirt that was well-trodden compared to the surrounding soil and gravel.

George waited until he and Ivy stood side by side on the doorstep before replying.

"Edward Gibson killed Kelly Tucker," he said, facing the old door in front of them that somebody had painted emerald green a long time ago. "I've never been so sure of anything."

He gave three loud knocks with the side of his fist, then stared down at her to reiterate the point.

A full minute had passed before they heard shuffling footsteps on the other side of the door, and eventually, the door swung wide open.

A large, mature woman who, George guessed, had grown old before her time, stood on the threshold. Her eyes were bright enough, but her hair was a limp, dirty-grey. She wore a worn flannel shirt with a rip in the collar, giving it the look of a street dog's ear.

"Now then," she said, her voice coarse and abrupt. The way she spoke wasn't exactly rude. It was more like they were interrupting an important task, emphasised by the dirty rag she held in her bloated hands.

"Detective Inspector Larson," George said, letting his warrant card fall open for her to view.

Her beady eyes roved from George's shoes to his eyes.

"Ah," she said knowingly, and exhaled long and hard.

"I wonder if we could take a few minutes of your time?"

"Unlikely," the woman replied. "Plenty to do. What's it about any road?"

George stepped back slightly to avoid crowding her.

"We're investigating two deaths that occurred during the flooding last night," he said, gauging her expression, but the woman had a poker face to match his own. "We're just seeing if anyone saw or heard anything suspicious."

George and the woman stared at each other in silence. Until, eventually, she sighed impatiently.

"So?" she asked.

"So, did you see anything suspicious last night, Mrs..."

"Ruth," she said. "I don't go by my last name. Not any more."

"Can I ask what it is anyway, Ruth?" He pulled at her like dough, to see how far she'd stretch. "Just for our records, you understand."

She gave him this one, but George imagined it was in exchange for information she'd refuse later.

"Hobbs," she said, then sighed once more. "Who died, then? Anyone we know?"

"Florence and David Tucker," George said quickly, before she had time to prepare a reaction. But she gave him nothing. "Do you know them?"

"Of course I know them," she said. "Live down the road, don't they."

"Do they?"

"Yes," Ruth spat. "They do."

She peered at a dusty old clock on the wall behind her, then with obvious impatience she stepped forward, forcing George and Ivy off of the doorstep and closing the door behind her. "You'll have to talk while I work," she muttered, her lips barely moving. "Things to do and all that."

"Of course," George said, stepping back with a sweep of his arm, knowing full well that she wouldn't appreciate being invited onto her own land. "We don't want to hold you up."

Ruth scoffed but didn't elaborate, and rather than walk, she seemed to waddle. Her huge frame rocked from side to side, emphasised by a slight limp.

They followed her around to the side of the house and over to a single wooden block in the middle of a courtyard, out of which a deep-seated hatchet protruded. She placed one foot on the block and pulled it out with a single yank, and from the corner of his eye, George caught Ivy's hand twitch over the pepper spray she kept in those endless coat pockets of hers. But he stepped to one side, putting distance between himself and the grisly old lady.

"So, Ruth," George said, eyeing as she placed a round from the nearby pile onto the block, then kicking it into place with a grubby, old boot. She was the kind of woman who clearly had well-hidden muscles beneath her plentiful flesh.

"How well did you know them?" George asked.

"Tuckers?" She said, pulling a grimace and shaking her head. "Barely. Waved when I saw them, I did. Nothing more."

"So you wouldn't know if they were having difficulties?"

"What kind?" Ruth replied. "Money, you mean?"

"Marriage," he replied. "Did you ever see or hear them arguing?"

"Even if I did, it'd be no business of mine," she replied, giving nothing away. "And none of yours neither."

"I agree. We're just trying to establish their last movements, that's all. Were you home last night, Ruth?" he asked, to which she stopped and stared hard at him.

"What are you saying?"

"Have you ever had reason to fall out with them?" he asked. "Or perhaps somebody else? Somebody from the village, maybe?"

"Not from round here, are you?" she replied, bearing the beginnings of a grin as she drove the little axe into the round, splitting it with ease.

George thought it best not to answer, not being one hundred per cent sure of the truth himself. In some ways, returning to The Wolds, seeing Tim, Peter Saint, and moving into the old house, did all feel like returning to an abandoned hometown. And yet he couldn't call it home. Not yet, anyway.

"There was a storm," Ruth explained. "Staying out of it, weren't I."

"Were you?"

"Aye, I was," said Ruth. "I was."

Then she took a particularly violent swing, and one half of the log landed at Ivy's feet. She bent, picked it up and held it out for Ruth to take, which she did, with the kind of quick grab that might cause splinters.

"Bloody road floods every year," said Ruth. "I'm not surprised the Tuckers drowned."

"I didn't say they drowned," George said, and this time, Ruth hesitated before swinging. "I said they died."

After the next crack of sharp steel through seasoned wood, Ruth took a break, slightly breathless, and rested her weighty arms on the upright axe. "What are you saying, Inspector... Lexon?"

"Larson."

"I'm a busy woman. Farm don't run itself, you know. What is it exactly you want from me?"

"It's not what I want *from* you, Ruth," he told her. "It's what I want *for* Mr and Mrs Tucker. I want to find out what happened to them. I want them to have justice, just as I would if I was standing on their doorstep discussing your untimely death. So, now we have that cleared up, perhaps you could tell us where you were last night?" George said directly. "Maybe then we can get on with our jobs and leave you to chop your firewood."

"I told you," she said, and her shoulders slumped with the kind of exhaustion most people felt at the end of the day, not the beginning of it. "I was staying out of the storm."

"Where?"

"Where else? Here. At home."

"And can anyone corroborate that, Ruth?"

Ruth stared at George, shifted her eyes to Ivy and back, and sneered the sneer of a petulant teenager who nobody trusted. Then she screamed a name, but it was more like a roaring bear.

"Connor!"

Immediately, from around the corner of the house, stalked a young man whom George guessed to be in his twenties. His thin, lank hair stuck to his skull through either sweat, grease, or even the remnants of last night's storm. He inched forward, as though trying to take up as little space as possible. He wore a dirty flannel shirt not dissimilar to his mother's, and as it was too big for his skinny frame, George wondered if it had indeed once been hers. He wrung his hands anxiously, in gloves that, even from a distance, appeared far too large for him.

Ruth shook her head at him, disappointedly. Her expression was not one that could be found on doting mothers at the school gates. It was more akin to hatred.

"Look, tell 'em I was with you last night, will you? So they can leave me in peace."

But Connor only continued to stare at George and Ivy as a shy child might.

"You police, are you?" he asked.

"We're detectives, son," George said. "I'm sure your mother will tell you, so I might as well. Sadly, your neighbours, Florence and David Tucker, were found dead last night. We're talking to the neighbours to see if anybody saw or heard anything unusual."

"Florence…"

"And David, yes," said Ruth. "Terrible, isn't it. Now tell 'em."

"Me and Mum watched telly," Connor replied quickly.

"What did you watch?" asked Ivy, speaking up for the first time, and Ruth glared at her.

"Emmerdale," said Connor.

"We're talking a little later than that, Connor," George said gently. "Around ten-thirty p.m. What were you doing then?"

George watched the boy's eyes move up and to the left. And although any psychologist would have agreed suggested that he was remembering, rather than lying, the relationship between eye movement and recall was a theory developed by Neuro-Linguistic Programming in the seventies, and it had since been debunked, leaving George to put his trust into his instincts.

"Taken," he said. "It was on telly. Finished just before midnight, I think."

"And then?"

"Then we went to sleep."

The boy's speech seemed to drag, like heavy boots trudging through thick mud, and George made a quick assumption that he'd struggle to lie. Ruth smiled at them with a dark, satisfied smile.

"Did you see any cars drive past, while you were watching the film?" he asked, fixing his gaze on Connor. The lad had not inherited his mother's poker face, and he gulped cartoonishly.

"The curtains were closed," he said. "I-I don't know."

George stared at the boy with steely eyes for a few seconds. Then he shifted his demeanour entirely to casual curiosity. "What's that?" asked George, pointing to a piece of tarp further down the yard.

"Will that be all?" Ruth spoke up.

Her eyes travelled from George's woollen sweater to his mud-specked tweed trousers to his best brogues that were now black with dirt. It hadn't escaped George's attention that Ruth's questions suggested that she had made up her mind about him already. She seemed like the kind of woman who boxed people as soon as she met them. And George doubted there were many boxes that fell into her favour.

George only smiled in reply, and waited for Connor to reply.

"It's just a tarp," explained Connor. "That's all."

"Fascinating," George said, and took a final look around. From where he was standing, he could see four or five outhouses up ahead, from stables to small, tin-roofed sheds. "Well, thank you for your time, Mrs Hobbs," he said, at which she scowled. Then he nodded at the boy. "Connor."

George didn't relish turning his back on Ruth Hobbs whilst she was in arm's reach of an axe, but he had to admit, her reaction hadn't been out of the ordinary. Many people didn't appreciate detectives knocking on their door. They often reacted in one of two ways – hostile, as Ruth had been, or scared, as Connor had been.

No, the only thing out of the ordinary, George noticed, as he and Ivy walked off the Hobbs property and back onto the still-wet road, was a beaten-up truck on the driveway with one of its headlights smashed. The kind of truck with a loud engine. The kind of truck that would stand out like a beacon in the blackness of a stormy night, it's one headlight lighting the carnage ahead.

CHAPTER EIGHTEEN

"So, what do you think?" he asked Ivy once the axe-wielding Ruth Hobbs and her less-than-fortunate son were out of earshot.

Ivy slowed to process her thoughts. "They both seem shady to me." She turned and sighed at the stunning but deteriorating old house. "And I think that house is wasted potential."

It could be glorious, George agreed. If only somebody fixed the brickwork, painted the front door, and trimmed the ivy that obscured the upstairs windows. Not to mention installing double glazing and central heating. It reminded George of a bigger, more livable version of his own Bag Enderby house on Church Lane. He wriggled his wet toes and remembered he had to go shopping for towels after work.

"Speaking of," he said. "What did you think of Connor?"

"The boy?" Ivy said. "You think he's wasted potential?"

He shrugged. "I think he'll never know his potential while his mother's alive."

Ivy stayed silent. George knew she thought he was lenient. They often held different opinions on their first impressions of people.

"So, do you believe him?" asked George.

"That Taken was on late-night TV again?" she said. "Yes."

George grinned. "And do you believe her?"

"Of course not."

"She's harmless," George told her. "No, people like that are bred to keep quiet. It's in their blood, Ivy. The air ambulance could have landed on their roof, and they would have told us they didn't hear it."

"They're up to no good, guv. Anyone can see that," replied Ivy. "She has a son who she clearly manipulates. He'll say anything she tells him to."

"Maybe," George said. "But is he smart enough to lie?"

"Yes," Ivy said, and looked at George. "Don't underestimate him, guv."

It was one of George's weaknesses, he knew, to give people the benefit of the doubt. It had been a hindrance in some cases and a help in others. He didn't jump to conclusions easily. But that sometimes made it hard to recognise a bad person when he was staring them in the face. In George's eyes, people were a spectrum of grey, and though the world liked to force people into boxes of black and white, he'd seen enough bad behaviour, to put it lightly, to know that people were complicated, and they came in many shades of grey.

He didn't believe in evil people. Only evil acts. But if anything, that made him judge the worst offenders even more. They had a choice. And they'd chosen to hurt someone else when they could have chosen not to.

Ivy, on the other hand, had specialised in criminal psychology. She'd interviewed murderers all over the country, helping create profiles and determine what made a killer. She'd told George spine-shivering stories about the acts of narcissists beyond hope. She wasn't afraid to label people as good or bad.

But these different perspectives made them a strong unit. Together, they saw suspects from all angles. And came to conclusions together.

Walking down the hill, George hesitated once more beside the fallen oak. There, now overseeing the sawing of the tree, hands stuffed into his police jacket, and watching the misting of his own breath in the cold air, was a familiar face.

"PC Byrne," he said.

The lad turned, saw George, and straightened to attention. George half-expected him to salute. "Inspector Larson," he remembered.

"Stand down, son." George smiled, presenting Ivy by his side. "This is DS Hart."

Ivy eyed the young man from head to toe, then nodded.

"What's happening here?" George asked.

"Fallen tree, guv,"

"Is that right?" asked George as Ivy tutted beside him.

"Fell down in the storm," he elaborated, glancing at Ivy. "We're removing it to re-open the road."

He eyed the men in helmets with chainsaws doing the hard work and looked back at PC Byrne. "And you're helping, are you?"

"I'm monitoring, guv."

George glanced down the hill at the gathering of officers who'd likely sent PC Byrne up the hill to get him out of the way. "Well, leave them to it for now," he said. "I need you to do a little job for me."

"Me, guv?"

"Yes, son," George said, and looked over his glasses at the boy. "You."

With the same youthful insecurity Connor Hobbs had shown in the yard, Byrne gulped.

"The Tucker house at the bottom of the hill." George stepped up to Byrne and pointed at the house the same way a father might point out a star. "The one on the left. It has one of those doorbell camera things. I want you to bag and tag any laptops in the house and take them to the station. They might have the doorbell footage." He looked at Byrne. "Is that clear?"

Byrne nodded. "Tucker house. All laptops to the station," he confirmed. Then he whispered, "I can do that."

"Very good," George said, patting him on the back. "I also want you to check the TV schedule for last night. See if the film Taken was on at about ten-thirty p.m."

"Oh, it was, sir," he said. "I watched it." Then Byrne leaned in and bent his head conversationally. "Great film."

In his peripheral, George saw Ivy's face break into an amused grin.

"I'll take your word for it," he said.

He turned to Ivy, spurred by a memory, feeling the first teasing moments of the investigation picking up speed.

"What was it that you found at the Tucker house? You wanted to show me something."

She answered by pulling a folded piece of paper from her coat pocket, which she unfolded, then handed it to George. He took it, and she jabbed a neat fingernail at the header at the top and said, "Tucker and Co. David's business. Might be a good place to start."

"Well it certainly can't do any harm," George said. "Let's pay them a visit." He turned to the young officer, who still lingered. "Which means I need one more thing from you, Byrne."

He straightened again, ready for anything.

"I need you to find Campbell. Tell her to expand the search and get a team together to look further downstream. We're looking for two missing people."

While Byrne seemed to process the words, he continued to look at George, hesitant.

"Is there a problem?"

"I just... I'm not sure she'll listen to me, that's all."

"Who?"

"PC Campbell," said Byrne, cringing. "I don't think she likes me very much."

George placed a hand on the officer's shoulder. "Tell her

Inspector Larson sent you. And buck up, son," he said, tapping the boy's face lightly. "You've got a job to do. We're not here to get along; we're here to work."

The little face-tap seemed to wake him up, and the young PC smiled weakly, then made his way down the hill.

"Two missing people, guv?"

"Sophie Gibson," George said. "I don't know where she is. Do you?"

Ivy shook her head. "And you think she and Lucy are…further downstream?"

She was right to use his euphemism. George wasn't ready to face the word *dead* when it came to Lucy Tucker. To face the possibility that he'd failed her, too. They stood staring ahead at the view of the two beautiful and ruined cottages, the haunted woodland behind one, and the clearing where the culvert overflowed beyond it.

"I don't know where they are," George said, hoping for the view to offer him the perspective he needed. "All I know is Florence and David Tucker are dead." These words, he needed to say aloud, to confirm it to himself. "And Lucy Tucker is still out there somewhere."

George turned to look Ivy in the eye, and she stared back at him, nodding as though she already knew what he was going to say next.

"I believe she has the answers to our questions, Ivy," he said. "So, we need to find her, and we need to find her fast."

CHAPTER NINETEEN

George drove while Ivy sat beside him, calling out the directions on her phone towards Ashby Puerorum. He wasn't a fast driver, and was rarely pressured to exceed what his common sense told him was a reasonable speed, having earned enough life and job experience to know that the blind corners of winding country lanes should never be underestimated.

"Next right, guv," Ivy said, and George did as he was told.

He glanced over at his number two, who peered up at the windscreen and between lengthy studies of her phone, focused on the job at hand, somehow managing to appear as though she had a good night's sleep, even though he knew differently. She would have been tossing and turning all night, anxious about her new start, keen to make a good impression, unlike George, who had very nearly called it a day and hung up his coat. The days of making good impressions were far behind him. These days, he would settle for staying below the radar, topping up his pension, and making a comfortable life for his golden years.

He could have stayed put. Perhaps he should have. But the forty-minute drive from Mablethorpe to the new station wasn't a journey that he'd relish taking every morning, especially as both he and Ivy were used to living two minutes from the station.

"How are you doing, Ivy? With the transfer, I mean? Think you'll stick it out?"

Amongst all his own ghosts that morning, he'd forgotten to even check in with her. It was *her* first day in The Wolds too, and he knew that her decision to follow him hadn't gone down well at home.

"Fine, guv," she said.

"How was the ride in this morning?"

"Fine," she answered. "Main roads were barely affected by the flooding."

"And Jamie?" George said, getting to the crux of the issue.

"He's..." She couldn't say *fine* forever. "He's disappointed, boss. As you know, he wasn't happy about the decision. He doesn't want to move here. So, for now, I'll just have to get used to the commute. It is what it is." George stayed quiet, knowing there was more for her to say. "He doesn't understand my commitment to...the job," she added with a brief hesitation, where George was sure she'd been about to refer to himself. That hesitation alone filled his heart. "He thinks it gets in the way of my commitment to my family."

"And does it?" asked George, confident that their relationship was open and honest enough for him to ask direct questions.

"I don't think so, guv. I love my family, the kids, Jamie. Of course I do. I just see myself as more than a wife and a mother. And I don't think that should be a problem. I mean, we moved to Mablethorpe in the first place so he could stay with the RNLI."

George remembered it well, a bright-eyed Ivy Hart turning up on her first day out of uniform, her hair frizzy, and cheeks rosy, still acclimatising to the sea air. He'd grown to know Jamie well enough, too. The four of them, Ivy, Jamie, George, and Grace, had endured many a Christmas party together. But he'd always seemed like the kind of man who needed attention, who wasn't quite comfortable being left alone at a party, always reaching for his wife's hand.

He knew Ivy protected Jamie from the darker experiences of the job, just as George had with Grace. That was one of the consequences of a career in the force. There were some things you were obliged to keep from your partner. Other things you chose not to. It was a myth of marriage, George believed, to tell your spouse everything. Why inject your nightmares into their dreams?

"And Hatty and Theo?" George said. "What do they think?"

Hart smiled. "As much as seven-year-olds can, they understand. They just want me around for school plays and summer fairs." She looked out the window. "I'll just have to make sure I'm there." Her phone pinged, and she glanced down into her lap. "Next left," she said quickly, causing George to swing into the turning a little too fast for comfort. "Sorry, guv."

The tarmac gave way to gravel, and George slowed before pulling up beside an open gate on which was a logo of a tree, its branches and roots coming together to form a circle. Beneath the logo, in a script-like font, the words *Your forestry experts* were printed. And above it: *Tucker and Co.*

"Here we go," George said, pulling into a space in what appeared to be less of a car park and more of a compound.

A strip of warehouses occupied the length of the land, with various vans parked in front of them, all white and liveried with the same logo that adorned the gate. A row of portacabins occupied the far side, with steel steps to each door and a permanent puddle before them like a moat.

Their arrival had garnered attention from a middle-aged man who looked out from the doorway of one of the portacabins as George and Ivy climbed from the car. Inquisitively, he trotted down the steps and strolled over to meet them halfway, eyeing them with curiosity.

"Now then," said the man, from ten steps away, then once he

had closed the distance, he reached out to shake each of their hands vigorously. "Can I help you?"

From his first appraisal, George judged him to be a man well used to manual labour, perhaps working his way into office life as the years had passed by. His suit was cheap and ill-fitting, and his dark hair had been combed back, more to get it out of the way than a preferred style. But a career in the forestry industry was all in the hands, George knew, and as the man before him scratched his chin, he revealed rugged knuckles, cracked with dry skin and bruises in his thick thumbnails.

"Detective Inspector Larson," George said, showing his warrant card. "This is Sergeant Hart. We'd like to have a word with whoever's in charge, if we may."

"If you're here to see David, you're out of luck, I'm afraid," he said, then looked at his watch. "Though I don't know where the bloody hell he is. Lazy git," he laughed.

Electing not to go for the jugular, George circumvented the root issue. "May I take your name, please sir?"

"Oh, sorry," he said. "Peter. Peter Mansfield. I manage the place. Is everything okay? There's no problem, is there?"

"Peter, I'm sorry to tell you that your employer, David Tucker, was found dead this morning."

The ghost of Peter's laugh faded slowly from his face, as though in disbelief at first. But George watched the realisation sink in the same way a shell sinks into the sand as the tide washes over it. Still, the sinking continued until the man's face had turned a deathly shade of pale.

"Peter," George said. "Are you all right?"

"I'm... It's just..."

"A shock, I know," George said. "Why don't we step into your office?"

Peter nodded silently and led them towards the portable cabin, giving George the chance to inspect the courtyard. A couple of men were loading a truck with timber, fence parts, and a dozen or so tree saplings with their roots wrapped in polythene.

For a port-a-cabin, the space was as nice as one could hope for, with a smattering of paperwork across two desks, a few mismatched chairs, and a small kitchenette to the rear. As learned from years of experience, Ivy quickly located the kettle, filled it with water, and switched it on, while George led Peter to one of the chairs, pulling the other closer to face the distraught man.

"What exactly do you do here, Peter?" George asked, opening with something simple, the kind of question he would have memorised from networking events, George supposed. "What's the business about?"

"Woodland management," he croaked, then cleared his throat. "Mostly. We offer fencing services too, for farmers and the like, weed control, tree planting, if that's what they need."

"And David is your only employer, is he?" George said, keeping the narrative in the present tense.

Peter shrugged and inhaled. "We're more like partners, really."

"So, you're the COO?" Ivy said, leaning on the kitchen counter and looking at Peter with faux innocence. "Of Tucker and Co?"

"David is the CEO," said Peter slowly, as though talking to a child. "I'm his number two. I don't really have a title."

"I see," she said. It was something Ivy often did — push for a reaction, especially if she felt George was being overly kind.

"Florence," said Peter suddenly. "Does she know?"

George licked his lips. This wasn't his favourite part of the job, far from it. "I'm sorry, Peter, but Florence was also found dead. Last night. We're treating both of their deaths as suspicious until we know more."

The man reeled in shock. He looked between George and Ivy with a fresh panic in his eyes, as though their presence had taken on a new meaning. "So what do you want from me?"

George leaned forward. "My primary concern right now is finding Lucy Tucker."

"Lucy..."

"Do you know where she might be?"

He shook his head slowly. "I have no idea."

"Do you know who she spends time with, perhaps? Friends? Boyfriends?"

"No," he said. "I don't know. She's just a kid."

Peter refused to look him in the eye. Perhaps out of guilt or shock, George couldn't tell. But when Ivy carried over two cups of tea and placed them on the desk, she then turned her back on Peter, giving George a look that made it clear she thought Peter wasn't being entirely honest.

"Mr Mansfield," George said, purposely switching to a formal last name. "Do you know anyone who might have held a grudge against David?"

"No," he said, picking at a loose-skinned cuticle. "Everyone loved David."

"When did you last see him?"

Peter inhaled but answered fast enough. "At work yesterday. He left about 4 p.m., I think."

"You think?"

"No. He did. I'm sure of it. Sorry."

"And where were you last night? Say between ten and eleven p.m.?"

"At home. I was with my nephew," he said, his eyes wide. "Sorry, you don't think that I–"

"We're just making enquiries, Peter," George replied. "These are just standard questions we have to ask everyone, so please don't read too much into them." The explanation seemed to appease Mansfield enough, at least, for him to nod and quieten. "You were with your nephew?" confirmed George. "What were you doing exactly?"

This time, Peter hesitated.

"Babysitting."

"Babysitting?" George said, letting his surprise become evident. "Now, there's an occupation you don't hear much of these days. How old is your nephew, Mr Mansfield?"

Peter made a show of calculating in his mind, whispering to himself, or more likely, for the benefit of performing to George.

"Three?" he said, staring down at George's brogues. "Something like that."

It was clear now that Peter Mansfield was avoiding eye contact, and George was growing tired of feeling his way through the dark. If Lucy Tucker was still alive, the first twenty-four hours were vital, leaving very little time for roundabout truths.

He needed answers. He needed them immediately. And he needed to find them for himself.

George sat back.

"I'm going to need a list of your employees."

Peter stared at the untouched cup of tea on his desk. "Of course," he said, but made no effort to move. George stood, stirring the man into action and startling him with the scrape of his chair.

"Now, Mr Mansfield," he said firmly. "If you don't mind." Mansfield stared up at George, reading the severe expression, and then opened his laptop. George stood over him, watching. And in the corner, Ivy sipped at her own tea, her eyes not once leaving Peter Mansfield's guilt-ridden face. "And before too long, we'll need something else from you," George said, and Mansfield looked almost fearful.

"What's that?" he asked.

"Somebody to corroborate your whereabouts, Mr Mansfield," George replied. "For our records, you understand."

CHAPTER TWENTY

"Thank you, Doctor Bell," George said, feeling the burn of Ivy's stare bore into his unshaven cheek. "You'll no doubt need some time to dig a little deeper? Shall we swing by tomorrow?"

"A whole day?" she said, her thick Welsh accent accentuating her surprise. "Tidy. I'll see you then."

"In the meantime, if you could get any swabs over to the lab. We don't have time for heel-dragging on this one."

"A day," she replied. "You can come again, Inspector Larson. It's not often you lot are so generous."

"Yes well, let's make it count, shall we, Doctor?" he said. "Until then."

"Until then," she replied, and ended the call, plunging the car into silence as George pulled into the station car park and, with half of the spaces to choose from, parked in a different place than he had that morning. It was his process of selecting his favourite spot, the one to which he'd grown attached. The one he'd be disappointed to find occupied on arrival. It was a process he went through for nearly every routine – work, the supermarket, even the town centre. It must have been what Ivy often called his OCD at play. Given the chance, he wouldn't have given it a name, but such was the modern way. A name for every little deviance. Even the little toe-rags that would no doubt amount to nothing were diagnosed with an excuse these days.

The spot he selected this time was a little closer to the fire escape doors to the stairwell. The downside was that he would have to walk through a huge puddle, so he ticked it off his mental list.

He and Ivy ascended the stairs in silence, and he wondered if she had any idea of his little process. She rarely failed to voice her opinions of him, so he deemed this particular quirk of his to still retain an element of secrecy. Besides, she was very likely contemplating a way to broach the topic of Doctor Bell's initial findings without coming across as smug.

But as soon as they pushed open the first-floor door, they faced a diversion.

"Ah, George," a voice called as soon as they entered the corridor, and he found Chief Inspector Long heading their way, with purpose, but boasting a friendly enough smile on his face to put George at ease. "Perfect timing. Let's have a quick meeting, shall we?"

Barely breaking his stride, George followed him down the corridor towards his office with Ivy in tow.

The floorboard outside of the incident room doors gave a loud creak as George passed over it, and he wondered briefly if it had done that before. He couldn't recall it, but then again, ten years was long enough for such insignificant memories to fade. But the idea struck him that many more memories may have slipped the net of old, grey matter. He paused long enough to peer through the little window in the door, just as the officers inside turned their heads to watch them pass. Like his Bag Enderby house, he'd have to relearn the subtle secrets of this station. And it seemed, when approaching this incident room, everyone knew you were coming.

In Tim's office, they sat just as they had that morning – Tim behind his own desk, George and Ivy on the two blue visitor chairs. And just as he had that morning, Tim clasped his hands together and got straight to the point.

"I need an update," he said. "Rose is on at me to organise a press release."

It was hardly worth complaining about the lack of time they had had. After all, in less than twelve hours, the body count had doubled, and Tim had worked his way up just as George had. He knew how it was sometimes.

"We, as in the wider team, discovered a second body blocking a culvert that was draining the road. Peter Saint suggested blunt force trauma. We're now treating both deaths as suspicious."

"Yes, I heard. David Tucker," said Tim, shaking his head. "I'm sorry, George."

"I barely knew the man."

"Yes, well, you know."

Tim had been there every step of the Kelly Tucker case. While he hadn't worked on it directly, he'd been around for every press release, every revelation of the inquiry. He had asked George how he was while they waited for coffee to brew. He had even volunteered his own officers for the numerous searches when needed. That was to say, he knew how the investigation affected George.

"My priority right now is finding Lucy Tucker," he said. "I've asked Campbell to organise a search team to look further downstream."

Tim nodded.

"PC Campbell. Good choice. She's a sharp one."

"I want her on my team," George said firmly. "And PC Byrne, too."

Tim exhaled a laugh. "Byrne?"

"And Campbell, yes," he said, leaving scant room to debate.

Tim held his hands up, as though relenting to a defeat George hadn't particularly fought too hard for. "If you want, George, they're yours. I'll let Kerrigan know." Then Tim frowned. "Why are you treating Florence Tucker as suspicious? Do you know something that I don't?"

"The pathologist called," George said. "She suspects foul play. We've made arrangements to view both bodies tomorrow."

"Anything else?"

"We briefly searched both homes, the Tucker house and the house opposite."

"Go on," Tim said, leaving George to continue.

"Sophie Gibson is also missing."

"Sophie Gibson? Good god," said Tim. "She still lives there?"

"It appears so."

"That must have been awkward," he mused aloud, then cleared his throat to pursue more of an objective discussion. "So, two bodies, both suspicious, two missing women," Tim said, confirming the state of play to himself. "Anything else that I should know? Key suspects?"

"We're really not at that stage, Tim."

"But between us, George. What are you thinking?" He leaned forward with a playfulness George didn't appreciate in this moment, as though they were playing a friendly game of Cluedo. "Top suspect so far?"

Still, George replied quickly. "Sophie Gibson."

At this, Ivy spun to look at him. It was rare for her to make such a reactionary movement. He understood her surprise, but not until Tim had asked did George realise himself that Sophie was at the top of his list.

Tim leaned forward, cautiously intrigued. "Why so?"

But George said nothing. He knew his assumption was biased. He knew it wouldn't hold up. Not with Tim, who needed solid answers for his press statement, and it certainly wouldn't hold up with Ivy, who'd already questioned his emotional investment in this case.

"George," said Tim slowly, "do you have a single thread of evidence against Sophie Gibson?"

His jaw ached from all the clenching. Surprised at the quietness of his own voice, George answered, "How could she not have known?"

Tim's eyes widened, as though he knew the route George was about to venture down.

"How could she have lived with that monster for twenty years and not known who he was?"

Tim sat back in scepticism. "George, that is *not* the investigation here. You just told me she's missing—"

"Missing?" George said. "Or on the run?"

"George—"

"What if Sophie killed the Tuckers and took Lucy?" George was leaning forward now, desperate to have his embryonic theory heard. "To kill her. Or worse, to do God knows what."

Tim leaned forward too, slowly. George knew he was trying to calm him. "You cannot blame a wife for her husband's crimes. Even if you could, Edward Gibson was never convicted. We must assume innocence. Least of all for Sophie Gibson."

"But—"

"No, George," said Tim, putting his foot down. "I don't want you pursuing this. It's a waste of resources. Follow procedure, collate evidence, build a theory." At this, he looked at Ivy as though asking her to ensure that George did just as he had asked. Then he turned back to his old friend. "You cannot force a theory to match the facts. You know that, George. It only wastes time."

Reluctantly, Tim glanced down at his watch, sighed, and then rubbed his forehead. He stood to initiate the meeting's end, then stepped over to the coat stand behind his desk and began pulling on a long, double-breasted navy overcoat.

"Search for Sophie Gibson, by all means," he said, straightening his collar. "But until there's evidence to prove otherwise, she's innocent. Do you understand?"

"Yes, guv," Ivy spoke up, saving George from having to do so.

Tim took it all the same, and George felt his sharp eyes on his neck as they left his office and walked slowly towards the incident room in silence. They had taken just a few steps when they were overtaken by Tim rushing towards his press conference in a flurry of coattails. Ivy waited until Tim had pushed through the door to the stairwell before speaking.

"You told me the two cases weren't connected?" she said.

"I know what I said, Ivy," George said, rubbing his eyes. "It's just a theory." He shook his head, shaking off fatigue like a dog shakes off rain. "But he's right. We don't have enough to go on."

The squeak of the floorboard had alerted the officers inside the incident room to their presence, and most of them turned to the door, expecting it to open. But at the sight of George and Ivy peering through the glass, they quickly looked away again, returning to whatever it was they were doing beforehand.

In the far corner, George spotted the young Byrne frowning at a laptop screen and tapping the same button repeatedly. On the other side of the room, PC Campbell was gripping her phone between her head and her shoulder, making notes with one hand and passing papers to colleagues with the other.

George breathed in the constant noise of the ringing phones, chugging printers, and the drone of chatter as though it were the familiar aroma of a roasting chicken. It was a sound that he'd heard most of his life - the hum of an incident room, its action and energy verging on chaos.

This time, he *did* ask Ivy the question on his mind.

"Well?" he began. "Are you ready for this?"

And, although he expected nothing less, she turned to him with a grin.

"Always, guv," she said. "This is the moment I've been waiting for."

CHAPTER TWENTY-ONE

"PCs Byrne and Campbell," Larson announced, taking immediate control of the incident room as soon as the doors had swung closed. The two officers looked up from their work, along with nearly every other head in the room. "With me, if you will."

He was such a paradox, Ivy mused. For the most part, he reminded her of Bill Nighy, a gentle and intelligent-looking man who bore his age with grace. But every now and then, he demonstrated a powerful command that belied his gentle nature, and one that she witnessed with awe every time, as if it were the first. It wasn't a coincidence that, in the past five years, she had watched nearly everything the actor had been a part of.

The room comprised three rows of four desks with a central aisle carving the spaces in two. Less than half the desks were occupied by various officers answering phones or sending documents to print.

George headed to the largest whiteboard in the room, which was conveniently unused and to the back of the room, behind Byrne's desk.

From the doorway, Ivy watched as Larson strode towards it, passing the astute Campbell on his way. She saw the young female officer scramble together a collection of papers and her laptop, fumble up from her chair, and scurry after him. PC Byrne, on the other hand, took a minute to process the instruction, then merely swivelled in his chair to face George at the whiteboard, tapping his pen on his teeth subconsciously. Before joining them, Ivy took a moment to take in the scene, to admire the way George had, in the space of a single morning, pulled together the fragments of a team.

He always looked most at home in front of a whiteboard, Ivy thought, with his back straightened to mirror the board's surface. His eyes darted between his listeners as though he relished their attention, and he held a marker pen in his hand the whole time he spoke as though it was a weapon he could draw on at any moment: a weapon that revealed the inner workings of his mind. She had always thought that, with his tweed trousers, woollen sweaters, and tendency for mentorship he'd have made as good a professor as he did a detective.

"Are you joining us, Hart?" he called across the room, and she made her way over to the board.

George looked between Campbell and Byrne, as if confirming his choices for a moment. "Chief Inspector Long has spoken to Sergeant Kerrigan, and you'll be working with me for the foreseeable. Any issues with that before we begin?"

Byrne glanced wide-eyed at Campbell, who stood with papers falling out of her hands, a look of confused joy on her face.

"Transfer, you mean?"

George looked down at him curiously.

"One day, maybe," he told him. "But for the meantime I need bums on seats. Think of it as an opportunity. By the time I'm done with you, you'll have a clearer picture of your careers. You both have a fine future in uniform. But, if you wanted to take a sideways step, this could be your way in."

Byrne stared at a spot on the floor as though imagining his future life in plain clothes. Whatever images were streaming through his mind, Ivy could only guess. But clearly, he was happy with the concept and started to nod his head, slowly at first, then enthusiastically, building to a reply of, "Yes, guv."

George turned to Campbell, eyebrows raised.

"Alright," she said very quickly.

"Good. But you should know that moving to plain clothes is not a promotion," George added. "I cannot emphasise enough that it is a sideways step, and if my career is anything to go by, it doesn't always end in a desk job and bird's muck on your shoulders. If that's what you want, then I suggest staying in uniform, especially in these parts. Clear?"

"Clear, guv," Campbell replied, and Byrne, still shell-shocked, appeared to be struck dumb.

"Right then," George said, with a deep breath and a quick glance up at Ivy. "Let's get started, shall we?" He removed the pen lid and continued without waiting for an answer. "Florence Tucker," he said, then wrote her name in the middle of the board and circled it. "Found dead in the floodwater outside her house last night. The pathologist has suggested her death is suspicious, but we're waiting to hear more. DS Hart and I will be attending the hospital tomorrow to garner a more detailed analysis, including that of the husband, David Tucker."

George wrote the name *David Tucker* beneath *Florence Tucker* and joined the two with a line.

"Cause of death?" Campbell asked.

"Blunt force trauma," Ivy said, the image clear in her mind, and Campbell nodded, clearly recalling the injuries she had witnessed that morning.

"To be confirmed by the pathologist," George said. "But yes, the initial examinations suggest so. For that reason, we're ruling out accidental drowning. It's quite possible that the flood water was used to make the murders look like an accident."

"But not very well," Ivy said, speaking on behalf of Timothy

Long. "Florence Tucker could have drowned, but David's body clearly showed foul play."

"Indeed," George said. "Which suggests?"

"Impromptu," Campbell spoke up. "It wasn't planned."

George pointed his marker at her. "Very good."

She glowed. Meanwhile, PC Byrne followed their fast-paced dialogue like he was watching a three-way tennis match. George, noticing this, brought him into the conversation.

"Byrne, I asked you to collect all the laptops at the Tucker house and bring them here. How did that go?"

"Done, sir," he said, and gestured at the three laptops on the desk behind his own.

"You managed to access them all?" George asked, his face mirroring Ivy's own surprise.

"Oh," said Byrne, his face dropping. "No, sir."

"Call me *guv*, son," George said. "I'm not your history teacher. Why didn't you take them to the tech team?"

"I did...guv. They said they didn't have time."

George strode over to Byrne's desk and picked up his desk phone. "What's the extension?" he asked, at which Byrne winced and looked up as though trying to remember.

"Erm..."

"114," Campbell announced.

George typed in the number and Ivy listened in to the one-sided conversation.

"DI Larson...three password-protected laptops...two hours ago, but I'll take as soon as possible...doorbell footage...DI Larson, that's Detective Inspector Larson...it's my first day in the station, not my first day on the job, thank you..." On each beat, George's face remained unchanged – collected and impassive. His voice didn't fluctuate. His hand didn't grip the receiver firmly or loosely, only as tightly as it needed to be held. "You can come down to the first-floor incident room to collect them...because I don't have time, son."

He hung up and cleared his throat, seeming to miss the awestruck expressions that spread around the room.

"Now then," he said, turning back to the board. "I want to talk about Peter Mansfield."

Byrne frowned. "The physicist?"

Everyone turned to look at him, even nearby officers who were not involved but obviously listening in, and Byrne withered under their attention. "Inventor of the MRI..." he said. "Nobel Prize winner...Peter Mansfield..."

"How do you know that?" asked Ivy, amused.

"Pub quiz," said Byrne, without further explanation. Then, when everyone continued to stare, he said, "I do them every Friday."

Ivy had yet to explore the local pubs of The Wolds but could quite believe that Byrne spent his Friday nights in one. Though she was a little surprised, not that he participated in pub quizzes, but that he remembered the answers.

"No, not the physicist," George said slowly, with a rare, worried frown. "Peter Mansfield, the business partner of David Tucker."

"Oh," Byrne said, then muttered to himself, "that makes a bit more sense."

George wrote the name *Peter Mansfield* on the board with a line to *David Tucker*.

"He claims the last time he saw David was at four p.m. on Friday night when David left work. That means, until we hear from Lucy Tucker, Mansfield may well have been the last living person to see David alive."

The progress was momentarily marred by a moody-looking man with a ginger beard, in smart chinos and a t-shirt bearing a single Rubik's cube, who skulked into their area at the back of the incident room. Without breaking flow, George pointed to the three laptops on the desk, which the man collected and carried off without a word.

"Then again," George said, tapping Peter's name with the back of his pen. "I didn't believe a word he said. Ivy?"

"Same, boss."

"Meanwhile," George said, turning to Campbell, "You should've received an email from *Tucker and Co,* a list of employees. I had him send it to your address."

"Yes guv, I did," she replied.

"I want you to run a check of the names. Flag any that stand out; any with previous, that sort of thing."

In response, Campbell finally relieved her arms of the jumble of papers, set her laptop down on Byrne's desk and knelt next to him, clicking on her emails.

"How about the car, Campbell? The black Toyota?"

"Registered under the name David Tucker, guv," she said, turning to face him once more. "Last seen on the River Lymm Road heading towards Somersby at 4:07 p.m."

She'd clearly memorised the time and the name of the road, waiting until she was asked to relay it. Ivy was impressed. George, too, it seemed, as he stared at the PC for a second longer than usual before offering his usual, "Very good."

"Which would fit with Mansfield's timeline that David left work at four p.m.," confirmed Ivy, loathe as she was to accept that Mansfield had told them at least one truth.

George nodded, and in his eyes, Ivy could almost see him set Peter Mansfield's name to one side in his mind.

"Now then," he said again, turning to face the board. He stepped back like a painter deciding where to add an extra brush stroke. "Ruth and Connor Hobbs." He drew their names to the right of the board, with a line that split off to touch both Florence and David's. "The neighbours of the Tuckers. Thoughts, Ivy?"

"Wouldn't trust her with a bucket if her son was on fire, guv."

"Why not?" said Byrne, leaning forward like he was ready for a story. "What's she like?"

"Did you ever watch *The Goonies?*" asked Ivy.

"Of course. It's a classic."

"You know the woman? Mama Fratelli?"

"Ah, yes," said Byrne nostalgically. "Face like a baseball glove?"

Ivy laughed. She found something quite amusing about Byrne. There was a naivety to him that she found endearing, and she couldn't tell if the next words from his mouth would be a surprise or a disappointment. It was almost fun to guess. "That's the one."

"It's not her face that concerns me," George said. "It's the words that spill from it." He returned their attention to the board with a tap on Connor's name. "Her son claimed they were watching *Taken* until just before midnight." George spoke up, talking over Byrne's open mouth before he could reiterate what a great film it was. "Doctor Saint estimated David Tucker's time of death between ten and eleven p.m., which makes them both each other's alibis."

"And Peter Mansfield?" asked Campbell, turning on her knees. "Where was he Friday night?"

"At home," Ivy answered. "With his nephew."

"So, he has an alibi?"

"If the alibi of a three-year-old counts," Ivy said.

"In court? No," George said. "And not with me, either," he said, and shook his head, "Still, I've never seen a guilty man turn quite so white when learning of a friend's death."

"So, three potential suspects," Ivy said. "Three potential alibis, all of which need corroborating."

George turned to face the board fully, frowning as though it held chess pieces in a game that he was losing. "There's just one problem."

"What's that, guv?"

He snapped the lid on the pen once more, and set it down into the little tray before turning to face them and plunging his hands into his pockets. "I don't believe a single bloody word they said," he replied, his tone as bitter as ever Ivy had heard him utter. "Not a single word."

CHAPTER TWENTY-TWO

"Now then," said Larson, stepping to one side and inviting the team to see the board in its entirety. "So far, we've spoken of Florence and David Tucker. But we also have two potentially missing women, both of whom I am extremely keen to talk to."

The melody with which he spoke again reminded Ivy of a professor explaining a complexity to his students. That was one of George's powers – to make people believe he had all the answers. Even, as Ivy knew well enough, when he did not.

"Lucy Tucker," George said, writing her name beneath her parents' names. "And Sophie Gibson."

He wrote Sophie's name in the top-left corner, in her own lonely patch of white space.

"As yet, we do not know the last time that either of the women were seen. But, we *are* assuming they still are alive. At least, we should be praying that they are. Campbell," George said, pointing at her again with his pen, "I asked you to expand the search team further downstream. Any news?"

"Nothing as yet, guv," she said, looking up briefly from the Tucker and Co employee list, at which George nodded, and she returned to her task.

George paused in his flow of thinking, and Ivy waited for him to bring up the old case – to write the names *Edward Gibson* or *Kelly Tucker* on the board. But he didn't. She watched him carefully, and as though he felt her gaze, and possibly assumed it to be a far-reaching scope for Long's watchful eye, he moved on cautiously.

"Unfortunately, we don't have much to go on," George said. "But maybe if we can find the person who killed Florence and David, it will bring us to Sophie and Lucy. For now, that's all we can hope for. Let's start with the basics – credit cards and mobile phones. Let's see if we get a hit there."

George looked at the board wistfully, and Ivy considered his vague language. Hope, she knew, was not something he usually put his money on.

"Guv," Campbell said urgently from her kneeling position on the floor. Given the rugged, scratchy carpet, Ivy could only imagine the kind of indented skin patterns she would have on her knees when she eventually stood again. "I might have something here."

Both George and Ivy stepped over to look over Campbell's shoulders at the laptop screen. Byrne swivelled his chair too, but over-spun in his enthusiasm and had to correct himself.

"Jason Connolly. He's got previous. Two counts of aggravated assault."

"Is that him?" George said, narrowing his eyes at the little photo in the corner of his file. "Pull it up."

As soon as the young man's face filled the screen, Ivy saw the recognition in George's eyes. The boy's spikey hair and hollow cheekbones. He opened his coat jacket and retrieved a photo slotted into his inside pocket, then held it up in front of the laptop screen. Ivy glanced between the two images, growing surer by the second they were the same person. The photo in George's hand might have been a mugshot, the way the boy glowered straight-faced at the camera lens if it hadn't been for the young girl planting an affectionate kiss on his cheek.

"Jason Connolly," George said, carrying the photo over to the board and attaching it with one of the little blue magnets gathered in the bottom-left corner. He then wrote his name beneath the image, with a line to Lucy's. "Quite possibly the boyfriend of Lucy Tucker."

"How do you know that, guv?" asked Ivy.

"I found that photo in Lucy's bedroom. There are tons of them. And that condom you sent to the lab, Ivy," he said, now pointing his marker at her. "I'll bet you anything it's his DNA."

George's expression now held the same growing excitement she had seen countless times before, either when he made breakthroughs in an investigation or was offered the specific single malt he liked in a pub. Forget hope, Ivy thought. This was an actual lead to Lucy. They were getting somewhere.

With that thought, Byrne's desk phone rang. He answered it with a sweet but unprofessional, "Hello-o?"

The young man frowned with concentration while listening to the voice on the other end.

"Tech support, guv," he said. "They've located the doorbell footage. The browser on one of the laptops was bookmarked, and the credentials were cached."

"See, that wasn't so hard," George told him, despite Ivy knowing that the more technical explanation would have meant almost nothing to him. "Have them send the last twenty-four hours to yours and Campbell's email addresses, will you?" Then he nodded at both of them in turn, Byrne to relay the message and Campbell to provide her address to the caller.

Ivy watched the two PCs work together for the first time. They jostled to both be heard over the phone. But at least they both seemed eager and, in their own ways, capable. They could yet make a good team, given time. But time, also, would tell.

She remembered her first foray into detective work – the

excitement and magnitude of processes. The feeling of having what seemed like a million tasks running through your mind at once, both those that were allocated to you and those you could do on your own initiative, the little insights that would help you stand out above the rest. It was a feeling she still knew well. But like other sensations, such as fear and guilt, the art was learning how to control them.

George waited until Byrne had hung up the phone before he allocated tasks.

"Campbell, get onto the lab, will you?" As he spoke, he wrote his phone number on a scrap piece of paper. It was their first day, after all, and Ivy doubted their details had been shared throughout the station yet. "I want the DNA in that condom confirmed." He handed her the paper. "Call me as soon as you know."

George turned. Suddenly, he had the vitality of a man half his age. Any fatigue that he might have displayed only an hour ago had dissipated, and she watched with affection, absorbing his energy.

"Byrne." At his name, the young PC swivelled once more, this time stopping himself in time to face George. "I want you to look through that footage with a fine-toothed comb. Any movement outside the house, any visitors, any comings or goings from twelve noon to midnight on Friday, I want to know about it."

While he talked, Byrne scribbled down the simple instructions in the notebook on his desk.

George waited patiently for him to finish before adding, "Then, I want you to call Katy Southwell in CSI. Get me an update. Tell her you're working with me and don't take no for an answer this time. I don't want to be calling her later because they were too busy for you. Do you hear me?"

"Yes, sir," said Byrne, with military-like emphasis. "Yes, guv," he corrected himself, a little less sure of himself. "Will do," he whispered in that way; Ivy had noticed he liked to confirm something to himself in a quieter voice.

It hadn't escaped Ivy's attention that Campbell had been given far fewer duties, and she assumed it was George's way of giving her a chance to demonstrate initiative, to spend her time as she saw fit in a way that would push the investigation forward. These unspoken opportunities were George's speciality, and had served Ivy well. After all, she had elected to transfer halfway across the county to work with him.

"Ivy," George said, turning to her with a grin. "You're with me."

"Jason Connolly, guv?"

"Jason Connolly," he confirmed, and turned to the boy's profile on Campbell's laptop to write his address. Then, in a rare show of his rank over her, he pulled his car keys from his pocket, threw them to Ivy in an easy, underarm throw, and said, "Warm the car up, would you? I'll be down in a minute."

So enlivened was she by George's burst of energy, and shocked at his subtle rank pulling, that Ivy turned to do as he had asked, and made her way across the room under the curious gaze of several other officers. At the incident room door, she thought to glance back where she found George with his back turned, speaking quietly to Campbell, and with some obvious urgency. The young PC was attentive, and she nodded with earnest.

Ivy turned to leave before they realised she was watching, and from the stairwell window, she watched the length of the corridor, hoping for George to visit the toilets before he hit the road, which, as a man in his sixties, he often did. Her intuition paid off. Through the diamond-printed glass, she saw George exit the incident room, then turn right towards the restrooms at the end of the corridor.

Ivy took her chance.

She walked into the incident room and headed straight to where Campbell was standing at her desk, about to make a call.

Ivy stopped on the other side and pressed down on the telephone's hook.

"What did he say to you?" she asked quietly, but failing to hide the paranoia in her voice.

Campbell looked up, her eyes widening in surprise, both to see Ivy back in the room, and to see the urgency in her eyes. "Who?" she said, failing to feign ignorance.

"Who do you think?" Ivy said. "I saw DI Larson speaking to you. Did he give you an instruction?"

She looked around the room self-consciously, at the officers who were going about their duties, perhaps hoping that one of them had noticed the interaction. Ivy, on the other hand, ignored them, fixing her eyes only on Campbell, who then stared at a spot on her desk, seeming to hesitate before making a decision.

"I'm sorry," she said, looking deep into Ivy's eyes, woman to woman. "He said to keep it to myself."

CHAPTER TWENTY-THREE

The easy-listening music formed patterns on the blank canvas of her mind. They swirled and sparkled like fireworks. The woman's voice was a Catherine wheel in the left-hand corner, the piano melody a rising rosette that burst into the chorus and split into a shower of tangerine and sapphire sparks. It was a sight to behold; an escape.

The radio had been on for a few hours now, and Sophie had slipped into a calm, meditative state that she was sure was borne of exhaustion, though deep down she felt that her calm state belied her predicament – tied to a chair with chills that had travelled through her bones, unable to feel her numb, bound legs. But even now, she doubted Connor's intentions. And her gratitude for the radio, the thrill of the small win still cheered her spirit.

She opened her eyes, listlessly, like swimming up to the water's surface, and she found Lucy sitting opposite her. She too, had closed her eyes. Yet, where Sophie had found calm, Lucy wore a deep frown.

Sophie imagined her at a firework show – arms crossed sulkily, or with her head buried in her phone, thinking she was too old for the blazing symbols of hope in the darkness.

There was a noise from outside, alien in her imagined world. A creak, and Lucy's eyes shot open in fear. She looked to Sophie, rather than at the door, as though Sophie had the power of protection.

Still, Sophie felt compelled to act.

"Connor?" she whispered, unsure why she was whispering. To protect him? To protect herself? "Connor, is that you?"

Eerily, the door creaked open at the push of a scrawny elbow, and Connor entered carrying a tray of plates and drinks. His thinning, blonde hair was still stuck flat to his head. Either he hadn't bathed since the storm, or it was his usual appearance. If possible, he looked even muddier than he had that morning, as though he'd been working in the mud all afternoon.

She sighed a long breath of relief at the sight of him. At least Connor had been expected, and in such a surreal situation as this one, better the devil she knew. The fact that he was carrying food suggested that their release was far from imminent. And although no tantalising aroma accompanied his arrival, only the harsh cold of the post-flood winds, to wet her lips, and to feel some kind of liquid in her throat would be heaven.

He placed the two paper plates and two plastic cups at their feet, the kind designed for picnics or children's parties, and then the tray, on which was a plate of bland, instant noodles. Still, she'd never wanted food more.

He ran the few steps back to the door, glanced left and right through the open entrance, then pulled the door firmly shut.

It was torture – to see the meal at her feet, out of reach. She doubted the move was purposeful. She doubted he had the intelligence to devise such torture. And when she peered up into his young face, she found only puzzlement. He looked between the two plates and the two bound women as though facing a riddle – the grain can't travel with the chicken, the chicken can't travel with the fox...

"Connor," Sophie said. "We haven't eaten all day. Please. Untie us. Let us eat. We promise not to run." She turned to Lucy, who appeared more frightened than eager to eat. "Don't we, Lucy?" Eventually, the girl nodded enthusiastically, still gagged and speechless.

In the background, the slow piano pop song was coming to an end and fading out, soon to be talked over by the presenter introducing the next segment, and Sophie wondered if the scrawny young man might realise what they had done, and perhaps discover Lucy's free leg.

"And she needs her mouth to eat, Connor," Sophie added, nodding at Lucy. "She's not going to scream. We just need food." She looked into his shallow green eyes, hoping her sincerity was getting through. "Please."

The next segment on the radio was the news, the presenter announced, and the soundtrack turned serious – two dramatic *ba-dums* before diving into the headlines. "And now for your news at five with Alison Hayes."

Five p.m., thought Sophie. *Good God, we've been here for 17 hours now.*

That meant she hadn't eaten for at least twenty-two hours. She was a woman of routine, something Edward had struggled with, and when she wasn't able to stick to her regular eating schedule, her body noticed with obvious severity. Lucy, too, looked between Connor and the food with desperate eyes.

He seemed to sense their hunger and, after his slow deliberation, deemed them safe to untie. But not before he dragged the spanner beside Lucy's foot towards him with a muddy boot. It was a clear warning, and one they should heed.

He began with Sophie's ankles, and the relief was immediate, immeasurable, and immense, like removing a hair-band that's been on your wrist all day. She peered down at the tentacle-like marks on her skin. But those would fade, she knew. She was more worried about her knees.

While Connor moved to untie her wrists, Sophie slowly

stretched her legs, feeling barely any sensation in them at all save for an ominous creak of sinew and gristle.

'...*the aftermath of last night's flooding has caused devastation throughout Lincolnshire*,' the radio continued. '*Here's Ben Adams to tell us more.*'

Connor struggled with her wrist knots. He had tied them well, and perhaps in her efforts to escape, she may have pulled them tighter.

The radio then switched to a second voice, one with the background noise of wind in the trees and passing cars sloshing through standing water. '*Hi, Alison, I'm here on Somersby Road where the flooding was particularly bad last night, blocking off this thoroughfare between Harrington and Somersby...*'

Sophie's stomach lurched.

Connor stopped struggling, and his head cocked as he tuned in. Sophie watched his shadow on the floor grow as he stood up to his full height. And from the panicked look in Lucy's eyes, he was staring at the radio. Perhaps he hadn't noticed it before.

They were just down the road, doing a radio report right now. Outside her house, while she was tied up in a workshop only five minutes away.

'*Not only did the flooding cause numerous traffic problems throughout the area, but tragically, two bodies were found here in the early hours. Police are presuming them to be a couple who drowned while trying to escape in their car, which was found half submerged in a deep gully.*'

Her mind swam before she'd even processed the words. Our bodies are always one step ahead, she thought vaguely, thinking she might faint. But soon enough, she understood.

"Oh god," Sophie muttered almost subconsciously.

'*Their house is behind me now, and I can see the devastation the flooding has caused, the level of the water line, and yes, it would have been difficult to escape the raging torrents that must've passed through here.*'

Sophie felt the onset of shock. It was all she could do to stare at the girl opposite, whose face had drained of blood as quickly as water escaping the collapsed side of a paddling pool. She shook her head back and forth.

"No, no, no, no, no," she cried, until her entire body shook with denial, and she peered up helplessly.

"Lucy..." Sophie began, searching for the words. Anything to reassure her, to comfort her, to join in her denial. *It's probably not them. It's a different couple. They were travelling through when the flood hit.* But Sophie's eyes, one step ahead, had already filled, and tears rolled heavily down her face. She wished her damn arms were free. Not to comfort Lucy, but to wipe away her own tears, to demonstrate what the girl needed most — strength.

But from somewhere deep inside Lucy's body came a long and deathly moan, guttural and in pain. It came from the very essence of the girl's being. Wherever it was that souls waited, it came from there. It travelled through her bones, escaping in the way thunder escapes a brooding cloud.

"Turn it off, Connor," said Sophie.

He stepped around Sophie to study Lucy.

"What's wrong with her?" he asked.

"Connor, turn the radio off!"

But it was too late. The next sentence from the news reporter confirmed their fears, and Sophie let her head fall back in despair as she gave a last thought to the Tuckers, once friends, neighbours, and suffering parents – were now dead.

'A statement from the police suggests that their daughter is believed to be one of two missing women in the area, thought to have disappeared during the heavy rainfall...'

At these last words, Lucy gave a cry that Sophie hoped she'd never have to hear again in her life. It was a wail of pure misery, a scream of absolute despair. She began jumping in her chair frantically, and the chair legs knocked and scraped against the concrete, squirming like a trapped, wild animal. Huge gag-like sobs rose out from her throat. Her shoulders shook like she was undergoing some painful, terrifying transformation.

"Lucy…"

"I'll turn it off," Connor decided too late, in a sad voice that sounded like he thought it might help. He walked over to the shelves, moving behind Sophie to keep his distance.

In the background, so mesmerised was she by the first throngs of grief gripping the teenage girl in front of her eyes, Sophie almost missed the reporter's final words before Connor turned it off.

'Police are imploring anyone in the vicinity on Friday night between ten and eleven p.m. to reach out to Detective Inspector Larson with any information that might lead to these two missing women—'

CHAPTER TWENTY-FOUR

The car ride from the station to Jason Connolly's house in Spilsby was the second almost silent car journey of the day. In the five years she had worked with George, they had never, that Ivy could recall, shared such a tense and secret-riddled day. If this was what her work life was to be like in The Wolds, then perhaps Jamie had been right. Maybe she had made a mistake in coming. After all, what was it that George trusted Campbell with that he couldn't trust Ivy with?

Ivy turned the question round and round in her mind, uselessly, indulgently, her tense reaction to its lack of answers only adding to the moody atmosphere of the car. And then, as if to emphasise her doubts, her phone began to vibrate and Jamie's name appeared on the screen.

George turned his gaze from the road at the distraction.

"Mind if I take this, guv?" she asked.

"Go ahead," he said.

They were doing that overly polite back-and-forth perfected by married couples who had something to fight about, but were not ready to fight just yet.

"Hi ya, love," Ivy answered the phone, hoping she sounded cheery.

"Mummy!"

Ivy's whole body relaxed at the high-pitched voice of her little girl.

"Hatty!" she said, copying her tone and smiling at the darkening countryside through her window. "How was your day, sweetie?"

"Theo stole my Lego socks."

"No, I *didn't*," came the indignant voice of her son in the background. "They're mine."

Ivy closed her eyes, rubbing the bridge of her nose. "The blue ones are Hatty's; the green ones are yours, Theo."

"See," came her daughter's voice, "I *told* you."

Then came the sounds of jostling over the phone, followed by, in the background, a deep, male voice telling them to stop. The phone line settled again and Hatty continued.

"Daddy wants to know if you'll be home to make dinner."

Why he couldn't have called to ask her himself? Ivy could only guess. Maybe he was hoping that Hatty's innocent voice would inspire more of a guilt trip?

Ivy looked at her watch – 5:18 p.m. It was unlikely they would be done and back at the station before 6:30 p.m. Then she had the forty-minute drive back to Mablethorpe. She didn't answer the question, just said, "There are fish fingers in the freezer. Tell Daddy to put them in the oven and to microwave some peas. I'll be back later, okay?"

Via their children wasn't Ivy's ideal form of communication with her husband, but until he was ready to sit down and talk properly, it would have to do.

"Okay," said Hatty unconvincingly.

"Look, Mummy has to go, okay? I'll see you later."

"To tuck me in?"

What was worse – admitting failure or risking a lie? Ivy took a gamble.

"Yes, sweetie, I'll be back to tuck you in."

"Okay, bye, Mummy," said Hatty, echoed by Theo in the background, trying to say it louder than his sister. "Bye, Daddy," she told Jamie, then waited for his response.

But Ivy heard only a few seconds of crackly silence before the call disconnected.

She rested it back on her lap and continued to stare out the window at the passing fields. The cold dampness of dusk was settling in once more. Any leftover puddles, swamped parks, or burst river banks would now have to wait for the morning and hope for the sun's rays to continue to soak up the damage.

In her peripheral, Ivy felt George's stare move continuously from the road to the side of her face. But, she knew, he wouldn't say anything until she turned to meet it.

"Next left," was all she said, checking the directions on her phone.

Jason Connolly's address was less of a house and more of a static caravan on a derelict patch of land. Not too far away, just around a corner and behind a thick hedge, was a two-up-two-down cottage. There was no fence between the caravan and the house, suggesting that the land the caravan occupied belonged to the owners of the house.

Still, the owner of the caravan clearly craved independence, having spray-painted a house number on his bins and the outer wall facing the street. *211-B Woodlands Avenue* – the address matching that on Ivy's phone.

Outside, tied up and large, like a threatening guard dog, a motorbike took pride of place. Not being overly familiar with motorbikes, she deemed it pretty standard. It certainly wasn't one of those easy riders, and it most definitely wasn't a sports bike. The thing might have even been a classic, if it hadn't been for the bright blue plastic around the handlebars and wheels that, in her opinion, only made it look tacky.

George pulled up on the street, and without a word between them, he and Ivy got out the car and strode up to the caravan in stony silence. George reached up and rapped on the door twice – one more than an accidental bang against the door, but no more than absolutely necessary. It was answered quickly, as if the knocks had been expected, and in the doorway, undeniably, stood the same man from the photograph George had taken from Lucy's bedroom. But in the flesh, he wasn't a man, really. More of a boy, no older than seventeen, and dressed in a white t-shirt and long sports shorts, despite the temperature not being higher than five degrees, even inside a thin-walled caravan.

"Jason Connolly?" asked George, taking his silence as confirmation. "I'm Detective Inspector Larson. This is Detective Sergeant Hart." The boy's eyes darted between them both indifferently. "I wonder if we could ask you a few questions? Can we come in?"

For a moment, it looked like he might refuse, but then he wordlessly walked out of view, leaving the door open. They climbed the three metal steps and entered, finding the boy perched on a long, half-circle sofa at the front of the caravan, rolling a cigarette. Usually, George would ease the tension by pointing out something he liked about somebody's home; an eye-catching painting or defining feature of the house. She watched him study the dingy and smoky caravan in search of something but then give up.

"Are you familiar with a Lucy Tucker, Jason?" he began, and then waited.

Jason twisted the cigarette in his hands, then rolled.

"I am," he replied.

"We're having trouble locating her, and we're led to believe that you and her are in some kind of relationship. Is that right?"

"What does that have to do with me?" Jason spoke up eventually, responding to the first question, but not the second.

"Do you have any idea where she might be?"

Jason licked the cigarette paper. People like Jason probably thought they looked masterful at this point of rolling, but Ivy always felt it held the same awkwardness as licking a stamp in a post office.

"She's at home, isn't she?"

"No, Jason," George said. "She isn't. She hasn't been seen since the floods last night." At this, Jason lit his cigarette with shaky hands. "When did you see her last?"

He inhaled and grimaced, as though the heat burned his throat. He spoke in the same moment of exhaling, so his words emerged in a cloud. "Couple of days ago," he said.

"Okay," George said, glancing back to check that Ivy was making notes. "And when was the last time you stopped by her house?"

Jason tapped his cigarette ash onto the table impatiently. "Are you deaf, old man?" he said, looking up at George. "I just told you, a few days ago."

George nodded. It wasn't the first time he'd been called an old man, but he had thick skin, and the way to handle individuals such as Jason Connolly certainly wasn't by reacting to their hollow jibes.

"You know, I always liked motorbikes," he said, staring through the window at the one outside.

Connolly appraised George, from his smart brown brogues to his woollen sweater, his neat, grey hair. He scoffed. "Is that right?"

"Oh yes," George said. "Not to ride them, you understand. But as a detective, you tend to pick up on things that another man wouldn't. It makes your job easier. A long, blonde hair on a jacket lapel. A Timberland boot print." At this, Jason glanced at the pile of shoes in the hallway. It didn't surprise Ivy that George had noted the footwear. Timberland boots were popular with manual workers, which was why George liked them, easy to associate a shoe with a crime. "The smell of a perfume," George continued, then moved his eyes to Jason. "The sound of a motorbike."

Jason took a drag of his cigarette and began tapping his foot.

"Very recognisable engine, you see," George continued.

Jason stopped tapping his foot. "What's your point?"

"My point, son, is that your motorbike was on Somersby Road on Friday night less than one hour after Florence and David Tucker had been killed?"

Jason stilled, his eyes fixed on George, like an angry lion or a scared gazelle. Ivy couldn't tell yet. But his next words revealed fear, not fury.

"What did you say?" he said quietly.

Ivy thought it was a threat, a reaction to George's accusation. But George knew better. The question wasn't what Jason was reacting to. The part he'd picked up, the part that had turned his skin grey, was something else entirely. And George reiterated it.

"You heard. David and Florence Tucker. Lucy's parents," he told him. "They're dead. I think it's time you started talking, Jason."

CHAPTER TWENTY-FIVE

"Dead," Jason repeated in a whisper.

"That's right," George said, softening at the boy's solemn reaction. "Dead."

A flash of panic crossed his eyes. "So, where's Lucy? Is she okay?"

"That's what we're here to find out."

"Well, what are you wasting your time here for?" Jason stood from his seat, cigarette left forgotten and charring the table. He flung his arm out, gesturing wildly. "You should be out there, bloody well finding her."

Ivy stepped forward, a silent warning for the boy to calm down. They had never verbalised the agreement, but she felt it her responsibility as the younger of the two, that in the event of what he called an escalating altercation, she would be the one to take control of the situation. Although, due to his infinitely calm persona, such occurrences were rare, preferring verbal and more gentlemanly de-escalation techniques.

"We *will* find her, Jason," George said, and with his sure, earnest voice, even Ivy believed him, despite Lucy's dwindling chances of survival with every tick of the clock. Jason clearly did too, and he sat down, dispirited. "But first, I need to know what you were doing on Somersby Road on Friday night."

Jason picked up his cigarette and took a drag, brushing the ash from the table to the floor. "How do you know it was me?"

"It was a motorbike. I heard it. I saw the headlight."

"So? I'm not the only biker in Lincolnshire."

"But it *was* you, wasn't it, Jason? Why else would someone visit an empty road nearing midnight unless they knew someone living in one of the three houses there?"

"What?" Jason's head snapped up. "Are you accusing me of something?"

"You tell me, Jason. What were you doing there?"

But the boy stayed silent. He stared at the glowing end of his cigarette. His shoulders hunched a bit further. His head bowed a bit lower. He was withdrawing. George switched tactics.

"We saw your name on the *Tucker and Co* employee list. What do you do there?"

"Warehouse," said Jason, speaking to the cigarette, then stumping it out on the table where it might cause a knot-like wood marking on the cheap furniture. "I load the vans, drive to sites, deposit materials. All that."

"Do you enjoy it?" George asked. "The job, I mean?"

Glass-eyed, Connolly stared up at him. "It's a job."

"And is that how you met Lucy, Jason? Working for her father?"

"None of your business," he muttered.

George switched again.

"What about David? Was he a good boss?"

Jason shrugged. "Doesn't really do much. Just sits in his office." Ivy noticed this often, people switching between past and present tense when they just learned of a death. It was a real-time reveal of the brain trying to process. Working out if the dead person still existed in this world right now or not. Connolly stared at George, defiant, and George stared back, resolute. "But that's always the way, isn't it? The big boss sits on his arse while people like me do the grafting."

"Is it?"

"Yes," Connolly replied sharply." "It is. You should know. What office is your boss sitting in right now?"

Always preferring to be the one asking the questions, and not answering them, George replied with a curt smile at the boy's intuition.

"What about Florence Tucker? Did you ever meet her? Did she come by the office at all?"

"No," Connolly said, already rolling another cigarette. "Has her own job, doesn't she. A teacher."

Ivy could swear she saw a few green marijuana buds between the tobacco, not enough for a strong smell but enough to hit the spot. It was a bold move, thought Ivy, lighting up in front of two police detectives. She stared at it until he noticed. Jason licked the paper while keeping eye contact, then rolled it together with a smirk.

"What about meeting David and Florence as Lucy's parents? Get invited round for tea, did you?"

Connolly snorted a laugh but chose not to elaborate.

"What?" asked George. "They didn't approve of the pair of you?"

"Not good enough for their precious Lucy, am I? Bit too rough round the edges for their type, if you get what I mean."

Ivy sensed a commentary on class in the statement, some-where; something about the Tuckers' standards, their status. Their house was beautiful. A million pounds, or near as damn it. Then again, with a daughter of her own, Ivy doubted class had much to do with the Tucker's reservations.

"Nope, no one's good enough for David Tucker," Connolly continued of his own accord. The topic had clearly grazed a nerve and stirred the young man into a rant. After all of his prodding, George had struck gold, and he let the boy talk himself into a corner. Which didn't take long. "David pays-his-employees-late Tucker. David seven-days-of-holiday Tucker. David fires-you-without-notice Tucker—"

"Fires you?"

Connolly came to a stuttering, spitting end to his rant like an old car spluttering to a halt.

"Jason, did David fire you?" asked George.

The boy kept quiet, his lips pursed. He'd learned a lesson he wasn't about to repeat.

"When did it happen?"

Jason didn't reply.

"It can't have been long ago," George said, turning to engage Ivy instead, as though they were having a harmless, casual conversation. "Peter Mansfield only gave us the employee list this morning. Jason was still on it, wasn't he, Sergeant Hart?"

Using her title was reserved for public displays, or to make a point of rank, and she was grateful for his selection. The last thing she wanted was for an individual like Jason Connolly to know her name.

"That's right, guv," she joined in.

Still, Connolly remained silent.

"Which means, I'm going to guess, that he fired you in the past week. David Tucker struck me as a man who keeps up to date with his paperwork, after all. Don't you think?"

"A week tops, guv," she said, answering on Connolly's behalf. "Probably sooner."

"Sooner, yes," George said, nodding his head and stepping forward like a queen about to secure checkmate on a cornered king. "Say, Friday?" A tall man, George, stared down at the hunched-up Jason Connolly, forming an imposing sight. "Is that when David fired you, Jason? On Friday? The same day that he was killed?"

Connolly hadn't moved. He just let his cigarette drop ash on his bare-skinned thigh. But at this, he finally coughed, and said, "No comment."

It was a tactic he was familiar with, clearly. Something he knew he should do, and one that had perhaps been advised to him by men more experienced in matters of the law. But the advice had been recalled just a little too late.

"This isn't an interview, Jason," George said. "You invited us in. You want us to find Lucy, so, help us. Why did David Tucker fire you?"

"No comment."

"For sleeping with his daughter?"

"No comment."

"For not showing up to work?"

"No comment."

"For being high at work?"

At this, Jason stared back at him with the same expression Ivy had seen hundreds of times on the faces of young, careless, rude young men – a look of realisation, a realisation that they had underestimated George Larson.

Jason stubbed out his second cigarette.

This time, and with the same raised-hair vitriol of a cornered cat, he spat, "No comment."

The silence lasted for at least half a minute, and Ivy watched on with amusement at the pair, ready to step in if Connolly made any sudden movements. But this was what men did, she knew, stared each other down like circling dogs establishing the alpha. Rarely did such a demonstration of testosterone escalate beyond a hard stare.

She was about to lose patience with the performance when the front door burst open.

"Jason," called a voice from the doorway. "Jason, I need to talk to you."

A man burst into the caravan's living area, eyes only for Connolly. It took Ivy a moment to recognise the man with his messy hair that had been neatly combed back, as though stressed hands had been running through it all day. His eyes were bloodshot, his shirt's top buttons were undone, and his tie hung loosely as if it had been tugged away to give him air.

"Not now, Uncle Pete," Connolly replied, peeling his eyes away from George to glare at the man.

But the man needed no explanation and had fallen mute of his own accord. He glanced between George and Ivy as though they were ghosts, haunting his life, following his footsteps. His eyes, somehow, had grown even more bloodshot, like the shock of seeing them again had burst a blood vessel.

Finally, George looked away and turned his attention to the older of the men.

"Hello, Uncle Pete," he said to Peter Mansfield and then held out his hand. "Inspector Larson. How lovely to see you again."

CHAPTER TWENTY-SIX

In shock, Peter Mansfield did actually take George's hand before getting a grip on himself. It came as no surprise to George that Mansfield wasn't an honest individual; that much had been evident during their first interaction with the man. The question was, why?

"Wh-what are you doing here?" Mansfield asked.

"Oh, we're just getting to know your nephew, Mr Mansfield," George told him, pulling his coat breasts together to indicate to Ivy that it was their time to leave. They had all the information they needed for now - almost.

George turned to Connolly once more.

"Jason, I'll remind you that my primary concern right now is finding Lucy Tucker," he said with the same sure, earnest voice that had resonated with the boy earlier. "And I'll ask you one last question."

Jason looked up at him, ready to listen, George figured, if only for the sake of his girlfriend.

"Do you know anyone who might have reason to hurt Lucy or David, or Florence, for that matter?"

It took the lad a few seconds, and George could almost see the cogs turning behind his eyes. It was a simple question. Yet for some reason, Jason Connolly had many factors to consider before answering it.

"No," he said eventually. George's nod was a formality, just as Connolly's response was a lie. However, Connolly had more to say. "But I can tell you one thing, Inspector." George looked down at the lad, whose face had contorted into a violent scowl. "If I find out that someone has hurt her, I'll kill him."

This statement, by contrast, George absolutely believed.

"Well, that clears that up," he said, turning to the uncle, who had closed his eyes in despair at his nephew's reckless response. "Mr Mansfield," he said quietly, "why didn't you tell me your nephew worked at *Tucker and Co*?"

Peter gaped like a fish, then said, "I didn't think it was relevant."

"You didn't think it was relevant that your nephew was dating your business partner's daughter? I asked if you knew who Lucy spent time with."

Again, he gaped. "I suppose, I forgot."

George laughed. "You forgot. And did you also forget to tell me that David *fired* Jason on Friday?"

"Now, that was a misunderstanding," Mansfield said before Connolly could stop him.

In his peripheral, George saw Jason throw his hands up and sink back into the sofa. Mansfield looked between George and Jason, his face displaying an artful blend of panic at saying too much, and confusion at the whole affair.

"And what misunderstanding would that be?"

But Peter Mansfield wasn't willing to step into the same trap twice.

After a few seconds of silence and with Mansfield avoiding his eyes like a shy schoolboy, George continued.

"Very well," he said, and nodded once at Ivy before following her to the front door. "You'll be hearing from us, the pair of you," he called over his shoulder. "Very soon, in fact."

With that, George held open the door for Ivy and they made their way down the steel steps and towards his car. The night had fully settled in the time they had been inside the caravan, and in the darkness, the motorbike's headlight grill resembled the mangled and bared teeth of a guard dog even more. Neither he nor Ivy rushed to George's car, even though the two men watched their every move through the window, perhaps to ensure they left, George now reasoned, Peter Mansfield's property.

With plenty to discuss, considering everything they'd just learned, the return journey to the station was far less quiet than it had been on the way there. For that, George was very grateful. He was grateful, too, that it was Ivy who spoke first.

"So, we have a motive, means, and opportunity," she stated the facts. "Jason Connolly. He was fired by David, you saw his motorbike at the scene of the crime, and the road would've been empty not long beforehand."

"True," George said. "I'm not sure what he had against Florence though."

"You heard him. Not good enough for the precious Tuckers. Both of them seemed to be standing in the way of his relationship with Lucy." The pace of Ivy's words matched the churn-speed of his own thoughts. "Or maybe Florence just got in the way? Maybe she caught him?"

"The shock on his face though," George added, shaking his head. "It was almost as convincing as Mansfield's."

"You know my thoughts on this, guv. People lie in all kinds of ways. We've seen narcissists cry their eyes out over the death of a victim only to confess to the crime later on. You can't trust reactions."

"You're right," George told her. He'd been caught out before, trusting emotions over facts. Perhaps it was because he found masking his own emotions easy that he found it hard to believe others could do the opposite, to display their emotions so openly, even when they were false.

"Saying that," Ivy said, "he did seem genuinely concerned about Lucy."

"Not concerned enough to tell us the truth when I asked if he knew anyone who might hurt her," George said, noting that he and Ivy had surreptitiously switched roles.

It was all part of the dissection, bouncing between the role of devil's advocate, like a couple dissecting an evening with friends on the car ride home; who drank too much? whose marriage was on the rocks?

"True," Ivy agreed. "He was lying. I'd have money on it."

"So why lie?" George asked. "If he cares about Lucy, and if he really wants her to be found, then why not tell us if he suspects someone?"

"Maybe it's someone he's also close to. Say, oh, I don't know, his uncle?"

George turned his headlights to full beam, acceding that the roads were unfamiliar, and even less so in the dark. He wondered if, for the rest of the time he lived here, whether he'd be able to disassociate the darkness from the flooding, so impactful his welcome to The Wolds had been during the previous evening.

"Possibly," he said. "Quite possibly."

It didn't take long for them to reach the station, the roads being empty. People were likely choosing the warmth and safety of their homes as they processed the trauma that the deluge had stirred. Some were likely staying with friends or family, on sofas or in spare rooms, unable to return to their ruined houses, their lives turned upside down in the space of a single night.

George pulled into the parking spot close to the stairwell door, the space that he had decided on earlier that day.

"Still, we're no closer to finding Lucy Tucker," he said, turning off the engine. He looked at his watch. "Nearly twenty hours since David and Florence were killed. We're running out of time."

Ivy turned to him with those kind eyes of hers, offering the same warmth roasted chestnuts did on a winter's evening. "We'll go to the pathologist first thing tomorrow. Hopefully she'll be able to shine some light on the matter."

The decision did little to relieve George's guilt, which was often the case during the first few days of an investigation. He felt he should be out there, on his hands and knees, hunting for Lucy, or questioning anyone and everyone. And he had done, in his younger years, when sleep and rest were further down his bodily priorities.

"We've done all we can do for tonight, guv," Ivy continued. "The search team is still out there looking. The best thing we can do for her now is get a proper night's rest and start again tomorrow."

"You're right," George said, but this time, it was to move on. There was one more thing he could do. He had one more card up his sleeve before calling it a night.

Ivy eyed him with the same suspicious and curious expression that she had worn all day. The line between what he was telling her and what he wasn't was larger than it ever had been. This place held many a buried secret, his failures, his life choices. And there was only so much he was willing to share.

And she knew it.

"Goodnight, guv," she said, reaching for the door handle.

"Goodnight, Ivy," George said, offering her the most reassuring smile he could and hoping it reflected in his eyes. "See you in the morning, eh?"

She offered the flash of a smile that suggested her unease, and then closed the door. George watched her walk across the car park to her own car and waited until she had settled inside before fishing his phone from his pocket.

It rang three times, enough time for Ivy to leave the station car park, onto the black road, and into the darkness, leaving the wispy remnants of diesel fumes in the air.

She answered the phone with a fast, straightforward, "Yes, guv?"

"Campbell," he replied, curtly. "What have you got for me?"

CHAPTER TWENTY-SEVEN

George placed his bags-for-life on the wobbly kitchen table and stretched his shoulders, silently contemplating which would last longer, the bag or his old body. But what had seemed to be an amusing little tangent in his mind turned morose, and he wondered if he would die in this house. The thought was quick and dark, and he shook it off, dismissing the notion as fatigue dulling his senses.

In one bag was a collection of new towels, navy and white, the colours that Grace had preferred for such soft accessories. In the other was a collection of groceries that he believed he could work with, given the house's limited cookware. Thankfully, there was a pot in a cupboard, along with a severely scratched frying pan, an old chopping board and a handful of utensils.

The first job of the evening was to check the oil tank. A delivery of fresh oil might take a few days, and he prayed that whatever was in there was still good enough to see him through. The tank was in the garden, a few feet from the boundary wall, and with the help of his little Maglite, he prized the lid off and peered inside. The torchlight reflected off the slick surface, but it was almost impossible to gauge the amount. So he kicked the side of the hardened plastic tank and saw the ripples in the oil writhe and then fade. It was enough for a few days at least, he thought, making a mental note to check again at first light.

Back in the house, he fired the old boiler up, waiting tentatively for the sound of the ignition, which took a few terrifying moments, until at last it jumped into life. He gave the old thing a pat on the side and laughed to himself before reentering the kitchen and dumping his coat over an old stool. He rubbed his hands together and watched the cold escape his breath. He'd been too tired the previous night to notice the cold, having stripped off his wet clothes, and wrapped himself in his old scratchy blanket. Crouched beside the radiator near the back door, he turned the dial until a menacing gurgle sounded as the hot water forced its way in for the first time in God knows how long. He eyed it for a few seconds, until eventually, the gurgling settled and the very bottom of the old radiator warmed.

He rolled up his sleeves and prepared to eat. By God, he'd earned it. Not trusting any of the cutlery until he had washed it all, he resorted to life as a student. For a knife, he used the penknife his first sergeant had bought him when he'd passed his NPPF exams, slicing the mushrooms and onions and garlic and then giving it a good wipe, before folding it closed and sliding it into his pocket. Once he had rinsed the small pan, he put some water on to boil, before frying the vegetables in a little skillet that had been hanging above the worktop on an old butcher's hook. Once the water had begun to boil, he added some penne pasta and hunted for some kind of plate or a bowl.

Some combination of two vegetables and a carbohydrate was the limit of George's culinary skills. Grace had always been the chef at mealtimes, leaving him to work through their selection of vinyl records. But for now, all George had in the way of music was the whistle of the wind through fissures in the windows and doors, and the mysterious creaks upstairs that he put to the back of his mind.

He closed the last of the kitchen cupboards, having found no sign of a plate or bowl.

With each second in the old house, his shopping list grew in length, and often expense. A record player, for example, loud enough to reside in the living room and still be heard in the kitchen. And now, of course, a cutting knife, some decent plates, and cutlery should be added to the list.

He settled on mixing the pasta with the vegetables, added a dollop of pesto, and then ate straight from the pan, stabbing pieces of penne with his pocket knife. He hadn't eaten this way since before he married Grace, when he lived in a tiny townhouse in Lincoln with five housemates, none of whom had considered investing in a plate set. George couldn't help but laugh to himself.

If Grace could see him now.

He left the pans soaking in the sink, promising to buy the tools to wash them properly, and then grabbed the bag of towels and headed upstairs. He placed it on the bed, and after a few moments to take in the room, he decided that some artwork would warm the cold, dark room. With the heating on, George tracked its moans throughout the house. It was like following a voice; he went where it sounded loudest, promising to add a radiator key to his shopping list, to give them all a good bleed.

He found the noise loudest in the master bedroom, where he felt his intrusion the strongest, knowing who it had once belonged to. It was that same feeling of trespassing he had felt in his own parents' bedroom, knowing it was out of bounds.

He closed the door respectfully, and returned to the room he had claimed as his own, then ran the shower. After a minute or so, the hot water trickled through, and the thought of a nice hot shower became the highlight of his day.

In his excitement, George stripped off and stepped into the running water, giving a loud sigh of relief. He felt like he'd been cold-through for twenty-four hours and could have stayed there for the entire evening.

Dry and refreshed, George changed into fresh pyjamas, his slippers and a dressing gown; the one Grace always said made him look like Arthur Dent. Remembering to skip the rotting step, he made his way downstairs, smiling at the mess, and the dust, and the filth, and the God knows what. He smiled because none of it mattered. The house was warming through, and with it, George's spirits.

He walked over to the fireplace and wiped its surface with an index finger, finding the layer of dust reminiscent of snow along a fence. If the dust in the old house had been snow, he would have enough to build a decent snowman. Cleaning products, he added to his list; duster, polish, vacuum cleaner.

He returned to the kitchen and retrieved his pièce de résistance — a bottle of ten-year-old Talisker, which he could almost kiss. And then, with a side thought, he added a nice new decanter and glasses to his list, preferring to drink his whisky from crystal. But for now, the old enamel camping mug that he had brought with him would do. George poured a healthy measure from the bottle, feeling like a ranger in the wild.

He settled down on the sofa that reminded him of his grandma's old house, where every soft furnishing had been floral of some description, from the wallpaper to the curtains. Deciding the old sofa would have to go, he considered a few places nearby where he could buy something brown and leather. He'd get some more blankets too, chequered and wool, he thought, like the ones that Grace had liked.

There was, much to his disdain, a small part of him that wanted to throw the list away, hire a van, and bring everything from Mablethorpe.

But another part of him, a far stronger force, treasured his house in Mablethorpe. The house that had been theirs. He preferred to keep it all exactly how it was; how she remembered it. Although he was unsure why. As a memorial? A shrine? How long would it take for that house to become like this one?

Unlived-in, dated, with rotting steps. He couldn't bear the thought of his and Grace's home turning to dust, but couldn't quite face pulling it apart either.

As he often did when emotions ran fierce, George sipped at his whisky and turned his thoughts to the investigation. Perhaps it was his mind's way of seeking distraction, but it had been too long a day to reason anymore. Feelings rose to the surface faster than logic, their buoyant force far stronger. Images that he couldn't quite keep at bay swam to the surface like carp on a hot summer's day. Harsh torchlight washing over Florence Tucker as she lay in a ditch. David Tucker's bloated corpse blocking the drainage culvert. Edward Gibson holding a dead fish. Sophie Gibson, Lucy Tucker, Kelly Tucker, they all stood in a line in a white space. Out of context. Because he didn't know where they were. He couldn't even imagine where they might be. Not one of them.

George so wished Grace was around to ground him. She was good like that. He closed his eyes and wished for her to be there when he opened them, crossed-legged on the rug, knitting a scarf, or reaching out to steal a sip of whisky. But when he opened them, there was only her absence, of course. The empty fireplace, the empty rug, the empty house.

His wristwatch suggested it was ten-forty p.m. Twenty-four hours before, he had been at home in Mablethorpe, sipping a whisky, wishing for Grace, in his favourite armchair which he'd sat in - he did the math's — at least three-and-a-half thousand times. He was even sitting in the same position, facing the fireplace. The February weather was the same. The stressful headache of a brand new investigation was the same.

But nothing was the same, of course. Nothing was the same without Grace.

CHAPTER TWENTY-EIGHT

An oncoming car flashed Ivy as she waited to pull into Lincoln Hospital car park. It was only when she was partway through the manoeuvre that she noticed the driver was George, and she gave him a polite wave. So committed were they both to being punctual, they had arrived fifteen minutes early, leaving enough time to navigate the hospital in search of the pathology department.

If any other man behaved with such gendered chivalry, it might grate on her. But with George, she found his old ways only endearing. It was all about the intention, and his, she had to remind herself after the previous day, were rarely anything but good.

He pulled into the space beside her and they both opened their doors to climb out, as if the move had been rehearsed or choreographed. It was this type of unconscious synchronicity that kept Ivy feeling so connected to George, even during the more recent and difficult days of their relationship – him not trusting her, her resenting him for it.

The decision had been made during the long and sleepless night, whilst staring at the ceiling and listening to Jamie snore beside her. Today was a fresh start. If George didn't want to let her into his secret, that was his prerogative. In the same way, she didn't want to tell him how bad things really were at home.

The problem was that George didn't owe her his secrets, and today, she would try not to make him feel bad about it. Part of her sensed that some subconscious part of her had been expelling her own domestic tensions on the only man who had stood beside her during the past five years.

"Morning, guv," she said, as brightly as she could for someone who had slept for less than five hours.

She was still adjusting to her Wolds schedule, waking at five-thirty to make breakfast, get the kids up, do some chores, and then leave the house to arrive by seven. This was compared to the days in Mablethorpe, when they lived two minutes down the road to the station.

"Morning, Ivy," he replied, walking her way.

He looked fresher than the previous day. His hair seemed softer and cleaner, his eyes brighter, his clothes, well, his clothes were the same as ever — a combination of wool and tweed. He was sporting a light jacket with elbow patches, a sleeveless wool vest, and one of his faintly striped shirts beneath.

The man needed a trilby, she thought to herself. If they had lived a few decades before, then she might have bought him one.

"How was your journey back last night?" he asked, as they walked in step towards the hospital entrance.

"Oh, not bad," she lied.

It was when she had arrived home that the problems started – Jamie's reluctant eye contact, his focus on the TV, his silent good-night, going to bed early, and pretending to sleep when she finally joined him. The kids had already been asleep, too. Hatty had tucked herself in badly, with one leg out the covers. Theo had been lying on his stomach, thumb in his mouth, despite her efforts to stop the habit.

"How about you?" she deferred. "How's the rental?"

Why George had chosen to rent a place nearby instead of

staying in Mablethorpe, Ivy understood well enough. She wouldn't wish her commute on anyone. Let alone the domestic problems it inspired.

"Not bad," George said, though she felt there was an appendix, much like her *not bad* had. "You know, basic."

"Ah, yes," Ivy said. "All IKEA furniture, white plate sets, and *Live Laugh Love* posters?"

George laughed. "Exactly."

"Where is it again? Over Hagworthingham way?"

"Yeah," George said. "Just one of those small modern builds. One bedroom. Not much, but enough for me for now."

"And back to Mablethorpe for the weekends. Not a bad set-up. I suppose Grace is enjoying some alone time in the house during the week?"

"Ah, you know Grace," George said, with the same affectionate smile that arose anytime he mentioned his wife. "She loves her alone time. I imagine she will have knitted me a dozen scarves by the time I get home."

Ivy shared in his smile. Grace had knitted Theo and Hatty some type of garment every Christmas since the year they were born – from tiny socks to toddler hats, and even gloves that they still wore to school on wintry days.

The floods had settled into the land and showed no signs of leaving. Deep puddles lined the roads, and the car park was awash with a glistening blanket of oily water, despite the sun's efforts, there was only so much warmth it could offer. Both Ivy and George's hands were deep inside their pockets as they crossed the car park.

Inside the main building, two painted lines on the floor flowed throughout the building, red and green, with the supposed intention of helping visitors find their destination. But somewhere in the middle of the building, a mysterious yellow line was added into the mix, and a blue one too.

George stepped up to the counter near the doors. The receptionist took a second to break from the chat she was having, then looked up at him. Ivy took the chance to analyse the small-print directions. She wasn't sure pathology would even be on a sign designed for patients.

"Thank you," she heard George say, having been given the directions, then nodded at Ivy for her to follow.

Ivy noted the patients as they passed – some in bandages, some walking, using a drip stand as a crook, tubes up noses and in forearms, some with bleeding sores or yellowing legs. For a detective, it was far from the most disturbing sights she had seen, and she smiled at a few of the older patients she passed, knowing how joy could lacking in life when spent in hospital.

"What was the pathologist like then?" asked Ivy as they walked the red line. "When you talked to her on the phone?"

"Oh, seems like a sweet girl," George said. "Welsh by the sounds of things."

"Lovely," Ivy said, reminiscing about her childhood spent in South Wales on the Gower. Days of headland walks and chips on the beach, and polystyrene cups of tea while the wind blew hot tea-drops onto her fingers. Everyone she had ever met in Wales had a welcoming, merry quality to them, homely and sweet. Welsh, thought Ivy, that was a promising sign.

At the end of the long corridor, the lines split like crossing train tracks.

"Christ," George muttered.

Ivy looked around them, but suddenly, the corridor appeared to be void of life.

"Follow our nose?" she suggested.

"I suppose we'll have to," he replied, taking a gamble on turning right.

After two or three minutes of dead ends and wrong turns, they sheepishly returned the way they had come, taking the left turn instead, where, clearly seeing they were in need of help, a nurse slowed to help them, her eyebrows raised, too busy for words.

"Pathology?" George said. "We seem to have got turned around."

"Can't miss it," she said, pointing straight ahead and then she rushed off, leaving them with a friendly smile. Ivy and George followed her directions, which eventually led to a large double door, on which was a small sign that read *Pathology*.

George sighed, relieving any pent-up stress. He was a man who liked to know where he was going, Ivy knew. As if to tease them, the doors opened into a long, glass-sided corridor that seemed to take the sounds of their footsteps and amplify them, which seemed to heighten the silence between them.

George knocked twice and waited. But nothing happened. As humbly as possible, Ivy reached forward and pressed the buzzer.

Still, she couldn't help letting a small laugh escape. George softened beside her and let out his own. The door was opened almost as slowly as Ruth Hobbs had answered her door. The pathologist was clearly in no rush.

When it did finally open, far from the sweet Welsh welcome that Ivy had been expecting, the pathologist, a squat woman with wild, yellow hair, facial piercings, and a dragon tattoo reaching up from inside her smock, looked them up and down.

"Now then," she said.

The common Lincolnshire greeting sounded strange in an accent that made the *o* sound like two syllables and the *w* sound like a whole new syllable. Her scrubs were rolled up to her biceps as though she'd been elbow deep in something before they had knocked, and between her long, plastic gloves and the sleeves, the far reaches of some deathly tattoo was visible.

"Larson?" she said, and George nodded politely, but it did little to raise a smile on the young woman's face. "You're late."

CHAPTER TWENTY-NINE

"Scrubs are in the cupboards," Pip said, leaving the door open and walking towards the single door off of the little reception area. "Clean your hands too, will you?" She nodded at the hand-cleaning station.

Ivy headed straight for the cupboards, but George stopped in the middle of the room, taking in his surroundings. Then he turned to the pathologist. "You must be Doctor Bell," he said, at which she turned around. "We spoke on the phone."

"I am," she replied, slowly.

"And this is Sergeant Hart," he added, gesturing to Ivy, who nodded curtly.

Bell stared at them both, sizing them up, as though offering her name was a privilege. "Call me Pip," she said, in a friendly tone that belied her perceivable mood. "The others do."

Then she exited the room, letting the heavy door swish closed behind her.

George turned and raised his eyebrows at Ivy. Silently, they agreed that she wasn't quite the field-frolicking little Welsh girl they had both expected. If there was anything their jobs should have taught them, it was not to judge people. But that was a very hard habit to unlearn.

They changed into disposable overalls, washed their hands, donned gloves, and Ivy tied her hair back with the trusty hairband she always kept on her wrist.

"Ready?" George asked.

"As I'll ever be," Ivy replied, and George was reminded of Ivy's reluctance for the part of the job they were about to endure. Even the sight of David Tucker's body blocking the culvert had turned her stomach, although she had done well to hide it. But at least then it had been in context, surrounded by the aftermath of the storm, where all around it had been in turmoil and devastation.

But when bodies were laid out as they were in such places, on stainless steel benches in a sterile environment, with no other purpose than to be opened and examined, the imagination filled in the blanks. And while others seemed better at overcoming their fears and trepidations, Ivy struggled, and the signs were as clear to George as the skin on the back of his hands. She must have seen dozens of bodies laid out on slabs, and never once had she asked to be excused. Such was her tenacity.

George pushed open the single door to the mortuary, and this time he entered first, as though to block Ivy from any sudden, unsightly images. But she stepped around him, refusing to be protected, and he was glad to find the two bodies on adjacent gurneys were still covered with sheets.

"Now then, who's up first?" said Pip, rubbing her hands together with a casualness that wouldn't have helped settle Ivy's sickly stomach.

"Let's start with Florence Tucker," George said.

"Ladies first it is," said Pip, stepping over to the gurney closest to them. "Ready?" she asked, looking at Ivy as though knowing when to recognise a fainter.

"Of course," Ivy said professionally.

Slowly, Pip pulled back the sheet to reveal Florence's ghostly body in full. Ivy hadn't been there when the body had been discovered, and George was grateful that Florence had suffered far fewer injuries than her husband. It was an easier transition for the younger Sergeant to deal with, before David Tucker was revealed.

"So, Inspector Larson–"

"Call me George, please," he interrupted.

"So, George," Pip said, adapting quickly. "As I mentioned on the phone yesterday, at first glance, the victim appears to have drowned. But upon further examination..." she continued, and George was almost mesmerised by the lull of her accent. She steepled her stout little fingers beneath her chin. "I'm not sure it was an accident. In fact, I'm certain it wasn't an accident."

George stared down at Florence with sadness. He could remember the woman's face clearly, under all kinds of emotions: desperation, terror, anger, and anguish at her daughter's disappearance. At least now, with her eyes closed, she appeared to have found peace.

"I'd assumed drowning," George said. "I didn't look much closer. The conditions weren't exactly optimal."

"Well, you wouldn't," said Pip, in a kind enough way, as though picking up on his emotional state. "Nearly missed it myself, I did. Many would have."

He noted the humble brag, but said nothing.

Without warning, Pip rolled the body towards her, so that Florence was on her side, much the same as one might toss and turn on a sleepless night. "Here. At the back of her neck, look, will you? What do you see?"

George donned his reading glasses, bent a little, and peered at the spot.

"I don't see anything."

"A slight darkness to her skin in two spots," Pip said, as if she thought him incompetent. "Just below the hairline, see?"

She adjusted her pork sausage digits, and two tiny bruises came into view.

"Ah, yes," George told her, squinting as though analysing the brushstrokes of a painting, trying to note an expert opinion, the touch of a shadow that spoke of the artist's intention. "I think I see. What are they? Bruises?"

"Bruises," said Pip, lowering Florence's body with a surprising gentility. "Or fingermarks to be precise. Which suggests?" She paused, clearly hoping for one of them to finish the sentence.

"Someone held her down," Ivy said, trying to make up for her squeamishness with insight. "They pushed her head down with their hands."

"Right," said Pip. "This is what made me suspicious."

"That's all?" George said. "Is that enough to go on?"

"When was the last time somebody touched the back of your neck hard enough to leave bruises?" Pip asked.

Taken the wrong way, the question could have been deemed as quite intrusive, and from the look on Ivy's face, she was thinking the same. "It's a very untouched part of the body," Pip continued. "Especially when it's hard enough to cause bruising. It's not like a leg that can be bumped into a table by accident. Touching somebody's nape is quite a purposeful move."

"And you'd be prepared to testify to that effect, would you?" George asked.

"I would," she said flatly, as if daring him to argue. She reached for one of Florence's limp hands and held it up for them to see. "The dirt beneath the nails indicates a struggle, but that's not conclusive, of course. What *is* conclusive is the pulmonary oedema. Then, of course, there is the hypoxemia, which means that blood flows through under-ventilated portions of the lung–"

"Okay, okay," George said. "I get it."

"You don't want to hear about the adrenal gland?" Pip asked.

"No need," George replied, aware of Ivy's paling skin tone. "You'll add this to your report, I would hope."

"I will," Pip replied, then stared down at Florence with a certain tenderness, and George considered what she had said, surmising that to know a body so well, even postmortem, relied upon a strange connection and empathy. It was a true insight.

"Her death can be ruled a drowning, yes." She pointed at the chasm in her chest, which seemed to stare at them. "But accidental? No. Somebody held this poor woman's head beneath the freezing water. She didn't drown, Inspector. She *was* drowned."

George nodded soundlessly at the analysis. Ivy, too, was clearly impressed. "Shall we move on?" Pip asked, making her way over to David's body, as casually as suggesting the next bar in a pub crawl.

George and Ivy followed silently, both controlling their own reactions; George's emotional attachment, Ivy's churning stomach.

"Ready?" Pip asked Ivy again.

"Yes," she said, again with as much professionalism as she could muster.

Once again, Pip carefully peeled back the sheet covering David's body, and as expected, Ivy looked away, finding a spot on the ground to stare at it, in much the same way that twirling ballerinas were trained to focus on a single spot in the auditorium to maintain balance. The wound had been cleaned, leaving just a gaping hole, surrounded by pale white flesh.

"He wasn't so lucky," Pip announced. "However, this cause of death is much clearer."

"Blunt force trauma," George answered.

"That's right," Pip replied, softly. "And in case you were wondering, I found no indication of drowning, no pulmonary oedema, no signs of hypoxemia. The victim's heart had stopped before he entered the water. But look at his hands. Washerwoman hands."

"What's that?" George said politely, as though he'd misheard.

"Washerwoman hands," Pip repeated. "Shrivelled skin, look. It means he was left in the water for longer than his wife. Several hours more, in fact."

George studied David Tucker's hands, likening them to how he imagined his own might look in years to come. But, unlike his own, they hadn't bounced back. They would stay that way, at least until the body decomposed.

"So doesn't that mean he died in the water?" asked George.

"No," said Pip. "Washerwoman hands happen regardless of whether the victim died in the water, see? The skin continues to react to its surroundings. Even after the heart stops."

"Even with all the bloating?" George asked. "Doesn't it kind of..." he said, searching for the least descriptive explanation. "Push the wrinkles out?"

"Even with all the bloating," Pip replied. To his side, Ivy leaned onto the empty gurney behind them. "But the interesting thing about this one," Pip continued, removing a pen from the top pocket of her lab coat and circling the head wound. "Is the angle of the wound, see? It's wider nearer the top of the skull–"

"Which indicates?" George asked, already seeing where she was leading them.

"That the attack came from above. Which suggests?" she countered.

"That the killer is tall," Ivy said, now gripping the table. "Or at least taller than David Tucker was. By several inches I would imagine."

"Precisely," said Pip.

"Time of death?" George asked, keen to move on.

"I'd say that Doctor Saint's initial report was accurate. Between ten and eleven p.m. Myself, I'd go for the middle of the hour. Ten-thirty-ish."

"And they both died at the same time?"

"Within minutes of each other, yes," answered Pip.

"All these scratches on his body," George began, pointing to

David's arm, where thin marks lined his skin. "Does that indicate a struggle to you? Do you think he fought back?"

"No," Pip replied, shaking her head. "The report said he was carried by floodwater. What, half a mile? Through a culvert? These are from pipes, Inspector, loose debris, stray objects in the water." She pulled one of David Tucker's hands from beneath the sheet, revealing broken fingers that pointed in all manner of directions. "But unlike his wife, I can find no sign of a struggle."

"Fingernail analysis?" asked George.

"In progress. I'll send you the results to be sure," Pip replied. "Now then." She moved on with vigour, as though impatient to focus on what she knew for certain, as though building to a finale. "Notice the wound. It's big, no?" Ivy didn't need reminding. "Suggests a larger, rounded weapon."

"Like a bat?" confirmed George.

"Sure." Pip shrugged. "I'd suggest a bat. Something hard and smooth." She turned to the stainless steel trolley to her side, on which lay a number of bagged items too small to identify from where George stood. "And then there's this."

Pip held up a clear zip bag, which she passed to George, who examined it and then handed it to Ivy.

"Broken glass? Where did you find it?" he asked Pip.

"In his hair," Ivy said. "Trapped in there by the blood. Lucky it wasn't washed away, really."

"A vase?" Ivy said. "Or a bottle, maybe?"

"I analysed the glass," said Pip. "It's magnified by some degree, but it's too thin to be a drinks bottle, which is what I thought it was at first."

"So, Pyrex? No... Or..." Ivy said, clearly grateful for the distraction. "Glasses?"

Pip reached out, took the bag for her, and clicked her fingers. She smiled up at George, and nodded at Ivy.

"She's good."

"I know," he replied sincerely, and she picked a small set of reading glasses from her breast pocket.

"In fact, it's from a pair like these," she said, holding up the spectacles for them to see. "These are mine. I only use them for reading. It's going to be impossible to gauge the prescription exactly, because the fragment is so small, but I think the glass found in David Tucker's hair is from a pair of reading glasses. The glass is convex."

"Doesn't help us much," George said. "Half the people around here must wear glasses, and who doesn't have a spare?"

"True," said Pip, pocketing the glasses. "But you're not just looking for any glasses, Georgie boy." At this, George raised his eyebrows. In amusement or annoyance, he wasn't sure. Either way, he'd met someone even less concerned with titles than he'd always been. "Oh no," she continued, her accent adding drama to her closing statement. "You're looking for someone who is long-sighted, which, by the way, David Tucker was not."

CHAPTER THIRTY

Sophie woke with a jolt. Her head snapped, reacting to her dream; a slap in the face, a sudden fall, a car soaring into a body of water. She wasn't sure what. But when she felt the cool, damp air around her, the dream faded into insignificance.

She remembered reading once that such dreamlike behaviours were the body's way of protecting its host; a hypnagogic jerk. The dream carries the individual to the verge of death, triggering an adrenaline rush to rouse them from sleep. The theory was probably an urban legend by now ‑ unproven. Still, she was on the verge of something; delusion, death, madness? It could be any one of them.

Two bright and shiny glints in the gloom marked Lucy sitting quietly opposite her. She blinked away the remnants of sleep to study the young girl's mood, and found her expression blank, and those bright and shiny glints were sore and bloodshot. But she was no longer crying, and that was progress.

Such a mess. Such a tragedy. It was never supposed to have happened this way.

Sophie's tongue searched the far reaches of her mouth for moisture, but found only dryness, and a rank film covering her teeth. She stared at the empty cup on the floor, longingly, and recalled how Connor had scurried away before she could ask for more. The cold noodles, too, lay untouched at their feet.

She wondered how long it had been since, after what had seemed like an eternity, Lucy had wept herself to exhaustion, and her body or her mind had succumbed to fatigue. At one point, the young girl had struggled to breathe between sobs, and Connor had finally removed her gag for fear of the girl choking on her own misery. He'd untied their arms so that Sophie could comfort her, and so they could eat. But after witnessing a teenager's entire world collapse in front of her eyes, Sophie had lost her appetite. At some point, she had slipped into her own restless sleep, and she put to the back of her mind the thoughts of what Connor had done while they had both slept, having re-tied both of their arms in their slumber.

She looked to the radio for the time, but Connor had pulled the plug from the wall, and she stretched her neck left and right, searching for him in her peripheral. It ached from the cold and gave an ominous click. She hoped her bindings hadn't trapped a nerve somewhere.

Still, Connor was nowhere to be seen.

Light spilled beneath the workshop door, and she guessed it was well past sunrise. Eight or nine o'clock, maybe? If she listened closely, she could hear distant noises in the yard. Sweeping, perhaps?

In the time it had taken for Sophie to get her bearings, Lucy hadn't moved an inch. She had barely even blinked in her catatonic state of grief.

"Lucy?" she whispered, unsure of what she wanted to say. Part of her just wanted to remind the girl that she was here. That she wasn't alone. "Did you sleep okay?"

The teenager remained motionless for a few seconds. Then she shook her head.

"I've been thinking," she said.

Her voice was neither quiet nor loud, soft or hard, mild or tense. It was breathy and hollow, like a whispered echo in a cave. Her eyes still didn't shift.

"About what?" Sophie asked, encouraging the girl to talk.

Talking was an important part of grieving. Sophie knew that well enough. People had to talk about their lost ones, about their feelings. They needed reminding of their own existence, that they were loved. Nobody had ever talked to Sophie about Edward. Nobody had asked for funny stories, her favourite memories, or what she missed most. They never asked how she was holding up, whether she was coping, or what she was thinking.

That lack of interaction had silently devastated her. With nobody to turn to, she had never felt more alone. A magnificent man had left this world forever, and she had been the only one who cared. The only one who had grieved for Edward Gibson.

Yes, Lucy should talk about her parents. David and Florence. Her grief, her memories. But with her next words, it became clear that wasn't what Lucy wanted to discuss at all.

"You," she said, finally abandoning her spot on the floor to stare into Sophie's eyes. "I've been thinking about you."

The directness of it caused a shiver down Sophie's spine.

"Me?"

Lucy narrowed her eyes. "Who are you?"

Sophie laughed. She knew it wasn't an appropriate response, but somehow it offered some tiny relief to the growing tension rooted deep within her chest.

"Lucy, you know who I am. Sophie Gibson. I've lived next door to you your entire life."

Lucy continued to stare at her, as if she hadn't heard a single word.

"Who are you?"

"Lucy–"

"Who are you?"

"Listen," Sophie said. "I'm just as devastated about your parents' death as–"

It was Lucy's turn to laugh, and it was far from involuntary.

"Sophie, they hated you. They *hated* you. You should have heard the way they talked about you. The look on their faces every time you walked past the window. Every time they drove past your house. They would shrivel up into these little prunes of hatred. It was so *ugly*. Do you know what that's like? To have that level of hate brewing in your home for ten years?" Sophie stayed silent. The image of laughing with Florence over a Sunday morning coffee flashed through her mind. She closed her eyes against it and felt a tear roll down her cheek. "Do you?"

"No," Sophie croaked.

"And now I can never ask them why. Because they're dead. So, you need to tell me, Sophie. You need to tell me why they hated you."

Sophie stayed quiet, suppressing those terrible rumours about her Edward. She would not indulge in the lies. She would not let them pass from David and Florence to Lucy. Who would it help, anyway? Not Lucy, that was for sure. Not to know why her parents had loathed Edward, and by proxy, Sophie. How they'd blamed her for standing by her husband. For excusing him. Those lies could only cause more harm. They needed to die with David and Florence.

"It was about Kelly, wasn't it?" Lucy said, forcing Sophie to keep eye contact. "Everything dark in that house is about Kelly." She shook her head, her frown softening, her eyes once more developing that sparkling sheen. "You know, they never explained to me what happened? One day, I had a younger sister, the next day I didn't. There are no photos of her in the house. They can't bear to talk about her. All that's left is that creepy, little bedroom that nobody ever goes in. And I just had to keep on living, pretending, as though I'd always been an only child." She leaned forward, her sadness turning to anger. "Do you have any idea how messed up that is?"

"Lucy," whispered Sophie. She couldn't even imagine. "I'm sorry—"

"Don't apologise to me," spat Lucy. "Just explain it. Just tell me the truth."

But Sophie couldn't. She couldn't repeat those allegations. She couldn't go back to that place — the dark, lonely chasm in which she had dwelled following Edward's death. Only in the last few years could she even walk through the village without people whispering, or crossing the street.

"All the time we've been in here," Lucy continued, "you've told me to trust you. But how can I?"

"You *can* trust me, Lucy."

"No," said Lucy, deciding something for certain. "See, I've been thinking. All night, I've been thinking. And it doesn't make sense."

"Lucy, please—"

"No, you *insisted*, Sophie. That we come here. It was *your* idea."

Sophie reeled. "Lucy, it was the only safe place."

"*Safe?*"

Lucy pulled her arms to highlight the restraints.

"Dry, then!" said Sophie. "You remember how it was. We almost drowned. We would have frozen to death. I was trying to find somewhere dry, that's all. Do you really think I *wanted* to come here?"

"We could have kept going along the road—"

Sophie shook her head. "No—"

"Yes! We could've found help. Jay would've seen us." She paused, and Sophie could see the story escalating behind her eyes, shifting her perspective of the situation, and her anger abated as she processed the thought. "Or did you know he was coming? Is that why you brought us here?"

"You're being ridiculous."

"Ridiculous? This whole thing is ridiculous. We're tied up in a lunatic's workshop, for Christ's sake. And you know what?" She leaned forward, huffing with rage. "You know what, Sophie? You seem weirdly relaxed about it all."

Sophie's mind raced, trying to find the most logical argument, trying to calm the girl down, for her to see her side of it. "Connor thinks he's protecting us. I don't know why. But that's what he thinks. He doesn't want to hurt us."

"How do you know?" she yelled. If Lucy's hands were free, Sophie imagined she would throw them up incredulously. "How do you know what he's thinking? Unless..."

Again, Lucy's eyes darkened with new possibilities. There was something wild and manic in them, sleepless, conspiratorial. She'd lost it, thought Sophie. Grief had turned her mind. Just as it had with David and Florence, turning them against her.

"Did you plan this with him?"

"Lucy, come on."

"Is that what this is? If you trust him so much. What is it, some sick kidnapping fantasy?" Her eyes widened, her pupils dark holes. Her voice quietened with anger or fear, or both. "Is this what you did to Kelly?"

Sophie tried to throw her arm out to point at the girl, but the restraints stayed, twinging her shoulder muscle like the tip of a dagger.

"I would *never* have hurt Kelly. I loved that little girl."

"See, I don't believe you," said Lucy quietly, then she broke and screamed. "I don't believe a word you say!"

"Lucy, shush."

"See. *See!* Why are you telling me to be quiet? We *should* be making noise. We *should* be trying to be found. Why don't you want us to be found, Sophie?"

"Who's going to hear us scream?" she said. "Who's going to hear us except Connor? Is that what you want?"

"He's *lying*, you old bint. He's mental." Then she leaned back and laughed a laugh that was almost a sigh. "But you know that already, don't you?"

"You're starting to sound paranoid."

At this, Lucy laughed. A full-belly laugh, like she genuinely found the situation funny. "If there's a time to be paranoid, I think it's now, tied up in the local moron's workshop."

"Lucy," she scolded.

But the girl just leaned forward, moving onto the next stage of her conspiracy theory. "Where had you been? The other night in the flood. Why were you at the house?"

"I mean, I... I," she stuttered, knowing it didn't help, "I came to get you. All of you. To make sure you were safe," she said, desperate to provoke even an ounce of reason. "In case you've forgotten, I saved you from drowning."

"Me, sure. But Mum and Dad? What did you do to them?"

"Lucy, you can't be serious."

"The radio said they drowned escaping in their car. That meant they left before we did, before I'd got back from Jay's. So where were you?"

She couldn't believe this was happening again. The wild, hollow allegations. But this time, not on someone she loved. On her. About people she loved, as though she had ever wanted anything but the best for David and Florence.

"Lucy, look at me," she said, staring into her agitated eyes, sure to say the next words as though they were absurd. "I did not kill your parents."

Sophie saw the same hatred in Lucy's eyes that she had seen hundreds of times in the eyes of her parents, as she leaned forward and spat, "I don't believe you."

"Lucy–"

"I don't believe you."

"I loved Florence and David like–"

"I don't believe you."

"I would never do anything to hurt you or your–"

"I don't believe you."

"Lucy, let me talk, for God's sake."

"I don't believe you," she said, the words grating on Sophie's mind the more she spoke them. "I don't believe you," she repeated, triggering a whistle like a kettle behind her eyes. "I don't believe you! I don't believe you! I don't believe you!"

Sophie reached boiling point.

"Well, what about you?" she yelled. "Where were you that night, hey? How do I know you weren't involved? Or that chavvy boyfriend of yours?"

Some of Sophie's spit had landed on Lucy's cheek, and she could do nothing to wipe it away. Sophie's chest heaved, holding the weight of Florence and David's death, Kelly's death, Edward's death. So much death. All remembered only by her. All sitting right between the lungs that worked so hard to keep her breathing, day after torturous day.

Lucy leaned back, looking almost smug.

"And there it is. The ultimate sign of guilt. Passing the blame," Lucy said, almost pleased with her analysis.

"You're wrong, Lucy."

"Do you know what?" she said, her face an ugly sneer. "I hope he comes back, and I hope he does you first." Her eyes widened, and her lips pulled back to bare her teeth. "Because I want to see you suffer."

CHAPTER THIRTY-ONE

George stepped over the creaky floorboard and shoved through the doors so quickly that the officers inside barely had time to look up before he was striding across the room, filled with purpose. Such was his obvious demeanour that without asking, Campbell and Byrne stopped what they were doing and headed to the whiteboard at the back of the room of their own accord, where Ivy was waiting.

George selected a pen from the tray beneath the board, gave it a quick test in the corner, and then turned to face his team — Ivy, Campbell, and Byrne.

"Byrne," he started, giving the lad no time to become flustered. "Any updates from CSI? I presume they've been through the house by now, not to mention the car and the, um, item that Sergeant Hart and I found in Lucy's bedroom."

"Yes, guv," he said. "I spoke to a Katy Southwell," he said, checking the notebook on his desk. "She said she'll have the report for you later today."

George nodded.

"Well, it would have been nice to have them ready for this

morning, but this afternoon will suffice. Keep on at them, will you?" George said. "And what about the doorbell footage?"

"I've been through it all, guv, and made notes."

George nodded, waiting for more, which sadly, wasn't offered freely.

"And?"

"Not much movement all day. Couple of cars drove past on the road. A few birds in the garden setting the camera off." George looked up and caught Ivy's eye. She grinned back shamelessly as Byrne referred to his notes again. "David Tucker returns home at four-twenty-seven. Followed by Florence Tucker at five-fifteen."

"That's more like it," interrupted George, positively conditioning the lad to stick to the facts that mattered. "Anything else?"

"There's a visitor around seven p.m. A man. I'd say mid-fifties. He talks with David on the doorstep for about fifteen minutes." Byrne was reciting from his notebook now, flipping through the pages as if it was a menu in a restaurant. "Then nothing for the rest of the evening. The storm picks up at about nine-thirty. After that, it's just rain and wind until midnight. Can't see past the doorstep really."

"Okay." George nodded. "Not bad. Show me the man."

"The man, guv?" said Byrne, looking from George's stern expression to Ivy, for some kind of support.

"The man that David spoke to. Did you save his image?"

"Oh." Byrne looked to his notebook, as though it might hold more answers. "No, guv."

George felt his patience being pulled between urgency and mentorship. But this is what he'd signed up for, taking the lad under his wing. He'd wanted to see for himself why some of the other officers clearly didn't respect Byrne. He wanted to decide for himself whether or not there were grounds for such a lack of confidence. He was a bit slow, that much was true, but he just needed the confidence to trust his initiative. Like plants, George found, individuals like Byrne needed nurturing to flourish, a rich soil in which to plant their feet. Provide that, and the lad could be shaped and pruned into something that George could be proud of.

"Find him on the tape," George told the boy, nodding at his laptop, "and pause it. I want to see his face. If need be, we can run it through facial recognition. That man might well be the last person to see David Tucker alive."

"Yes, guv," Byrne said, and turned to open his laptop.

He had dropped the *sir*, at least, one unfurling petal at a time.

"Campbell," George said, moving on. "How about the lab? Have they been in touch?"

The question was somewhat for show. During their previous night's conversation, they had spoken on the topic and, unlike Byrne, she had demonstrated the need for far less need for nurturing. He already knew what she would say. But Ivy didn't, and he told himself he was giving her the courtesy of being updated, rather than deceiving. Still, he didn't like it.

He was a fine actor. Not a particularly expressive one, but precisely for that reason, quite able to hide his own character, if needed, in place of a pretence. He didn't enjoy such deception and manoeuvring, that was all. It was important to be genuine – to know thyself. In that knowledge were values and integrity. Spending prolonged periods of time pretending to be somebody else ran the risk of losing sight of those all-important values. Which was why, in his experience, Hollywood actors were often quite lost.

"Lab confirmed that the DNA from the condom was Jason Connolly's."

"As expected," George said, nodding at Ivy. "We had the pleasure of meeting Jason last night," he explained to the rest of his team.

"What's he like, guv?" asked Campbell, a fine actor herself.

"A piece of work," Ivy added, arms crossed and leaning against a free desk. "And a liar."

George clicked his pen lid. "Jason Connolly is courting Lucy Tucker, whose parents didn't approve."

"Courting, guv?" Campbell said, with a wry smile spreading across her face.

"What would you call it?"

"Dating. In a relationship with."

"I see. Well, add to that the fact that David Tucker fired him on Friday," he said, turning to the whiteboard and drawing a line from David to Jason. "And we've got ourselves the beginnings of a motive." He turned to face them again. "Now, when I was there on Friday night, I heard a motorbike. Campbell, you might remember. It stopped at the top of the hill, where it turned and left the scene," he said, adding *motorbike at 11:35 p.m.* to the side of Connolly's name. "The same kind of motorbike as the one sitting outside Jason Connolly's caravan."

"So you think he killed the Tuckers?" asked Byrne, skipping a few steps ahead.

"I heard the bike about an hour after their death. I'm not sure even Jason Connolly would be foolish enough to return to the scene of the crime so soon afterwards."

"Maybe he left something?" Campbell said, a suggestion she had relayed during their call. "He returned to get it, saw the traffic patrol, got spooked, and left? Remember, he rode off as soon as I started to walk up the hill."

"Possibly," George said, just as he had the first time. "Either way, he denied being there at all."

"Well, he's guilty then, right?" said Byrne. He'd tapped the space bar on his laptop and swivelled in his seat to re-enter the conversation. "Why lie if you have nothing to hide?"

"People lie for all kinds of reasons," Ivy told him. "Fear, love, hate. It's not always guilt."

"We need to add another connection," George said, keeping

them on the investigation, and then drew a line between Jason Connolly and Peter Mansfield. "Jason Connolly is Peter Mansfield's nephew."

Byrne gasped, as though in a courtroom drama, and they all looked at him.

"We didn't know that, right?"

Campbell rolled her eyes, and Ivy fought back a grin, while George studied him with curiosity.

"No, we didn't," he said. "Not until last night, when Mansfield stormed into Connolly's caravan saying they needed to talk."

"Talk about what?" asked Byrne.

"We don't know," Ivy said. "He shut up as soon as he saw us."

"Well, that's it then, isn't it?" Byrne said, looking between the three of them as though waiting for the instruction to go and arrest one or both of them right now. "We can bring them in? They're clearly in it together."

If only it were that simple. If only the narrative was enough. If only suspicious behaviour and red-flag characteristics coupled with a guilty look in the eye would hold up in court. Then Edward Gibson might've died behind bars where he belonged.

"Sadly, our opinions, no matter how well established, aren't anywhere near enough, son," explained George. "We need evidence."

He turned back to the board and in the top-right corner, wrote *pathology*.

"And that brings us to the..." George bounced his head, struggling to find the right word. "*Charming* Pippa Bell and her analysis." He relayed the facts as he wrote them, sticking to the key points. "Florence Tucker was indeed drowned. However, it appears that somebody held her head beneath the water, judging by the bruises on the back of her neck," he said, scribbling fast – *Florence, drowned, bruises*. "David Tucker, however, died from blunt force trauma and remained in the water for hours after his death. The two were killed within minutes of each other. And in case that wasn't enough for us to chew on, Doctor Bell found a fragment of glass in his hair."

David, blunt force, glass.

And beneath that, he wrote and underlined the word *glasses*.

"Glasses?" Byrne said.

"Glasses," George repeated, tapping it with his pen before turning. "That's our evidence."

Byrne looked incredulous, and George raised his eyebrows at the boy. "Just some glasses? Is that really enough to, well, kill someone?"

"They aren't the weapon," Ivy said, stepping in. "The weapon was something like a bat, or a rolling pin, or a glass bottle. Something hard and smooth, which sadly, most of the county have in a cupboard somewhere."

"Well, maybe," he said, his face reddening. "Mum keeps a good drinks cupboard."

Byrne was at that age when items such as cooking utensils, or pieces of furniture, or drinks cabinets were way down the priority list, especially when he was on what George assumed to be a fairly low pay grade.

George moved the conversation on.

"It indicates that there could have been a struggle, despite Doctor Bell claiming that no such thing took place. So, I've asked Campbell to relay the news to the search team…" At this, Ivy flicked her attention from the board to George. He could see the question behind her eyes. *When?* But she blinked it away and stared back at the board, only a slight frown revealing her true thoughts. "If we find the broken glasses, we could find the owner."

"So, until we find them," Byrne said, following along like it was a maths problem, "we can't touch Jason Connolly or Peter Mansfield?"

George paused.

"He's right, guv." Ivy caught his eye and shrugged. "But we *could* bring them in for questioning, couldn't we?"

That wasn't quite what Byrne had said, but Ivy was kind to pretend it might have been.

"No," George said, deciding. "I don't want to bring either in until we've got something concrete. We've got twenty-four hours once we do, and I want to be prepared enough to use that time wisely."

He turned back to the whiteboard, thinking, but mid-spin, he stopped when something on Byrne's laptop caught his eye. George stepped towards it. For a moment, Byrne obviously thought he was staring at him and recoiled a little, but then he followed George's gaze to the screen with relief.

"Who's that?" George asked, and Byrne checked the screen.

"Oh, it's the man, guv," he said. "I paused the video recording. This is the visitor David Tucker talked to on Friday night."

"That's not just any man," Ivy said, stepping forward to peer over Byrne's shoulder. "That's Peter Mansfield."

"Yes," George said. "Yes, it is."

"You wanted concrete evidence," she said, turning to George with her eyebrows raised. "That's pretty concrete to me."

CHAPTER THIRTY-TWO

"That's it," George announced after a few moments to deliberate. Gently, he rapped once on the table, where another man might have banged it with his palm. "We've got him."

Ivy and George turned in unison and gathered their things, ready to go.

"But why?" Campbell asked. It was one of the first times that Ivy had seen her question a decision. "Just because he saw David Tucker three hours before he died?"

"No," George said, buttoning his coat. "Because he lied about it."

"Peter Mansfield told us that the last time he saw David Tucker was when he left work on Friday afternoon," Ivy explained, then pointed at Byrne's laptop. "This directly contradicts that."

"But why would he lie?" said Byrne, catching up. "And why speak to David Tucker at his house when they'd been at work all day together?"

"That," George said, straightening his collar, "is exactly what I plan to ask Peter Mansfield once you've brought him in."

Byrne's eyes widened. "Me, guv?"

"Yes, you, Byrne," George said.

"You've arrested someone before, surely?" asked Ivy, watching his face crumble with worry.

"Of course I have," he said, a little too quickly. "But mostly, they were just drunks and lowlifes. Not, you know, murderers."

"Potential murderer," Ivy corrected him.

"Oh, potential murderer, yeah," Byrne said. Then he muttered to himself, "That's alright then."

"Campbell, stay here," George said. "Collect everything you can on Peter Mansfield for me, ready for questioning as soon as we get back." Ivy watched him pause and wondered if he'd dare to mention a task related to whatever he was keeping from Ivy. But in the end, he said, "And anything on Jason Connolly too, while you're at it."

"Byrne, Ivy, you're with me."

He made to leave the room with urgency, but then his demeanour switched to something slower, more hesitant; the car journey perhaps, and being on the road for an hour or so.

"But first, I think I'll hit the little boy's room."

Ivy grinned. She knew him well.

"Yeah," said Byrne, his face pale. He looked as though he could also do with a moment before heading out. "Me too."

That left just her and Campbell in a far quieter incident room with only four or five officers scattered about, most of them busy with their own work. Still, their little nook at the back of the room was far from soundproof. But Ivy had something she wanted to say, something that had kept her awake. Still, she advanced quietly, preferring the conversation not to be overheard.

She opened her mouth to speak, and Campbell appeared grateful for a break in the awkward silence.

"A word?" Ivy said, gesturing to the glass partition of an under-used storage space.

They hovered there for a few seconds in the furthest corner of the room. Such conversations didn't come easily to Ivy. In her experience, they were the most vulnerable of all.

"I wanted to apologise, Campbell," she said eventually. "For how I spoke to you yesterday. It was unprofessional. If the guv had told you something, then I'm sure he had a reason, and you were right to do as he asked."

She meant it. She trusted George, even if the sentiment was exclusive. She had to. Campbell stayed quiet, as though absorbing the apology.

"Thank you," she said.

Ivy smiled, feeling a little lighter. If they were going to be working together in the long-term, then perhaps it was best to start off on a good foot and set a precedent of open communication. But as she turned, Campbell called her back.

"Sergeant," she said, and for the first time, appeared a little uneasy. "Can I ask you something?"

Ivy turned fully to face the PC, noticing the anxious way in which she wrung her hands.

"What is it?"

Campbell took a deep breath. "I've been in uniform for seven years now. I have a Professional Policing degree from UCL." She shook her head, hesitant about what to say next. "Byrne is barely out of college. I think he's been here a year."

Ivy still waited for the question.

"Why did Inspector Larson bring him onto the team?"

Ivy stared into Campbell's hurt eyes. She seemed like a woman who considered other people's success her own failure, and in the ruthless hierarchy of the force, it was a trait she would have to grow out of – and soon, especially as a woman. It wasn't a fair world. But it was one she could learn to navigate with patience and resilience, and, with Ivy's help.

"Look, Campbell," Ivy said, taking a step forward. "If there are two things I know about the boss, it's one, he loves a project. He likes to fix things. Make them better than they were before. He sees it as his duty, and in a job as thankless and open-ended as this one, it's not a surprising hobby. And two, he sees the potential in people. Even if they don't see it in themselves." She bent her head to catch Campbell's eye. "It's your job to support him. You know that, don't you?"

Campbell nodded, and then frowned. "Support who? DI Larson?"

"No," Ivy said with a smile. "Byrne." She straightened. "It's *my* job to support DI Larson."

Then, with a friendly smile, she turned to leave, but not before a defeated sigh escaped Campbell's lips and she called once more, "Sarge?"

Ivy turned to face Campbell again, this time with raised eyebrows.

"He asked me to look into Sophie Gibson," Campbell told her, her body relaxing as if a great weight had been lifted. "I'm to focus on the last decade. He said to look for any misdemeanours, any suspicious circumstances. Anything we could use to bring her in." She paused. "And he said to do it discreetly."

Ivy shook her head. Of course. After their meeting with Chief Inspector Long, he hadn't dropped Sophie Gibson after all. He had simply stopped revealing his suspicions to Ivy. She'd seen it before, George letting his emotions rule his motives, but never before had he hidden it from her. Lucy and Sophie had been missing for over twenty-four hours. They simply didn't have time for vendetta-led goose chases.

Ivy leaned back against a desk and sighed. "And?" she asked.

"Sarge?"

"What did you find? On Sophie Gibson?"

"Oh," Campbell said. Then, with a shrug, she revealed exactly what Ivy had expected. "Nothing at all. She's as clean as a whistle."

CHAPTER THIRTY-THREE

The route to *Tucker and Co* was clear in George's mind from the previous day. Still, Ivy sat beside him in the front seat, ready to provide directions if needed. In the backseat, sitting in the middle like an only child, was Byrne. He leaned forward to peer through the windscreen as though they had a family bet on who would be the first to spot the sea on the horizon.

In his mind, George reeled through what they had on Peter Mansfield. The man had lied to them yesterday, and now they had proof of his deceit. If it was evidence that Tim Long wanted, then the doorbell footage was the catalyst that George hoped would open more doors. He was following procedure, gathering evidence, building a theory, just as he had been asked - or, more accurately, as Long had demanded.

But maybe Tim was right. This was the way things should be done. After all, Campbell had found nothing on Sophie Gibson. And even if they found her, they had no reason to treat her as anything but a victim. She was clean.

He looked out over the waterlogged fields, thinking how easy it would be to drown somebody, or to conceal a body in a flooded ditch. Even for someone escaping the flood to catch their leg on a hidden tree root, only to succumb to the freezing water.

George blinked away the images.

He had to keep hope. He had to believe that Lucy Tucker was still alive.

If Sophie Gibson wasn't involved, which he had to consider, then questioning Peter Mansfield was their best chance of finding the missing women. What if he had killed the Tuckers? For some personal vendetta, or a business issue, or even a family drama? He might know where Lucy is. Then, after all this was over, George could reconsider the Kelly Gibson case, perhaps with a chance of finding peace for the poor dead girl.

And he could finally move on because, clearly, he hadn't.

He wondered how long the lack of closure had been lying dormant within him? His entire ten-year stint at Mablethorpe? Was this all it took? A few days back in The Wolds to realise he'd carried its weight around for a decade?

Like yesterday, George almost missed the turning to *Tucker and Co*, and again, he swung into the entrance too late and too fast, and once more Ivy's expression revealed all she was thinking.

He drove up the lane at speed, forcing him to focus on navigating the road and for Ivy to grip the handle above her door. Poor Byrne slopped from side to side like seawater in the backseat.

The five-bar gate was open, and George brought the car to a halt on the courtyard's loose gravel, a few yards from Peter Mansfield, who stood in the middle of the yard, chatting to one of his warehouse workers, and broke away at George's dramatic entrance. The two men's eyes met through the windscreen, and George saw his face descend into a place of fear. It was a look George recognised. It was the look of somebody who knows what's coming next.

George and Ivy removed their seatbelts and climbed from the car, followed a few seconds later by Byrne, who then clicked open and closed the handcuffs that he kept on his belt, as though double-checking his tools for an upcoming magic trick.

George did a sweep of the area. Warehouse workers paused loading vans, a man George presumed to be a supervisor held a clipboard to his chest as he watched the three police officers stride across the yard towards Peter Mansfield. George had expected to see only one other recognisable face – Jason Connolly, climbing down from one of the vans, enjoying his reinstated position. But he was wrong.

Because there were two recognisable faces.

Over by the portable offices, Connor Hobbs was busy with a broom, making small post-winter piles of leaves. He wore the same green fleece with a tree logo as every other employee, and like everyone else, he too stopped what he was doing. He leaned on his broom to watch them from across the yard with an empty-eyed curiosity.

Having not personally inspected the employee list, George wasn't surprised that Connor's name had slipped through the net. But there he was, clear as day. An employee at David Tucker's company. How neat and tidy, he thought, and then pushed the newfound fact to the back of his mind, for the time being, at least.

Keeping Jason in his peripheral vision, he focused on Mansfield, and from the way Ivy moved her hand to her belt, George took comfort in knowing that she was keeping an eye on the young rogue.

George made a beeline for the eldest of the men, who calmly finished his conversation and pointed the young worker in the direction of the warehouses. Then he straightened and turned to face George with a dignity he hadn't shown much of until now, like a prisoner, ready to face his fate.

"Peter Mansfield," George said. It wasn't a question. "Remember me? Inspector Larson."

To his relief, Mansfield offered no snide retort, which

suggested to George that this wasn't his first brush with the law. It was as if he knew that George had a legal obligation to identify himself and was familiar with the ritual that followed.

George had hoped that Byrne would have stepped up by now, ready with his handcuffs. But he had to physically turn and nod at the lad, who whipped the cuffs from his belt in such a smooth motion, George imagined he'd practised it at home in the mirror.

"Peter Mansfield, I am arresting you on suspicion of murder."

At this, Byrne stepped forward. He pulled Peter's arms behind his back with the same gentle politeness of a tailor measuring a man's sleeve length.

"You do not have to say anything. But it may harm your defence if you do not mention when questioned, something which you later rely on in court. Anything you do say may be given in evidence."

Surprisingly, Peter stayed silent. He didn't struggle at all, and George imagined he'd been expecting the visit ever since the first visit. Ever since they had informed him of David's death. Ever since he'd remembered that he'd been the last person to see him alive. Ever since he'd lied about that fact, and especially since running into George and Ivy at his nephew's caravan.

In his peripheral, Connolly started towards them all, not unlike a lion prowling before the attack, sticking to the corner of a gazelle's eyesight as if daring it to make a move.

"I've seen him," Ivy said, making it clear that she would stand in the young man's way.

George recognised the look of relief on Byrne's face as he led Peter to the car and remembered his first major arrests. Not the little ones. The domestic cases, the assaults, or the possession of cannabis, but the big ones. The murderers, the rapists, and even a few hard nuts that were involved in organised crime. Those had been terrifying, and like Byrne, George had been full of doubt. But the lad had done it. It was over, and in the end, it had been easy. But then again, nobody learned much from the easy ones, and Byrne was in need of a lesson or two.

"You don't have a right to arrest him," came a voice.

"Jason," George said, turning as though greeting an old friend. "You know, I'm somewhat surprised to see you here. Thought you'd be down the job centre by now."

"Got my job back, didn't I?"

"Oh, I imagine you did. And yes, I do have the right. We need reasonable cause, son, and believe me, we have it."

Jason stared at him, deep in the eyes, then he moved his mouth as though chewing gum and spat on the ground. It landed not far from George's feet.

George figured he needed three good reasons to arrest Jason Connolly, and spitting on the ground like a thug didn't count. But he had the motorbike, the motive, and the criminal record. George decided it was enough. It wasn't a whim. It had been in his mind to kill two birds with one stone on this jaunt to *Tucker and Co*. Jason's hostility just made it an easy choice.

"Byrne," George called casually to the young PC who was just pushing Peter Mansfield's head into the back of the liveried car. He closed the door and scurried over.

"Guv?"

George's eyes had not left Jason Connolly the entire time.

"Him too."

He nodded at Jason Connolly, then leaving Ivy to oversee the affair; he let Byrne step up and approach the man who'd just widened his stance to that of a boxer's, unfurling his arms from across his chest, and was now stretching his neck.

George returned to his car and watched as Byrne unhooked a second pair of handcuffs and approached Connolly as if he were a snarling dog. Now *this* would be the lesson Byrne needed, he thought, and glanced across to the liveried police car, where Mansfield sat silently in the rear seat.

"Come on, Byrne. He won't bite," he called out, which,

although it raised a smile on Ivy's face, was more for Connolly's benefit than Byrne's, and the pair of them made it clear he had been heard. "Not unless he wants to add a five-year sentence for assaulting a police officer to his charge sheet." He smiled at Connolly. "Is that right, Jason?"

"You're making a mistake," he replied, then nodded at him wide-eyed. "A big mistake."

"Oh, I doubt that very much," George replied as he made his way back to his car. He opened the driver's door, then looked back as Byrne was placing the cuffs on Connolly's wrists. "But, as you probably know, I've got twenty-four hours to find out."

CHAPTER THIRTY-FOUR

The five of them spilled into the custody suite in a flurry of drama.

George led, nudging Mansfield towards the custody desk with a gentle hand. Ivy followed, gripping Connolly's handcuffed wrists with the same tight reins as a rider leading a stubborn horse to the stalls. Byrne entered last, with one hand holding George's best handkerchief to his bleeding nose, the other held out in front of him, reaching for obstacles that he couldn't see with his head held back, facing the ceiling.

"Now then," said the custody officer behind the desk, a rosy-cheeked, curly-haired fellow who boasted the confidence of a man who had seen it all. Still, he stood straight, as if pleased by the entertainment.

George didn't have time for introductions. The custody clock was now well and truly ticking.

"Two arrests," he said, as the man pulled across a custody form on his desk, picked up a pen, scribbled something, then shook it, put it down, and picked up another.

"Name?" he asked Mansfield, as politely as if checking in a hotel guest.

George nudged him once more.

"Peter Mansfield," he said quietly.

"And you?" asked the custody officer, looking over George's shoulder.

"Jason Connolly," Ivy replied, when all Jason emitted was a low mumble.

"And what're you both in for?"

So light was his tone, George half expected him to ask, *business or pleasure?*

"Suspicion of murder," George said, meeting the officer's eyes and hoping to convey a seriousness he felt was lacking in the interaction. Any gravity was lost, however, by the sound of Byrne accidentally kicking a fire extinguisher behind them and releasing a soft moan. "You can add assaulting a police officer to Connolly's sheet, as well."

"Leave them with me," the custody sergeant said.

He clicked at two officers out of sight behind the desk who approached the handcuffed men.

"Careful with that one," Ivy told the officer, as she handed Jason over. "He's a biter."

Together, George and Ivy watched them disappear down the corridor to the cells, Mansfield with his head down and resigned to his fate, Jason struggling at any chance he saw. With a sigh of resignation, George turned to Ivy, raised his eyebrows, and exhaled through his mouth.

"Thanks for stepping in," he said.

"You're welcome," she replied. "I had an idea he was going to try something."

"Yes, well, if you hadn't been there, then I imagine poor Byrne would be dealing with slightly more than an elbow to his face. He didn't upset you, did he?"

"Who?"

"Connolly," George said. "You know, with all that rubbish he was spewing about mothers and pigs and...well, the sexual stuff. You know?"

"It did bother me as it happens," Ivy said, and she seemed to poke her jaw out in defiance. "But I suddenly felt better when I had him face down on the car bonnet. I think I felt something click. A rib, maybe?"

George turned to the custody sergeant, who wore a knowing grin. He was younger than George, more Ivy's age – mid-thirties. He was a handsome lad with a smooth-skinned face and bright green eyes beneath his dark curls. Clearly, he'd been entertained by the affair, as though he rather enjoyed the job that most officers didn't.

"Sergeant Robson," the man introduced himself, then added, "Dan." He held out his hand. "You must be Inspector Larson."

"That's right," George replied, shaking the man's hand.

Robson turned to Ivy and waited for an introduction.

"Hart," she said. "Sergeant Hart."

She shook his hand too, and George could swear that Robson winced a little, as though Ivy had gripped his hand more firmly than usual.

"So, where do you want them?" he asked, crossing his arms, as though asking about the weather, or perhaps hiding Ivy's grip marks.

"Peter Mansfield straight into interview one," George said. "He's had enough time to think."

"And the feisty fella?"

"Leave him in the cell to calm down."

"Let him stew, eh?"

"Sure," George said, without indulging in the joke.

"Ivy," he said, turning to her and nodding at Byrne, who'd settled and gone quiet. "Take him to the medic, will you?"

"Sure, guv," Ivy said.

"Who's the medical assistant in this station, son?" he asked Sergeant Robson.

"That'll be Handley," he said. "Second floor. Lovely lady. Good with a needle."

"Good," George said, then turned back to Ivy. "Meet me in interview room one when you're done."

With that, Robson disappeared to process his new guests. Ivy stepped over to Byrne, who had picked a wall to hold on to.

"Come on, you," she said, taking him by the arm the same way she had when handling Connolly. George watched with interest as they headed upstairs to the second-floor corridor, with Byrne inexplicably hobbling.

"Why are you limping?" he heard Ivy ask before the door shut.

George took a moment to prepare himself for the interview. He couldn't go in feeling frazzled. He needed a strategy. Ideally, he would have taken a few moments with Ivy and written a plan. But there wasn't time. And all the while, at the back of his mind, one nagging thought plagued him.

Lucy Tucker is still missing.

Instead of heading upstairs, George saved his energy and slid his phone from his pocket, and as always, she answered quickly.

"Campbell," he said, not waiting for a reply, "I want everything you've collected on Peter Mansfield. Bring it downstairs to custody, would you?"

"Yes, guv," she said, amidst the rustle of paperwork, as though she couldn't even wait until the end of the call. "Coming now."

He took another deep, calming breath, thinking through the remnants of a strategy. It took Campbell so little time to burst through the stairwell doors holding a thick manila folder that she had to have run. He had to grant it to her. They had been gone less than an hour, and she'd collected a decent amount of information. She handed it to George, and he flicked through it only to find that it hadn't been fleshed out with empty pages, which was a classic trick to make the folder seem thicker. Instead, the notes were ordered and stapled where necessary.

"Very good," he told her.

The front page was a helpful summary, and so he read through the key points in silence; Mansfield's criminal history, his work life, his family, his associates. Of course, George would rather have time to garner more on the man, but it would have to do.

Campbell smiled and lingered.

For a moment, he thought she might expect to be invited to join him in the interview, and that time would almost certainly come. But not yet.

Instead, the door to the stairs opened again, and Ivy appeared as if she'd dropped Byrne off as fast as she could to avoid missing the interview.

"Go and check on Byrne," George said to Campbell. "He took an elbow to the nose. We're pretty sure it's not broken. But I'm sure he'd appreciate the moral support."

"Yes, guv," Campbell said.

The disappointment at having to deal with Byrne's nosebleed over helping conduct an interview was clear. But she looked at Ivy before leaving, and the two women exchanged glances as if they had an understanding that George wasn't privy to. He smiled inwardly. Such progress could only be a good thing.

Ivy straightened her sleeves. She often wore plain, unbranded clothing that was dark in tone, even on her days off. She wore a navy blazer over a white blouse, and black trousers over black boots, preferring the flexibility they offered over a pair of smart shoes. He had rarely seen her wearing jewellery except for a watch and a wedding ring. Her loosely curled hair sat neatly on her petite shoulders, but she was always ready to tie it up at a moment's notice.

They faced the custody suite corridor side by side, waiting for the green light from Robson.

"How's the lad?"

"He's fine," she said, shaking her head and then paused, and George waited for her to speak the words on her mind. "You're sure about him are you, guv?"

It was somewhere between a statement and a question, as if she wasn't willing to question his judgment, but felt maybe that he should question it himself. The truth was, he wasn't sure. PC Byrne was inexperienced, unreliable, and almost incapable. Yet he had that underdog quality that George found extremely endearing.

"Ask me some other time," he said, without meeting her gaze.

The corridor to the interview rooms opened and Robson leaned through.

"He's ready for you," he said, as though Peter Mansfield was the host and they were his houseguests.

Robson led the way to interview room one, where he pushed the door open for George to enter first, and Ivy followed close after. Peter Mansfield sat at the table wearing a surprisingly calm expression. It was the opposite of how he'd looked the previous day when he had burst into Connolly's caravan; wide-eyed and with hair tousled. George imagined it would be a relief for him to finally sit and tell his side of the story.

The first thing Ivy did was to step forward and undo Mansfield's cuffs, although she did so with very little grace, and he rubbed at his wrists, choosing not to verbalise his thoughts, regardless of how evident they were by his expression.

George slapped the folder onto the table and took his seat while Ivy prepared the recorder. She clicked the button, and they waited for the long buzzer to sound and then stop before George proceeded.

"This interview is being recorded and may be given in evidence if this investigation is brought to trial," he began, and then relayed their location, the date, and read the time from the wristwatch that Grace had bought him for some long forgotten birthday. "I am Detective Inspector Larson, and with me is Detective Sergeant Hart." He looked over at Mansfield. "Please state your full name."

"Peter Mansfield," he said quickly.

"Good, thank you," George replied. "And have you been offered legal assistance, Mr Mansfield?"

"I don't need it," he replied. "I've done nothing wrong."

"Good good," George said, opening the manila folder, "So without further delay, Peter–"

"Didn't you hear me? I didn't kill David," he burst out. "And I certainly didn't kill Florence." George noticed his phrasing, as though killing David could at least make sense, but killing Florence couldn't. Both he and Ivy stayed quiet, allowing the suspect to speak. Then Mansfield leaned forward in his seat, and George imagined him pulling a card from his sleeve and placing it on the table, such was the way he began his next sentence.

"But..." he began, letting his words falter.

"But what?" George asked, still perusing the order of the files. He looked up at the silence, wondering what excuse Mansfield might start with.

"But..." Mansfield said, swallowing hard and taking a deep breath before looking up into George's eyes with undeniable sincerity. "But I know who did."

CHAPTER THIRTY-FIVE

"Well, we'll get to that, Mr Mansfield," George told him, dismissing the man's card as soon as he had played it. There was no way he was going to fall into the trap of letting Mansfield dictate the pace and topic. No, that wasn't how this was going to work. At this, Mansfield slumped back into his chair. "For now, I think we should establish your whereabouts on Friday night."

Mansfield appeared perplexed.

"I told you where I was."

"Oh, that's right," George said. "You told us that you were babysitting. Is that right?" Mansfield bit his lip, but said nothing. "You also stated that the last time you saw David Tucker was when he left work on Friday afternoon, around four o'clock, I believe."

"Right," Mansfield said, and George closed the file, offering a moment's silence for the man to correct his earlier statement.

But no such correction was offered, and George's hand had been forced.

"Perhaps then, you would like to tell us why you lied to us about the last time you saw David Tucker?"

"I didn't," Mansfield said, automatically. "I didn't lie."

"You told us you last saw him at work on Friday, when David left at about four o'clock."

"Yes, I did," Mansfield replied. "He did. David left at four."

"David did leave at four, yes, Mr Mansfield, I quite agree." Peter sat back again, relieved. George had rarely met such an expressive man. The problem was aligning his expressions with the rubbish spilling from his lips. "But the last time you saw David was at his house later that evening at seven o'clock, wasn't it?"

"What?" Mansfield said, exhaling dramatically. "No."

"Then why does the doorbell footage obtained from the Tucker house show you on his doorstep, Peter?" George said, putting on his most convincing *confused* expression. "We did get the right house, didn't we, Sergeant Hart?"

"It's the right house, guv," she replied, her tone flat and certain.

Peter's dramatic indignation evolved into wordless mouthing beyond the ability to lie.

"Mr Mansfield," George said, as he removed his glasses and leaned forward slowly. "This is going to be a very long interview if you keep lying to me. And I don't know about you, but I'd like to get home on time today."

Peter's head snapped up, as though being free to go home today wasn't a possibility he'd considered.

"So, why don't we come to an arrangement?" George said. "You stop lying to me, and I won't build a case around the blatant contradictions recorded on tape. Instead, I'll actually consider your side of the story. So long as you tell it truthfully. How does that sound?" His condescending tone wasn't always an effective approach, but for Mansfield to take the interview seriously, he needed a device to spark some truth from the man. Or as Grace would have put it, he needed a firework up his backside. "So, let's try again," George continued. "Did you, or did you not, pay a visit to David's house on Friday night at around seven o'clock in the evening?"

It was obvious that Peter's instinct was to lie, but he stopped himself just in time, so only a small mumble escaped his mouth. Then he thought for a few seconds. Then he spoke, and for the first time, George believed it to be the truth.

"I did," he said softly.

"Right," George said, with a long exhale. "And for what purpose was the visit?"

"I went to talk to him about Jason."

"Alright," George said. "What about Jason, specifically?"

"David fired him," Mansfield said. "I didn't find out from Jason until after work. I wanted to see if I could change David's mind."

"Why did David fire Jason?"

Mansfield hesitated and scratched at the marks the handcuffs had left on his wrists.

"It was a misunderstanding. That's all."

"What was the misunderstanding about? Must have been pretty serious."

It was clearly a topic Mansfield was loath to discuss, and he stayed silent, looking between Ivy and George, clearly torn between helping himself and helping somebody else, namely his nephew. He leaned back in his chair, and George began to get the impression they were losing him, and so switched tactic.

"Mr Mansfield, why did you tell us you were babysitting your nephew on Friday night?"

Mansfield let his head hang back with something akin to shame, or perhaps fatigue.

"I panicked, okay? You'd just told me about David. He was my friend. I was..."

"You were what?"

"Devastated." Mansfield's head snapped to attention, reminding George of an old wooden doll he had as a child, whose limbs hung limp until a string was pulled, when they snapped into place. "David was my business partner. He was my best friend. I panicked."

"Devastated," repeated George, making a note of the word in an empty space in the folder. "You say you panicked. Why? What were you doing on Friday night?"

Again, Mansfield hesitated. It was clear that this honesty game would lead him into trouble. But, being a terrible liar, he was running out of options.

"I was with Jason."

"Your nephew?"

"Yes," Mansfield said, the word tinged with impatience.

"And Jason is, how old, Mr Mansfield?"

He gritted his teeth. "Seventeen."

"I thought so," George said, sitting back and turning to Ivy as though they had made a playful bet on the topic, before turning back to Mansfield, "Because he looks a smidgen older than three years old to me."

"Like I said," Mansfield said. "I panicked, all right."

"And what were you and Jason doing together on Friday night?"

Mansfield said nothing and stared at the recording.

"It must have been something naughty," George said, maintaining the childlike talk, "to make you panic when a police officer asked you about it."

Again, Mansfield said nothing, and folded his arms to accentuate his silence.

"Well, let's put a pin in that one," George said, turning over some papers in the folder. "For now, I'll just assume it's the same answer you refused to give me about why David fired Jason." He looked up from the papers. "Shall I?"

Mansfield shuffled in his chair uneasily. But still maintained his silence.

"It says here that you've been at *Tucker and Co* for twenty years, Mr Mansfield," George said, and he gave a low whistle. "Since it was founded. That's a long time."

"*I* told you that," Mansfield said.

"Did you?" George replied innocently. "How did you and David meet, exactly?"

"I worked for him," Mansfield said freely, with no reason to lie or to feel conflicted about telling the truth. "At first, I was in the warehouse." He shrugged to signify that it no longer mattered. "I worked my way up to partner. David had the business skills, but he needed someone who knew the work, somebody who knew the customers."

"Very impressive," George said. "And were there any disagreements during that time?"

Mansfield scowled at the prospect.

"Disagreements?"

"Well, twenty years, Mr Mansfield. That's as long as a successful marriage. It's the emerald anniversary, I think. Is that right, Hart?"

"Don't ask me, guv. We'll be lucky to hit the ten-year mark, let alone twenty."

"Surely you had spats, arguments, fights?" George asked, directing his question at Mansfield. "Every relationship must have its ups and downs."

"We didn't have any fights, Inspector Larson, no." He paused at the end of his answer and puffed out air shakily. "We were close."

"Close?" George said, raising his eyebrows.

Mansfield seemed angered at the insinuation. "Friends," he spat. "Who do you think was there for him? Who do you think helped him through everything he went through?" he said, his voice breaking. "When Kelly..."

George felt his face grow dark, like it had passed beneath the shadow of a cloud. "When Kelly what?"

"When she went missing," he said, frowning, visibly alarmed at the look on George's face.

George resumed his usual passivity. This time, Ivy was the one to shuffle uncomfortably at his side. She took the reins while George collected himself and adjusted to the shift in conversation.

"Peter," she said softly, and George recognised her voice as one she used only with her children or suspects she was manipulating. "Our main concern right now is finding Lucy Tucker. She needs to know what's happened. We need to make sure she's safe. If you know where she might be, then it would work in your favour if you mentioned it now."

"I don't know where she is," Mansfield said, his eyes moistening. "I promise."

"Does Jason?"

"No," he replied, shaking his head. "I asked him. He doesn't know. He's worried sick. He..." He looked up, eyes now only for Ivy. "He was with me all Friday night. He has nothing to do with this."

George was ready to re-enter the conversation. More than that, he was ready for Peter's theory. Ready to hear what he really knew.

"Then who does?" George said. "You said you know who killed David and Florence. Go on then. Who was it?"

Mansfield switched his gaze to George. The tears were no longer flowing, set solid with a bitter hatred. George knew what he was going to say before Mansfield spoke; such was the hatred etched into his face, a hatred he recognised.

"Sophie Gibson."

But the name from the lips of another man sounded so obviously biased. Her name, so tainted with local history, so saturated in a communal hatred and regret, was almost impossible to take seriously, and in that moment, George empathised with his old friend and new boss, Timothy Long.

"And you have evidence to support that claim, do you?"

"I know it," he said, punching his chest. "And you do, too."

"Do I now?" George said quietly.

"Inspector Larson," Mansfield said, staring deep into George's eyes. "I remember you. I remember you giving press conferences, and organising the searches. I was there at each one. I was by David's side as he searched for his little girl. I was the one holding the man up." His eyes narrowed and some of the balance shifted in his favour. "The moment I saw you, I remembered. You worked Kelly's investigation. You were the one who failed her."

He spoke passionately. All the lies were gone, and he spoke what George considered to be his most honest words yet.

"You know all about Sophie Gibson. What her monster of a husband did to that family." Mansfield lowered his voice, spitting his vitriol all over the table. "And she didn't even have the decency to hide away in a hole somewhere. She stayed in plain sight. Lived across the road. Shameless. Torturing them one day at a time. Well, now we know why, don't we?" He leaned forward and stabbed the table with his finger. "She was plotting her revenge. Biding her time. And now they're dead." He spoke the last word with a sob he could no longer inhibit. "Maybe Lucy too. Sophie's finally done it."

George swallowed his emotions. "Finally done what, Mr Mansfield?"

Mansfield shook his head, and George saw in his expression an unrivalled anguish and bitterness that contorted his face into somebody new.

"She's finished what her husband started," he said, his wild eyes glancing at the door briefly. "And she's out there somewhere, as free as a bird."

CHAPTER THIRTY-SIX

In the corridor, George and Ivy stood in silence for a few moments. She observed his mannerisms as he leaned on the white wall with the two blue stripes, removed his glasses, rubbed his eyes, and exhaled a slow, meditative breath.

"You agree with him, don't you?" she said.

George waited until he'd wiped his glasses with the sleeve of his jumper and put them back on his nose before replying.

"I don't agree with him, Ivy," he said, deciding to be honest. She could see it all, anyway. "I just recognise how he's feeling. It's hard not to blame Sophie Gibson for the Tuckers' deaths. Just like it was hard not to blame her all those years ago."

"Did David and Florence know?" she asked, frowning as though she'd never actually considered the answer. "You say you knew that Edward Gibson was abusing Kelly Tucker. That it became clear in the inquiry after her disappearance. Did her parents know?"

"Everyone knew." George sighed. "Kelly often played in the woodland behind the Gibson house. Witnesses placed Edward in the woods at the same time. Even his wife confirmed it. The Tuckers told the court about scratches on Kelly's arms." He paused and swallowed a sickness in his throat, his face a picture of disgust. "Bruises, and...other injuries." His furtive glance filled in the details, and her silence beckoned him to continue.

"It was clear from the inquiry following Edward's death that this wasn't a one-off. Edward Gibson had been abusing Kelly Tucker for years. Right under their noses. The inquiry made the whole sordid affair public knowledge, so yes, the entire village knew. The entire area even. The only one who didn't accept it was Sophie Gibson."

It was accounts like the one George retold that inspired all kinds of horrific scenes in Ivy's mind, and each time the young girl in her imagination became clear, it was her own daughter.

"The tragedy is that only after Edward Gibson had killed himself and Kelly was beyond saving did the truth come out."

Ivy frowned with a new thought. "What if he didn't?"

"Didn't what?"

"Kill himself." She pushed off the wall and started pacing. "You saw the hatred on Mansfield's face. I've seen it on your own, guv." At this, George cocked his head curiously, and she shrugged apologetically. "I have. And that was just a hatred for his wife. I can only imagine how people felt about Edward Gibson."

"What are you saying?"

"What if someone found out about the abuse *before* Kelly Tucker went missing? What if Edward's death wasn't a suicide at all?" She stopped pacing and turned to him. "What if it was a lynching?"

"The thing is," Ivy said diplomatically. "It doesn't make a difference either way. If Edward killed himself or not, Lucy Tucker is still missing. If Sophie is involved or not, we have no idea where she is. We have to follow the leads. It's all we can do. If we start to deviate from the process, guv, we'll be chasing our tails, just like you were ten years ago."

"I know," George said. "I know."

He stared at the wall opposite and pushed his head back

against the cold concrete. Ivy took up a similar position on the other wall, not opposite him, just in his side view, so he knew she was there.

"So, what have we got?" George said, shoving off the wall and taking a few steps to gain some clarity. "What have we just learned?"

Ivy straightened, ready to talk it through.

"Mansfield went to David's house to talk about Connolly being fired."

"And we still don't know why." George turned on his heels. "What else?"

"Mansfield and Connolly were together all of Friday night."

"Which we still haven't confirmed."

"Mansfield doesn't know where Lucy is."

"And you believe him?"

Ivy hesitated for only a second.

"I do," she said, to which George nodded.

"I do too." He winced, frustrated. "Not much to go on, is it? I'd like to know why Connolly was fired. We need confirmation on whether they were together or not." He switched his mindset from the emotional road it had taken with Ivy to a practical, list-like format, something Ivy recognised and admired. "I want the number plate of that motorbike. I want to know where it went and when on Friday night. Let's run an ANPR check for any *Tucker and Co.* vehicles, including Mansfield's car."

"We need to revisit Jason Connolly's caravan, guv."

"We do," George agreed, eyeing the custody suite in which Connolly was locked.

"Mansfield might not know anything, but I don't trust Connolly as far as I could throw him," she reasoned. "For all we know, Lucy could be in his caravan."

"You're right," George said. "Talk to Campbell, see if the warrant has come through," he said, striding towards the custody door. "Then we'll interview him. And this time, I want answers."

Before they reached the end of the corridor, Sergeant Robson poked his head through the door.

"Guv's here to see you," he said, holding the door for them, then followed them into the custody suite where, at the desk, Chief Inspector Long was standing, reading through the custody forms for Peter Mansfield and Jason Connolly.

"Just bumped into PC Byrne," he said, monotone, and without looking up. "Looks like he's been through the mill."

"Nothing he couldn't handle," George lied.

"So, you've arrested a Jason Connolly and Peter Mansfield," he said, and then finally looked up and into George's eyes. "Would've been nice to know."

George nodded. "You're right," he replied, not quite apologising. "It happened quickly. Next time I need to make a decision, Tim, I'll come to you for permission. Perhaps you'd care to join in the interviews, as well?"

"There's no need for that, George," Long told him, and Ivy watched the two mature men strike some sort of balance. "What's the plan now?" he asked.

"We're going to conduct a search of Jason Connolly's caravan," replied George.

"I presume you have a warrant."

"There's a chance that Lucy Tucker is inside," George told him. "She might still be alive. I don't need a warrant where preventing death or injury to a person is concerned."

"Good," Tim replied, seeming placated, if not cautious. "So there's no sign of them?"

"Not yet," George replied, shaking his head. "Nothing from the search team, no call-ins from the press conference. Nothing." George threw him a bone to chew on. "The pathologist has identified the weapon that killed David Tucker as something hard and smooth, perhaps a bottle, or a bat, or something. She can't be sure."

"All right, then," Tim said, eying George carefully. "Keep to the process on this one, George. Emotions will be running high."

"Guv," George replied, before gesturing for Ivy to follow him into the car park.

Long stepped aside to let them pass. But he didn't let them leave without having the last word.

"George," he called, and both George and Ivy turned as one. Long was clearly torn between offering George the loose reins he deserved and reminding him of their current positions. "Be careful out there, mate."

CHAPTER THIRTY-SEVEN

Bringing a car to a stop outside Peter Mansfield's house, George and Ivy took a moment to appraise the building. It was an old house that had been extended and then rendered to a smooth white finish, which was a tragedy, George thought. To make an old house look new removed all the charm and character. But when he considered the house he was staying in, he could understand why Mansfield had felt the need for an overhaul. The harsh winds and rain that tear through the county could age a building, and left to its own devices, rot and damp, could set in like an incurable cancer.

An Audi A4 was parked on the driveway, and before he had even asked, Ivy was noting down the number plate.

Beyond the garden gate to the side of the house stood a modern glass conservatory, surrounded by a patio marred by winter debris, and lawns that would benefit from the first cut of the season. Even so, the finish was quite lovely, and George imagined it to be a suitable home for an unmarried, middle-aged man who enjoyed an element of seclusion.

With his mind wandering to all manner of tangents, George followed Ivy around the thick hedge that separated Mansfield's house from the small, unloved paddock in which sat Connolly's caravan, where Mansfield's renovation efforts had clearly waned. The concrete hard standing beneath the static home was cracked and stained, and the caravan had faded to a dull, nicotine yellow. It was a stain on an otherwise spectacular property, and one quite underserved of the views across the Wolds.

"Makes you wonder, doesn't it?" George said quietly. "Mansfield puts in all that effort to make his house as nice as it is, and then his nephew comes along and dumps this thing behind it. He must really love his nephew."

"Either that or Connolly has something on him," Ivy remarked.

"Now now, Ivy," he replied. "We can't paint him with every dirty brush in our bag."

The motorbike was still parked at the foot of the steps, and Ivy made a note of the number plate.

"Send them over to Campbell, will you? Ask her to find out if they were on the road on Friday night."

"Will do, guv," she replied. "Although there aren't too many ANPR cameras in these parts. It's not the city, you know?"

"All we can do is follow the process," he told her. "We tick boxes. Nothing more, remember?"

George watched Ivy inspect the motorbike. Perhaps looking for blood, dents, or long, blonde hairs. George could only guess. He pulled his phone from his pocket, found the number he was looking for in his recently dialled list, and hit the green button.

"Guv?" came the response after a single ring.

"Campbell," he said, catching Ivy's eye. "Sergeant Hart is going to send you a couple of number plates. Have them checked will you? ANPR, the works."

"ANPR? You'll be lucky," she replied.

"I doubt it," he told her. "But you never know. How's Byrne doing, anyway?"

"He's..." she began, and he imagined Byrne breathing through his mouth at his desk, perhaps with two cotton wool balls stuffed up his nose. "He's fine, guv."

"Good. Let's keep him busy. Tell him to go back to *Tucker and Co.*" George said. "Let's get him back on the horse, as it were. Ask him to find whoever's in charge in Mansfield's absence and compile a list of all number plates registered with the company." He heard the sound of her note-taking over the line and waited until the scribbling stopped before continuing. "Run all of them through ANPR too, and see if there's some kind of log book. They must have some way of knowing who drives what vehicle. I want to know who was on the road, at what time, where they were going, and when they got back. Do you understand? The priority is finding out where Peter Mansfield and Jason Connolly were on Friday night, if they were together, and what they were doing. Okay?"

"Got it, guv," she said.

There was a hopeful determination in her voice, like she was excited to prove herself. It was a commendable quality, if not overly keen.

"Good. We'll be back in an hour or so," he told her.

It was a tight time limit. But if Campbell wanted to prove herself, George would give her every opportunity to do so. If it was a challenge she wanted, he was willing to give her one.

"Yes, guv," she said, confidently enough.

He ended the call and walked over to Ivy.

"Anything?" he asked, touching the handlebars.

She shook her head, and they turned to face the static home. The door was locked, but with just two solid shoves of her shoulder, Ivy broke the flimsy bolt that kept them out, and the door swung open, slamming against the inside wall. It wasn't what George would call high security.

It was moments like these that George was especially grateful for Ivy and her young, resilient body, being unsure how many more doors his ageing shoulder was capable of shoving through, if any.

They worked in practised silence, with Ivy taking the bedroom to the right and George the living room. Everything was as it had been the day before, except perhaps with a stronger, lingering stench of cigarettes. The ashtray on the kitchen counter overflowed with dog ends, none of which bore any sign of lipstick. He recalled his previous day's visit, and how the ashtray had been near empty in comparison, surmising that Connolly had been stress-smoking.

But the thing that really caught his eye was a large ordnance survey map of the area. He donned his reading glasses and crouched for a better look, noting that Jason Connolly didn't really fit the description of an avid hiker, a thought supported by the red circles made by a marker, which were far from rambling spots.

One circle he recognised well – the Tuckers' house. Another circled a building not far away, and George recalled the large, run-down farmhouse that belonged to Connor Hobbs and his mother. The map denoted the main house and a number of smaller squares that represented the various outbuildings.

Between the Tucker house and the Hobbs was a single, red line, along which Connolly had written the number ten, presumably the amount of time it took to get from one place to the other.

There were more scribbles in the map's margin. *11:30 p.m.,* which George recognised as the approximate time he had arrived at the Somersby Road diversion on Friday night. Or, perhaps, from Connolly's perspective, the time he had turned up on his motorbike.

Above it, another time had been scrawled. *10:50 p.m.,* which meant very little to George, as he would have only just left Mablethorpe. Other than that, it fell into the window that Doctor Bell had provided for the time of death.

Without touching the map, he removed his phone from his inside pocket, turned on the camera, and held it over the markings, taking various close-up photos, as well as a few wider shots to get the full picture. Taking the images on his phone stretched his technological capabilities. Still, it did the job.

Leaving the map where it was, he opened a few drawers, but found nothing but rolling papers, unopened bills, and chocolate wrappers. Nothing of great interest. The place was a mess, littered with empty milk cartons, beer cans, and dust balls in the corners of the skirting. In a word, the place was a mess.

Still, George remembered himself at that age. He'd never been as slovenly as Connolly, of course, but he hadn't been as fastidious as he was now.

"Why are you living alone?" he muttered to himself, considering the young lad was a mere seventeen years of age. But before he had time to consider the question, Ivy called out to him.

"Guv," she said, and then arrived in the doorway, her face bright with promise. "You should see this."

George studied her for a clue, quickly surmising that the find was not Lucy Tucker or Sophie Gibson, but was crucial nonetheless.

"It's not Lucy," she said, as if reading his mind. "In case you were wondering."

"Worst luck," he replied, allowing her to lead the way, where he found that Ivy had made no effort to cover her tracks. She had pulled the covers off the bed, upturned the mattress, and left the contents spilled across the floor.

"Ah, you've been thorough, Ivy," he joked, but found her expression stoic, and she nodded at the little built-in wardrobe.

"Take a look," she said.

George stepped closer, and found that Ivy had not so much removed the thin back panel as ripped it off, judging by the splintered wood. For good reason, it seemed. Because concealed in the space between the wardrobe and the wall, a black holdall had been stuffed.

"Curiouser and curiouser," he said as he crouched. The zip was open, providing a clear view of its contents. He turned back to Ivy, who smiled knowingly.

"What do you think?" she said.

"I think Jason Connolly has a lot to answer for," he began, as he pushed himself to his feet with a groan. "And unless he has good reason for that, he's going to prison for a long time."

CHAPTER THIRTY-EIGHT

In light of Mansfield's attempts at controlling the line of questioning, George began Connolly's interview with a power move. He dropped the holdall onto the table, slap bang in the middle as if it was an exquisite dining table centerpiece, and there it remained while Ivy began the recording, and George recited the place, date, and time.

"This interview is being recorded and may be given in evidence if this case is brought to trial," he said. "I am Detective Inspector Larson. Present is Detective Sergeant Hart." He peered over the bag at Connolly. "Please state your full name."

"Jason Connolly," he muttered, slumped so far back in his chair that George was surprised he wasn't sliding off.

"Robert Speakman," the duty solicitor to his side announced.

George found, after so many years in the force, that the faces of duty solicitors merged into one. They were often grey-haired men who wore faded navy suits with their top button unfastened and their tie pulled a touch too tight. More often than not, they carried an old-fashioned briefcase containing a handful of paperwork and too many pens. Robert Speakman was no exception. Except his suit was a dull brown, reminding George of the seventies. Nothing in particular of the era, just the seventies in general.

Perhaps it was a sign of Connolly's familiarity with police procedure that he had demanded a solicitor from Sergeant Robson the moment George had called, telling him to prepare the young lad for an interview. Yet George assumed that Connolly was either much smarter or had more to hide than his uncle.

"Jason," George said, diving straight in. "Do you understand why you're here?"

"No comment," Connolly replied.

"Well, for the record, you have been arrested on suspicion of the murders of David Tucker and Florence Tucker. You do not have to say anything. But, it may harm your defence if you do not mention, when questioned, something which you later rely on in court. Anything you do say may be given in evidence, and for the record again, that includes *no comment*."

Connolly flicked his eyebrows once, which, in light of his responses so far, was progress.

"Your uncle informed us that you were fired from your position at Tucker and Co. on Friday, Jason. Why was that?"

Connolly smirked.

"No comment."

"What were you doing on Friday night?"

"No comment."

"Were you with your uncle, Peter Mansfield?"

"No comment."

"He said you were."

"No comment."

"Very well," George said. He opened the manila folder that Campbell had run downstairs to hand him as soon as he'd entered the custody suite. He slipped out one of the photos that she'd printed off, showing a local traffic light camera, in front of which were Peter and Jason in a *Tucker and Co.* van, its large, green tree logo on the bonnet.

He slid it towards Jason, notably avoiding the bag that was in his way.

"This is you and your uncle in a work van on Friday night, is it not?"

"No comment," Connolly replied, quieter than before, eyeing the photo. Still, his solicitor nodded, as though Connolly was sticking to a plan that they had previously agreed upon.

"See, I'm confused, Jason," George said. "I thought you had a motorbike. Why were you using a work van?"

Connolly seemed tired of responding with a boring, *no comment*, and reverted to silence.

"Bit late to be working, isn't it? Late on a Friday night?" George said. "Is that why David fired you, Jason? For using work vans out of hours?"

Again, Connolly remained silent. He glanced up at the clock on the wall, perhaps calculating how long until they had to release him. He began to chew on the inside of his cheek – more like a gnaw, as one might pass the time in a waiting room.

"By the way, that's a nice caravan you've got," George said, switching tack. "Bachelor pad, is it?"

At this, Connolly only glared at him.

"Run away from home, did you?" George asked, to which Connolly scoffed. It was a sound, at least; progress still. His solicitor heard it too, and he shuffled in his seat before glancing at George and then Ivy. George stared right back at him, then at Connolly, before he pulled the thread.

"Parents kick you out, did they? Did they grow bored of your behaviour?"

"They left," he spat. There it was. His parents. Connolly's weak spot, his loose link, his Achilles heel. "Buggered off to Spain, didn't they."

Clearly, Connolly wanted to establish his position as the victim in the affair.

"Weren't you invited?" asked George innocently. "It seems odd to me that they should just up and leave. Do you speak to them at all?"

"They said I was old enough to look after myself," he replied. "And no. Not often, anyway."

"So, your Uncle Peter took you in?" Connolly suggested, to which Connolly simply shrugged.

"Lets me live in the kennel in his yard, more like."

"Perhaps he thought the static home suitable accommodation for his young nephew," George offered.

He was close to offering some kind of comforting statement, perhaps selecting one of the more positive features, albeit for the recording's benefit. But, in light of the squalor he had witnessed, there was barely anything he could add.

"I found this in your living room," he said, generous with his wording. He slipped another photo from the envelope and pushed it forward to sit beside the second. It was the photo of the map on Jason's coffee table that George had emailed to Campbell for printing.

The lad sat up, clearly angered. "What you going through my stuff for? Don't you have to have a warrant or something?"

Robert Speakman leaned over to whisper a reminder to his client, but Connolly flinched away from his breath in his ear and swatted the air as though swatting a fly, scowling at him.

"This is a murder enquiry, Jason, and we had reason to believe that Lucy was inside," George explained reasonably. "Now, do you want to tell me about this map?"

"She's not," he said.

"I know that now," George replied, then flicked his eyes downwards. "The map?"

Connolly shrugged, leaned back and folded his arms.

"These red circles," George said, pointing at them with the end of his pen. "Local sightseeing spots, are they?"

Connolly scratched his ear, as though still irritated from his solicitor's whisper, but still, it seemed to serve as a reminder.

"No comment," he regressed.

"Jason," George said, taking off his glasses and leaning forward much as he had with the boy's uncle. "You do understand that we're looking for Lucy, don't you?" Connolly averted his eyes and held his jaw clenched, as any teenager might. "And every second I waste here with you is a second I could be out there finding her."

He let the words permeate, and then pushed the bag towards Connolly, as if it was an olive branch, a sign he was done playing games and was ready to get to the point, and hoped that the feeling was mutual.

"We found this in your wardrobe."

"Found what?" Connolly replied, to which George simply glanced down at the bag. "It's not mine," he said, and Robert Speakman noted something in his paperwork.

"It's at least five hundred grams," George threw out a number, knowing there was at least a kilo of weed in there. "A hybrid strain by my reckoning. Blue Haze, maybe or–"

Connolly snorted a laugh through his nose, and looked George up and down again, from the parting in his hair to his unfashionable glasses and then to his woollen sweater.

"You don't know what you're talking about,' he said with a smirk.

"And you do, do you, Jason?"

The implication was clear. They stared each other down for a few seconds longer. But George sensed the boy had lost his edge. He didn't feel quite so dangerous, and not nearly as aggressive. He looked worn out, like a toddler who'd spent all morning screaming and just needed a bottle of milk and a little nap.

Ivy took up the moment.

"Jason," she said, "do you want to hear my theory?"

He moved his gaze from George to Ivy, and offered a curt response.

"Not really."

"I think you've been using *Tucker and Co.* vans to distribute drugs to local businesses and individuals under the guise of legitimate business deliveries."

"No comment."

"I think David found out and that's why he fired you."

"No comment."

"I think your uncle tried to get your job back, and David refused."

"No comment."

"I haven't asked you a question, Jason. I haven't asked you to comment on anything." She picked on his misunderstanding of the situation, suggesting he wasn't as smart as he thought he was, and Connolly squirmed in his chair. "The question I will ask you, however, is a simple one," she told him, and then paused. "Do you love Lucy Tucker?"

The question caught both George and Connolly off-guard, and the boy blinked as though something had flown into his eye and then swallowed hard.

"Come on, Jason. Give us something here," Ivy said. "Are you, or are you not, in love with Lucy Tucker?"

"Yes," he croaked to which Ivy leaned forward, frowning as though she was genuinely concerned.

"Then why are you making it so difficult for us to find her?"

Connolly looked up slowly, then focused on her. His eyes resembled his uncle's, worried and moist.

"I didn't kill anyone," he said.

"I don't think you did," she said. "But we need to know what you *did* do. Otherwise, we'll waste time here instead of finding out who *does* know where Lucy is. Do you understand that? Whether guilty or not, your behaviour, your job, and your relationship with Lucy places you at the top of our list. We simply must establish your whereabouts and what you were doing. If you can't do that, then we can't charge anybody else and expect to get a conviction, can we?"

He let out a shaky exhale.

"You know how this works, Jason. Any defence lawyer will tear us apart if you're still a suspect," she told him, then glanced at his legal rep. "Isn't that right, Mr Speakman? Unless your client is alibied, then any court in the land would see him as a viable suspect, thus discrediting any efforts to convict another party."

"It was just me," Connolly said, perhaps just to shut her up, and for the second time today, George reminded himself that Jason Connolly was just seventeen - a boy whose parents had left him to fend for himself.

"I got to know the customers. They asked if I wanted to get involved. We had the vans. We were going to these places anyway. I thought, why not? A side job, that's all. More money than Tight-Ass-Tucker paid us anyway."

At this, his solicitor scratched between his eyes in despair.

"Uncle Pete had nothing to do with it. He was just trying to protect me. That's where we went on Friday, to the supplier. To tell him I was done. I was out." Then he nodded at the bag, licked his lips, and added quietly, "After this one."

George watched him. The lad's whole demeanour had shifted. He was refusing to look them in the eye for fear of breaking down. His knee bounced as his foot tapped anxiously on the floor. If Jason was lying, then perhaps an acting career would have been more advantageous than working for David Tucker.

"And Lucy?" Ivy said.

"I don't know where she is," Connolly said. The build-up of tears in his eyes now spilled over his fiery lids and plopped onto the table. "I promise, I don't."

"What's with the map, Jason?" asked George, to the point.

"I want to help," he said, looking at the photo of his some-what pathetic investigation work. "I want to find her."

"What are these timings?" George pointed at the scribbles in the margins.

Jason sighed. He looked too tired to fight anymore. "This is the time Lucy left mine," he said, pointing at the *10:50 p.m.* "She was at the caravan when I got back with Uncle Pete. She has a key. We watched TV for a bit. Had a few drinks. Then she left at ten-fifty. I remember looking at the clock, working out when she'd get home."

"And this one?" George pointed at the *11:30 p.m.*

This time, Jason hesitated.

"Jason," George said in a tone somewhere between a warning and an encouragement.

He shook his head. "That's the time I went to Lucy's." He met George's eyes. "On my motorbike." His face filled with a visible regret. "I made her walk home. It's only ten minutes. But I'd been drinking and smoking. I didn't want to ride my bike, especially not in the rain."

George could almost see the memories of Friday night being relived behind the boy's eyes. Connolly threw his elbows onto the table and buried his face into his hands.

"But then the storm got worse," he continued. "Like, really bad. And she lives in that dip in the road. I just wanted to check she was okay. But then..."

"You saw the police diversion," George finished.

"I got scared." When he looked up, it was Ivy's eyes he went to. "And I left," he said, openly crying now. "I just left her, and now I don't know where she is."

Ivy leaned back and sighed, as though she felt deeply for the boy. It wasn't that George didn't think she cared, but he knew her well enough to know that she often exaggerated her reactions during interviews. It was part of the game.

George took over for the final question.

"Jason, this is important. Can you think of anyone at all who might want to harm Lucy?"

Jason's face turned dark. "I know exactly who," he said, with a similar determination to his uncle. His face screwed up into a familiar hatred, too. "That freak," he spat. "The weirdo she lives next to."

"Who, Jason?" Ivy said.

She frowned, as though she wasn't sure of the answer. George shouldn't have been so sure himself, because when Jason opened his mouth, the name that followed was not the one he had expected to hear.

"Connor," he said. "Connor Hobbs."

CHAPTER THIRTY-NINE

"So, we've got nothing?" said Byrne insensitively the moment George had relayed their interviews with him and Campbell. There was no evidence of his nosebleed, except for some dried blood in the wispy hairs on his upper lip.

The incident room was much busier in the afternoon when various shifts crossed over. Almost every chair was occupied, and although the team were mostly ignored in the room's corner, the incessant ringing of phones and names called across desks was so maddening that George could hardly hear himself think.

"We can rule out Peter and Jason," Ivy said, arms crossed and frowning at the board. "If they were on camera on the A158 by Lincoln at eleven twenty-five, there's no way they could've made it on time to Somersby Road to kill Florence and David. Anyway, the security cameras at *Tucker and Co.* picked them up at eleven-thirty dropping the van off at the yard."

"I didn't realise they had cameras," George admitted. "Good spot."

"It wasn't me, guv," she replied, and her eyes arced towards Byrne, who was studying his image in his camera phone, picking at the dried blood on his lip.

"Well done, Byrne," he said. "That's what I call using your initiative."

The young PC smiled, reddened, and then set his phone to one side, while George uncapped his pen, and was about to strike a neat, red line through both names on the board. But something told him otherwise, and he deemed a cross beside each of their names more suitable.

"So that's it?" Byrne confirmed. "They were just dealing drugs, were they?"

"Just?" said George. "There must be a kilogram in that bag." He turned and clicked at Byrne. "Speaking of. Find out who to pass them onto. Tell them to go down to the custody suite and to speak to Sergeant Robson. They've got a Jason Connolly waiting for them in interview room two and a big bag of weed in an evidence locker. That should help them hit their targets for a while."

"Yes, guv," Byrne replied, lifting the receiver of his desk phone. He was at least improving at admin tasks, thought George, even if his arresting skills needed work. "What do you think will happen to them?"

"Oh, they'll be bailed until the magistrate sees fit to deal with them."

"Bailed. Are you saying they'll be free to walk the streets? Won't they be remanded?"

"It's a kilo of weed, Byrne," he told him. "It's hardly the bust of the century. Now go on."

George considered the number of hours they had wasted on Mansfield and Connolly. Only today, at least four hours. That was two hundred and forty minutes. Or – George stared at a white space on the board as the numbers turned over in his mind – fourteen-thousand four-hundred seconds, during each of which, Lucy Tucker had been lost, God knows where, and enduring God only knows what.

Like a rainbow offering a glimmer of hope in the grey, the

creak of Campbell crossing the threshold travelled through the incident room's hum, and she rushed over to their spot at the back, handing George a file.

"Thank you, Campbell," he said, taking it and opening it immediately.

He held the file with the same fragility as an ancient, dusty book plucked from a forgotten shelf. The flimsy folder was a decade old and had been touched by his own oily fingers hundreds of times. He remembered its specific details – a dog-eared corner, a coffee stain on the bottom-right-hand side. He thought if he smelled the cover, he might find the aroma of old cigarettes. It was the right file, all right. Except now there was a layer of dust on the spine, gathered from its home in a filing cabinet for the last ten years.

Ivy eyed it in his hands, and he avoided her until she spoke out.

"Guv?" she said, conveying her entire thought process in that single syllable.

She knew what it was, that much was obvious. But George ignored the unspoken question. He just turned to face the whiteboard, ready to give it a restyle.

But Ivy wasn't willing to let it go.

"Guv, I thought we weren't considering the old Kelly Tucker case."

It was a reminder, not a question, and he didn't reply. Instead, he used the red marker again to start noting more names in an empty space to the right of the board.

Kelly Tucker. Edward Gibson.

"*Guv?*" she repeated, her tone harsher than it had been, demanding a reply.

George turned as fast as any man his age could. Yet to anyone else, it was more akin to a cargo ship returning to port.

"What, Ivy?"

"We agreed to let it go. To focus on the current investigation. To follow the leads."

George raised his arms, as though highlighting the empty space, and all the leads that filled it. "What leads? Connolly and Mansfield are a dead end. This *is* our lead," he said, holding up Kelly Tucker's old file and flapping it back and forth. "What else have we got?" He hadn't raised his voice, but even he recognised the desperation in it. "Really, Ivy," he continued. "Give me a lead and I'll follow it. Do you have one?"

She shook her head, whether in answer or in disbelief, George wasn't sure. But when she uncrossed her arms and dropped them, he saw his own desperation mirrored right back at him.

"No, guv," she admitted. "I don't."

"All right then," he said, and turned back to the board, where he added the date of Kelly's disappearance, and a crude map of the Gibson and Tucker houses, the road between them, and the woodland behind the Gibsons. Campbell and Byrne had watched his and Ivy's altercation in silence. The tension lingered, and when he turned back to face his team, he caught them wide-eyed, like worried siblings.

"Ten years ago, Kelly Tucker, four years old, the youngest daughter of Florence and David Tucker, went missing."

He tapped Kelly's name and looked straight at Byrne, a subtle reminder to keep up. There was no time for lagging.

"The same night Kelly disappeared, Edward Gibson, Sophie Gibson's husband, killed himself. There was an extensive search for Kelly but her body was never found. In the weeks after, there was an inquiry. It became clear that Edward Gibson had been abusing Kelly Tucker in the woodland behind his house."

The three of them watched George's storytelling like campers around a bonfire. Ivy too, though her eyes were a little misty, as though she was only half-listening, half indulging him.

"And you think that investigation," Campbell said, nodding to the right of the board, "is connected to this one?" She nodded to the left side.

"Well, I can't be certain," he said, glancing over at Ivy, who clearly disagreed. "But in light of recent events..."

As though to break the tension, Ivy's phone rang. She blinked away her thoughts, and then held it up, as though asking George's permission. He nodded.

"Jamie?" she answered, turning her back on the team and walking a few steps away. In the bustle of the incident room, privacy was limited, and no matter where she stepped, they could all hear her. "What is it? I'm at work."

Sensing the inappropriateness, George drew their attention to the file in his hand with a polite cough.

"And that's what Peter Mansfield thinks too," confirmed Campbell. "That the two cases are connected. That Sophie Gibson is involved."

"Yes," he said slowly, not enjoying being tarred with the same brush as Mansfield. "It's hard to believe that Sophie didn't know what her husband was up to. And now," he said, shaking his mind of the biased hatred on Mansfield's face, "Maybe she's followed his lead."

"What about the Hobbs?" said a voice at George's side.

"What about them?"

"You said that Connolly suspected Connor Hobbs," said Byrne.

"They work together." George shrugged. "Connor's a little... socially inept. Jason Connolly probably doesn't like him. I wouldn't trust the character judgement of a man like Jason Connolly."

"Well, were the Hobbs involved in the Kelly Tucker case?" Byrne asked, looking down at his notebook. "I mean, they live just up the road, don't they?"

George looked down at the PC. He had his notebook on his lap and pen poised like a curious student, and the sprawl of messy handwriting suggested that he'd been taking notes as George spoke as though he was giving a lecture.

"Now that's a good question," he said.

George opened the case file in his hand to find any mention of the Hobbs, with half of his attention on Ivy, whose voice had raised slightly and had shifted in tone to brash and defensive.

"*You're* too busy?" he heard her say. Then, after a pause, "They're your kids too, Jamie."

His attention switched back to the file. There was one page of notes on the Hobbs, which he skimmed. Two personal statements had been condensed and labelled as pretty much useless, stating that the mother and son had never seen anything suspicious, minded their own business, and barely even acknowledged their neighbours. George certainly didn't remember them being involved in the inquiry. It didn't seem necessary at the time. The character statements against Edward Gibson and various dog-walker witness statements had been more than enough.

But one thing caught his eye. George spoke aloud the names of the registered members of the household, as it was noticeably longer than he'd been expecting. "Ruth Hobbs," he said, tapping her name already on the board. "Connor Hobbs," he said, tapping the name next to it. "Molly Hobbs," he said, with no name to tap.

He wrote it down instead. *Molly Hobbs.*

"Who's Molly Hobbs?" Byrne asked, his own pen poised to note the name down.

George turned the page over, finding the other side blank. "I have no idea."

Paper-clipped to the top left corner was a single photo of a tall, thin man with wet, blonde hair leaning on a tractor wheel in the recognisable Hobbs yard. George turned it over and read aloud what was written on the back in small, block capitals. "Roger Hobbs. Deceased."

He added *Roger Hobbs* to the board, and in the space of a

minute, the odd family from the top of the hill had doubled in size.

"Connor's father?" asked Campbell, nodding at the new name.

"Looks like it." George squinted at the photo. "No, definitely," he said. The man could easily have been Connor Hobbs in ten years with his wide-set eyes and lank hair.

From where she stood near the window, Ivy's voice rose ten decibels or more.

"I'll be home when I'll be home."

And with that, she ended her call with more of a slap than a press of the red button on her screen.

She stood with her back to them for a few seconds, yet her fury had permeated the room. Even the incessant desk phones seemed too nervous to ring. From where George stood at the board, her heaving chest was evident, and her shoulders rose and fell like an industrial pump – with anger or embarrassment or anxiety. He wasn't sure which.

He whistled at Byrne and drew the lad's attention away from her, saving him from being caught gawping. Byrne squinted at the board in faux-concentration and even raised his hand to his chin like The Thinker.

Ivy cleared her throat and then turned on her heels, less like a cargo ship and more like the crack of a whip, and stormed back to them before glowering at the board. She crossed her arms and perched on a nearby desk.

"Who's Molly Hobbs?" she retorted.

"I don't know," George said. Then he pulled his jacket from the back of a chair, swung it over his shoulders and offered her a smile that he hoped she would take as a helping hand. "Let's go and find out, shall we?"

CHAPTER FORTY

The brickwork was stained with damp, like a dark shadow spreading upwards from the foundations. The paint on the front door was chipped and lifeless. And as if to confirm the old building's surrender to nature, patches of ivy clung to the walls like varicose veins.

He had a faint recollection of visiting the place during the Kelly Tucker investigation, but nothing strong enough to chisel a memory worthy of retention into his old grey matter. With such an obvious target, George's sights had been blinkered. The lines of inquiry had been so clear, it was both a miracle and tragedy that nobody had picked up on Gibson's behaviour before it was too late. He had barely covered his tracks at all, and in the light of such a beacon, George had been blind to any menacing cliffs that lay out of sight in the darkness.

Ivy had barely spoken during the short drive. He imagined that if he touched her arm, the static charge would be intense enough to create a spark. Her brooding emanated fury the same way a storm cloud emanated thunder. An energy that rumbled and growled from somewhere deep within her displayed in the tension of her arms, her rigid back, and her intense stare at the view outside her window.

She was in no obvious hurry to leave the car, preferring to linger in the company of her thoughts.

George considered broaching the subject of Jamie, the kids, her home life, which, he was quickly realising was in a more dire situation than he'd initially thought. But something told him she wasn't ready to talk about it. Not yet. And he knew better than anyone that the job was an effective, if not an especially healthy, distraction from personal issues.

So, instead, he drew her attention with a simple question.

"Are you ready?"

It took a few moments for his words to forge a path through the clouds, but eventually, they did, and she nodded before slowly turning to face forward, exhaling like a weightlifter preparing for a personal best.

"I am," she said, as she shoved the door open and climbed out with a heavy sigh. George followed suit, and the two of them walked up to the Hobbs' front door in silence.

The yard was just as it had been the day before—wild and unkept, the rain storm having enriched the rust that clung to the random farm equipment into a terracotta red. They followed the same line of well-trodden ground up to the house, where George knocked twice on the big wooden door. They had been forced to wait during their last visit, but this time, the door was answered in haste, fretfully almost.

"Hello?" said Connor, sticking his head around the frame.

"Hello, Connor." George smiled. "We were just passing by and wondered if we could ask you a few questions. Can we come in for a moment?"

Connor clung to the door in a clear state of indecision. He glanced over George and Ivy's shoulders, then over his own, and then, with a last moment of hesitation, he gave in.

"Alright," he said. "Mum's not here."

"That's all right," George said. "It was you I wanted to speak to."

Again, Connor peered over their shoulders. Then, to George's surprise, he stepped over the threshold, forcing Ivy and George from the doorstep, just as his mother had.

"Let me just..." he muttered.

Leaving the door ajar, Connor skulked across the yard to a generator tucked into a corner. It was large, green, and industrial-looking, covered by the overhang of one of the many outbuilding roofs. He yanked at the cord a few times before it rumbled groggily into life. But once it had, he eyed it for a few seconds, as though making sure that it remained running, and then skulked back over to them. The noise was ugly and metallic, and if it was the only source of power for the old property, then George understood why it had been placed as far from the house as possible.

Offering no explanation, Connor re-entered the house, leaving the door open for them to follow.

The inside was just as dingy and unkempt as the outside. The hallway was long and dark and it seemed as if every single floorboard creaked beneath their feet, as if the house protested their unwelcome presence. Yellowed wallpaper peeled at the edges, and the furniture was old, not in an interesting vintage way, but in a wobbly, folded-paper-under-legs kind of way. It was mismatched, unordered chaos that could so easily have been charming had there been a sense of care in the house; which there wasn't.

George and Ivy followed Connor along the tunnel-like hallway and to the right, which led into a large, L-shaped living space, which seemed to breed shadow. It was a pleasant enough day outside, yet the curtains were closed and looked as though they might exhale a great breath of dust at the slightest touch. The colour scheme was one of gradual evolution or decline, rather than the result of a positive decision; rustic greens, browns and reds, all of which were shades darker than they had originally been. Almost everything seemed to be covered in such a thick layer of dust that it seemed to taint the very air George breathed.

It was enough to rival even George's house in Bag Enderby. But at least he had a plan for that.

He looked over at Ivy, who viewed the room with a look akin to sadness. Her gaze followed the thick, wooden ceiling beams, which might have once been beautiful features, along with the once grand fireplace, arched windows, and shiplap panelling, all of which lay beneath a veneer of grime.

Connor didn't offer them tea or biscuits. He just sat on a striped crimson armchair beside the fireplace. George mirrored his actions, choosing a floral two-seater which bore cushions so slack that he wondered if he would stand without assistance. Ivy chose not to sit, and George rather hoped that she would make tea. Not that he was thirsty enough to drink from a cup in the house, but she might use the excuse to take a look around.

"Connor," George said, finding the lad's dull eyes. "I'll get straight to the point. You're aware that Lucy Tucker and Sophie Gibson are missing. Unfortunately, we've been forced to dig out the old Kelly Tucker investigation. You remember that, don't you? You remember the girl?"

"I do," he said. "I was a boy back then, but I remember."

"Well, while we were looking through the old files and statements, I noticed an unfamiliar name." Connor cocked his head, the way a collie might when expecting a treat. "We're here to talk about Molly." He studied Connor's face carefully for a reaction. There was something like a wince of pain as his eyebrows arced. "She's your sister?" pushed George.

There was that wince again at the mention of his sister, and he gave a soft grumble.

"Yeah."

"Is she here?" George asked, innocently looking around as though she might be playing a childish game of hide and seek.

"No," he replied, as though the answer had been obvious, and the question redundant.

"Oh," George said, feigning disappointment. "Where is she?"

"She doesn't live here anymore."

"Where does she live, Connor?"

Connor's wince had developed into a bemused frown, as though he had never thought to locate the girl.

In reply, he merely shrugged.

George looked at Ivy, which was enough to convey his thoughts. They weren't going to get much from Connor. Best to do their own research. She got the hint immediately.

"Shall I make some tea?" she asked.

In their time together, George had found that this tactic worked only when Ivy offered to make the tea. People were more likely to believe that a woman would automatically resort to domestic duties, even in somebody else's home. And if there wasn't another woman present to challenge it, nobody questioned it at all.

"Yes, please, Ivy," George said. "Just black for me." He smiled and looked to Connor, inviting him to express his own order.

"Yeah," he said, looking between George and Ivy and copying the routine. "Black for me."

Ivy left the room casually and George heard her commitment to the part; the pouring of water from the kitchen sink, the switch of a kettle, and the clink of cups being pulled from a cupboard. All the while, her roving eye would scan the room.

All the while, George sat and smiled at Connor, contemplating his next move. He'd always found it surprisingly hard to win against those who didn't know how to play chess. Their moves were so random and erratic that they stumbled on success. In contrast, he would overthink their intentions, impressed at their unpredictable gameplay, when in reality, they were just busy remembering which pieces could travel in which direction.

The way to Molly, he thought, might be the long way around.

"Connor," George said, repeating his name to build a rapport. "How well do you remember Kelly Tucker? I mean, she only lived down the road."

"A bit," Connor replied.

His eyes were so unreadable, so lacking in depth, that it was impossible to tell if he understood the question, the situation, the stakes, the circumstances, let alone gauge the sincerity of his response.

"Did you ever play with her when you were a kid?"

"Yeah," said Connor. George waited and stared at him, wanting more. "We used to ride our bikes together."

"And Molly? Did she and Kelly play together too?"

"Yeah," said Connor. "All the time."

"And Edward Gibson?" George said, curious. "Did you know him?" At this, Connor's face revealed a hidden depth. His eyes filled with a darkness that George hadn't expected, like a dark trench beneath a reef.

"Yes," he said.

"I get the feeling that you didn't like him, Connor? Or didn't trust him, maybe?"

Connor's fists tensed into tight, thick balls. A single, bulging vein travelled from between his knuckles halfway up his forearm, reminding George that he was alone in a room with a young man who could probably pick up a bale of hay and carry it above his head.

Still, he wasn't afraid to push.

"Why, Connor? Why didn't you like Edward Gibson?"

George doubted that Connor was the type of man to read the papers or to stay abreast of local news. Anyway, he would've been a boy at the time, no older than ten years old. Even if Ruth had told him, even if they communicated about local affairs, would he even remember?

"He's a bad man."

Though slightly unnerved at the use of present tense, George guessed it was more of a linguistic mistake than a suggestion that Edward Gibson was still alive. After all, George had seen him with his own eyes. His body swinging like a wayward kite hanging from a sturdy limb. So engrossed was George in digesting the young man's words, tone, and disposition that Connor's following statement came as a pleasant, albeit shocking, surprise.

"He hurt Kelly," he said, and then came that wince in the forehead once more, as if he was fighting some inner demon. "And Molly. He hurt my sister."

CHAPTER FORTY-ONE

"Lucy?" Sophie hissed.

But the girl hadn't spoken in hours. She hadn't even looked her way. She had barely even moved, choosing instead to gaze at the ground, frowning, clearly going over and over the conspiracy theory against Sophie growing in her mind. Sophie hadn't said much either. She had spent her time wondering how to put things right, how she might get Lucy back on her side. But, not knowing her any more than her physical description, she had devised no plan.

"Lucy, I'm sorry," she said, deeming an apology the best place to begin; so long as it was genuine. "I never should've said those things. I never should've—"

"Accused me of killing my own parents?"

It was a reaction, at least. Though she'd said it quietly and still refused to meet Sophie eye to eye.

But maybe Lucy hadn't been developing her conspiracy theory. Maybe she hadn't been thinking about Sophie at all, because the next words that came out of her mouth had nothing to do with her.

"Do you remember Molly Hobbs?" she asked.

"Sure," said Sophie, then backtracked. "A little bit."

"She was smart," Lucy mused.

Whether Lucy hated Sophie or not, Sophie couldn't tell. Maybe those things didn't matter anymore, when they only had each other to talk to. What else was there to do?

"I don't really remember," Sophie said, not having given the child a thought in years. But she saw her now, in her mind's eye. A sweet young girl frolicking among the daisies by the stream.

The daisies, she thought, and her ravenous mind wandered further afield, to the small, gold chain adorned with daisies that hung from her bedroom mirror. It had been one of Edward's treasures. Something that had belonged to his mother. She blinked away the image, sure that, to Lucy, it looked like a tick, like someone with a mental illness, twitching at the intrusive thoughts they can't escape.

"She was smarter than her brother," Lucy said, her lip curling at the thought of Connor Hobbs. "She had that beautiful, curly, blonde hair, remember? God, she was so cute."

"I don't really remember," Sophie repeated, her mind's eye drawn to the image of the necklace as if it rested proudly on a heaving chest, with its pendant glimmering in the sunlight. She missed him, she thought, grateful for the distraction. She was always missing him; after all, that was why she had hung it from her dressing table mirror. To honour his memory, to remember him as a good son and husband. A loving man. Someone who had cared for his mother, and who had treated his wife with the same long-lasting care.

"We used to play together all the time, me and Kelly and Molly," Lucy continued. Her eyes had glazed over, and Sophie found her lost in childhood memories, the kingdom where, in the words of Edna St Vincent Millay, nobody ever dies. "We'd build little dams in the stream, climb trees in the woods, make daisy chains."

"Daisy chains?" Sophie repeated, surprised by the moment of synchronicity, and Lucy stared at her briefly.

"Do you think this is what Connor did to her?" she asked, and Sophie gave the notion some thought.

"No," she said, her words slurring a little. "Edward loved Molly. I don't think he'd have done anything to hurt her."

"Who?" Lucy said, her expression twisting in confusion, and Sophie realised her slip.

"Connor," she corrected herself. "Connor loved Molly. He wouldn't have hurt her, surely?"

"Then where did she go?"

"She went to live with her father," Sophie told her with a sigh. "I remember your mum asking Ruth once." At this, Lucy closed her eyes, as though not quite ready to hear about her parents. "And Ruth said that she'd gone to live with her father. Rupert, his name was. Something like that. "No, Roger. That was it. Roger Hobbs."

In a brief demonstration of teenage impatience, Lucy's eyes rolled as Sophie struggled to recall a name that no longer mattered. Such was Lucy's indifference to the anecdote that Sophie nearly chose not to pursue the tangent. But she did so, if only to savour the interaction.

"I remember him, if only vaguely," she began. "If you think Ruth and Connor keep to themselves, then the dad had been a veritable hermit. We'd see him in the distance on his tractor sometimes, but we never spoke." She gave a laugh, hoping to inspire the girl, but clearly she would have to try harder. "Then, one day, it was his lanky son we saw out there. We didn't think anything of it. At least, not until Molly went."

"I think Connor did it," said Lucy, with the same suspicious hatred that she had directed at Sophie.

"Did what?"

"I think he kidnapped Molly. I think he kidnapped Kelly. And now he's kidnapped us."

Sophie wasn't sure that, as a fifty-five-year-old woman, she even qualified as being kidnapped.

"Connor won't hurt us," she said for what felt like the hundredth time.

"How can you be so sure?"

That hateful suspicion writhed in the girl's voice once more. Sophie stayed silent, unwilling to feed it with speculation.

"Come on, Sophie. You seem to have all the answers. What happened to them? To Molly? To Kelly?" Lucy said, staring at her now with urgency. "Because whatever happened to them, Sophie, it's about to happen to us. We need to get out of here," she said, flicking her eyes around the workshop with the same determination she had shown when reaching for the spanner with her foot. Christ, that seemed like weeks ago now.

Sophie leaned back, resting her head on the back of the chair.

"If you want to make some futile escape plan, then go ahead," she told her.

"Aren't you going to help? You can't just sit there and stare at the ceiling, Sophie," Lucy said. "Help me find a way out of here. Maybe if we jump about hard enough, we can break the chairs?" Sophie opened her mouth to respond, but as she struggled to find the words, Lucy's head snapped to one side, and she shuffled herself upright. "Did you hear that?"

There were voices. Two of them being carried across the yard outside by the breeze. Then, the sharp rap of two knocks on a big wooden door.

"Oh my God," Lucy said, staring at Sophie. "Somebody's here. Maybe they're looking for us?"

Sophie tuned into the noise. It was definitely voices. Someone was at the door of the farmhouse.

"Should I scream?" Lucy asked.

"No," Sophie said, her heart beginning to pound in her chest. "Don't scream, not yet."

But Lucy ignored her. She sucked in a huge breath, her face

tightening as she readied to give it everything she had. But then there was a new noise, alien and mechanical, and close. An ugly and deafening engine rumbled into life, like rocks in a washing machine, and like a single violin in an orchestra, Lucy's feeble scream was lost in the midst of the mighty raucous.

CHAPTER FORTY-TWO

The narrow and steep staircase was little more than a tragedy, Ivy thought. Beneath the scratches and dust were hand-carved spindles, perhaps a century old, that, with a little love and care, could be transformed into a marvel that new build houses often lacked. The stairs were solid, and as grimy as the place was, it had a strength to it, not unlike that of Ruth Hobbs.

The kitchen had held very little of interest, save for a wasted central island, hewn from some old oak around the time the house had been built, a few hanging copper saucepans, and some mud-caked wellington boots beside the back door. The room was almost an extension of the yard. It was a farm-worker's kitchen, used for quick cups of tea and grubby-fingered glasses of water. But it wasn't a family space by any means.

The upstairs, too, was far from family orientated. She tracked the muddy footprints that had merged to create a crusty layer of dirt on the carpet. The walls were mostly blank spaces between peeling wallpaper, with only a handful of misplaced black-and-white photographs; mainly of the house, the farm, and people who had long since been laid to rest. There was little colour to any of the rooms, nothing that popped, anyway. Nothing that invoked a smile.

Most of the rooms were the same: dull and near-empty, with nothing of note except for old, iron-framed beds that wouldn't have looked out of place in a Victorian hospital, and chests of drawers that could have come from the ark. But it wasn't the decor or furnishings that occupied her mind so much as the old battle-axe who she dreaded finding her snooping around. With every room she entered, she was sure to knock first and call out.

"Ruth? It's Sergeant Hart. Are you in there?"

One particularly thin door, which looked like a closet, opened to reveal an even narrower staircase, which presumably led to an attic space. But it was passageways in old buildings such as the Hobbs' house that inspired curiosity and fear in equal measure.

It was hard not to compare the homes she visited to her own, which was a small, coastal terraced house, with bricks thick with salt, and a gusty sea breeze that seemed to find the nooks and crannies, slamming doors at random intervals. But it was, at least, bright and colourful, with painted handprints pinned to the fridge, photos of Theo and Hatty in bright, summer outfits, and faded bunting that still lined the garden from last year's barbecue, flapping incessantly.

With a tug in her chest, she recalled the photo beside her bed of her wedding day, and how the airborne confetti caught the sunlight in a myriad of vivid shades. But more than the colour, the smiles were bright and true. And now they had faded like the bunting in the garden.

With every day that passed, remembering the good times seemed harder. Something had been lost, she knew, a spark, a shared secret, hope, surprise, and wonder. Like the passageway before her.

She pushed on up the narrow staircase, through the oppressive weight that seemed to lurk in the gloom.

"Ruth?" she called, reaching the small landing. "It's Sergeant Hart, are you in there?"

From the fresh pile of dirty laundry, the sleeping laptop, and the unmade bed, Ivy surmised the room was Connor's. The dormer curtains were open, and although the window offered a stunning view over the yard and the fields beyond, scant light reached the corners of the room.

Beside the bed, in the same honoured spot of affection as Ivy's photo of her and Jamie, was a photo of Connor as a child, with an even younger child beside him. Connor was much the same, just scaled down. The same blonde hair, the same blank eyes, and the same oversized clothes.

But the girl beside him intrigued Ivy. She held Connor's hand and sucked her thumb, the same way Theo did when he slept. She too, had a head of thin, blonde hair, but bright, intelligent eyes. She looked straight at the camera, while Connor seemed to look just above it. She wore cord dungarees and wellies, and Ivy's mother might have suggested that the girl needed a good, hot bath. Ivy snapped a photo of the framed image, then pocketed her phone to study later.

Beside the photo, leaning against the wall was an old, limp rag doll, also blonde, with red ribbons in her frayed hair. One of its button eyes hung from a thread, and the stitched smile she imagined it once boasting was now a grime of loose cotton. It was not a toy that Ivy would place beside one of her children, hoping for them to sleep soundly.

She moved back to the window and peered down, counting five outbuildings forming a courtyard to one side of the house.

At the whistle of the old kettle, Ivy hurriedly retraced her steps to the kitchen where, using an old tea towel to protect her hand, she lifted the kettle from the old stove and turned off the hob. She filled a tired-looking teapot with tea bags from a caddy, then filled it with water.

"It's just brewing," she called out. "Won't be a minute now."

She hadn't expected a reply, but George was a gentleman, after all.

"Thank you, Sergeant Hart," he called out, which she surmised was all part of the charade.

She stepped through the stable door and out into the muddy yard, where the rumble of the generator was loudest. There were no power lines to the property, and she wondered what life was like living off-grid, deducing that they had known no other way.

She could just make out the corner of a water trough, suggesting that the buildings to her left had once been stables. Directly ahead, a large barn-like building commanded the space with its eye-like hatch and davit arm peering down on the three steel-roofed constructions, maybe tool houses or workshops that stood beside it. Not particularly familiar with farm life, she imagined them containing a collection of old machinery, not like the relics that were dotted around the yard. But while most of the outbuildings had open doors, one, she noticed, the furthest of the three, was padlocked shut, and with its proximity to the generator, she surmised it was used to store the fuel. Although, given how rickety the building appeared, she was surprised it had survived the storm. It looked as if it might blow over with a strong enough huff and puff.

Ivy started towards the flimsy-looking outbuilding. Her curiosity grew with every step. Yet it was dashed at the sound of a deep voice.

"Now then," it said, stopping Ivy in her tracks, and she turned to find Ruth Hobbs, hands on hips, staring at her as if she'd just insulted the old battle axe's mother or spat on her grave. "Help you?"

She strode towards Ivy, coming to a stop a few feet before her, then squared her shoulders. Her deep-lined face was scrunched up in fury; her thin lips pursed and thick eyebrows kissing in a heavy frown.

"I, er..." Ivy stuttered, surprised at her own reaction to the woman, having faced far more dangerous people than Ruth Hobbs. But there was something about the woman's demeanour. She had a childlike-nightmarish quality, like a Roald Dahl character. "Connor, let us in."

"Connor?" she growled, after a moment's deliberation.

"That's right," Ivy told her, regaining some confidence.

"Where is he?"

"He's speaking to Inspector Larson," she said, which helped to remind her of their purpose and roles. They were police detectives, and this was a murder investigation.

Ruth raised her eyebrows.

"Alone?"

"That's right."

With this, Ruth's lip curled, and she huffed like a bull before heading straight for the house. But what Ivy called after her stopped her in her tracks.

"We're here to talk about Molly," she said, feeling the balance of power shifted in her favour.

Ruth turned slowly, her eyes narrowing as if she was playing the statement over in her mind. "Your daughter?" Ivy clarified. "Molly Hobbs."

The old woman stared at Ivy, clearly struggling with some inner conflict. Perhaps she was taking it all in. Finding Ivy on her land, going through her things, poking into her family history. It was enough for anyone to feel exposed; resentful even.

"Are you now?" Ruth asked with evident restraint.

While Ivy had to raise her voice to be heard over the generator, Ruth's carried effortlessly.

"Where is she, Mrs Hobbs?" Ivy said. "Where's your daughter, Molly?"

Whether she winced at the memory of Molly, the use of her marital name, or the intrusion itself, Ivy couldn't be sure. Either way, she was clearly in a state of inner turmoil.

"She's with her father," Ruth spat, eventually. "Now, get the hell off my property."

But before Ivy could ask whether Mr Hobbs lived nearby, where that might be, or inquire as to the last time she had seen him, Ruth rushed towards the kitchen door, ready to drag her son away from George's prodding questions, leaving Ivy alone with the generator's dull scream, and an uneasy throb in the back of her mind.

CHAPTER FORTY-THREE

They met at the front of the Hobbs house, Ivy seeming as pleased to be leaving the property as George was. "You look like you had a similar welcome as I," he told her.

"She's not what you would call warm and bubbly, is she?" Ivy replied.

"No, she's not," George agreed. "I haven't heard language like that for a while, I can tell you. It's enough to make your eyes water. Do you know, she ordered me off her land? She would have dragged me off, given half a chance, too. Said that she'd had enough of us poking around. What did you say to her?"

"Oh, you know," Ivy replied as they strolled along the quiet lane, as if enjoying the springtime weather. "I said you were inside talking to Connor."

"And that's all?"

She grimaced a little, allowing half a smile to reveal itself.

"I might have asked her where her daughter was."

"Ah," he replied. "Now I see."

"I didn't see any point in lying," she said. "I found a photo of Connor and a young girl beside his bed."

"His bed? So you had a good look around, then?"

"I wouldn't say it was a good look. I had the time it took the kettle to boil, but it was enough to build a mental picture of them."

"And?"

She gave a laugh and puffed out her cheeks.

"They remind me of a film I saw once, about a group of teenagers who get lost in the wilderness in the US. They stumble on an old shack where a few inbreds live. Of course, they're picked apart, one by one, until it's only the pretty brunette left alive, and she makes a miraculous getaway."

"Sounds grisly," George told her. "I'm more of a Gone With The Wind type of man, or The Dambusters. Much calmer."

"Less cannibalism?"

"Much less cannibalism," he agreed. "So I think we can agree that Molly was his sister."

"Ruth didn't argue," Ivy replied. "She didn't pretend not to know what I was talking about. What about you? What did Connor have to say for himself?"

"Do you really want to know?"

"Of course," she said. "I didn't just creep around the house of horrors for the fun of it, you know?"

"Kelly wasn't Edward Gibson's first victim," George told her. "Which I think I knew all along."

"Oh?"

He sucked in a deep breath, wondering how best to retell his findings.

"During the inquiry, other allegations against Edward Gibson had arisen, sexual comments to co-workers, friends' suspicions about the way he had acted around their daughters. You know, the usual grooming techniques. He'd tutored GCSE maths in the past, and most of those contracts had ended prematurely, very likely due to his inappropriate behaviour, but he was never questioned publicly, and nobody ever outed him. Mostly, Edward Gibson was considered a creep when he was younger. But nobody had stepped in to take it more seriously."

"And Connor told you all of this?" Ivy said, her expression conveying her disbelief.

"No, of course not. He only knew the older, middle-aged Edward Gibson who had, on the surface at least, become more respectable. He'd been able to fool decent members of society and befriend good people. People like David and Florence Tucker. He'd even fooled his wife, Sophie."

"Again, Connor told you all of this?"

"No, all Connor did was reaffirm my suspicions, Ivy. You know, people like Edward Gibson have no trouble deceiving adults. But children? Now, they're a different story. They have a nose for it, you see. He told me about when they were all kids. About how they used to think him a little weird and run away from him if he showed up where they were playing."

"But they never told anybody?"

"Who would they believe, Ivy? An upstanding member of the community, or a bunch of kids?"

Ivy mulled the backstory over, and he wondered if he'd won her support, finally.

"And then what did he say?" she asked.

"That's it. He didn't say much else," replied George. "We went into his part-time job at Tucker and Co., how David treated him. But there's no motive there. If anything, David was doing the lad a favour by taking him on. Most of the farm has been sold off, and what's left doesn't bring in much of an income, and he's not likely to change career paths and become a doctor, is he?"

"He'd have to wash his hands first," Ivy remarked, and the smile they shared felt good.

"You?" George said. "Anything else to report?"

"Not really. Nothing that would hold up in court, anyway," she said. "Did he mention Molly, at all?"

"I brought the topic up," he replied. "According to Connor,

Edward Gibson had been sniffing around her. Although it troubles me that he didn't say anything ten years ago, it doesn't change much right now."

"Like you said, guv, it's likely that more people kept quiet than came forward."

"True enough," he agreed. "Nobody wants to put their child through all that questioning, do they? It just sickens me that Edward Gibson will never be punished for his actions. However long the list of his abused children grows, that fact will never change."

"Did he say what happened to her?" Ivy asked.

"I was getting to that when Old Mother Hubbard barged in," he replied. "Not that it matters now, and not that it matters to Lucy Tucker either, come to think of it."

"So, in summary?" Ivy pushed, and he realised he'd been dallying, a sign of his age, she supposed.

"You should have seen the look in Connor's eyes when he was talking about Edward Gibson, Ivy. Genuine hatred, it was."

"But how does that hatred correlate to the deaths of Florence and David Tucker?" she asked. "Are you leaning towards Sophie Gibson being involved?"

"However backwards Ruth Hobbs and her son are, there's simply nothing to suggest their involvement." At the crest of the hill, George stopped and looked down over the gulley where the Tucker and Gibson houses were, now empty of water and void of life. Ivy stopped beside him, waiting, as she did for him to continue. "The truth is, Ivy, that I'm struggling to believe we have any more to go on now than we did twenty-four hours ago. All we've done is narrow down our options, and we're left with little more than a suspect we haven't seen hide nor hair of. Connolly and Mansfield are up to their neck in God knows what, the Hobbs, well, you know my thoughts about them."

"Actually, I've been thinking," Ivy said, thoughtfully. "If David's company was involved in some kind of drug distribution, that could give us any number of suspects."

George stayed quiet. He appreciated her effort. But at this point, her refusal to acknowledge the role of the old case in the new one was starting to feel passive-aggressive. Then again, even to George, the links between the two were tenuous at best.

"I suppose," he acceded.

"If David Tucker prevented Connolly from distributing the weed, and let's face it, we're not talking about a little bag here; it would disrupt the entire process. Maybe that upset somebody higher up the food chain? Maybe enough for them to go after David. Maybe David got involved somehow, and like we said before, maybe Florence just got in the way."

George nodded, then heard himself sigh, something he never used to do quite so often.

"That's a lot of maybes."

"I'm not sure what else we have to go on, guv."

He didn't disagree. Their lack of evidence was infuriating. Either David and Florence's murderer was extremely adept at covering their tracks, or the ferocity of the storm had done it for them.

George looked over at the fallen oak that no longer obstructed the road. The chainsaw-wielding workers had removed any straggling branches. All that was left was the thick trunk and its huge, knotted roots. It was always strange to see the roots as they were, up in the air, unearthed like some terrible secret.

He walked closer, taking in the sheer size of the tree.

"Hard to believe, isn't it?" he said. "That something so huge could be uprooted by a single storm. It must have been there fifty years or more, and a single storm, which was more wet than windy, managed to take it down."

Carefully, he climbed into the ditch and up the other side, where he pushed through a break in the hedgerow and stepped into the field, followed closely by a far more agile Ivy.

There was something sad about the fallen tree, with its limbs cut back and roots in the air. It reminded George of the elephants in an old Wilbur Smith novel he had read once. It had been set in Africa, and Smith had described scenes of carnage, as entire herds of elephants were brought down for their ivory.

The tree wasn't too dissimilar to one of those great beasts. Wise and all-seeing. Maybe that was it. Maybe with the lack of any concrete evidence, he was drawn to its wisdom. This tree had very likely seen it all from its perch on top of the hill. It had seen Edward and Kelly's sickening walks in the woodland. It had seen the Tuckers' daily hatred of their next-door neighbour. It had seen the Hobbs toiling through every season, the dwindling of their family from four to three to two. And who knew what else?

"If only trees could speak, eh?" he said. "If only we could take a statement from them."

"Guv?" she said, and he saw her concerned expression and shook his head dismissively.

He followed its trunk to the roots and traced their vein-like pathways through the air. Most were as thick as his forearm, but some were as thick as this thigh. A great collection of congealed dirt, insects, and leaves had risen up with the roots, as though to emphasise their interconnection with the tree.

He couldn't help but relate. How long could he survive the harsh winds of this job? How long until this investigation, congealed with all his memories of the last ten years, uprooted him completely? How long until he gave up and fell to the ground?

"Guv?" Ivy said.

George turned. He'd almost forgotten she was there. In his dark, old thoughts, her light, youthful face was a pleasant reminder of hope. But right now, it was lined with concern. She was on her knees further beside the great hole the roots had left behind, and she held something in the air.

Something alien to the natural landscape.

"Is that...?"

"Gold, guv," she said. "I think it's a bracelet. I just saw it on the ground," she explained, standing up and handing it to him.

George gently brushed away the soil, but there were no identifying features. It was a simple, thin, gold-link chain; pure gold. It would never rust.

Together, George and Ivy turned on the spot, scouring the ground for any more finds, bending, pushing around leaves with their feet as though they'd lost something. The bracelet could be nothing. Or it could be the first piece of evidence they'd found.

Maybe there was more.

If the sun hadn't been setting at that exact moment, causing long finger-like shadows across the fields, George might have missed it. But it caught the sun and sparkled, grabbing his attention. It could have been mistaken for the dew on the grass. But no. He looked closer. It was more solid than that, and he bent down to pick it up.

"Found something?" Ivy called from the far side of the hole, and he held his find up for her to see.

"It's–"

"Glass," he replied, holding it up to the light. "Convex." He looked across the chasm at his old friend, seeing a new light.

"Jesus."

"This is where it happened, Ivy," George said aloud, seeing the space as if with fresh eyes. The oak was more than just a fallen tree now. It was a crime scene. "This is where David and Florence were killed."

Then George remembered something, a passing observation he had barely noticed at the time, let alone thought about twice. He handed both the glass and the bracelet to Ivy as though in a trance, then started back towards the road, rapidly picking up speed.

"Guv?" Ivy called after him, and he heard her footfalls in the debris behind him. "Guv, wait for me."

CHAPTER FORTY-FOUR

"Guv?" Ivy said as he stormed ahead and as if he was a much younger man, he tore through the hedgerow, leaped across the ditch, and strode back onto the road, offering her to run after him. "Guv?"

For each of his strides, Ivy had to take two fast steps.

They were headed down the steep hill towards the two empty but beautiful houses.

"Sophie Gibson," he said.

Ivy wondered if it was a habit, that he just had to blurt Sophie's name out whenever he had a rush of adrenaline. She needed more than that. She'd heard the name enough times in the last two days to know George tended to turn on Sophie whenever they reached a dead end. She needed to know why. And why now?

"What about Sophie Gibson?"

"It's hers," he snapped.

"What is?" Ivy said, following George as he snapped through the police tape and then barged through the garden gate. "The bracelet?"

George shoved his way through the unlocked front door into Sophie Gibson's house. He stopped in the hallway, and Ivy watched his chest rise and fall, and for a moment, she felt the pang of concern that was becoming increasingly familiar. He wasn't a young man. He shouldn't be exerting himself so much. But then she saw on his face an expression of immense satisfaction, like a hunter who had cornered his prey.

And now it was within reach.

"Not the bracelet, Ivy," he said, nodding at the table in the hallway.

Ivy followed his eyes to the collection of things by the door, the kind of things anyone living in the country kept ready to use; a shoe scraper, a doormat...and a high-powered torch with a broken lens.

"Jesus," she said, for the second time in what felt like minutes. She dropped to a crouch for a closer look, eying the crimson stain on the torch body. "It's blood, guv." She turned to offer him a winning smile. "You were right."

He was far too polite to say I told you so. Not to Ivy. But there was a sparkle in his eyes that told her he was thinking it.

"Sophie killed David and Florence," Ivy said slowly, introducing this newfound narrative to herself. George nodded patiently as she caught up. "Up by the fallen oak tree. She used this torch to hit David. That's the glass we found. Then she drowned Florence. And then..."

Here, Ivy's story faded.

"How did the bodies get down to the bottom of the hill?" he asked, as if he knew the answer but wanted to hear it from her.

"The water," she said. "Sophie pushed David and Florence's bodies into the flood water. That carried them downhill. Florence got caught in the ditch at the bottom, but David was carried all the way through to the culvert."

George nodded along with her story.

"Oh my god," Ivy said, her mind catching up with the news.

"What?" he asked.

But this time, Ivy didn't explain. She darted upstairs and

headed straight for Sophie Gibson's bedroom. It was still there, straight ahead of her, dangling as naturally as a string of moss from a willow branch. She leaned forward and gently unhooked the necklace from where it hung. It was light and short, too tight for an adult woman's neck. There were daisies every few inches, too - a child's flower.

She heard George's slow steps behind her, patiently catching her up. She took her phone from her pocket and browsed to the last photo she'd taken; the one of the picture by Connor's bed, and then she zoomed in on the little girl's neck where a thin necklace hung. The details were still quite blurry. But with the real thing in her hands, the similarities were unmistakable.

Ivy turned around holding the necklace in one hand and her phone in the other.

"This is Molly Hobbs'," she explained. "I found the photo in Connor's bedroom."

"And that's her necklace," he finished. "We'll need to have the image analysed."

"Goes without saying," she said, pocketing her phone.

"I also want forensics on that torch. Make sure that blood is David Tucker's," he said. "And I need to see Sophie's fingerprints on it too. And check for any others."

Ivy nodded along.

"My thoughts exactly," she said, but he hadn't finished.

"I want CSI at that fallen tree up the road. Find out exactly what happened there. And bag that necklace," he said, nodding to the one lying limp in her fingers. "This could be what we've been waiting for, Ivy."

Ivy pulled out one of the plastic bags she always kept in her large coat pockets, and bagged it.

"I want to know everything about Sophie Gibson's day-to-day movements." His voice was rough and fast. "Where she goes, what she does, who she spends time with. Any suggestion of any place she might be keeping Lucy Tucker, search it. They don't have transport. They haven't been seen. They can't have got far."

"Yes, guv."

Ivy prepared to delegate the tasks, reaching into her pocket for her phone, where her fingernails caught on something.

"Guv, wait," she called.

George peered up at her, mildly irritated that she had broken his train of thought, and she felt a pang of guilt that she had doubted him all along. She had questioned his bias, his emotional investment, and his motives. But that empathy, his ability to follow his emotional instincts as well as those borne of intellect. That was what made him great.

"The bracelet," she said, carefully pulling out the thin, gold chain that she had found by the roots of the fallen oak tree. "If that necklace belonged to Molly, then who does this one belong to?"

"Or more to the point," he added, "to whom did it used to belong?"

CHAPTER FORTY-FIVE

She fingered the thin gold bracelet on her wrist, turning the chain over and over. A comfort mechanism, perhaps.

The deafening noise had stopped. The ringing in their ears had faded, along with Lucy's apparent determination to escape, which Sophie could only be grateful for.

"It's pretty," Sophie said, and Lucy glanced up to find Sophie gesturing at her wrist.

"Oh," she said. "Thanks."

"Was it a gift?" Sophie asked, preferring this calm, thoughtful version of Lucy. Her more energetic or petulant teenage moments were far more challenging.

Lucy gave a heavy sigh.

"My parents got it for me." She caressed the bracelet as if cherishing a memory. "I've had it since I was a kid. I have one and Kelly had one. I think they were a set that belonged to my grandma."

"Do you remember her?" asked Sophie.

"No," said Lucy. "She died before I was born."

Sophie smiled at the response, but she didn't rephrase the question.

"I don't remember much about Kelly, either," Lucy said, as though she had understood Sophie's question but had been stalling. "I was only six when she died."

Sophie considered her choice of word. Died, but chose not to dwell on the fact that the girl's sister had never been confirmed as dead. Her body had never been found, and that had been Sophie's argument all along; Edward's defence. "But you must, right?" Lucy said. "Remember her, I mean."

She looked up at Sophie with eyes searching for comfort. After all, memories of her loved ones were all the teenager had left. They were all gone now. Florence, David, Kelly. All dead. Lucy was the only remaining Tucker.

"I remember her, yes," said Sophie. "I remember her well, in fact." Of course, she remembered Kelly, with her long eyelashes and sharp cries and her love for butterflies. She decided to be true to her memories. Only those positive recollections that were crystal-like, so clear that they created prisms of colour on the white walls of her mind. "Your mum and I used to walk into the village with the two of you. You would run ahead, picking the leaves from trees, and then you'd bring them back to show me, as proud as could be." In Lucy's eyes, Sophie saw a realisation of the depth of their relationship. To Lucy, Sophie was just the weird lady next door that she wasn't allowed to talk to. But Sophie had known Lucy forever. Before everything. Before prejudice and betrayal and hatred. In happier times. "She was a lovely little girl," Sophie said, picturing Kelly's huge blue eyes. She looked up and smiled at Lucy. "You both were."

Lucy swallowed hard. Kelly, Sophie imagined, was the loved one that she had grieved for the least. The death of her parents would be far more devastating than a sister she barely remembered.

But Sophie knew grief.

She knew it wasn't always discernible. It would all merge

together with all manner of sorrow, whether the loss was a husband, a daughter, or anyone, really. It all meant the same.

"And what about you and your husband?" Lucy asked innocently. "Didn't you want kids?"

So, Lucy had never been told about Edward. Perhaps Florence and David hadn't told her the truth about the man she had married. The man she had loved.

No, Sophie had to remind herself. Not the truth.

The lies.

Sophie thought hard before answering. They'd never wanted kids. That had been the line they had used. Having each other had been enough. But then, there was a time, wasn't there? Yes, she did remember a time when she'd wanted a daughter. Someone to spoil, to dress, to see herself in, and to learn from her mistakes. The memory stirred a wolf-mother-like growl in her stomach. An instinct she had repressed for what seemed like a lifetime.

"Edward never wanted kids," Sophie found herself saying. "But I did."

"Why didn't he want them?"

Sophie shook her head. She stared at the bracelet on Lucy's wrist, and thought of the second of the pair.

"I don't know why," she said, and for the first time since he had been alive, she dreaded to think what Edward would have been like as a father. She had always told herself he would have made a perfect dad; a goofy playmate, a wise adviser, a loving protector. But maybe that was because she was so tired, and so hungry, and so thirsty, or blind to the truth. Either way, a new picture of her late husband was forming, like a face emerging from the gloom.

"I think he didn't want to face that side of himself," Sophie said. "To see what he was capable of doing to his own kids."

She felt a single, heavy tear escape from her eye and roll down her cheek. It felt like an escaped memory, a repressed thought, a tear that she had been holding back for a decade.

Lucy frowned at her.

"What do you mean?"

But before Sophie could say anything more, before she could choose to either backtrack or confess everything she now knew, there was a rattle of metal, and the workshop door opened. Even in her state of insight, her survival instincts stirred. She swung her attention to the doorway, swayed by the promise of food. There was only the instinct to eat. But with dread, she saw that Connor carried not food, but an old, creepy rag doll.

"Hello," said Connor awkwardly, as though he was joining a meeting late. He stood there fumbling with the doll, his head bowed.

"Connor," said Sophie, hoping she had sounded strong, but hearing nothing more than a beg, a plea for food. Weakness.

But he ignored her, seeming only to have eyes for Lucy, who in turn, looked between Sophie and Connor, as though Sophie might translate what was going on, or what he was thinking.

He closed the gap like an eager child and then held the doll for Lucy to see.

"Do you want to play?"

She stared at him for a few seconds, a growing look of horror on her face.

"What?" she said, leaning as far back as her restraints allowed, and baulking at his touch as he placed the doll on her lap, then stepped back as though expecting something to happen, as though he was expecting the doll to burst into life.

Still, Lucy looked between Connor and Sophie, not understanding. He wrung his hands nervously, watching Lucy with wide, expectant eyes; the eyes of a child. One dressed as a farmer. In his mother's old work clothes. Sophie studied the doll, and its fraying, blonde, curly hair, tied with little red ribbons.

"Connor?" Sophie said, hoping to draw his attention away from Lucy. She spoke softly. Motherly, she thought. With kindness. "Connor, is that Molly's doll?"

He said nothing, remaining still with his head bowed and his grubby hands fumbling with nothing.

They were a trio of sadness. Each of them trapped in their own ways, in an old, dark and damp workshop. All processing a lifelong trauma with nobody to blame, nobody to serve justice for everything that had happened. All with their own useless coping mechanisms.

Sophie had lied to herself, denying her the truth. Lucy lashed out the way teenagers do, brandishing a vicious tongue as her only defence.

And Connor, it seemed, regressed to something Sophie could only describe as childhood.

And for the first time, too tired to deny the truth, Sophie understood the cause of their sadness. She realised why all this was happening. Why all their lives had been so full of loss and tragedy?

Because the man she had married, the love of her life, that tall, blonde city boy, Edward Gibson, her Edward, had not been a perfect, beautiful, honourable man after all.

He'd been a monster.

CHAPTER FORTY-SIX

George sat back on the floral monstrosity of a sofa, placing his enamel mug of whisky between his thigh and the armrest, caring more for the dog-eared file on his lap than the furniture.

He handled it the way a librarian handles a first edition, with a duty of care. Perhaps if Grace had been there, it would have been a novel on his lap. She could always relax him, helping him to separate life and work, home and the incident room. But she wasn't there, and he was, and all he had to read was an old case file that had subconsciously haunted him for the last decade.

After dropping Ivy at the station where she would delegate the tasks, he had headed back to his ruined little house in Bag Enderby. It wasn't home; not yet, anyway. What he needed was space to think, which the incident room, with its perpetual hum of voices and printers, and chiming phones, failed to provide.

He needed to stare at the squares for a while, consider all the options, and how the game would change depending on what piece he moved next.

There had been a sense of relief, of course, to have found evidence against Sophie Gibson. To move forward, if only a few steps. But he had moved forward into the gloom. Pieces were missing, and infuriatingly, he couldn't visualise the end.

And just as she had for the last forty-eight hours, Lucy Tucker weighed heavily on his mind.

All the evidence in the world mattered not a single iota. Sophie Gibson could rot in prison, her husband could finally be found guilty, and they could even find Kelly's remains. But unless Lucy Tucker was found and fast, then none of it mattered a jot.

Search teams had been scouring the area for days and found nothing. Soon, he would have to call them off. He knew the process. Tim would tell him to scale the investigation down, and although Lucy Tucker's file would remain on his desk, it would soon be covered with new files unless, much like the file in his hands had been, it was archived.

George closed his eyes and listened to the instincts he'd been encouraged to ignore, instincts that guided him to the old file. But before he could open it and read through the decade-old statements for the thousandth time, there came a knock at his door. Two knocks. The first to grab his attention, the second to confirm it hadn't been the wind.

He stayed for a minute, frowning at the wall above the fireplace. It was almost impossible for him to have visitors. The mind had always fascinated him, and that moment was not different, as images of Sophie Gibson or Kelly Tucker at his door became clear, and then faded to the realms of ridiculous.

Out of curiosity more than any other purpose, George placed his whisky on the floor, placed the file on the sofa, rose from his seat, and approached the door with trepidation.

The old, creaky door needed a tug, reminding him that one day he would need to plane a fraction of an inch from its width, and it opened with a judder, revealing the last person he had expected.

"Ivy," he said, surprised at seeing her and not hiding his delight.

She peered up at him from beneath a weighty frown.

"Campbell got me your address, guv." She sniffed. "Hope that's okay?"

"It's fine," he told her, preparing to be caught out in a lie. "Come in, come in."

He stepped to the side, welcomed her through the door, and watched as she appraised the room, from the ancient, dusty ceiling beams to the dark and creaky floorboards. If his mistruth had been apparent, then her expression hid her feelings well. She looked tired, more than confused, angry, or hurt.

"Can I get you a drink?" he asked, realising that he would have to surrender his mug, being the only available drinking vessel that he trusted. Unless, of course, he cleaned the cup he had used that morning. But he'd have to find it first.

She shook her head, and the polite smile that followed was brief but true.

"Are you okay?" He knew the answer, of course. He knew why she had made the journey from Mablethorpe, why she wasn't with her family, and it didn't need voicing.

Instead of answering, she strode to the windowsill, where he thought she might stare into the evening. But she turned towards the kitchen with a cup in her hand. The cup he had used that morning. The one he'd thought nobody would notice. Because Grace wasn't here. Because he was alone. Because nobody cared if he left an empty mug out on the windowsill.

She carried the mug through the living room as though familiar with the layout already, and George followed slowly, watching as she placed it in the sink. He found the whole act surprisingly touching. It was something Grace might have done.

At the sink, she stilled and stared into the drain.

"The lab report's in," she said, still not answering George's question.

"Go on," he replied, not willing to let go of his original question, but curious to hear more.

"There was no DNA beneath David Tucker's fingernails," she said. "So Pip's assumption was correct. There was no struggle."

"And?"

"She inspected the finger-marks on the back of Florence Tucker's neck more closely. She thinks Florence's attacker was female or a small male."

"Anything else?"

"Byrne followed up with Katy Southwell." At this moment, she paused and glanced at George, and they shared a look of mutual admiration for the PC. "They found that the fingerprints on the front of David's car belong to an unidentified person."

"All right," George said. "When we get Sophie's prints from the torch, run it against the fingerprints on the car. I'll bet they're a match."

Ivy frowned. She turned and leaned on the sink, and spoke the narrative out loud.

"David and Florence were escaping the flood. They drove to the top of the hill. And for some reason, they got out and walked into the field to the tree. And there, they were attacked by Sophie."

"Yes," George said. "Then she pushed their bodies into the downhill flood water. And pushed the car down the hill. It would only take a few shoves with the handbrake off."

"Okay," Ivy said. "But why did they stop?"

George imagined the scene, using his own experience of the storm that night. It had been hard to see. Hard to hear. The whole world had felt surreal. Veiled by a shower-wall. Roaring. Messy and unpredictable.

"Maybe they saw Sophie," he said. "Maybe she needed help."

But he could hear his own doubts in his low, slowing voice, and Ivy confirmed them.

"The Tuckers? Stopping to help Sophie Gibson? I don't see it."

Neither did George. That was one of those missing pieces.

Why had the Tuckers stopped? What had caused them to get out of their car in the middle of a storm? Why walk into the field?

George imagined Ivy's silence was a sign that she had more to say to further dampen his spirits. But what she said next only warmed him.

"Guv, can I stay here tonight?"

She didn't meet his eyes, and he hoped she didn't feel ashamed to ask.

"You don't need to ask," he told her.

"I just thought I'd give Jamie some space because…" she began, then shook her head and laughed the kind of laugh that surpassed tears. "Well, because he asked for it, actually."

Even though, in all the five years they'd known each other, George and Ivy had never hugged, he knew that this was the right moment for it to happen. He took one long stride towards her and gave her shoulder a squeeze, the way a father might console his daughter. And she turned to him, shaking her head in disbelief. She fell into his open arms, allowing her head to rest on his chest, and silently sobbed.

"It's okay," he said, gently rubbing her back. "Let it out. Let it all out."

CHAPTER FORTY-SEVEN

She settled into the armchair across from George which, like the sofa, was a hideous, floral affair, and from her straight back, and perpetual adjustments, he guessed it was just as uncomfortable. She had cleaned the only other mug in the house, and he was pleased to see that she was comfortable using it as a make-do whisky glass. They both took a long sip, converting their emotional states into something more logical.

"Sorry about that," she said, a statement he assumed was referring to her minor display of vulnerability. He shook his head a little. Enough for her to see, but not to dwell. Instead, he raised his mug to her.

"To friends," he said. "Present and gone."

"To friends," she replied, and once more they drank. After a few seconds of wincing at the Talisker's comforting burn, Ivy nodded at the file on the sofa. "All right, guv," she said. "Talk me through it."

Casually, George flipped open the file. He could have referred to old statements. He could have spread them out on the dirty floor for them both to pore over. But instead, he closed the file and cleared his throat.

"What do we know?" he asked.

"Guv?"

"What do we know?" he persisted.

"Well," she began, and he might have seen a spark in her eye. "We thought the glass found on David Tucker's body was from a pair of glasses, but we now know it to be from the torch, which, I might add, not only matches the injuries to his head, but also has blood stains."

"We're sure about it being the weapon?"

"I am," she said. "There are six D-cell batteries in that torch, that's enough weight to cave in a skull without a doubt."

"What else?" he asked.

"We have to reason to believe that Florence Tucker was murdered by a female; Sophie Gibson is still missing, as is Lucy Tucker. We've been through her bank statements, credit cards, and everything else we can get our hands on, and we're certain that Gibson has no other properties. The only vehicle registered to her is still on the driveway, so either she had the help of somebody else, or she went on foot."

"And where does that leave us?" George said, and admired the way in which she read his expression, searching for the actual question he was asking.

"It means that we're inches away from nailing Sophie Gibson, guv."

"Except that we don't know where she is, and therefore we can do nothing about it."

"That's right," she said, then sipped once more. "It's not lost on me, you know?"

"Sorry?"

"The similarities," she said. "You knew it was Edward Gibson all those years ago, but could do nothing about it." She shrugged, and her lips pulled taut. "Now, we know that Sophie Gibson murdered Florence and David Tucker, and there's nothing we can do about it."

George nodded at the irony and returned to the basics.

"Ten years ago," he started. "Edward Gibson abused and killed Kelly Tucker."

"Abused, yes. But killed? We don't actually know that."

This was how it worked. George set up the facts, and Ivy played devil's advocate. Although George knew it in his bones, he appreciated how subjective his conclusion was.

"You think she's still alive?" he asked. "You think Kelly Tucker is still alive?"

"Possibly." Ivy sighed. "She could have escaped, got lost, kidnapped. Someone else could have taken her. Someone else could have killed her."

She leaned forward to rest her elbows on her knees, swirling her cup and staring inside as though it might reveal the answers, like tea leaves.

"Because, why would Edward Gibson kill and bury Kelly Tucker and then kill himself?"

"Because of guilt," George said. "He didn't mean to kill her. Or he didn't want to."

It was obvious. He was frustrated to be questioning this part of the case already. There were enough mysteries. But the murder of Kelly Tucker by Edward Gibson was not a mystery. It was unmistakable.

"Okay, but why bury her, guv?" pushed Ivy. "Why go to the effort of finding somewhere, digging a hole, or discarding her body at all? Why not just leave her where she died and then kill himself? It's not like he'd have to face the consequences, is it?"

George shook his head. He couldn't remember ever considering it.

"Well, what about your lynching theory?" he asked, questioning his own theory. "What if somebody else killed Kelly Tucker and buried her? What if whoever it was, was caught in the act by Edward. And what if that someone killed Edward and made it look like a suicide?"

Ivy swirled her cup again, more desperately this time.

"That's a lot of what-ifs," she said, mirroring his earlier comment, and George pinched the bridge of his nose. "The thing is, guv, we're talking about ten years ago now. Anything is possible. What we need is probable. And if we can't even solidify the key points of what happened, how were we supposed to find justice in any of it?"

"Very eloquent," he replied, masking his true thoughts.

"I think we just need to accept the possibility," Ivy said slowly, "that someone else might have killed Kelly Tucker." George looked up and into the eyes of the woman he trusted more than anybody, except Grace. "Because something doesn't add up."

He nodded to appease her enthusiasm, but the possibility had shaken him. If he'd considered this possibility ten years ago, could things have been different? Would he even be sitting there at that moment? If he hadn't assumed that Edward Gibson was the only guilty party, if he hadn't been so blinded in his hatred for the man, would David and Florence still be alive?

"Go on," he said.

"Sophie," she replied. "Sophie could have killed Kelly Tucker." George leaned forward, hoping for a vague memory to reveal itself. "Think about it. They didn't have any children. Maybe they couldn't? Maybe she was so traumatised by being barren–"

"We don't know that she is barren."

"Imagine she is," Ivy said. "Just for a moment. Imagine that she couldn't have children, and the only house within half a mile is opposite, filled with the sounds of joy and love, and children's laughter."

"It would be torture," he acceded. "But it doesn't help us. Even if we do find her, she's unlikely to hold her hands up to another life sentence, is she?"

They sat in silence for a few minutes, stewing over the options. Finding the bracelet and glass by the fallen oak tree, seeing the torch in Sophie's house, it had all been a rush of adrenaline. They'd been on to something. But now that rush had ebbed, and they were left with a fatigued contemplation of what it all meant. And how it all connected.

They needed to think in silence and together until something clicked.

While Ivy frowned at the ceiling, George flicked through the file, hoping for a big, red answer splayed across one of the papers like the word CONFIDENTIAL.

And it came in the form of the old photo of Roger Hobbs.

"The thing that bugs me," he said, developing the idea as he spoke the words, "is Molly Hobbs."

Ivy looked at him, her eyebrows raised.

"Molly and Kelly were around the same age, judging by Connor's photo."

Ivy leaned forward, matching his posture with her elbows on her knees.

"So?"

"So, if your neighbour killed himself and the news spread that he'd been abusing the little girl next door, wouldn't you worry about your own child? Connor practically told us that Edward had abused Molly, too."

Ivy shrugged, urging him to continue.

"So, why didn't they report it?"

It was a simple enough question. One, they should have asked Connor. One, they should have asked Ruth while she was chasing them off her property.

"Are we sure they didn't?" Ivy said.

"There's nothing here," George said, holding up the single page in the file about the Hobbses. "It would've been flagged. There were no recent allegations against Edward Gibson. Only Kelly's disappearance and those that came forward during the inquiry. There's no mention of Molly Hobbs."

"So, how did Connor know that Edward was abusing Molly?" Ivy asked.

"Hurt. He said Edward hurt Molly. But we can assume that's what he meant." George sighed. "And I don't know. I couldn't get anything else out of the lad. He closed off, and she came in."

"What if he saw it?" Ivy said. "What if he caught Edward abusing Molly and..." She grappled the empty air in front of her, gripping her hands as though a reasonable theory was just within reach.

"And killed Edward years later?" George shook his head. "That doesn't make sense."

Ivy's train of thought switched tracks.

"Ruth Hobbs doesn't seem like a woman who trusts the police. Maybe that's why she didn't report it. She was biding her time and eventually took matters into her own hands."

George shrugged.

"Maybe," he said. "But if you knew your daughter was being abused, you wouldn't bide your time. You'd act immediately. As soon as you found out. Otherwise, the abuse could continue."

Ivy set down her whisky and rubbed her temples with the same frustration as trying to remember a word or work out a brain teaser. "Well, maybe that's why Molly went away."

George frowned. "What do you mean?"

"Well, maybe Ruth knew that Edward was abusing Molly," she said. "So, she sent Molly away to live with her father. To protect her."

He'd lost her. Up until now, they'd been on the same page, following the same theories, even if they did keep coming to dead ends. But now, he was lost in a cloud of possibilities, truths, and wonders, from which a single thread teased at him.

"Ivy, what do you mean that Molly went to live with her father?"

"That's what Ruth told me," Ivy said, frowning back at George. "That Molly's with her father."

George set down his own whisky slowly, purposefully.

"That's what she said? Molly is with her father?"

"Yes," Ivy replied, clearly not understanding the problem. "I mean, I couldn't get an address or anything. But we could track him down. Get Campbell on it in the morning. Molly will be in her teens, I suppose. She might still be living with him."

George cast his mind back to the incident room. He remembered holding up the photo of Roger Hobbs and reading the word deceased on the back. He hadn't written it on the board, though, and Ivy had been on the phone to Jamie. She hadn't heard that part of the conversation.

"Ivy," he said, leaning forward. "Are you sure those are the exact words Ruth used? Molly is with her father?"

"Yes," Ivy said, frustrated that she was missing something. "Guv, what is it?"

George stared at her, some but not all of the pieces falling into place.

"Roger Hobbs is dead."

Ivy sat back, processing this new information with quick darts of her eyes.

"Eh?"

"He's dead," George repeated, and he searched for the photo in the file, holding it out to her face down.

Her eyes widened, and he smiled at how fast she had fallen in with the evolved theory.

"So that means..."

"That Molly is dead too," George said quietly.

Ivy paused. Then she threw her hands up incredulously. George shared in the absurdness. Another body to add to the count.

"Then...when?" Ivy's head shook. "Why? How did she die? And where is she? Surely, if anything had happened to her, then–"

"They would have found her when they were looking for Kelly Tucker?" George finished, and she nodded. For each answer they discovered, it seemed to spawn even more questions. Even more doubt. But they were onto something. He knew it. The answers were there, teasing him, showing themselves, and then slipping into the fog. He slapped the old file onto the floor and dropped to his knees, spreading the individual documents out with a few careless sweeps of his hand. No longer was it the first edition to be cherished. It was muddied with grief, and loss, and torment, and the answers lay in the mud.

The map was a crude photocopy, adorned with red pen, blue pen, and even pencil, each denoting the areas that had been searched.

"Here," he said, stabbing his finger at the image. "It's bloody here." He tossed the paper at Ivy and checked his watch before reaching for his coat that hung over one of the grimy dining chairs.

"What? she said, not following, as he slid into his brogues. "Where are you going?"

"We're going out," he told her and then downed the remainder of his drink, feeling the burn and savouring it like penance. "I know where she is," he said, and could have laughed at the sound of those incredible words. "I know where Kelly Tucker is."

CHAPTER FORTY-EIGHT

"All right, Connor," said Lucy, and she smiled down at the doll in her lap. Her voice had softened, as if she had surrendered to his needs. "I'll play with you."

Connor's face broke into a grin, the joy on his face marred only by a sliver of doubt. He stepped forward as though testing her sincerity.

"What are we playing?" she asked. "Is it a tea party?"

He cocked his head in wonder. It was uncanny, Sophie thought, to see a grown man behave in such a way. Lucy grinned up at him, her eyes glistening. But it was all Connor could do to look at her in wonder.

"Well?" she said and made a show of tugging on her restraints. "I can't very well play like this, can I?" Gone was the bitter snarl that Lucy had adopted when accusing Sophie of murdering her parents. It had been replaced with a girlish voice, sweet almost, and one that she had clearly relied on to get her own way. "Shall we play on the floor? Maybe you have a blanket?"

As usual, Connor looked to Sophie as though asking for permission. In reply, she shrugged, hopefully conveying a message between up to you and why not?

Connor hesitated, and once more, Lucy peered down at the doll.

"Does she have a name?" she asked.

It was enough to convince Connor of her intentions. He reached into his pocket and pulled out a flip knife, the kind a farmer might use to remove the deep weeds around a crop. Stepping forward, he flicked it open with a practised hand, bent down, and eagerly began cutting the ropes around Lucy's ankles and wrists.

Over his head, Lucy locked eyes with Sophie. That steely determination to escape had returned the glint in her eye, and she nodded once as if to confirm it. But there was something else there besides hope; grief, loss, anger? Revenge, maybe?

Sophie hoped that Lucy's single nod was a promise that she wouldn't abandon her. But that hope was fading, translating the gesture into something else entirely. An affirmation that Lucy hadn't forgotten, perhaps, her conspiracy against Sophie. Or a reminder of her childhood of being told not to trust the lady next door.

Lucy closed her eyes, only to sigh in relief as the ropes were cut, and she rubbed at her wrists in glee.

Sophie could only imagine the relief. The bonds itched, pained, and restricted any kind of movement. It had been like wearing tight socks for days, or when she had slept with her watch on by accident. All she wanted to do was scratch at the deep grooves in her skin.

Connor stepped back and let the ropes dangle from his grip. He eyed Lucy like a wild animal that he'd freed from its cage. And, as if to reassert his position, he adjusted his grip on the knife, keeping it close by his side.

Slowly, Lucy rose, rolling her shoulders, and stretched her legs and her arms, inciting a few clicks from the girl's knees. But Sophie knew it was nothing compared to the sounds her own knees would make when the time came.

If the time came.

Then Lucy committed to the act. She dropped to her knees, and then, just as the young Molly Hobbs might have, she walked it across the concrete floor. It was a surreal dynamic. Sophie watched Connor's manipulation. She admired Lucy's control, how she seemed to understand the man, and how she revealed nothing of her plans to either of them. Connor dropped the ropes and knelt on the ground before her, though he did so heavily, as though he'd been overcome by emotion. Like a parishioner kneeling at an altar. Defeated. Devout.

Lucy made the doll dance over to him and jump onto his thighs. She let out playful 'oohs' and 'aahs', as though the doll was speaking. But beneath that heavy frown was a focus on her peripheral. She was biding her time. Searching for an escape, for an opportunity, for a weapon.

Again, and innocuously, Lucy stood. She made the doll climb the chair leg that she'd been bound to for three days. From there, it jumped from the seat to the nearby shelving unit, bouncing past the radio, and over the spanner that Lucy had worked so hard to drag close, only for it to sit uselessly at her feet. Then the doll took a flying jump to the workbench, where Lucy's smashed phone still lay, broken and black-screened.

Sophie watched in horror as the doll swayed along the work surface. Connor followed like a transfixed puppy. She could only imagine what he was thinking, to see that doll come to life once more, in the hands of a young girl that he could pretend was his lost little sister. He seemed happy enough, but he was being tested, and it could be a fatal mistake to test the limits of his intelligence. But he showed no sign of distrust, so lost he was in the joy. It was a sick sight to witness, tragic and horrifying.

Finally, through all the performative flouncing, Sophie saw the goal in the doll's little escapade; an open toolbox at the end of the bench.

"La la la, la laaa," Lucy sang, as Connor climbed to his feet for fear of missing out.

But Lucy stopped the doll, turned it to face Connor inquisitively, and then threw it into the air. His arms floundered as he scrambled to catch it, letting his guard down for just a moment too long. The knife fell from his grip and clattered on the floor, bouncing beneath the workbench. A fraction of a second was all it took for Lucy to plunge her hand into the toolbox, grip onto a hammer, and then smash it into Connor's skull. For a split second, his expression conveyed only shock before he collapsed to the ground, and the hammer fell from Lucy's bloodied fingers.

It took but a moment for the significance of her actions to hit home, and she gazed down at Connor's still body in something between horror and pride; an expression that should form on the face of no girl her age. The workshop was silent. Not a single breeze blew the trees outside or rustled one of the tarpaulins.

Realising that she was holding her breath, Sophie swallowed hard, if only to wet her throat, and her wide eyes fell on the rag doll at the tip of Connor's fingers.

"Jesus, Lucy," she said. "What have you done?"

As if the words had roused Lucy from her trance, she snapped into life. She leapt over Connor, heading straight for the door.

And then she stopped, as the fingers of doubt claimed a place in her mind, and she studied Sophie's expression, perhaps searching for one final clue as to her guilt. For a moment, Sophie thought the girl might free her, and that they might escape together. She could see them in her mind's eye, springing towards their homes, to safety, hand in hand, maybe.

But she lingered just a moment too long, and as Lucy turned to make her escape, a hand-hewn from the farmland gripped her ankle, and she fell with a heavy thud to the floor.

"No!" Sophie yelled, as Connor pulled himself to his knees with a groan. Lucy kicked out with her free foot, connecting with his chest, but still he held fast. He seemed dazed, unable to move, to think, or act in any way except to hold on to her ankle.

It was all Sophie could do to shuffle in her chair across the rough, concrete floor, hoping to break the connection, or cause a distraction. Anything. She rocked sideways, lifting the chair legs into the air, until finally, gravity had its way, and she fell onto them both.

In the time it had taken for Sophie to regain her senses, Lucy had scrambled to her feet. She stumbled towards the door, her legs succumbing to fatigue and adrenaline in a single deadly shot, and she crashed into the door, shaking it wildly as she searched for the deadbolt.

But Connor was onto her, scrambling over Sophie on the ground. Lucy fought with the rusty deadbolt, kicking at the door in frustration as Connor, with one hand on the side of his head, the other gripping the workbench for support, staggered across the room like an old drunk.

Helpless, useless to all and sundry, Sophie could only warn her, and pray that she would escape.

"Lucy, he's coming."

"No," he slurred. "No, stop. I need to look after you."

But Lucy was wild now. She reached for the nearest thing to hand, an old, rusty weight beside the door, which she slammed down onto the bolt once, twice.

The tinkling of metal on concrete came on the third strike, followed closely by Connor crashing into wall shelves. Paint cans rattled and fell to the floor, and an old picture smashed on the concrete. Soon enough, his arms wrapped around Lucy while her legs flailed in desperation.

And then Sophie saw it. The knife he had used to free Lucy. It was two feet away beneath the bench. She rolled, shoving herself from where she lay on her right, and fell with a thud onto her left. It was there, somewhere behind her. She groped blindly amidst the cobwebs and God knows what else, until she felt the cold, reassuring kiss of steel on her fingers.

The pair near the door rolled and writhed, with Lucy lashing out any way she could, with anything and everything she happened by, while the farm-strong Connor held fast, taking kick after kick and blow after blow.

The knife was sharp and cut through Sophie's bindings with ease. But there was no time to savour the sensation of freedom, no time to rub her wrists or ankles, and no time to ease her aching knees into action.

She threw herself at Connor with everything she had, connecting just as he grappled Lucy onto her knees, and the three fell forward into a heap. In the momentum, the knife flew from Sophie's hand, lost to a dark corner of the workshop. Connor bucked, releasing his grip on Lucy, and Sophie groped for his eyes with her free hands. He yelled and climbed to his feet, and together, they crashed backwards into the workbench where, with a shrug of his shoulders, he flung her from his back onto the tools and mess, where she rolled to a stop.

A rush of cold air found Sophie's grazed skin. It was a moment of clarity. A defining event in three lives. And Lucy stood on the threshold, staring at Sophie with a look that weighed in equal parts of regret, revenge, and rebellion. She lingered there, briefly; defiant, triumphant, and tenacious.

"Go!" Sophie screamed. "Run, Lucy."

But she hesitated long enough for Connor to rub at his eyes, regain his sight, and allow his body to sag with defeat.

"I just want to look after you," he said, his voice weak and broken.

And then she turned and fled into the night.

Snakelike veins swelled within the sinew of his lean arms as he gripped the workbench. He bowed his head, tears falling from his eyes, and he mumbled over and over as a madman might.

"I just want to look after you. I just want to look after you."

From where she lay, sprawled across the workbench, Sophie watched the man's demise, not with glee but with hope. Hope that the ordeal would soon be over, that he would get the help he clearly needed. That Lucy may have the strength of mind to gather what remains of her life and begin anew.

"You lose," she told him, and laughed at the notion of the last few days being nothing more than a game.

Slowly, he shook his head in denial, then straightened. And for a moment, Sophie thought she caught the remnants of the child within. But it vanished in a flash, replaced by ugly hatred as he raised his fist into the air.

"No, you lose," he told her, his voice whispered and hoarse, and his body tensed as he prepared to strike.

"I lost all those years ago, Connor," she said, and he paused long enough to hear what she had to say. "When my husband killed two poor, innocent little girls."

And then he struck.

CHAPTER FORTY-NINE

Connor knew the woods at the bottom of the hill better than anyone. And he knew its secrets better than anyone. Those terrible woods held only darkness.

But soon, it would be bathed in light.

His well-adjusted eyes scanned the shadows for movement, his keen ears ready to hone in on the slightest crack of a stick underfoot.

How long had it been? How long since that time? When sunlight had streamed through the canopy, when their feet had trampled the carpet of daisies, and that whimper had carried through the trees?

He could picture her now. He could picture them all. But her, the Tucker girl, he could picture so clearly.

He had looked after her, just like he had looked after Molly.

And they had played.

Crack.

His head snapped to the source of the sound, to a space between the trees, to where the stream was narrow enough to cross. And there she was, her shadowy figure stumbling over the roots, falling, and scrambling, only to fall again.

She was barefoot, he recalled, having taken her soaked shoes off in the workshop.

"I want to take care of you," he called after the girl, and he saw her pause, look back, and then start off in a hurry.

It had been a warning. He hadn't meant to spook her.

But she didn't understand. She didn't know. And how could he explain it to her? What would he say?

No, all he could do was keep her safe.

His long legs made light work of the limb-like roots that served to slow her escape, and before her chance came to cross the still-swollen stream, she was within grasp. But he held fast, not wishing to hurt her or cause her to fall.

"Stop," he said, pleading with her. "There's no need to run. I won't hurt you."

"Get away from me," she screamed, turning her back on her escape, and she faced him, her eyes wild and body trembling with fear. She reached for a long, hanging branch and pulled hard on it, until it yielded, and she held it, daring him to come closer. "You're sick, Connor. You won't get away with this. Not now."

He fingered the open wound on the side of his head, and it throbbed at his touch. Warm, sticky blood was congealing. She had done that. She had hurt him.

"Don't come any closer, Connor. Just back off."

"You hit me," he said.

"And I'll hit you again," she warned, although her trembling voice belied the sentiment behind the words.

"I just want to look after you," he told her, reaching out for her, pleading with his eyes.

And she swung the branch at him, forcing him back.

"Don't you see?" he asked, daring once more to reach for her. And again, she swung. Harder this time, her aim truer, her conviction absolute.

But he caught the stick mid-flight and growled at the pain before tearing it from her hands and tossing it into the undergrowth. She cried and held her splintered fingers, and Connor took a single step forward, approaching her as if she were a wild beast.

"Don't you see?" he said again. "Don't you see that I'm trying to protect you, Lucy?"

"Protect me from what, Connor?" she whispered. "From who?"

He glanced over his shoulder, at the hill that led back to the farm, to the workshop, then back at her.

"From her," he hissed, and then made his move.

He reached out for her, held onto her, pulled at her, and then...pain, dull and sudden, and darkness.

It took a moment for him to comprehend his whereabouts. Weightless, lying on the damp ground as the forest swirled about him. A bright light burned his eyes, and a heavy boot crushed his chest, before another connected with his cheek, his nose, his groin, and he folded, scrambling away, his fingers groping through the storm debris. Leaves, sticks, twigs, and filth. And all the while, the blows rained down, hard and violent, for what felt like forever. Was this hell? Maybe it would never stop. Maybe he was destined to crawl through the filth for the rest of time. Maybe this was his punishment. To endure the devil's silent wrath for eternity.

Until a heavy boot rolled him onto his back, and he stared into the powerful light as if the heavens had opened. But angels wouldn't hawk a mouthful of phlegm and spit it into his face.

And the two silhouetted figures who stood over him had no wings.

CHAPTER FIFTY

The biggest danger in speeding along the country lanes in the dark was the risk of hitting a deer. The bends could be learned; they were constant. Pedestrians, should there be any, should have the sense to step onto the verge. But deer had a habit of freezing in the middle of the road.

But even if he saw one, George doubted he would brake, such was the grip his determination had on his senses.

He didn't like to drive with such reckless abandonment, but the answers to decade-long questions were at the tips of his fingers. And if he was right, then maybe, just maybe, they would lead him to Lucy Tucker.

Hopefully, before it was too late.

Either way, he would not leave Lucy Tucker unfound for one more night.

Beside him, Ivy flicked through the old case file. She hadn't seen it yet, he realised. He'd kept it close to his chest. But now he was glad it was in good hands. He had looked through it so many times by now, he couldn't see the wood for the trees.

But he saw it now.

And, soon enough, she would see it too.

"Guv, help me out here, will you?" she said.

"What?" he said, his eyes darting between the page in her hands and the perilous road. "What did you say to me? Back at the house. What did you say?"

"I said that Molly Hobbs was dead," she replied.

"After that," he said. "You questioned if she was dead or not."

A few inches of still water sat in the gully where David and Florence Tucker had once lived, and the car tore through it, waking the sleepy night. He slowed at the hill, searching the trees to his right for something.

"I wondered why they hadn't found her when they had looked for Kelly Tucker," Ivy said, clearly noticing that they had slowed, but letting events unfold naturally. He drew the car up to the side of the road, where two men with chainsaws had made light work of the fallen tree and had piled the logs at the roadside, ready for collection. "And then you tossed me the map."

He applied the handbrake and switched off the engine before reaching for the interior light. Her eyes were dark and heavy, and the light revealed deep worry lines, but the cause was momentarily forgotten. It was a problem for another Ivy, another time. She held the map up to the light.

"What do you see?" he asked.

"Looks like a search plan to me," she said, her finger tracing the various hand-drawn lines. She focused on an area circled in red. "This is the detailed search. This is where I'm guessing you thought that Kelly Tucker had been killed, or she was buried, or something."

"Right," he agreed, and she moved to the pencil line.

"I'm guessing this is the dog team? They would have covered a larger area in shorter time." She looked up for confirmation, and he nodded.

"Very good," he said. "And what do you notice?" She shook her head and focused hard on the sheet of paper, as George often did when just a clue or two from completing the Sunday crossword. "Where are we now?"

"Where are we?" she asked. "On the map, you mean? We're here." She fingered the spot on the hill where they had stopped. "It's blue," she said, more to herself. "The dogs didn't search this area. It's open farmland. It was searched, but not like the other areas. They didn't come through here on their hands and knees."

He stared at her, unsmiling, and she looked past him into the night.

"The tree?" she said. He reached for the file, and once more, it was a first edition. Precious. Sacred. All-knowing. He found the sheet of paper he was looking for and handed it to her. He'd read it a hundred times, maybe more. He'd even cried over it one evening, at failing the girl it described.

"This is Kelly Tucker's profile," Ivy said, and he swallowed hard.

"Read it."

He stared ahead now, through the windscreen, and he pictured David and Florence out there in the howling wind and beating rain. He could see them. He could even see the looks on their faces as they worked to drag the fallen tree from the road in near darkness.

"Blonde hair, blue eyes, three feet six inches," Ivy said, and then flapped the paper around like it was a throwaway paperback. "This is her description, guv. It's been ten years."

"Read it," he said, still clinging to the image of David and Florence.

"She was wearing a yellow t-shirt, blue shorts, pink shoes, and..." She paused, and Ivy's gaze intruded on the image in his mind. He let them go. David and Florence, he let them go. He knew now.

"And?" he said, prompting her to finish.

"A gold bracelet," she whispered, and with that, he grabbed the torch from the door pocket and climbed from the car.

The verge had been well trodden by the men with chainsaws, but he picked a path through to the ditch where he found the footholds he had used earlier that day to leap the short distance.

"Guv?" Ivy said, coming after him as he scrambled up the other side. "Guv, you're not making sense."

"We found it here," he said, holding a hand out to help her across the ditch. "The bracelet. It was here all along."

"So one of the Tuckers had it?" she said. "What are you saying, that they dropped it during the storm?"

"No," he said, finding the spot where Ivy had spotted the fragile gold chain. He marked it with the heel of his shoe. "No, that's not what I'm saying at all."

Her face twisted a little as the only alternative surfaced, and she stared down at the mud.

"No," she said in disbelief. "No, guv…"

But he had come too far to be deterred. There was no time to wait for officers with spades and lights, and all the paraphernalia they might need. They could come and finish it. For now, all he needed was an answer. He was on his hands and knees, clawing the earth.

"Guv, come on," Ivy said. "This is ridiculous."

"Go if you want," he told her, and stopped long enough for her to see the conviction in his dampening eyes. "I need to do this, Ivy."

She lingered a moment, as if deliberating. Then, just as he was about to drive his hands into the soil, she placed a hand on his shoulder.

"Move," she said, applying some force to his shoulder, and reluctantly, he made room for her. She knelt beside him and forced her strong hands into the earth, dragging it this way and that. They worked together, him with the torch between his teeth, both pairs of hands working frantically.

But that delicate sense of camaraderie, as wonderful as it was, lasted only a few brief moments, until she stopped abruptly. Frozen like one of those deer.

And that look in her eye, that look he recognised so well, was confirmed without doubt when she gently scraped back the earth to reveal the crown of a hard, smooth skull.

George fell back onto his backside and wrenched the torch from his teeth. He shone the light on that unmistakable curvature, and Ivy moved back, as if it might spring to life at any moment.

"Jesus Christ, guv," she said. "Jesus bloody Christ."

Had he not had that drink, he wondered if he might have felt differently. If perhaps he might have experienced some overwhelming elation. It had only been the one drink, and not even a full measure at that, but still, maybe it had marred his emotions, somehow. Maybe he was numb after all these years. He had hoped for more. He had hoped that by closing this decade-old chapter in his life, he might be reborn, reinvigorated.

But he hadn't the time for such experiences. This was not his night. This night belonged to Kelly Tucker, to David and Florence, and to Lucy.

And as if by divine intervention, his thoughts were confirmed. A single scream sang through the trees, and Ivy snapped upright, her eyes bright and wild in the gloom.

"What the hell was that?" she hissed.

"It has to be her," he said, scrambling to his feet to stand beside her. "That's Lucy Tucker."

CHAPTER FIFTY-ONE

George and Ivy rushed back to the road.

It was hard to trace the source of the scream with any precision. In the surrounding countryside, its echo had bounced between trees, across fields, and from giant rocks that jutted from the hillside like fractured bones. But it had come from beneath them somewhere. Ivy was sure of that, at least.

"The houses," she said, then ran before George could argue.

She sprinted ahead, down the hill, her arms flailing to maintain balance until her feet splashed into those few inches of water that the car had ploughed through not twenty minutes before. She paused there, unsure of which way to go, and George's leather-soled brogues announced his hastened approach with a slap, slap, slap, and then a splash as he joined her, breathless yet no less determined.

"Which house?" he said, between raspy breaths, to which she could only have hazarded a guess until the next cry sang out, pained and ghoulish in the night. George stared into the trees. "That didn't come from one of the houses."

"No. It came from over there," she replied, pointing into the woodland beyond the Gibson house.

"And it was male," he called out, doing his best to keep up with her. "She's fighting back."

There was a hope to his tone and in his words. But she dared not to crush it by voicing her concerns. Not now, when they were so close.

Ivy sprinted past Sophie's house and straight into the trees, slowing to navigate the gnarled roots at her feet. They rose like twisted arms, ready to tighten around a wayward ankle and drag her to the ground. George's torchlight bounced back and forth, stilling occasionally when he stopped to find a path. They moved forward together, Ivy slowed by the roots and the debris that still clung to the trees and undergrowth, George hastened by the aid of his torch, and in some degree, she considered, by memory. How many times had he searched these woods whilst looking for Kelly Tucker? How many times had he left this place disheartened? How many nights had he contemplated his next move, with each subsequent sleepless night proving more and more futile?

"Shh," he hissed, and she stopped in an instant. Ahead, the trees became clearer. A light was blinking, providing only brief and tantalising snapshots, moments in time, but with clarity, nonetheless. It was disorienting. Like strobe lighting in a nightclub, flickering on and off and on, lighting the trees in a series of flashes.

The thrill of fear slipped into Ivy's bloodstream, moistening her palms, her back, and quickening her breathing.

George killed his torchlight and crept forward, spying not one but three figures, revealing themselves for the tiniest of moments in the flickering light, the reason for which soon became evident. Two of the figures were kicking at something on the ground, the torch waving about with the effort.

"That's enough!" George cried out, and he stepped forward, switching his torch on to illuminate the scene. Hands rose to shield blinded eyes, and the melee ceased. To the side of the action was a fourth figure, smaller than the others, and caught between joining the attack and stopping it, clearly relieved that somebody had arrived to make the decision for her.

"Lucy, is that you?"

Slowly, the girl lowered her hands, and George redirected the beam. She was barefoot with filthy jeans, her hair hung in strings about her face.

"Yes," was all she said. A single word that, for Ivy, marked the beginning of the end. She rushed forward, spurned by the promise of success, to hold the girl in her arms, to tell her every-thing was going to be okay.

"Are you hurt?" George asked, to which the girl shook her head.

"I'm okay."

"And you two," George continued, gesturing for the two men to lower their hands. "Let's see who we have here, eh?"

Slowly, their hands dropped to their sides, but their heads remained held high.

"I might have known."

He shone the light onto the ground, where Connor Hobbs stared up at the sky. His nose had been bloodied, broken, most likely, and aside from the unseen injuries, he had a deep wound to the side of his head that had clearly been caused by something other than a boot.

"You two," George said. "Step away from him. Over here, now."

Reluctantly, Jason Connolly and Peter Mansfield ambled over to him, but not without Connolly spitting the contents of his foul mouth onto Connor's face.

"Knees," George told them.

"What?" Connolly said, incredulous.

"On your knees, Connolly, or I'll put you down there myself, and by God, don't think I won't."

They hesitated, as if each of them was waiting for the other to drop first, and then Mansfield set the tone, which was enough to convince his nephew to follow suit.

"Ivy, if you please," George said, and she led Lucy to them, resting her against a tree before restraining the two men with the zip ties she carried in her pocket. "Call it in," he told her, before turning his torch onto Jason and Peter, who cowered away from the harsh light. "Is somebody going to tell me what's going on here?"

His voice had the same stern quality as a headteacher's. But Connor's injuries had been caused by a ruckus that was far more serious than a playground scrap. He was covered in blood. Some dried, some wet, having drained across his features in torrents.

Nobody said a word. Jason Connolly glanced nervously around him and shuffled his feet, Lucy whimpered into her hands, and Peter Mansfield was the only one to look George in the eye.

Ivy knew the warning signs, the darting eyes, the weight on the front foot. Jason Connolly caught her stare as she grinned at him. "Don't even think about running, Connolly," she told him, shaking her head, and as a result, he switched tack to one of defence.

"He was going to hurt her," he said, throwing his arm out to point at Connor. "The creep!" Then, once more, he spat at Connor, and the phlegm turned in the air, landing on the ground just above the boy's head.

Connor only wheezed in defence, holding his ribs.

"He did it," Connolly said, looking at George now. "He had her all this time."

Calmly, George blinked once, then turned his attention to the girl, who, the most passive in the situation, had been somewhat ignored until now. Even in the darkness, Ivy could see the wave of relief that had washed over George's face. He seemed to study her, as if she might not be real, and that the whole affair might be a dream, and he would wake in his chair with his enamel mug of whisky.

"Lucy," he whispered. The girl raised her head, which she'd been resting heavily on the tree trunk, as though, like a newborn, she hadn't the strength to hold it up on her own anymore.

"Yes?" she said, which seemed to take George by surprise. "Do I know you?"

George didn't reply. What could he possibly say? Did he know her? Can you know really know someone from afar? Could you delve into their family history, their trauma, and grief, and not know the person?

"You're Lucy Tucker," he said quietly.

"Yes," said Lucy, still unclear as to who they were.

"I'm Detective Inspector Larson," he explained, then gestured at Ivy. "This is Sergeant Hart. We've been looking for you, sweetheart."

At this, Connolly scoffed.

"Did a great job, didn't you? She escaped by herself."

"And if you'd been a bit more cooperative, perhaps we might have found her sooner," Ivy said, turning on the teenager.

"So, this is my fault, is it?" He sneered at Ivy and climbed to his feet with his hands behind his back. "I told you. I told you it was that freak." He nodded at where Connor was lying on the ground. "If you'd just done as I—"

"We don't just follow the whims and wonders of drug dealers, Mr Connolly," George announced, his voice cutting through the affray. "Now, I suggest you get back on your knees before you find yourself on another altogether more serious charge."

But Connolly hadn't finished. He leaned in so close to Ivy that she could smell the weed on his foul breath.

"You were useless! If me and Uncle Pete hadn't been here, if we hadn't been watching Connor's house, if we hadn't seen Lucy run to the woods, she'd be dead by now. Or worse." Then he looked her up and down, and spat, "Pathetic."

Ivy stepped forward, but George was the one to drag him back to his knees.

"Spitting at a police officer carries a three-month sentence, Mr Connolly–" he began, but then his warning glare shifted into something altogether different, and Ivy followed his gaze.

In the midst of their arguing, Lucy Tucker had slumped against the tree and collapsed to the ground. Ivy rushed to her side.

"She needs a hospital," George said, as he crouched protectively beside the girl. "Lucy, come on, sweetheart. You're safe now. Talk to me."

"What's wrong with her?" Connolly called out, walking on his knees to be close to her. "This is your fault. I told you about him."

"It's no use passing the blame, Jason," George told him. Then he turned to the girl he'd been searching for nearly fifty hours. There she was. Within reach. "Lucy, come on, darling. You need to wake up for me."

Ivy's call was answered in less than two rings.

"It's me," Ivy said. "Are you awake?"

"I am now," Campbell replied with a groan.

"I need an ambulance at the Tucker house," Ivy told her.

"Right," came the reply with barely a nanosecond of hesitation, followed closely by the scratching of bed sheets. "Anything else?"

"Uniformed support."

"How many?" Campbell asked, to which Ivy gauged the situation before her.

"Send anyone you can get," she replied. "This isn't over yet."

Lucy Tucker stirred, but the girl barely had enough energy to open her eyes.

"Let her be, for God's sake," Mansfield spoke up, as Ivy pocketed her phone.

"I'm going to find out who did this to her," George told Connolly, as if to reassure and calm the lad. But his words were met with nothing but a vile hostility.

"Are you mental, old man?" he said, turning on George. "Who

the hell do you think did this to her? The freak who chased her
through the woods and threw himself on top of her. Look at
him."

As if to accentuate his point, Jason turned to where Connor
lay behind them on the ground, then did a double-take. He shuffled round on the spot, searching the immediate vicinity.

"Jesus," Ivy said aloud, and she witnessed the moment that all
the elation and hope that had raised George's spirits crumpled.
"Connor's gone."

CHAPTER FIFTY-TWO

The low branches whipped Connor's face, stinging his skin, leaving what felt like hundreds of tiny cuts, insignificant against his already broken body. His face was raw, his bruised arms and legs ached, and the sharp stabbing pain in his rib cage meant that he could barely take a breath to fill his lungs.

He pushed on through the trees, stumbling and scrambling. He fell often, but clambered to his feet when his body allowed, half-running, half-crawling his way to the edge of the woods. He welcomed the breeze that rolled over the open field and licked at his open wounds, cooling the sweat on his forehead.

Ahead, the old farmhouse sat at the crest of the hill, with two lit windows like demonic eyes watching his every move, lights that he followed like a moth to a flame.

He pulled himself up onto the fence, clutching his chest, then fell to the ground, landing heavily on his back in the mud. For a second, he just stared up at the stars, wondering; if he lay there long enough, would he slip into a deep sleep? One from which he might never wake?

But there were engines now and headlights over at the road, and he dragged himself to his feet one last time.

The generator hummed its baritone tune, throbbing and thrumming as it did each night. The workshop door was ajar, just as he'd left it, and with a quick glance up at the house, he stumbled through the doorway.

Sophie was still. Clad in only her nightshirt and denim jacket, she was sprawled across his workbench exactly as he'd left her, and he sighed with relief at the sight.

He hadn't considered her before, not when Lucy had been there, with her nice hair and bright eyes. But now they were alone, and she was peaceful; he saw her as if for the first time.

She had a motherly face, warm and kind, and lined only around her eyes as if her skin had been stained by sadness. Her shirt was pulled tight across her chest, and he saw her for the woman she was.

Her bare legs were pale in the low light, like a porcelain doll's, and gently, he ran the back of his finger across her cold skin. Beyond her knee, her thighs were soft and lush, and he held them, his body juddering at the sensation, the connection.

And then he parted them, and a soft, involuntary groan rose from his loins to his throat, like a bubble seeking the water's surface.

She was still and silent, and a trickle of blood ran across her forehead from the cut in her eyebrow. It was nothing. He could make it better. He could take care of her.

Her buttocks were cool to the touch, soft, like a child's.

"Connor?"

His hand snapped to his side, and he froze, refusing to face the familiar voice.

He wondered if it was some inner part of him calling for him to withdraw his hand before he did something he might regret, like the cartoon he had seen once, where a little angel and a devil had sat on opposite shoulders, each vying for their host to pay heed.

"Connor?" the voice said again, and this time, he did turn.

The large square doorway framed her broad shoulders, and she stepped into the room, allowing the weak lightbulb to reveal the disgust on her face. Her fat arms hung by her side, and she tapped something against her leg. The hatchet from the woodpile. She seemed to enjoy the fear that took over him when he recognised what she had in her hand.

"What have you done this time, boy?"

"Nothing, Ma," he said. "I was just looking after them."

She took a step forward, into the dim light from that single bulb, and peered past him to Sophie, her eyes running over her bare legs.

"You disgust me," she hissed.

"No, Ma–"

"You're filth," she spat, taking another step, and her face twisted into one of absolute horror.

"I was looking after them, that's all."

"Them?" she said, and Connor silenced. Her head cocked to one side, and her eyes narrowed. She glanced around the room briefly before teasing his gaze to meet hers. "Them, Connor? Who's them?" He said nothing and picked at the dead skin on his hand. "Answer me, boy. I'm your mother, damn it."

But she wasn't his mother anymore. She hadn't been for years. Not since Molly. She was Ruth, that's all. Ruth Hobbs. The animal he lived with. The animal he spent every day trying to please.

She held the hatchet out at him as if to make her point.

"You will answer me, boy."

"No, Ma–"

"What have you done?"

She stepped closer still. He could shove past her and run. He could be out of the door and away into the night in a heartbeat. He was sure he could.

But then Ruth would be alone with nobody to look out for her.

"Move," she said, eying the bare legs behind him.

"No, Ma, don't."

"Move, damn it," she hissed, and her teeth bared in a sneer, lighting that brush of soft down on her upper lip. Slowly, he stepped to one side, further into the room, further from the door.

"It's the Gibson woman," she whispered in wonder, then stared at him. "What were you going to do, Connor?"

"Nothing, Ma–"

"Tell me what you were going to do if I hadn't found you."

"Nothing, Ma. Honest."

"You were touching her–"

"No, it's not like that."

"I saw you, Connor. You were touching her," she said, that sneer of disgust lingering as if to accentuate her point. "You had your hands all over her."

"I didn't."

"Is this what you do?" she said, her cold eyes wandering to his naval. "I should have cut it off long ago. I knew you were bad when you were born. I could smell it on you."

"Ma, don't–"

"I should have put you in a sack and dumped you in the river like the puppies."

"No, stop–"

"You're worse than your father was. I should have known nothing good would come of you." She stepped away from Sophie and closed in on him, trapping him as he'd trapped the girls. "You're pathetic."

"I'm not–"

"Say it," she yelled. "You're pathetic. Say it, damn it."

"No," he whined.

"And the Tucker girl? Kelly. What did you do to her, Connor?"

"Nothing, Ma. Honest, I didn't."

"Did you touch her too? Did you touch her the way you just touched her?" She nodded backwards at the workbench, gesturing at Sophie Gibson. "Do you like that, Connor? Do you like it when they're helpless? Does it make you feel like a man?"

"I wasn't–"

"Take it out," she said, and her sneer faded. Her great, slumped shoulders straightened, and she seemed to grow a few inches in height. She nodded at his groin. "Go on," she said. "Take it out."

"Ma, no–"

"Take it out and pull it tight," she said, raising the hatchet in the air. "Go on. Put it on the bench."

"I didn't–"

"Maybe this will stop you. God knows I've tried everything else," she said.

"Ma, I'm not like that."

"What about Molly, eh?" she said. "You think I don't know what you did to my little girl? To your own sister. You're an animal, Connor. Tell me. Tell me you're an animal."

"I'm not. I didn't do anything."

"Didn't do anything?" she wailed. "You killed your own sister–"

"No…"

"You're a monster, Connor."

"NO! I didn't kill her." Connor banged the workbench, his frustration building like a volcano inside him. "You didn't listen to me. You never listen to me."

"And then you killed that little Tucker girl. Didn't you, Connor? I saw you. I saw you do it."

Connor remembered that night even now, even in his surreal, swirling state of existence, his sight blurred with blood, his head throbbing, his breaths tight and wheezy. It hadn't been him. He'd seen it with his own eyes.

"I didn't kill Kelly," he said. "I didn't."

"You did!" she screamed, leaning in, pushing her face so close to his he breathed her rank breath. "You touched her. You used her," she said. "And then you killed her, Connor. "

"NO!"

"You put your hands around her neck, and you squeezed the life from that poor girl."

"No!" he screamed, and he shoved her so that she stumbled backwards.

"I didn't kill Molly," he told her, finding conviction in his actions.

He looked to the lifeless rag doll on the floor. She was face-down. A sob escaped his throat.

"Then who did?" The voice wasn't Ruth's. It was gentle and caring. Motherly. Behind her, Sophie Gibson rose, her eyes streaming with tears. "Who killed Molly, Connor?"

But he just shook his head. He couldn't bear to think about it.

"Who killed Kelly?" said the same soft voice. "Who killed Kelly, Connor?"

But at this, Ruth turned on Sophie. She glared at her, as though Sophie was disrupting some private domestic dispute. As though it was none of her business. It was, of course. It was all of their business. They were all connected by these horrifying events over the past ten years, whether they liked it or not.

Ruth took a step forward. She lifted the hatchet in her hand. Whether a threat to Sophie or a genuine attack, Connor couldn't be sure. He couldn't move. He couldn't protect her. Not physically. But he could still talk. He could still reveal the truth.

"She did," he said, so quietly that he wasn't sure if they would hear.

But both women turned to face him, both in their own state of shock. As if Sophie couldn't believe the truth had finally been told, and Ruth couldn't believe he'd betray her. "She killed Kelly," he said, staring at the woman he had once called mother. "I saw it."

A silence followed this revelation. He had never said those words, not aloud. Not even to himself.

Ruth stared at him in disbelief, then her face softened and

crinkled with mild amusement. A laugh escaped her yellow teeth, quiet at first, then louder and louder, as if she had never found anything so funny. But it stopped like a hatchet splitting wood, and her lips pursed like little, spiteful prunes.

"And who would ever believe you, Connor?" She took a step towards him. "Who would ever listen to Connor the gormless wonder?" She was closing in on him once more, making him feel small, making him cower like a dog, forcing him to look away in shame, forcing him to surrender to the alpha. "Prove it," she spat. "Because no one will ever believe you. You're worthless."

But where before he might have cowered at her spiteful tongue and her vile accusations, something had shifted inside him. Her words were harmless now. He had said it aloud. He had told the world what he had wanted to say for years.

"How could you?" she said, shaking her head in disappointment. She said the words slowly, looking down at him, sneering. Her arms were tense, the hatchet poised. "How could you do this to me, after all I've done to protect you?"

His fists clenched, like the restless legs that kept him awake at night. He just had to move them. He just had to lash out. The energy was soaring through him. The anger.

"Say it, Connor," she told him. Ruth had switched into play mode. He recognised it. She was having fun. She enjoyed this part. "Tell me you're pathetic. Tell Sophie the truth. Tell her what you did. Doesn't she deserve to know the truth?"

"No, Ma," he said quietly.

"Tell her how pathetic you are."

"Ma, don't do this."

"Ruth..." said Sophie, clearly sensing the climax.

"SAY IT!" Ruth screamed, and it seemed as if every muscle in her face had tensed. Her eyes bulged, and she raised the hatchet once more.

Something inside of him rose up from the very pit of his stomach, spurned by hatred and sadness, loss and guilt, and the lies that he had been forced to live, day after day, year after year.

And he shoved her as hard as he could. She stumbled backwards, slamming into the bench on which Sophie sat. She growled at the pain and straightened, the fires of hell burning bright in her eyes.

He searched frantically for a weapon and found one at his feet, waiting for him to pick and use, like a fated sword. The hammer Lucy had used to hit him. He picked it up and faced Ruth. They were no longer mother and son. They were no longer a family forced to live a life of seclusion to bury a decade of lies.

She tensed as a bull might, focused on its prey, her great shoulders bulging in preparation. She gripped the hatchet in her hand.

And then he saw it.

Behind her, a bare and slender arm rose into the air just as she took her first step. The glint of a blade, his blade, shone in the weak light.

And then buried itself into her back.

Ruth stopped, the hatchet held high and an expression of horror frozen on her face, as if Sophie had merely pressed a button to pause time.

But the reprise was short-lived. Before Connor could even consider getting out, Ma's eyes saddened then narrowed, and she rocked from side to side as she turned to face Sophie, who backed away as far as she could, pressing herself against the shelf that held the truth-telling radio.

"You," Ma said, and she coughed once at the effort.

Her arm tensed, and she prepared to drive the hatchet down.

And Connor swung the hammer.

CHAPTER FIFTY-THREE

Sophie watched in horror as Ruth Hobbs' body twitched once and then stilled on the concrete floor. She had fallen as a sleeping cat falls. She looked dead. Sophie hoped nobody else had to die. She hoped that this could all just end. Without anybody else getting hurt.

How had it got to this point? How had three households caused each other so much pain?

She closed her eyes and said a silent prayer to Lucy.

Send help. Send it soon.

But Connor had other ideas.

He was crouched beside his mother, sobbing like a child, like the child that had asked Lucy to play with him.

"It's over, Connor," she said softly, but he didn't budge an inch. He smoothed his mother's thick, grey hair, tucking it behind her ear, and then stroked her face, his grubby finger tracing the deep lines in her sallow skin.

A breeze from the door caught Sophie's bare legs, and she covered herself with her night-shirt. She eyed the doorway and the dark night beyond.

Letting her leg slip from the workbench, Sophie eyed Connor

to gauge his reaction, if any. But he was lost to the conflicts of grief. She knew the feeling well. It was something she would recognise for the rest of her years.

She eased herself to the bench's edge, mindful of the myriad of tools that threatened to betray her stealth.

This is it, she thought. She could hop from the bench and run.

How far would she get? Was it dark enough to lose herself? Was it dark enough to find someplace to hide, to sleep, to pray for a passing car?

And as if the heavens had heard her, a tinkle of rain danced on the old, tin roof, light at first, but growing in weight with every passing second, as if a great storm cloud was moving in to wash the stain from the earth's surface.

"No," he said, his voice authoritative now, and her head snapped his way. He stared up at her from beside his mother, then glanced at the doorway briefly. "No."

"Connor, it's over."

"You can't leave," he told her, no longer the man-child but a man in control of his destiny.

"You don't have to do this, Connor," she said. "It's over. It's all over. I heard what she said. What you said."

He rose from his crouch like a dark shadow against the wall, and in a few short steps, he put himself between her and the door, his chest rising and falling as panic set in.

A vehicle sped along the distant lane, and a soft, blue light lit the courtyard twice, and then faded with the sound of the engine.

"Give yourself up, Connor," she said, hoping to ease his mind. Hoping that enough of that child inside remained to manipulate, to coerce, or to convince. "I'll tell them what she said. I'll tell them what she did–"

"No," he screamed, then flinched at the doorway as if he'd heard something, or his paranoia had. He seemed jittery. Restless.

Panicked. And he rushed to the shelves, brushing them clear with a sweep of his hand, tearing old sheets from piles of old machinery, and poring through boxes, discarding them as useless.

Until he found what he was looking for, and he held it with obvious doubt.

"Connor, no–"

"You can't leave," he screamed at her, and there was a wildness in his eyes. "None of us can."

Frantically, he unscrewed the cap on the jerry can and sniffed at its contents.

"Don't be stupid, Connor. Look how far you've come."

"None of us can leave," he said, with a new calmness, as if the decision had been made.

"I won't say a word then," she said. "How about that? I won't tell them. I'll say that you helped us. That you took care of us."

He began with the doorway, dousing the old frame in petrol.

"I'll tell them I don't remember anything."

"None of us can leave," he said, his voice monotone and almost robotic. And then he drenched the shelves, the table, the machinery.

"Don't you see?" she said. "You'll be a hero, Connor. You kept us safe."

He paused at the words, as if by some miracle she had pierced his stubborn and delusional shell. But it was short-lived, and he tossed the can to the back of the room, where the rest of its contents gurgled into a puddle in the shadows.

"The farm is yours now, Connor. She's gone. I'll tell them what I heard. That it was her who killed Kelly. That it was her who killed Molly."

That name was a knife that pierced his heart like the one that was still stuck in his mother's back. He rummaged among the chaos on the table, and Sophie saw her chance. She could make it.

She lowered her feet to the concrete floor, easing herself from the bench, and she took a single step, eying the darkness outside, the rain, the cold, and the unknown. Slowly, she moved out of his peripheral, the tease of the storm every bit as enticing as the shade of a tree on a summer's day.

And then she ran.

And then she felt it, the snag of her nightdress on some sharp corner of the bench, and tore the material. Hell, she would rip it from her body if she had to. She tore it free and prepared to run.

But it was too late.

He faced her, closing in, his eyes two dark pools, as if his mind belonged to something else, some being not of this world.

And with a single swipe of the back of his hand, he knocked her to the ground.

"It's over," he told her, as she rolled onto her back, crawling from him, further into the room, closer to Ruth Hobbs' body. He followed, as a child might follow a pet, curious and unafraid. Then he saw what he had been looking for on the bench where she had been. He grabbed it with a shaking hand and stared down at it, its contents rattling with every tremble of his body. A few matches fell to the floor, but he held one tight, and held it up to the light like it was the answer to everything. The holy grail. And then he struck it. "None of us can leave."

CHAPTER FIFTY-FOUR

"Don't do it, Connor," a voice called out over the rain on the roof. It was familiar yet distant, like it belonged in a reoccurring dream.

The voice was neither angry nor gentle. It was a command. An affirmation. An instruction from a man who seemed to understand.

The flame burned in Connor's fingers, and he turned to face the voice, the shape in the doorway, as it moved into the light. It was the detective, the tall, old man with the focused, soft eyes. The one who had been kind.

"Connor," he said again. "Put the match down, son."

But Connor didn't. He held his arm high, out of reach of all. He could hear the little flame flickering. "It's over now," he said.

"Not yet, it's not," said the man. George, that was it. George something or other. "But how it ends is all down to you."

The man took his eyes off Connor for the first time, glancing between Sophie and Ruth on the floor. He made a show of inhaling. Then he turned his eyes back to Connor. "I know it wasn't you," he said. "You're not in trouble."

Connor hadn't thought he was. He hadn't thought about going to prison or being punished or getting into trouble. Because he wasn't planning on surviving this. It was too much. It was all too much. It was time to end.

"You don't know anything," Connor told him. "Nobody knows anything."

"So let's talk about it," he replied, and there was something in his voice that Connor recognised. A softness, like his father's. His fingers burned, and Connor dropped the match to the floor. Sophie gasped, scampering backwards, further into the corner of the room, until Connor placed a boot over the dying flame.

"That's it," the detective said, taking another tentative step forward.

"No closer," Connor told him, and he fumbled for a fresh match from the box.

"We can talk about this, Connor," he replied. "Nobody else needs to die."

"I need to die," Connor said. "Don't you see? I do. I deserve to die."

"I don't believe that for a moment," the man said. Larson, that was his name. George Larson. He remembered it now. "I don't believe that anyone needs to die."

"I could have stopped it. I could have saved them."

"Saved who?" Larson said. "Saved Kelly?"

The tips of his fingers no longer burned, but that heat now lived behind his eyes. He blinked away the tears, but the fumes stung, and new tears ran in their place.

"Come on, Connor. Who could you have saved? David and Florence?" he said, taking another cautious step. "Kelly?"

"Stop," Connor told him. "Don't come any closer."

"Or was it Molly that you could have saved? Is that who it was?"

"All of them," he screamed. "Don't you see? I did it. I'm worthless. I'm pathetic."

"Oh, I don't believe that for a second," Larson said calmly.

"I did. She heard it," Connor said, pointing at Sophie in the corner. "She heard it all."

"Tell me about the storm," Larson said, taking another tentative step, forcing Connor further into the shadows. "Tell me what happened."

"I told you already," Connor said.

"No, you told me a lie," Larson said. "But that's okay. We all tell lies from time to time. Myself included. Tell me what really happened."

"No, I can't," he said, and an involuntary sob swelled in his throat.

"We found oil on the bonnet of David Tucker's car, Connor," Larson said. "You were out there, weren't you? You were out there in the storm."

"No–"

"Do you know what else we found?"

"No, stop–"

"A bracelet. Just out there in the mud near the fallen tree."

"Stop it. You can't know."

"It was Kelly's bracelet, Connor. Wasn't it?" Larson said, speaking softly, as Ruth used to do on those days when she had spoken about Molly. "You burned her, didn't you?"

"No," Connor whined, shaking his head. All he had to do was to strike the match, and it would all go away. He wouldn't have to hear it.

"Do you know what I think happened?"

"Stop," Connor pleaded. "Please, just stop."

"I think David and Florence were escaping the flood," Larson began, and he came to a stop beneath the light bulb. "I think they climbed from the car to move the tree."

"No–"

"You know the tree I'm talking about, don't you? You can see it from your house," Larson said, but Connor shook his head, wishing it would all stop. "I think they found her. I think they found their daughter's remains. I think the storm felled the tree, and they unearthed her. Imagine that, Connor? Imagine trying to escape a flood, imagine trying to save your life, and discovering your daughter's body out there."

"I was looking after her," Connor screamed, and Larson smiled softly. Deep shadows grew in the corners of his eyes. "I was looking after her, that's all." Larson said nothing, and raised a hand to a commotion at the door, beckoning somebody to step away, to wait in the rain. Connor recalled the evening that had haunted his dreams for a decade. The faces. "It was late," he began. "I heard something out there."

"Where?"

"In the woods."

"What were you doing?"

"Just walking," he said. "I like it out there. It's where we used to play. Molly and me."

"The woods near the Gibson house?" Larson asked. "Is that right?"

Connor nodded.

"I heard her crying. I heard..." He paused, trying hard to banish the cries from his head, but it was relentless.

"What did you hear, Connor?"

"I heard them. I heard her crying," he said, then peered across at Sophie. "And I heard him."

"Who, Connor? Be clear for me, now," Larson said. "Who did you hear? Was it a man?"

"It was..." Connor started, his chest growing tighter with every word of truth he spoke. "It was Edward Gibson."

———

He could picture the scene. He knew the woods as well as any of them, just as well as Sophie Gibson, Kelly Tucker, and even Connor Hobbs. And he had spent long enough staring at the images of Edward Gibson for the memory of his face to have been etched into his mind for eternity.

But it wasn't the image of his face that George now recalled. It was his body hanging from the tree, swinging in the breeze. Perhaps it was a memory that Sophie, too, had recalled, as she sobbed in the corner of the room, in the darkness, alone with her cruel thoughts.

"Did he see you?" George asked, to which Connor nodded, his face a picture of shame. "And what did he do?"

"He ran," Connor replied, a string of saliva hanging between his lips. "He ran, and I took her. I carried her."

"Where?" George said. "Where did you take her, Connor?"

The young man shrugged and stared at the floor.

"Here," he said. "I looked after her."

"You looked after her?"

"Yeah. We played," he replied. "I fetched Molly's doll, and we played. I took care of her."

"But now she's in the field beside the road," George said. "Where David and Florence found her."

"She shouldn't have run," Connor said helplessly. "She should have stayed here, where it was safe."

"But she did run," George said. "She did run, but she didn't get away, did she? You couldn't let her get away. She had to be stopped, didn't she?"

"It wasn't my fault," Connor screamed. "I was looking after her. It wasn't my fault."

"Just like David and Florence's deaths weren't your fault. Is that right, Connor?" He opened his mouth to speak, but held his tongue, squeezing his eyes closed at the memory, at the pain it had caused, and at the betrayal. "Tell me about the storm. Tell me why you went out there?"

"I can't," he mumbled.

"Tell me why you pushed David and Florence's bodies into the water, Connor," George said. "Tell me why you pushed their car down the hill."

"You wouldn't get it."

"Tell me why you planted the torch in Sophie's house."

Connor stared at him, his eyes boring into George's, as if seeking how much he knew.

"You did what?" Sophie said from the back of the room, and she emerged from the shadows. George appraised her from afar. She was injured and hobbling, but she was alive.

She, too, stared at George, but not with fear, like Connor did. It was a look of recognition and of shame.

"You okay, Sophie?" he asked, to which she nodded.

"George Larson," she said, as if it was for her own benefit more than anybody else's.

"The torch that was used to bludgeon David Tucker to death, Sophie," George began. "Connor planted it in your house. Perhaps he was trying to shift the blame. Perhaps he was hoping that we'd find it and we would blame you." He shrugged once and gave a heavy sigh. "And if I'm honest, it worked. For a while, at least."

"Because of Edward?"

"Because you always defended him," he told her. "Because ever since your husband took his own life, your life has been nothing but misery. I'm right, aren't I?" She waited a moment, as if she was digesting the words, then with a resignation, she nodded. "The thing is, Sophie, your husband might have been guilty of terrible things, but he wasn't a murderer."

"How did you know?" Sophie said. "How do you know it wasn't him?"

"I didn't," he admitted. "I didn't know. In fact, I was sure it was him. I was sure right up until this evening." He stared at her and then at Connor. "Nobody in their right mind would leave a torch beside the front door when they head out into a storm, Connor."

"It was broken," he replied, then realised his mistake.

"Nobody could have moved that tree on their own, either," George said. "Nobody except, perhaps, a young man who had spent his life working on a farm. Somebody who has the strength of two men."

Connor's eyes shifted uneasily, and his fingers turned the unlit match around and around.

"You see, when we arrived during the storm, the tree was off the road. Why would David and Florence stop their car in a flood if the tree wasn't blocking their path?" Connor closed his eyes, perhaps reflecting on his mistakes, mistakes that had been made during a single terrible night. "Are you going to answer me, Connor?"

The young man shook his head, still twirling the match around in his fingers.

"You can't look after them all, son," George said, and he nodded at the great lump of a woman who lay still on the floor. "You can't protect them forever."

CHAPTER FIFTY-FIVE

"She was just sat there, staring at the wall," Connor said, and he gulped at the image that haunted him. "I asked her if she was okay. I asked her what happened. But she wouldn't tell me. She didn't talk. She didn't say anything."

The match was warm in his clammy fingers. It was his way out. It didn't matter anymore.

Nothing mattered.

"She was sitting in the armchair, but her hair was wet. It was late, and it was my job to keep the generator going. I saw the torch was missing. I kept it by the door to fill the generator up. I do it before we go to bed, so it lasts until the morning. But it was gone. She shouldn't have gone out there." He stared up at Larson, hoping at least for some sympathy. Hoping that he would be kind enough to understand.

"She went out to fill the generator," Larson said, and Connor nodded.

"I was going to do it. I always do it. It was my job."

"But your mum did it during the storm, did she?" Larson asked, then continued before Connor could respond. "Your mum went out there to fill the generator with fuel, and she saw David

Tucker's headlights." He waited for Connor to speak, but there was nothing he could add. "And she saw where they were, didn't she? She knew Kelly was buried there."

"She probably just went to help–"

"She went there for one reason and one reason alone, Connor," Larson said, and then let the certainty permeate.

"When I saw the torch on her lap, I knew. I don't know how," he said. "I just knew. She had that same look on her face. The same stare."

"So, you went outside, and you saw the headlights, and you thought you'd make things right," Larson suggested. "You wanted to look after her?"

"I didn't know what else to do," Connor said. "I saw what she'd done to them. I couldn't leave them there. I thought the water would carry them off."

"And you did this with gloves on," Larson said. "The same gloves you wear to fill the generator. That's why there was oil on the bonnet of the car."

"I just wanted to fix it. I just wanted it all to go away."

"But?" Larson said, and he eyed Sophie in the corner.

"But when I got back, I saw the door was open," he replied, and nodded at the heavy workshop door.

"And that's when you found Sophie and Lucy," Larson said, as if everything made sense. But it couldn't make sense. He couldn't know it all. "You wanted to protect them from your mum, Connor. Is that right? So that she wouldn't hurt them?"

Connor nodded, and for the first time, he admitted, "Yes."

"Like she had hurt David and Florence?"

"Yes," he said again.

"And like she hurt Molly?" Connor saw it now. He saw where he was being led. "You were just playing with Kelly Tucker. You were looking after her. Is that right, Connor?"

Connor nodded emphatically. "I just wanted to take care of her."

"But your mum thought you had..." he said, searching for the right words. "Done things with her. To her. Is that right? Why would she think that? What on earth would make her think you would do such a thing, Connor? Did you ever give her a reason to think that? Is there something I'm missing here?"

"No, I never did–"

"I mean, you're out here on your own. You're not married, are you? Maybe you were curious? Maybe you wondered what it felt like to be with somebody. Maybe you didn't want to die a virgin."

"I'm not a virgin. I know what it's like–"

"Your mum wouldn't have known that, would she?" Larson said, and then his eyes narrowed. "Would she, Connor?"

"You don't know anything," he said.

"Connor, if there's something I should know–"

"There's nothing you need to know!"

"Did you take care of Molly, Connor? Did you look after your sister?"

"We played. That's all. Molly and me, we played."

"But something happened, didn't it?" Larson said, and Connor recognised the scrutinising look in his eye. "I don't see how your mother would know about your...experiences, shall we say, if Molly wasn't involved."

"She did know. She took care of me."

"Connor, what are you saying?"

"She told me that I never needed to go looking for it. That if ever I felt...you know?"

"No, I don't know. Be clear."

"Whenever I..." He pointed at his groin. "She said that whenever I needed something, that she would help me."

"Your mother?" Larson said, and Connor nodded. "She touched you, did she?"

"She didn't want me hurting anyone. She thought that if she did it, then I wouldn't have to go looking for it. That I wouldn't leave her like Dad did."

He took a deep breath, turning the match over and over. He only needed to strike it once. It would all be over.

"Connor?"

He looked into the detective's eyes and saw nothing but sorrow, and a softness in his soul, like his father had.

"The marks on Molly's body. You didn't make them, did you?"

"She was bathing her," Connor said. "She was bathing us. Both of us. She saw something. A mark or something. Or blood. I don't know."

"Where?" Larson asked.

"On her body."

"Where exactly on Molly's body?" the old man said. He took a step towards him, and Connor held the match to the box, only for the man to crouch down. He picked up Molly's doll and seemed to study it for a moment before tossing it to Connor. "Show me," he said.

"What?"

"Point to where your mother saw the mark on Molly's body."

"I don't..."

"Point to the area on the doll, Connor," Larson said, raising his voice to be heard over the rain on the roof.

Connor held the doll that he had kept beside his bed. The doll that he could see, in his mind's eye, Molly playing with. Kelly had played with it, too. And Lucy. But none of them played like Molly had. Those had been special times.

He pointed to the area where the doll's legs were stitched to the torso, then held it beside him with the matchbox.

"But all you had ever done was look after her," Larson said. "You never hurt your sister, did you?"

"No," he said. "I wouldn't."

"Connor, I'm going to ask you a question, and I want you to tell me the truth. Do you understand?" Larson said, to which Connor nodded slowly. "What were you doing in the woods on the day you heard Kelly crying?"

"I was going to look after her, like I said. I was going to look after Kelly."

"Because something was happening to her?" Larson said, and Connor nodded. "And you knew what it was because the same thing had happened to Molly?"

Despite voicing her awareness of her husband's guilt, Sophie still seemed to crumple at the words, and a sob fell from her parted lips.

"It's true," Connor said. "I swear."

"Just stop it," she said, and she dragged herself around the bench towards him. "I can't bear to hear it—"

"It's true, Sophie," George said, and she stilled, shaking her head in disbelief.

"You," she said, turning on George. "You always had it in for him."

"And you were always in denial," he told her, meeting her hatred with cold fact. "I'm sorry, but you can defend him all you like, Sophie. I can prove what he did," he said. "The necklace in your bedroom. The one hanging from your mirror."

"You've been in my bedroom—"

"It's hers, Sophie," he said. "It's Molly's."

"No. No, it can't be. He told me it was his mother's. He said it was all he had left of hers."

"I'm sorry, Sophie," he said. "I am. I'm truly sorry."

"The daisy chain?" Connor said, remembering the little daisies around Molly's neck, and he smiled at the memory of her wearing it. Daisies had been her favourite.

"Can't we just leave it? Can't we just let them all rest in peace?" she screamed and limped forward, but Connor held his hands up, the match in one finding its way to the box in the other before the doll had even landed at his feet.

"Connor, you don't need to do this," said George. "You didn't hurt anybody, did you? Edward Gibson assaulted them both, didn't he? Tell me, Connor. Now is the time."

"You don't have to say it, Connor," Sophie said, but with barely an ounce of conviction in her voice. "You can make this all go away."

"Connor, tell me. I need the truth, now."

"Yes," he cried out. "I didn't do anything. Ma was only trying to protect me. I didn't want her to be alone."

"Edward Gibson hurt them, didn't he?"

"Stop," Sophie said, holding her hands to her ears. "Just stop."

"But she killed them. Is that right?" Larson said. "Your mother killed them all."

It was all Connor could do to look between them, his heart racing, the match ready to strike.

"Connor, tell me. I need you to say the words for me."

He lowered his hand to his sides. Part of him wanted to reach out, to rub her back. To help her.

"Connor?" Larson said.

"Yes," he screamed, and he dropped to his knees by her side and stabbed at his chest with his thumb. "She did it all for me. She killed them all for me. For us."

"All of them?" Larson asked, then softened his voice to a lullaby. "Even poor Molly?"

Connor still remembered the day. Remembering how she hadn't said a word to him, even when he had carried her body out of the house wrapped in an old towel. How she told him it had all been his fault.

"She always thought it was me," Connor said quietly, and he looked up at Larson. "She always thought that it was me who... you know?"

"And she was protecting you?"

"She said it was our secret. That we were supposed to be together," Connor said. "She said that nobody could ever come between us. That nobody could ever take me away."

He closed his eyes and pictured her in that hole in the ground. How he had kissed her forehead for the last time, and then filled the hole in the very soil beneath him. He stared at the detective, who waited to hear the words leave Connor's mouth as if he already knew what he was going to say. His hands connected before him, and the detective watched with uncertainty, like he didn't believe he was capable. It's over, he thought, as he struck the match and held the flame before him as he said those final words to Larson.

"Nobody," he said. "Not even Molly."

CHAPTER FIFTY-SIX

The heat was instant.

A rush of air being sucked into hungry flames.

The newborn fire licked at its world, tasting the wooden structure as a baby seeking to suckle, finding nourishment in the old, rotten wood.

And he watched. Connor, the lanky young man whose life had been robbed from him by his own mother's insecurities, stared wide-eyed.

"Sophie," George called, but she was trapped by the flames. A pool of petrol from the discarded can burned fiercely at her feet.

But she could have got through. He was sure of it. She could have run to him. Instead, she just stood there, as if she was contemplating the flames, contemplating the last decade.

Contemplating hell.

"Now, Sophie," he screamed.

It was as if she hadn't heard him. The old, damp wood bellowed smoke that rose around her, swallowed her, consumed her.

"Connor!"

He ran to the young man, who knelt beside his dead mother,

his face upturned to the cloud of smoke as one might savour the rain that follows a drought. George took hold of the boy's shirt and pulled. But Connor was strong and tore himself free with ease, before settling down beside his mother's body, his eyes open, as the flames raced across the ceiling beams.

Connor whispered something to his mother that George could not process in that moment.

The light bulb popped and a tinkle of glass fell to the floor, and somewhere near the shelves, a pressurised canister succumbed to the heat, exhaling its chemical contents in a spray of greens and oranges.

Hands grabbed at George's shoulders. Strong hands. And he knew them.

"Guv, get out. Come on," Ivy said, but he couldn't leave. He could not walk away. Not now. He was so close. With her jacket over her mouth, Ivy placed one arm around his waist, and she heaved.

"Connor," he called out.

"Guv, we've got to go."

"Connor, you don't have to do this."

And those eyes found him. He had found peace, and he watched calmly as hell rose, devouring the building with every passing second.

More hands grabbed onto George's arms, his shoulders, his waist, and his clothes, and he felt himself being pulled. He was a child again. Out of his depth in the frigid North Sea. Connor was his beach. Sophie was his beach. And those hands, those strong and relentless hands that clawed at him, were the unforgiving tide, pulling him further from sanctuary, from his mum, from his dad, from life.

A ceiling beam fell, the moment that rain touched his skin and they fell to the sodden ground in a heap, as a shower of sparks and embers, carried by the heat, rose and seemed to dissipate in the night air.

The flames reached a height of twenty or thirty feet, and a blanket of cloud lay in that space where hell's fury meets cold, hard reality.

They dragged him clear, and Ivy called a paramedic over. But all that was a dream. All that happened in the distance. It was background noise. The hum of life. No, his world lay inside the raging workshop, where growling flames danced and jived in victory. Where Sophie Gibson faced the truth. Where Connor Hobbs, the loner, lay beside his mother.

"Nobody can come between us," he had said. "I'll look after you."

There were no screams from inside. None that crossed the threshold, anyway. Only the cackles and growls of hungry flames, the pops and sprays of paint cans, and the hiss of air, feeding the fire.

"It's done, guv," Ivy said. And George let his head fall to the ground. He was wet and cold but numbed to the sensation. His body shook and trembled, but his mind was senseless. "Let's get you out of here, eh?"

He said nothing. It was all he could do to stare into the flames.

"Help me get him up," she told the paramedic, and once more, arms groped at his body, reaching under his arms, dragging him backwards and upwards. Away.

And then he heard it.

"Come on, guv. This man needs to check you out, okay?" He raised his hand to silence her, irritated at the distraction, and he shushed her. "Guv, it's over."

He shoved her off him and stepped closer.

"No, guv. That's not a good idea," she said, her voice distant, like Grace's in his dreams. Hands grabbed him once more, but he wouldn't be stopped. "Help me out here, will you?" Ivy screamed at anyone close enough to help.

But he shook her off, moving closer to the awesome heat that burned his eyes.

More hands. More desperate cries. More of Ivy's distant pleading.

And there he was. He appeared in the raging doorway as Virgil with Dante in his arms. He had guided her through hell and carried her into the icy rain. Into purgatory. Into life.

George whipped his jacket from his shoulders and ran to them.

"We need help," he yelled, as he wrapped it around Sophie's unmoving body. Connor fell back onto his haunches and watched helplessly as the two paramedics began working on Sophie. George put his shoulder beneath the young man's arms and beckoned for Ivy to do the same. Together, they hoisted him to his feet and dragged him clear of the heat, and as if infuriated at its loss, the fire raged with renewed ferocity. The roof gave, falling to the flames, and the walls seemed to linger there for a few moments, before tumbling down onto the remains of Ruth Hobbs, swallowing her, devouring her.

Consuming the evil inside of her.

CHAPTER FIFTY-SEVEN

A steady stream of silent tears spilt from Lucy's eyes. She was unblinking. Lost in a memory. Sophie followed her gaze to the small coffin as Kelly began her final journey, and she remembered her own day. The day she had said goodbye to her world. Edward hadn't been buried, of course. His grave would have been desecrated the moment the first shovelful of soil hit wood, and so she had watched the curtains close on him. It wasn't the same, somehow. But she was glad of it now. Now that she knew.

And then all that remained was memories, and what to do with those?

Kelly's was the last of the coffins. She was with her parents at last.

Only one Tucker remained, and she stood opposite Sophie, watching her entire family go into the ground.

She remembered how she'd cried at Edward's funeral. How his death had seemed like an injustice. A tragedy, even. But the truth was that he was nothing more than a coward.

There were happy memories that Sophie struggled to shake, tainted by evil, deceit, and the thought of his touch. Their wedding day, the house, the mornings in bed, the holidays, the dinners, and…the list went on. The memories lived on — good and bad — for eternity. That was her burden. That was the burden she had chosen to carry while standing at the threshold of hell. She recalled how she had pulled Connor from his mother's body. How she had begged him to come, and how he had held on, unwilling or unable to leave her.

"It was them," she had told him. "It was all Edward and Ruth. Not us. Don't you see, Connor? Don't you see that we have to live? We have to live so that they can die. We have to live so that this can end. The truth dies with us, Connor."

There was only one light in the darkness now.

Sophie looked over again at Lucy, remembering how they had sat in those same positions for nearly fifty hours, facing each other, facing their pasts, facing their futures.

Around them, a scattering of friends and acquaintances marked their respect. People she recognised but who hadn't uttered a word to her since that day. She wondered if they knew now. She wondered if things might be different.

And then she felt it. Those eyes. They were kindness. They were compassion. And they hurt, as did hers.

He was watching her. The detective. The old, lean, grey-haired man who had unpicked her story. Their story. The man who had lived and suffered, and beat himself up for not knowing, for not recognising the truth when it had been there all along.

And he nodded to her. Just once. But it was enough.

The reverend continued his sombre monologue, reciting from the good book, and she wondered what page he would read from during Ruth Hobbs' funeral. She wondered who would attend, or if her ashes might simply be cast onto the fields to be carried by the wind.

Gently, he offered Lucy a small bucket of earth. It was that time. The time during any burial that the reality truly hit home.

The noise of soil on wood.

But Lucy was still. The reverend, patient beyond words, looked to her. To Sophie.

She went to her. She stood at the young girl's side, and she touched her arm.

"Let's end this together," she whispered, and she took her hand, leading her fingers to the soil.

"But if I do this," Lucy sobbed, wiping at her eye with her free hand. "Then I'll always be alone."

"You'll never be alone," Sophie told her, holding her hand against the dirt. "Not while there's breath in my body."

CHAPTER FIFTY-EIGHT

"How are you holding up?" Ivy asked as she approached George at his car.

He stood with his hands in his pockets, and his jacket pulled tight around him, more for comfort than warmth.

"It's hard on the poor girl," he told her. "Life will be very different for her now. It always is."

"But she will have a life, guv," Ivy said. "She has choices."

"Oh, she does. I just hope she makes the right ones."

"Are you referring to Jason Connolly?"

"Partly, I suppose," he said. "He won't be away for long. A kilo of weed. I doubt he'll do any more than twelve months."

"What about Connor?" she asked, to which he shook his head.

"He'll go into the system. He's not right," he said sadly. "It's hard to recount the events without attributing some element of guilt in his favour. With any luck, a jury will see him for what he really is."

"And what is that?" She asked.

He gave the question some thought, and then smiled as he considered the kindest of answers.

"Lost," he said, and they both quietened for a moment.

"Should we talk to her?" Ivy asked, and nodded at the gathering beside the church.

"No, let's leave her. She knows how to find us if she needs us."

"It might be nice to say something, though."

George shook his head. "It's not my place."

"How do you mean? She hasn't got anybody else."

"My role was to solve a murder. If I followed up with every victim, witness, and family member on every investigation I ever worked on, I'd never get anything done."

"But this one was different, guv," Ivy said. "It meant something to you. You have to admit it. I've never seen you so close to an investigation."

"It was," admitted George. "But it's over now. I just wish I'd been able to solve it earlier. If I had found Kelly's body sooner, David and Florence would still be alive."

"It's not your fault."

"I know."

"Kelly's body could've been anywhere," Ivy continued. "You couldn't have ordered a finger search of the entire Wolds, guv. At least now it's been found, and she can finally be buried in peace. And she has you to thank for that."

"And you," he said.

"Yeah, right. If it was down to me, we would have been sitting in your house, drinking scotch while I moaned about my marriage," she said with a laugh. "By the way, were you going to tell me about the house?"

"What house?"

"The rental," she said with a knowing look. "Not exactly the new build you described, is it?"

"Oh, I don't know," he said. "With a bit of imagination, maybe."

"I see," she replied. "Well, maybe one day you'll trust me enough to let me in."

He grinned at her persistence.

"Thank you, Ivy," he said.

"What for?"

"For everything. For keeping me grounded. For challenging me. I'm not sure I would've gone anywhere but in circles with this one if it wasn't for you."

"Anytime, guv," she said, but quickly broke the moment by pulling away. It was something she did. It was an inability to face emotions. It was like she enjoyed the security of a defensive wall but wanted to peer into her neighbour's garden. "Are you going back to the house then, are you?"

"Not yet," he told her. "I've a bit of filing I want to do. You know?"

"The Kelly Tucker file?"

"It needs putting away," he said. "For good this time."

She nodded, then inhaled long and hard.

"You know, Ivy, I think I'm going to make a go of it," he said.

"Of what, guv?"

"Of this place. The Wolds. The house."

"Well, that's good."

"I think I'll pop back to Mablethorpe. You know? To grab a few bits from the old house."

"It does need some soft furnishing," she replied with a smile.

"If you ever need a place," he said. "I mean, if you don't mind having to fix a chair before you sit in it…"

"Thanks, guv," she said, before he could finish, and they enjoyed a moment's peace.

"Will you head home now?" he asked.

"Probably."

"How is everything?" he said, peering over her wall. "With Jamie, I mean."

Ivy stepped back, as though stalling for time. "Better," she said. "We're going to have a family weekend. Go to the wildlife park. Spend some time together with the kids. I'm sure it'll be fine. He just has to get used to me travelling for work, which he will. I'm sure it'll all work out for the best, guv."

"I'm sure it will," George said.

"Yeah," Ivy said. Then she looked like she was about to say something else, but thought better of it. "I'll see you on Monday, guv."

"You will, Ivy," he told her as she turned her back and walked away. "You most certainly will."

CHAPTER FIFTY-NINE

Fresh, salty sea air welcomed George as he breezed along the Alford Road, drinking in the views. He likened Lincolnshire to a three-course meal, with each course offering a flavour of its own yet complimenting the next. The Fens were mostly wild and flat, with far-reaching views filled with possibilities. The Wolds held secrets in its hills and gullies, and prized its guests with surprise, beauty, and seemingly endless green. And finally, the pudding. The coast. Wild, untamed beaches, rich farmland, and a pace of life like no other. It was the edge of nowhere yet had been the centre of their world.

His and Grace's.

George pulled into the car park and switched off the engine. He climbed from the car and took one more deep breath of sea air, as if for strength. In truth, he needed all he could get. To overcome the heartache, the fear, and the guilt.

"Heya, George," he was welcomed as soon as he stepped through the sliding doors.

The lobby was more of an entranceway than a reception. Mismatched armchairs sat to one side beside a large wooden bookcase, and the desk wasn't the kind he was used to. There was no tempered glass screen or stern-faced officer on the other side. It was a small, oak desk, behind which, in a comfy, armed desk chair, sat the ever-smiling Miss Dowdeswell.

"Morning, Susan," he replied, signing to check himself in.

Such a warm welcome always reassured George. He supposed that was the point; warmth and kindness. That was the point of it all.

"What's on the agenda for today?" he asked.

"Painting," Susan said, which George supposed was a good thing. It did, at least, resemble the past.

He smiled a thanks and headed down the corridor to his right to the door at the end, the one with the corner window overlooking the garden, where the birds sat and sang.

He knocked twice, once to get her attention, the other to confirm that the first hadn't been the wind or figment of her imagination. He took one more deep, salty breath and opened the door, where he stood, and just like he had during the journey there, he drank in the view.

"Hello, Grace," he said.

She didn't look up, choosing instead to focus on the painting on her easel, flicking her wrist, perhaps to cause the illusion of a sun-ray or wisp of cloud.

She was more silver-haired than brunette these days, with deep wrinkles and laughter lines around her eyes and frown lines in between. She'd been very freckly as a young woman, and though her arms still held the brown, pointillism-like dots, those on her face had merged into a permanent tan. She wore grey joggers and a thick maroon cardigan, not dissimilar to the colour of George's sweater.

But where once her vitality and charisma had drawn people close, to hear her stories and to buy her paintings, her shoulders were now rounded and hunched, perhaps from bearing a weight far heavier than she deserved.

But to George, she was and always would be, beautiful.

"Hello, darling," she said in her own time.

She turned to smile, and George searched her eyes for recognition. Some days, he was sure she knew who he was, but halfway into their conversation, it became clear that she had mistaken him for somebody else. Her brother, maybe. Who knew?

Other days, they just acted like strangers, getting to know each other for the first time. That was okay. It was all part of it. As long as she was happy.

Grace's Frontotemporal Dementia had been a long and slow development. The first signs had been ten years ago. Small things, like struggling to find the right word or getting lost on the walk home from town, a journey that she had made thousands of times. And after a diagnosis that had forever changed their lives, they had decided to move to the coast.

He had taken care of Grace on his own for as long as he could. But all the while, he had known that the day would come when he would have to ask for help. That had been the hardest part. The initial request. The admission of defeat.

She had grown agitated and withdrawn, quick to anger when she became confused. Old places were new to her, as were faces and voices. There had only been so much he could do. And it had been near-impossible to do it alone.

"I've just come from The Wolds," he told her, sitting down on the armchair opposite, from where he could watch her, from where he could admire her.

"Oh, The Wolds!" she said, looking up from her canvass. "My husband and I used to live there. Just outside Horncastle. Do you know it?"

It was one of those days. They would be strangers today, and as much as his heart sagged under the burden, he could only accept it.

"That's where I work now."

"Oh, it's lovely there. I grew up in The Wolds, you know?" she said, dabbing her painting with white dots that George supposed were the snowdrops outside the window. "In a town called Bag Enderby, if you can believe it."

George laughed. "Very Tolkien-esque."

"Yes. Isn't it just?" she giggled. "It was real though." She stopped painting and gazed out of the window, perhaps recalling a time. "Everybody was friendly, everybody said hello, and there was never any crime. Doesn't sound real, does it?" she added with a frown.

"Yes, it is real," George said, leaning back and staring out the window, hoping for his gaze to connect with hers. "I'm getting to know it quite well."

"It was a beautiful house," she continued, as if she hadn't heard a word he had said. "It was just across from St Margaret's Church." It was usual, but still fascinated George, that Grace could recall details from fifty years ago but not remember what day of the week it was. "I remember a stained-glass window above the front door, and you could see the whole of The Wolds from my childhood bedroom." She looked to him briefly with a care-free smile. "Imagine that."

"It sounds lovely," he said.

"It was," said Grace. "It was a lovely place to grow up."

Part of him wanted to tell her what a state that old house was in now. To remind her that she had inherited the house when her parents had died, and that he was going to fix it. He was going to fix it all. But that was the part of him that sought conversation. The part that clung to the old her. The her who, like the file he had not long ago returned to a drawer, was a memory.

He had felt her presence in Bag Enderby, her spirit, her youth. He'd heard so many of her childhood stories. It was like she haunted the house. And that's what he wanted. To feel close to Grace.

He pulled his eyes from the peaceful garden to look around the room. The walls were filled with canvases ranging in size from large Lincolnshire landscapes, like the one he had seen in Sophie

Gibson's house, to smaller, more abstract depictions of fading memories. George recognised his own face in some of the more shadowy artworks. Like she knew him, or her memory was teasing her with his image.

He found her staring at him, and although he smiled, she seemed lost.

"You should go," she told him, the words plucking at his heart-strings. "My husband will be here soon."

George took a breath and played along, as he'd learned to do. He teased her in the same way he did when they had been younger, speaking about himself in the third person.

"Your husband? What's he like?"

She hesitated, then said, "He's very protective of me. We've been married forty years."

"He must be a very handsome man," he said. "To have won your heart."

"Oh, he is." Grace smiled, remembering the man who sat right in front of her. "He's very tall," she said, then added, "and very clever. He's a policeman, you know?"

George crossed his legs and relaxed. She'd calmed down again and returned to her painting.

"Is he now?"

Grace nodded and looked between the snowdrops outside and her white-paint counterparts.

"Oh, he's very smart, is my husband." She looked up and smiled at him, her expression one of pride. "He solves crimes. Although, I should say he's a bit of a brooder. Doesn't always tell me what's going on up there, if you know what I mean?" She tapped her temple with a claw-like index finger.

George nodded, linked his fingers, and rested them on his stomach. He'd take that description of himself. For her, if nobody else, he wouldn't stop. If that's what she thought of him, if he made her that proud, then he wouldn't retire. He'd keep on, however challenging it proved to be. Until the day came, at least when there was no longer a need.

He'd be the man that Grace saw him to be.

"What's his name?" he asked gently.

"Who, dear?"

"Your husband. What's his name?"

"Oh, it's..." she began, and then stopped to stare at the floor for a few seconds, before looking up at him. "Do you know, I can't remember."

He smiled back at her, clenching his gut where the verbal knife had cut him wide open.

"I'm sure it'll come," he said. "I'm sure he loves you just as much as you love him."

"Do you really think so?" she asked with a girlish laugh, and she bit down on her lip in shyness.

"Oh, I know so," he told her. "I absolutely know he does."

The End

Click here to download book two - The Harder They Fall.

THE HARDER THEY FALL - PROLOGUE

The sunset over St Leonard's Church must have been one of the most spectacular that Richard Hawkins had ever witnessed, certainly of those he remembered in the Lincolnshire Wolds, or even the UK. The sky seemed as though it had been painted specifically for the twelfth-century church, so the fading light could illuminate the moss on its old, olive-green stones, and the pink sky might highlight the rosy tints of its stained-glass windows. In fact, there was little doubt that St Leonard's had been created in harmony with the nature that surrounded it at such a time when devoted design was paramount to serving God.

Richard eased the car along the rugged, fence-lined track, beneath the skeletal trees that hid the most prominent aspect of the church from view – its church tower. Through the blooming spring branches, it rose into view, majestic yet modest, and he parked in its shadow.

A low whistle escaped Richard's lips, and as if in reply, his wife Sarah gasped aloud.

"Oh my," she said.

It wasn't that the church tower was any more impressive than any other. Built on the highest hill of the village of South Ormsby, nature contributed to much of its commanding presence. In fact, standing at about forty feet, the tower was smaller than many, and compared to Lincoln Cathedral, which they had passed less than an hour ago, St Leonard's paled in significance. But to Richard and Sarah Hawkins, the church was a grandiose masterpiece, a prominent symbol of their life together. He laughed once, then let it fade.

"This is where it all began, Sarah," he said. "Right here." He glanced over at her. "Who'd have thought, eh?"

There was no car park, just an area of flattened grass on the edge of the graveyard, which was filled with disjointed graves that stood at jaunty angles like broken teeth. Many were so old that the writing upon them was illegible. Who died there, why, and when, and who loved them? Information that had been lost to time.

Richard turned off the engine. For a while, they sat in silence, looking up at the setting of their most treasured memory. The clock of the tower was around the corner, on the north side, so neither could visualise how long it was they sat there. But that didn't matter. It just felt good to be back.

"It's just the same," Sarah said eventually, leaning forward to take in the church through the windscreen.

"It's been here for nine hundred years," Richard told her. "The twenty years since we last saw it are just a minute in its life."

"That's what I always loved about it," Sarah said. "That we're part of its history now."

Richard turned to face his wife and leaned over to kiss her cheek. "Happy anniversary, love."

She turned her head so that his kiss landed on her lips, and she stroked his face. He was greyer and chubbier, but still as rugged and handsome as the day she'd met him.

"You looked so smart," she said, straightening the collar of his quarter-zip jumper, "waiting for me at the end of that aisle."

"I'll never forget it," he said. "My heart stopped. It stopped," he reiterated, "seeing you walk towards me. Nothing could have prepared me for that sight, and nothing will ever take it away."

Sarah smiled warmly, then closed her eyes and laughed. "In that god-awful puffy-sleeved dress? I must've looked like Little Bo Beep."

"Hey," Richard said, pushing her arm playfully. "That's my wife you're talking about. You looked beautiful. Like Princess Di."

She laughed. "God help us."

Richard laughed, and then his face turned serious.

"And he did, didn't he?" he said. "He helped us along the way. Every step of it, in fact."

"He did," Sarah said, touching her heart, lips, and head the way she'd been taught as a little girl, in gratitude and faith. "We've been blessed."

They returned to their nostalgic silence, holding hands in the car's centre console. The sunset was fading now, and the swirled pink had deepened to a denser, twilight blue, slowly fading into a darkness that waited on the edge of the world. The old stone walls had begun to merge with the sky, becoming less and less defined, more and more shrouded in mystery. The bats had arrived. They flitted in front of the windscreen on their journey back up to the church tower.

Richard squinted at the graves once more, trying to read the names, but even writing became lost to time eventually, he reasoned. Nothing could last forever. Not even words.

He sighed.

"Maybe we could be buried here too?"

"Richard."

"What?"

"Don't talk like that." Sarah shuffled in her seat, like an uncomfortable bird rearranging its feathers. "You know I don't like to think about all that stuff."

"But it'd be fitting, wouldn't it?" He turned to his pouting wife. "See, my life began the day I married you here. It's only right it should end here too."

Her face softened. "For everything, there is a season," she said, "and a time for every matter under heaven. A time to be born, and a time to die. A time to plant, and a time to pluck up what is planted. A time to kill, and a time to heal." Richard *hummed* along to her quoting scripture as if it was a song he liked. "But our time isn't yet, Richard. Not for a long time, in fact."

At this, they sat for a while longer in silence, something anxious growing between them, a nervousness that they might be too late or too early. Richard checked his watch.

"Are we?" she asked. "On time?"

"Seven o'clock," he said, showing her his wrist for her to check. "Right on time."

Richard put his hands in his pocket, feigning a casual indifference but wanting to touch the folded letter in his pocket, as though reminding himself it was real. He fingered the corners of it, running his thumb along the envelope's edge until it caused a tiny paper cut. He winced and whipped his hand out of his pocket to examine the slice, and then suck at the seeping droplet of blood, and the irony taste filled his senses.

Sarah didn't notice, preoccupied as she was with her own thoughts. It was dark now, and he could sense her growing twitchy, scanning the graves, or the spaces between them, at least, through which anybody could stalk and head towards their car.

"It's probably a present," she said, repeating the same theory that she had argued the whole drive over from Norfolk. "An anniversary present from one of our old friends."

"Maybe Father Wassall," he said, just as he had last time.

"Yes," she said, nodding out the window, then adding quietly, "that would make sense."

"Or a party," Richard said, repeating his own theory. "It's our fortieth anniversary, after all. Something to celebrate."

"Ruby," Sarah said distractedly.

"Ruby," Richard said, taking her hand once more to touch the ruby ring which he had slipped onto her finger as she woke that morning. He kissed her fingers.

But Sarah barely reacted. She was uneasy. He could tell.

"What time is it now?" she asked.

Richard had only just looked at his watch but made a show about doing it again for Sarah's sake, as though he, for one, was not worried about the passing of time, about whatever they were here for, about being late. "Five past seven," he said, showing her his wrist again.

Sarah sighed and frowned. "What did it say again?"

Richard didn't need to pull the letter from his pocket. He had it memorised.

"*You're invited*," he read, but his monotone voice failed to capture the points of exclamation. "Seven o'clock. St Leonard's Church. Let's celebrate! "

"Right," Sarah said in a similar monotone. "Well, where are they then?" Richard could hear her voice developing that dangerous tone of haste that occurred when she was anxious or impatient. "I hate surprises, Richard."

"I know you do, love." He squeezed her hand, but it lay lifeless, cold with nerves. "Look, they're probably waiting inside for us."

"Yes," Sarah said, eying the graves again. It would be dark soon, the kind of dark one experiences only in the countryside – deep and dense. "Maybe."

"So, do you want to take a look?" Richard said, unbuckling his seat belt. "The door should be open."

He reached for the door handle, but she grabbed onto his arm, and he turned to find her fearful, her eyes wide. "What's got into you?" But before Sarah could say, before her lips had even parted, before she could arrange her fears into some semblance of order, a dark shape in his peripheral caught his eye through the glass sunroof.

He thought it was a bat at first, but the movement was wrong. It didn't dance in the sky, or flit between the trees.

It simply fell from the sky, growing larger with every fraction of a second until it landed with a violent crash onto the car bonnet, shattering the windscreen and rocking the suspension.

They sat for a moment, both silent and aghast at the wide and lifeless eyes that seemed to stare through them.

And smeared across the head, trickling from its eyes, ears, and lips was blood the colour of their fortieth anniversary – a bright, ruby red.

Click here to download book two - The Harder They Fall.

ALSO BY JACK CARTWRIGHT

The DCI Cook Murder Mysteries

A Winter of Blood

A Secret to Die For

The Wild Fens Murder Mysteries

Secrets In Blood

One For Sorrow

In Cold Blood

Suffer In Silence

Dying To Tell

Never To Return

Lie Beside Me

Dance With Death

In Dead Water

One Deadly Night

Her Dying Mind

Into Death's Arms

No More Blood

Burden of Truth

Run From Evil

The Deadly Wolds Murder Mysteries

When The Storm Dies

The Harder They Fall

Until Death Do Us Part

AFTERWORD

Because reviews are critical to an author's career, if you have enjoyed this novel, you could do me a huge favour by leaving a review on Amazon.

Reviews allow other readers to find my books. Your help in leaving one would make a big difference to this author.

Thank you for taking the time to read *When The Storm Dies*.

Best wishes,

Jack Cartwright

AUTHOR

COPYRIGHT

Printed in Great Britain
by Amazon